CW00693483

Samuel Tay has retired from Singapore C[...]
that's another story.

John August is a guy who has saved T[...]
years. He's an American who may or may not do something for the CIA.

Now August wants to collect on all those favors Tay owes him. He needs
Tay's help to investigate a homicide.

'Whose homicide?' Tay asks.

'Mine,' August tells him.

Tay's little inner voice is shouting at him not to get involved. He's a cop, he
keeps telling himself, not a spy — well, at least he used to be a cop — but
he's bored and curious so how can he resist? Apparently, there's a woman
who knows who tried to kill August, and that's a good place to start if only
Tay can figure out who she actually is.

When Tay picks up the woman's trail, he follows her first to a beach resort
on the coast of Thailand that is surely one of the most notorious towns on
earth, and then on to Washington DC, another town that is equally notori-
ous, although perhaps for slightly different reasons.

Tay doesn't want to go to Washington since he doesn't like Americans very
much, but he's onto a murder plot that lies right at the heart of the American
intelligence establishment, and Washington is where all the answers are.

Washington doesn't frighten Samuel Tay. He's the kind of man who lives to
blow away the smoke and break the mirrors.

This time, however, Tay is going up against people who may be too powerful
to be exposed, people who know exactly how to protect themselves.

They'll simply kill Sam Tay if he gets too close to the truth.

WHAT THE CRITICS SAY
ABOUT JAKE NEEDHAM

"Jake Needham's the real deal. His characters are moral men and women struggling in an increasingly immoral world, his plotting is top-notch, and his writing is exquisitely fine. Highly, highly recommended." — **Brendan DuBois, New York Times #1 bestselling author with James Patterson of THE SUMMER HOUSE**

"In his power to bring the street-level flavor of contemporary Asian cities to life, Jake Needham is Michael Connelly with steamed rice." — **The Bangkok Post**

"Needham knows where a few bodies are buried." — **Asia Inc.**

"Tight and atmospheric, Needham's novels are thrillers of the highest caliber, a perfect combination of suspense and wit that will satisfy even the highest of standards. Jake Needham is a man who knows Asia like the back of his hand." — **The Malaysia Star**

"Needham writes so you can smell the spicy street food mingling with the traffic jams, the sweat, and the garbage." — **Libris Reviews**

"No clichés. No BS. Thrillers written with a wry sense of irony in the mean-streets, fast-car, tough-talk tradition of Elmore Leonard." — **The Edge, Singapore**

"For Mr. Needham, fiction is not just a good story, but an insight into a country's soul." — **The Singapore New Paper**

"Jake Needham has a knack for bringing intricate plots to life. His stories blur the line between fact and fiction and have a ripped from the headlines feel. Buckle up and enjoy the ride." — **CNNgo**

"Needham exudes the confidence of a man who has seen it all, done it all, and still bristles with energy and butt-kicking tales well worth writing about. He has found acclaim as one of the best-selling English-language writers in Asia." — **Singapore Today**

AND BROTHER
IT'S STARTING TO RAIN

AN INSPECTOR TAY NOVEL - BOOK 5

JAKE NEEDHAM

Always,
for Aey

The White House maintains that the right to self-defense, as laid out in Article 51 of the United Nations Charter and the Congressional Authorization for the Use of Military Force, passed September 14, 2001, may include the targeted killing of persons who are threats to the security of the United States, both in and out of declared theaters of war. The administration's posture includes the prerogative to unilaterally pursue targets in states without prior consent if that country is unwilling or unable to deal effectively with the threat.

- *FOREIGN AFFAIRS*

If you're going to fight,
fight like you're the third monkey
on the ramp to Noah's Ark.
And brother, it's starting to rain.

— T-SHIRT SOLD BY A BANGKOK STREET
VENDOR

AND BROTHER
IT'S STARTING TO RAIN

PART 1
ARPEGGIO

ONE

S AMUEL TAY STOOD in his small garden and frowned at the sky.

It was the color of periwinkle blossoms, and a few random puffs of cloud made him think of the last kernels of popcorn rolling around in the bottom of a blue lacquer bowl. The afternoon was tranquil, pleasant, and agreeable. Tay, however, was not about to be bamboozled quite that easily.

It had been raining steadily in Singapore for nearly a week, and when it rained in Singapore it was like God was draining His swimming pool. Tay was certain this unexpected exhibition of blue sky was nothing more than an ambush. God was going to have a little chuckle at Singapore's expense by luring the credulous and the trusting out of their houses and into the streets while He was preparing yet another deluge to pound them all into soggy submission.

Tay was neither credulous nor trusting. He wasn't buying it. This time he had God's number.

Tay went back inside and settled himself in the wingback chair where he read in the afternoons. It felt strange to be home every day now, separated from the life he had always lived, no longer the person he had always been. Not so long ago, there had been places he needed to be, people he needed to talk to, even on the weekends, but that was all done now.

For just a moment, he found himself wondering what was to become of him now, but he pushed the thought away as quickly as it surfaced. It was not a subject he particularly cared to ponder since it generally came accompanied by a feeling of mortality as cold and damp as a grave.

He had spent so many years reading in that chair that his forearms had rubbed the dark green leather of the armrests to the texture of fine silk and his weight on the seat cushion had shaped it into a precise mold of his ass. It felt as familiar against his body as a faithful, enduring lover. Or as familiar as he imagined a faithful, enduring lover would have felt if he had ever had one, which he hadn't.

He tugged the floor lamp a little closer to his chair and opened the Winston Churchill biography he had been reading, but he was disappointed to see that the extra light didn't do him much good. The book's print was still less distinct than he knew it should be. Was it even less distinct than it had been when he started reading the book last week? Surely not. That wasn't possible, was it?

Tay knew eventually he was going to have to face the fact that he needed glasses, but he was putting that day off for as long as he could. His body was in open rebellion already. His knees ached, he had developed tinnitus in both ears, and his bowels sometimes refused to function at all. Occasionally, God help him, he even had a strong sensation his teeth were itching, although he didn't see how that could possibly be true. He simply couldn't face the humiliation right now that his eyes were giving up the ghost, too.

Sometimes he wondered if this was all happening because of his retirement. He was no longer working, so perhaps his body had decided it no longer had to work either.

· · ·

THE BELL AT his front gate sounded and Tay looked up from his book.

It was Sunday afternoon and nobody ever came to see him on Sunday afternoon. Actually, no one came to see him much of any other time either he had to admit if he were being entirely honest about it. The bell ringer was most likely some aspiring juvenile delinquent who thought it was funny to ring the gate bells of houses occupied by perfect strangers and then run away.

Tay lived on Emerald Hill Road in a quiet neighborhood of dignified row houses, many of which dated back to Singapore's colonial days. Less than a hundred yards to the south, however, all that quiet and dignity was swallowed up by busy Orchard Road, Singapore's internationally famous shopping street and quite possibly the only thing about Singapore that most visitors had ever heard of.

Orchard Road was lined by dozens of massive shopping malls and an equal number of soaring hotel towers. Worse, at least from Tay's point of view, there was a clump of open-air bars and restaurants exactly where the serenity of Emerald Hill Road ended and the twenty-four-hour madness of Orchard Road took over, and they were among the city's most popular places for the young and the fatuous to hang out.

Motor vehicles were banned from the bottom of Emerald Hill Road where Tay lived and the street in front of his house was generally used only by pedestrians and a few bicyclists. During the week, it was mostly empty and peaceful, but on weekends all that changed.

The lure of free street parking led people headed to the Orchard Road shopping palaces to cruise the area to the north until they found a way to avoid the extortionate prices charged by the city's commercial garages. After they parked their cars, most of those people seemed to end up walking straight down Emerald Hill Road right past Tay's house. The trickle of pedestrians during the week swelled to a river on weekends.

And then there were the tourists. The weekends brought them out in droves, too. A lot of Singapore guidebooks described the houses along Emerald Hill Road as fine examples of early colonial architecture, and Tay supposed that was true enough. Still, finding groups of tourists taking photographs outside his front gate disquieted him. Once he had come home carrying his Saturday morning shopping and discovered a whole wedding party wearing long dresses and tuxedos gathered in front of his house posing for pictures.

Tay hated the weekends. The weekends made Tay feel like he was living in fucking Disneyland.

He ignored the bell and returned to his book.

WHEN THE BELL rang a second time, Tay was forced to reconsider his theory that some young thug was responsible. Could he really have an unexpected visitor?

Tay's house faced onto a small garden surrounded by a high, whitewashed brick wall. A tall, black iron gate opened to a walkway paved in red brick that led to his front door. Since he had no way of knowing who was at the gate without opening his door, Tay had thought about installing a camera so he could see who was there whenever the bell rang.

Once he opened the door to find out who it was, he was more or less screwed if it turned out to be someone he would rather avoid. There he was standing fifteen feet away from whoever it was and they were looking straight at him through the gate. After that, he could hardly slam his front door again and walk away no matter how devoutly he might wish to do so.

You've got to get that camera installed, Tay reminded himself. *You really have to.*

Of course, he had been reminding himself of that for several years now and he still hadn't gotten around to doing it. In his heart, he knew this new reminder would be forgotten as quickly as all the others he had given himself.

The bell rang a third time.

Tay sighed, abandoned his increasingly unmoored musings, and opened his front door to see who was there.

"UNLOCK THIS DAMN gate, Tay. If I stand out here any longer, Singapore's going to make me a citizen and I sure as fuck don't want that."

"John? What in the world are you doing here?"

John August just looked at Tay and pointed silently to the handle of the gate.

Tay noted with some satisfaction that August was apparently as skeptical as he was that the rain was really over because he was belted securely into a double-breasted khaki trench coat. Tay chuckled. August looked like an extra in a spy movie.

"You're a walking cliché, John."

"It's just a raincoat."

"No, it isn't. Given your associations, it's a cliché."

"You're probably right," August shrugged. "I just hate thinking about it that way."

Tay had known August for a long time, but the truth was he really knew next to nothing about him. It was obvious that he was somehow connected to American intelligence, and he had admitted as much on several occasions, but Tay had no real idea what that connection actually was.

The natural thing to do would have been to mark August down as CIA, but that had never felt entirely right to Tay. He was pretty sure August wasn't CIA. He thought it more likely August was something worse than CIA.

"What are you doing here, John? I didn't even know you were in Singapore."

"Of course you didn't."

"Well, it's just quite a surprise to find you standing at my gate."

August pointed to the gate's lock again.

"Stop babbling and open the fucking gate, Tay."

"Oh, yes. Sorry."

Tay trotted quickly down the walk and flipped open the locking bar underneath the handle.

"Inside," August muttered as he pushed past Tay and disappeared into the house.

In some people, Tay might have found that to be peculiar behavior. In John August, it seemed perfectly normal.

W HEN TAY FOLLOWED August inside, he discovered to his dismay that August had taken up residence in the wingback chair where he always sat. Tay took the wingback opposite August instead, but he wasn't at all happy about it. It was a chair he didn't like since its leather upholstery wasn't nearly as soft as that of his chair and the cushion felt unfamiliar against his rear end.

But what could he do? He could hardly demand that August trade chairs with him, could he? He wanted his chair back, he really did, but asking for it would make him look like a putz. Sometimes, he supposed, life just screwed with you and there was fuck all you could do about it.

Tay made himself as comfortable as he could under the circumstances and waited for John August to tell him what he was doing there. August hadn't dropped around to inquire into the state of Tay's health. He didn't do social calls. Something was up. Until August materialized at his front gate, it been a sleepy and untroubled Sunday afternoon in Singapore. Tay was fairly certain that was about to change.

"Why are you here, John? Or don't I want to know?"

"Oh, I think you want to know."

Tay said nothing. He just waited.

"I need your help, Sam."

That was unexpected. August had never asked him for any kind of help before, and Tay noticed that August hadn't looked him in the eye when he asked this time. Tay doubted that meant anything good was coming.

"You know I'll give you whatever advice I can."

"It's not advice I need."

Tay chuckled. "Don't tell me you want to borrow some money?"

August didn't even smile at that.

"Okay, I'm all ears," Tay said. He stretched his arms out on the armrests of the chair and arranged his face into what he thought was a polite expression of interest. "Tell me how I can help you."

"I need you to investigate a homicide."

"A homicide?"

"Yes."

"Here in Singapore?"

"No. In Hong Kong."

"Who was murdered?"

"I was."

TWO

TAY STUDIED AUGUST'S face for some sign he was joking. He found none.

"I don't understand, John."

"It's simple enough. Somebody tried to kill me and they think they succeeded. I need you to find out who it was."

"How am I supposed to do that?"

"Ah, well," August's eyes roamed the room, "that's where things start to get a little complicated."

Tay's living room was high-ceilinged with the air of an expensive men's club, which it was, more or less, although a club with the number of members strictly limited to one. At the back of the room, a pair of French doors and two traditional sash windows overlooked Tay's small garden. The other walls were shared between rosewood bookcases so tall that one of them had an old-fashioned library ladder attached to the front of it and a few oil paintings of remarkably dour-looking men and women that appeared to be vaguely nineteenth-century.

The floor was lightly colored hardwood polished to a high gloss, and in the center of the room was a very large rug, an antique Tabriz, woven in reds and blues so rich they made the rug glimmer as if it were somehow illuminated from within. Arranged on the rug were a low coffee table, square with a reddish-brown granite top, and a U-shaped grouping of a dark green leather upholstered couch and the two matching wingback chairs where August and Tay sat facing each other. Brass floor lamps with oversized cream-colored shades flanked both chairs, and the table was clear but for a heavy glass ashtray the size of a hubcap and two stacks of books.

"I can't just drop everything I'm doing here, John, and dash off to Hong Kong."

"You've got nothing to drop. You're not doing anything here. You retired a couple of weeks ago."

Tay had told no one about that. No one at all. Regardless, August knew. Just like he always seemed to, August knew. Tay protected his privacy by reflex, so whenever anyone said anything about him that had something to do with his personal life his first instinct was always to deny whatever it was, whether it was true or not.

But what was the point in claiming to August that he hadn't retired? August obviously already knew he was no longer a homicide detective in Singapore. However he knew it, he knew it, and that had something to do with why he was sitting in Tay's living room right now.

Tay shifted his weight in the chair and crossed his legs. He hated talking about any of this, but he owed August a straight story, he supposed. What was it going to be? The long version or the short version? He chose the short version.

"They offered me a promotion," Tay eventually said. "Deputy Superintendent in charge of traffic enforcement. They told me that remaining a detective in CID wasn't an option. I had to take the promotion or retire."

"They've wanted you out for a long time, haven't they, Sam?"

Tay hesitated, started to say something, but then settled for merely nodding.

"You were a cop in Singapore for... what? Twenty-five years?"

"Twenty-seven."

"And you were a homicide investigator in the Criminal Investigation Department for—"

"Sixteen years."

August exhaled heavily. He paused, seeming to contemplate the significance of that span of time, but Tay doubted that was what he was thinking about at all.

"I know it probably doesn't feel like it right now, Sam, but I think you're better off."

"You're right. It doesn't feel like it."

"You'll find another way to use your talents."

Tay said nothing.

"I might even have a few ideas," August added.

Tay had no idea what August meant by that, but something stopped him from asking.

"You never fit in here, Sam. It's as simple as that."

"I never tried to fit in."

"Yes, exactly. And good Singaporeans *always* try to fit in. They don't cause trouble, they don't rock the boat."

Tay gave a small shrug, but he didn't say anything.

"You have your own money so you didn't need the job," August went on. "They couldn't control you."

That wasn't exactly it, Tay knew.

Men in Singapore who rose to power, and it *was* always men in Singapore who rose to power, didn't control others with money and jobs. They controlled them with social pressure. Most Singaporeans were eager to be members of a common group, people in good standing with society, and they wanted to be seen that way. The group might be political, or social, or related to their employment. Whatever it was, they wanted to be a part of it. They needed its protection and its safety.

American and Europeans, particularly Americans, generally got Asia wrong. In the West, individualism was so much a part

AND BROTHER IT'S STARTING TO RAIN

of the culture that it was almost a form of religious faith. People wanted to get ahead, to stand out from others, to win the game. Most Americans couldn't imagine a society that worked any other way.

But Singaporeans generally weren't motivated to win the game. They were far more motivated by the fear that they might lose it. Individualism wasn't an ideal Singaporeans had simply not yet found a way to attain, which was the way most Americans looked at it. Individualism was a threat, a cancer Singaporeans wanted to see rooted out before it destroyed them.

Tay had been slightly suspect from the day he joined the police force because his father had been an American. His father died when he was a teenager, but that didn't matter. Tay's fellow cops still wondered if his American lineage made him different from them. Maybe he was really an individualist at heart and not a loyal member of the group like a real Singaporean would be. They never said that to his face, of course, but he could see them thinking it.

Tay didn't tell August any of that, of course. He didn't feel like having another of those philosophical conversations about the differences between Singaporeans and Americans. He was sick to death of them. So, he settled for shrugging again and waited for August to lose interest in the subject.

"You were the best homicide investigator Singapore CID ever had, Sam. The best they're ever going to have."

"Could we talk about something else, John?"

"Sure. How about we talk about what you're going to do now?"

"I'm not going to do anything now."

"Bullshit. That's not you."

"Just watch."

"You could go private. They do have private detectives in Singapore, don't they?"

"Funny you should mention that."

Tay pointed to one of the stacks of books on the table

between them. Three titles were plainly visible on the dust jackets. *The Big Sleep*, *The Lady in the Lake*, and *Farewell, My Lovely*.

"I've been rereading Raymond Chandler recently. I think I'm beginning to see myself as Philip Marlowe."

August's face crinkled in puzzlement. "Seriously?"

"No, but lend me your trench coat and maybe I can get in the mood."

August smiled at that, but not much. Tay liked knowing something he said had pushed August off balance, even if it was only a little. He didn't remember ever doing that before.

Tay had no idea where August was going with this business about his retirement, and he wasn't absolutely sure he wanted to know. His curiosity frequently had a mind of its own, however, and it spoke up before Tay could tell it to keep quiet.

"Why is the subject of my retirement suddenly so interesting to you, John?"

"Because that's why I'm here. I'm here to get you back to doing what you do best."

Had August somehow engineered a deal with the Singapore Police to reinstate him to the Criminal Investigation Department? Surely not. Still, August had all sorts of shadowy connections that made no sense to him and, if that wasn't what August was talking about, then what—

And that was when it dawned on Tay what this might really all be about.

"John," he asked, going very still, "are you offering me a *job*?"

THREE

"I NEED AN experienced investigator, Sam. I want you."

"I don't know what to say."

"That's easy. Say you'll help me out."

"John, I know I owe you more favors than I can ever repay, but right now I just don't see—"

"There's no one else I trust enough to ask, Sam," August interrupted. "It's got to be you."

To buy himself some time to think, Tay stood up and walked over to his French doors and looked out at his back garden. He was a little surprised to see that the sun was still shining and the sky was still blue. He sniffed the air cautiously, but there was no odor of rain in it. He had been certain there would be. Perhaps he had been too pessimistic. Then again, his personal experience was that pessimism was the only rational view to take of the future.

Tay had no idea what to say to August. He liked him. He even considered him a friend of sorts, as much as someone he didn't know very much about could be a friend. And he owed August. There was that, too. He owed him quite a lot.

Still, that didn't really change anything. Tay didn't want a job. Not any kind of a job. Not a permanent job, and not a temporary one. Even if he *had* wanted a job, he certainly wouldn't consider going to work for some agency of the American government that was no doubt engaged in daily outrages against civilization he would find personally appalling if only he knew what they were.

But how could he tell August that? You couldn't insult the work a man does and expect him to shake your hand and still think of himself as your friend, could you?

Perhaps the thing to do, Tay thought to himself, was simply to hear August out. Let him make his pitch, whatever it turned out to be, and then politely but firmly tell him no. Maybe he could say he had decided to take up golf or something equally stupid. August wouldn't believe him, of course, but he would probably be polite enough to pretend he did.

Yes, that's what he would do. He would hear August out and then say no. But first he needed a cigarette.

Tay opened the top left-hand drawer of a small Regency-style desk that sat just to the right of the French doors in exactly the same place it had been since he was a child living in this very house. He took out a new pack of Marlboros and a box of matches, broke the seal of the pack with his thumbnail, and paused to inhale the odor of fresh tobacco rising from it.

Tay enjoyed smoking. Smoking wasn't a habit for him, but rather his personal choice of meditative experiences. The whole process had a ritualistic quality that brought him peace. The crinkling of the cellophane wrapper as he peeled it off the pack, the whiff of fresh tobacco when he slit it open, the scrap of the wooden match against the box, and the indescribable feeling of the first wave of nicotine hitting his bloodstream.

He returned to the chair where he had been sitting, shook out a cigarette, and offered the pack to August.

"No thanks. I'm cutting down."

"Well, doesn't that make you special?"

Few things annoyed Tay more than the war of feigned morality constantly being waged against smokers. He blamed it all on the Americans, he really did. For some reason, America produced an inexhaustible supply of sanctimonious killjoys endlessly crusading to improve everyone else's life. He had absolutely no objection to anyone who wanted to improve his own life. What pissed Tay off was the insistence that those presumed improvements be imposed on him, too, whether he wanted them to be or not. And more often than not, the source of that insistence was some self-righteous American prick.

Tay took a match out of the box, lit the Marlboro, and tossed the spent match into the big glass ashtray. The first puff was always the best and then it was all downhill from there. The longer he smoked, the less enjoyable it became because each draw contaminated what was yet to come. Maybe everything got worse the longer you did it. Perhaps that was just the way life worked. Tay pushed the thought aside before he lost his balance and spiraled off into a succession of musings he knew would quickly turn morbid.

Tay exhaled a long stream of smoke directly at August.

"Enjoying that, are you, Sam?"

Tay just smiled. He took another puff on his Marlboro and cleared his throat.

"I've never asked you directly what you do or who you work for, John. I thought not asking you was rather like a professional courtesy, but maybe it was more than that. Maybe I just didn't want you to have to lie to me."

"I appreciate that."

"But you understand, don't you, in order to continue with this conversation, I'm going to *have* to ask?"

August nodded, but he didn't say anything.

"Are you a spy, John?"

"No."

"You're not CIA then?"

"When the going gets tough, the tough blame the CIA."

"I always thought you were probably CIA."

"No, you didn't."

17

August had him there.

Tay took another pull on his Marlboro. This time he tilted his head back and exhaled toward the ceiling.

"You're going to have to tell me who you really are, John."

August nodded slowly and sat there for a moment as if he was gathering his thoughts. Tay figured it was more likely August was trying to decide how little he could say and get away with it.

"A long time ago I was Delta Force, and I did some stuff in Afghanistan that I have no intention of telling you or anyone else about."

"Join the army, see the world, meet interesting people… and kill them?"

"Something like that."

Neither of them laughed. Neither of them even smiled. Tay made a little rolling gesture with his right hand and August continued.

"After I left Delta, I was a Paramilitary Operations Officer in the Special Operations Group of the Central Intelligence Agency for a while. In Agency jargon, that means I was an oper-ator, which is what the Agency calls—"

"I thought you said you *weren't* CIA."

"I haven't been in a long time, not since I've known you. These days I work for a private company, not the government."

"Have I heard of this company?"

"No, you haven't. There probably aren't more than fifty people who have." August paused and offered a rueful smile. "I guess now that's more like fifty-one."

"What does this company do?"

"We do what the government can't do."

"Such as what?"

August said nothing and his eyes drifted off of Tay's face.

"Then let me guess," Tay said. "You find people the govern-ment of the United States thinks are a threat, and you kill them."

"Not always."

"But sometimes."

"Yeah, sometimes."

Now it was Tay's turn to say nothing.

"Look, Sam, there is only one effective way to end a serious and unrelenting threat to your life or the lives of others. You kill it. Whether the threat is a stranger breaking into your home in the middle of the night or a madman in some Middle Eastern shithole planning to blow up New York City, the fix is the same. You don't propose negotiations. You don't issue a warning. You kill the bastard before he does terrible harm to you or somebody you love."

"You're scaring me here, John."

"Some men are morally opposed to violence, I understand that. But they are protected by men who are not. Do you understand *that*?"

Tay nodded, but remained silent

"Anyway," August shrugged, "somebody has to do it. Somebody has to be me. So, it's me."

"How do you know who to kill?"

"We act only on instructions from the highest authority."

"The *highest* authority? Well, that would be… who? God maybe? You're a messenger from God?"

August just looked at him.

"Or is that your way of telling me that this company works for the President of the United States?"

August continued looking at him.

"You know the President of the United States personally?"

August bobbed his head in a way that could have meant almost anything.

"But you *are* telling me, aren't you, that the President of the United States gives the order to kill people and you kill them?"

August just stared at Tay like he was trying to decide on the best way to dispose of the body.

"I can't believe I'm having this conversation," Tay said. "I really can't."

"Sure, you can. You know there's killing being done to protect you. You read about it in the newspapers all the time."

"The fact remains that—"

"But there's also killing done to protect you that you don't know about. The killing you don't ever hear about. I do that."

"People sleep peaceably in their beds at night only because rough men stand ready to do violence on their behalf?"

"George Orwell."

"Yes."

"And Orwell was right about that. I have done unspeakable violence on your behalf and you know nothing about it. Because of me and other men like me, you sleep unburdened by any knowledge of the brutality committed in your name."

Tay finished his cigarette and stubbed it out in the heavy glass ashtray on the table between them.

He needed something before this conversation went any further, but he wasn't sure what it was. He didn't want another cigarette. He wasn't really much of a drinker and he never drank during the day, although he did sometimes look forward having to a drink in the early evening.

He looked at his watch.

Just after 4:30pm.

Close enough.

FOUR

TAY WENT INTO the kitchen and rummaged around in the cabinets until he found a bottle of Bushmills Irish whiskey. He poured two fingers into a tumbler and added two fingers of water from the tap.

"What do you want, John?" he called back into the living room.

"How about a cup of tea?"

Tay walked to the doorway and stood there looking at August.

"Are you serious?" he asked.

"Of course I'm not serious. You got any beer?"

"I might have a bottle or two of Tiger."

"Tiger? I said beer, not a soft drink."

"You want it or not?"

"If that's the best you can do."

"A glass?"

"Bottle's fine."

Tay brought the drinks into the living room, handed the bottle of Tiger to August, and settled back into the chair with his glass of Bushmills. For a while, no one spoke.

August knew better than to push Tay. He also knew he

didn't have to. He had Tay's curiosity working for him. All he had to do was be patient and Tay would come to him. For his part, Tay didn't think for a moment that August was sitting in his living room to propose he join some secret mob of political assassins. August knew him well enough to know that was a nonstarter. So why was August telling him all this? Why was he *really* here?

"This company you work for," Tay asked when he decided the silence had gone on for long enough, "does it have a name?"

"Its formal name is Red River Consultants, but most people who know we exist just call us the Band."

"The Band?" Tay couldn't help snickering a little. "Really?"

"It was before my time," August shrugged, "but the way I hear it somebody started calling us the Band years ago and it just stuck."

"So, what do you call the guy who leads the Band? The Conductor?"

August just looked at him.

"Oh *shit*, John, tell me you're not serious."

August drank some more of his beer.

"You'll get used to it," he said.

"I'M OBVIOUSLY HAVING a little trouble with this, John."

"I can see that."

"I'm flattered you trust me enough to tell me all those things, I really am, but I'm confused, too."

"About what?"

"I don't understand *why* you're telling me."

"I'm telling you because you're the best investigator I've ever known."

"For God's sake, are we done dancing here yet, John? What do you want from me?"

"I just told you. Somebody tried to kill me. I need you to figure out who it was and then find them for me."

Tay exhaled heavily and looked away. He and August had been through a lot together. He owed him a great deal, maybe even his life. And if someone had asked him fifteen minutes earlier, he would have said he would do anything August asked him to do.

It wasn't just a matter of some sense of personal indebtedness. It was more than that. It was the friendship that had grown out of the things they had done together. Tay didn't have many friends. The few he had mattered a lot to him.

The thing was, August had never asked him for his help before, but now that he *was* asking, it felt to Tay like this was too much to expect of anyone.

Looked at one way, August was just asking him to figure out who was behind some kind of a threat to him and to the people he worked for. It would be an investigation pretty much like all the hundreds of investigations Tay had conducted in his career as a homicide investigator in Singapore. Something happened and you figured out who caused it to happen and then found them. It might be a little more difficult because he didn't know the territory he would have to work the way he knew Singapore, but not all that different. Not really. It was something he could do. Perhaps not easily, but he could do it.

Looked at another way, however, August was asking something much darker.

What would happen if Tay was able to identify and locate whoever it was August wanted him to identify and locate? Would August go around and talk to whoever it was and tell them to knock it off? Would August perhaps report the person's location to the FBI and that would be that? Of course not.

August didn't find people and call the law. In his world, August *was* the law, the avenging angel, the messenger of death. John August solved problems the old-fashioned way. He killed them.

Tay could understand how August could feel that what he was doing was right, he could even understand how in some circumstances he might feel that way himself, but it changed nothing. August would still be asking him to identify someone, find them, and mark them to be killed. Whatever loyalty he might feel toward August, he simply didn't see how he could do that.

He had been a policeman for twenty-seven years. For twenty-seven years he had brought criminals to justice. No one really understood what that had all been about for him. No matter how utterly compromised the whole process was, it was still about human decency and values. He went after those who committed crimes for all those who did not. He figured somebody should, and he wanted it to be him.

Tay wanted to explain all that to August and make him understand why he could not do this, but he wasn't sure how. So, he did what everyone does when they want to avoid bluntly turning someone away. He equivocated.

"I'm getting old, John. My knees hurt and I need glasses. I don't have what it takes to run investigations anymore. I'm retired. I'm through."

"Horseshit, Sam. Being an investigator wasn't just your job, it's who you are. You can't retire from who you are."

Tay had always been a digger, natural and obsessive. Sometimes he even saw himself as something of a grinder and he feared that might be true. More and more often he found himself wondering if he had always gotten by on hard work rather than talent. He hoped he had talent, but he wasn't certain of that anymore.

"You're wrong, John. I'm done. I've seen enough."

And he had seen enough, that was true. Too much really. Any cop who was on the job long enough had seen things he would never talk to anybody about. The things he had seen in nearly two decades of investigating killings followed him home and crouched in the dark corners of his bedroom and whispered to him when he tried to sleep. He did not like what they whispered.

That was what he wanted to explain to August, but he didn't know how to do it. He could barely explain it to himself except in a cascade of clichés. How could he ever hope to make August understand? He had no idea what to say.

August seemed to see that. Abruptly, he changed the subject.

"I've always liked this house, Sam."

Tay's thoughts flashed back to the only other time August had been in his house, at least the only other time that he knew of. August had suddenly appeared out of nowhere back then as well, although on that occasion he hadn't bothered to ring the gate bell. He had let himself in through the French doors from the back garden at a moment when Tay was fully occupied trying to fend off three heavies who had forced their way into his house to… well, Tay hadn't been entirely certain what they were there to do, but he was pretty sure it hadn't been to bring him a bunch of flowers. August's unexpected appearance had quickly settled the matter and the heavies bolted before they had the chance to do any damage. Tay owed August one for that, and he owed him for a few other things, too.

"It's a house with a certain gravity," August continued. "It feels anchored in a time that was better than this one."

"I inherited it from—"

"Your father. Yes, you told me."

Tay didn't remember telling August anything of the sort, and he wondered for a moment if he really had told him he inherited the house from his father and forgotten all about it or if August had found it out some other way. August was like that. Over the years Tay had kept noticing that August knew things about him, things that Tay had no idea how he could possibly know.

He had first been introduced to August by a woman who was the Regional Security Officer in the American Embassy in Singapore. She and Tay had been working together on an investigation of the murder of the America ambassador's wife. It was a particularly puzzling case because it hadn't taken Tay very long to discover that no one appeared to want it to be solved. Not Tay's bosses at Singapore CID, not the FBI who had stuck their noses into the investigation and tried to shut it down, and not even the American ambassador whose wife it was who was murdered and dumped in a room at the Singapore Marriott.

Back then, August had claimed to be retired from the United States State Department and told Tay he had bought a bar in Thailand just to give himself something to do. Tay had doubted from the very first that August was retired from anything, certainly not from the State Department, and he had doubted it even more when August pointed them in the right direction to solve the murder of the ambassador's wife.

Ever since then, August had turned up on a remarkable number of occasions just when Tay needed him most. Tay never really had any idea where he came from or where he went to. One moment he wasn't there, and then the next he was. That was how John August operated. He was a ghost.

Tay knew there was no point now in spiraling off into the sort of philosophical ramblings to which he was all too prone. That would accomplish nothing. He had already decided to let August tell his story so that's what he would do.

"I suppose you might as well tell me what happened, John."

A ND THAT WAS when August told Tay everything.
Well, almost everything.
John August never told anybody everything.

PART 2
EXPOSITO

FIVE

I T WAS A fine morning in Pattaya. Air as smooth and warm as melted butter, a sky as hard and blue as glazed porcelain, and a breeze off the ocean in which you could smell the sweetness of childhood. It was the kind of a day that promises better times are coming.

Pattaya is a cheerfully seedy little Thai resort town a couple of hours south of Bangkok that has a decidedly dodgy reputation. It offers visitors a few crappy beaches, some mediocre hotels, a prodigious number of bars, and quite possibly more prostitutes than any other single spot in the entire world.

It is also a place that has a perpetual buzz on, a place where violence is constantly lurking somewhere just beneath the surface. Pattaya is the sort of town that's always on edge and trying hard not to show it.

John August dawdled his motorcycle along Beach Road relishing the emptiness of the morning streets, the softness of the breeze, and the warmth of the sunshine. August rode an old Norton Commando, a 1971 model with a coal-black paint job that he kept tuned to perfection and waxed to a mirror-like gloss. He was certain the Norton was about the most beautiful machine ever made. It was a pain in the ass to maintain, of course, but then when was anything that beautiful ever easy to live with?

Back when August had worked out of the American Embassy in Bangkok, he had known a DEA guy posted there who was a real bike nut. The man had invested more than a year of his life and a ridiculous amount of money in meticulously restoring the Norton to its full original glory. Eventually the fellow's wife lost patience with him and laid down the law. She told him it was either her or the bike. The DEA guy offered August his choice. August picked the bike.

At the end of Beach Road, he rode straight ahead into what everybody in Pattaya called Walking Street. The road had an official name of some kind, he was sure, but he doubted anyone remembered what it was. Since it was closed off to vehicles at night, it had been called Walking Street by everyone for as long as he could remember. At night, Walking Street overflowed with the lost and misbegotten of the world and became the center ring of the circus that was Pattaya in the hours of darkness.

August goosed the Norton's throttle and smiled. Down here past the beach, the sea was blocked off by densely packed shophouses lining both sides of the road. Most of the buildings housed bars or restaurants and the thicket of neon signs arching out over the street looked like the tangled branches of a metal and glass forest. August loved to hear the guttural sound of the big 750cc engine echoing in the confined space. He felt a little silly every time he revved the engine just to hear it growl, but he did it anyway.

Walking Street in daylight was sharply etched by the unrelenting sun of Thailand and generally almost deserted. The few people on the street during the day looked a bit lost to August, as if they couldn't quite remember why they were there.

Occasionally, a few early customers could be seen scattered among the little open-air beer bars that were tucked away almost everywhere. These daylight customers were generally white men, mostly in their sixties or older, and dressed in wrinkled t-shirts and shorts that looked like they had been worn yesterday and maybe the day before, too. They were almost always sitting alone, a bottle of beer in front of them, and staring into the distance at sights only they could see. In the daylight hours, the loneliness of all those old men filled Walking Street like a fog. Sometimes it was so thick August could hardly breathe.

At night, Walking Street was a different place, maybe even a different planet. In the late hours, Pattaya heaved with partying mobs, the music boomed from a hundred open doorways, and the laughter rang harsh on the street corners. It was either a carnival of flashing lights or a neon nightmare, depending entirely on your point of view. Sometimes August thought he was too old for Pattaya, and sometimes he thought he wasn't old enough. He couldn't decide which it was.

A UGUST WASN'T JUST screwing around in Pattaya like most of the other foreigners who were there. He owned a bar he bought as a retirement gig after he stopped working for the government and he had renamed the place Secrets. A little cute maybe, but the irony appealed to him.

Secrets was a two-story shophouse painted dark green with brown trim. It didn't look much like the other bars in Pattaya because it wasn't. There were no flashing neon lights, no rock and roll booming through the door, just a modest entrance with a simple sign above it. Secrets was probably the only bar in Pattaya without a single go-go girl swinging from a silver pole and displaying her assets for the customers.

Instead, the place was dark and woody with a clubby feel to it. It was the sort of place that caused people to lower their voices without thinking about it, the sort of place where you expected a little Billie Holliday or maybe some Chet Baker to be playing quietly in the background, and it usually was.

Secrets served simple but decent American food. Breakfast

all day, thick burgers, dynamite chili, and a solid chicken-fried steak. It was a place that offered Pattaya's foreign community some relief from the soul-deadening shabbiness for which Pattaya was famous. Not that shabbiness was always such a terrible thing, at least not the way August looked at it. Sometimes shabbiness just meant the place had a little soul.

Secrets didn't open until four in the afternoon, although like most everywhere else in Pattaya the concept of opening hours was vague. If the door was unlocked, people could come in. If it wasn't, they couldn't. The door was almost always unlocked by late morning, but that didn't make a great deal of difference since the traffic was usually light until early evening. Foreigners in Pattaya generally didn't wake up until at least noon and few of them were willing to risk any form of serious perambulation for several hours after that.

August turned the Norton off Walking Street and rode about a hundred yards up a little *soi* that was too narrow for cars and trucks. When he stopped in front of Secrets, he killed the engine and locked the bike to a U-bolt he had concreted into the wall.

He grabbed his backpack off the back of the bike and stood for a moment looking up and down the *soi*. A tang of rotting garbage in the air blended with the ever-present aromas of raw sewage, burning charcoal, and fermented fish sauce. August smiled. The smells of Asia had become a part of him somehow. He wasn't sure how that had happened, but it had.

No one was in sight in either direction and the little *soi* looked lonely and sad. At night, Pattaya was like a raucous border town. Tijuana on the Gulf of Thailand. In daylight, it felt like somebody had moved the border.

I NSIDE SECRETS, THERE was a long wooden bar on the right with ten high-backed stools and a brass foot rail.

The rest of the space was one big room furnished with

comfortable-looking black leather chairs grouped around low wooden tables. The lighting was indirect and came mostly from the brass floor lamps with brown and white striped shades that were positioned discreetly around the room. It was bright enough for people to see each other, but dim enough to discourage surgery.

A man behind the bar was leaning on his forearms reading a newspaper, and August nodded to him.

"Morning, Woods."

Woods nodded back, but he didn't say anything. He was dressed in his normal ensemble of jeans and a black t-shirt, but this morning he had a blue bandana wrapped around his head and knotted in the back. August wondered for a moment what the significance of the bandana was, but he decided not to ask.

Woods was a former Navy SEAL with red hair and a thick red beard and he didn't talk a lot. Strangely enough Woods was his first name. No one had used Woods' last name in so long that on the rare occasion August needed to come up with it for some reason he generally had to stop and think what it was.

"Coffee on yet?" August asked.

Woods nodded again. He took a white ceramic mug off a shelf, filled it from the pot in the coffeemaker, and placed it on the bar in front of the last stool at the end, the place where August usually sat in the mornings. Then he went back to reading the *Bangkok Post*.

August pulled a MacBook out of his backpack, put it on the bar next to the mug, and tucked the backpack behind the foot rail that ran along the bottom of the bar. He sat down, flipped up the lid of the MacBook, and logged onto Secrets' Wi-Fi network. He took a long pull from the mug. The coffee tasted as good as it smelled.

There was a time when August couldn't imagine coffee in the morning without a newspaper in his hands, but he had adapted to the digital age. These days he could use his laptop to skim half a dozen newspapers from all over the world before he had even finished his first cup of coffee. It was a lot easier than folding the pages of a newspaper back and forth, and the lighting was certainly better, but the whole process still had one thing in common with reading printed newspapers. In both cases, after he was done reading, he usually wondered why he had wasted his time.

August checked his email. He found a pitch to buy cheap ink cartridges for laser printers, a proposal to invest a fortune for a Nigerian prince, and a promise that he could add three inches to the length of his dick. He figured he already had all the ink, money, and dick he needed. He hit delete three times.

After that, August logged into a website called the Chess Board that he visited regularly. The site hosted a community of chess players from all over the world and organized online games among them.

He checked the messages left for him on the board and found an invitation to play a game waiting for him from someone he didn't know.

That's where August's story got a little complicated.

You see, John August doesn't play chess.

SIX

AUGUST BENT DOWN and fished a pack of Camels and a box of matches out of his backpack. When he laid them on the bar next to his laptop, Woods lowered his newspaper.

"We got a gig, boss?"

"Are my habits that transparent?"

Woods shrugged, but he didn't say anything.

"There's a signal on the Chess Board," August said.

"I hope this job is somewhere good." Woods raised his newspaper again. "Hyderabad was a shit hole."

August shook out a Camel and lit it. Then he reached down the bar, pulled an ashtray toward him, and dumped the match.

A message at the Chess Board asking for a game was a signal to check the draft folder at an iCloud account to which he had access. Leaving instructions in the draft folder of an email service was a little bit more secure than actually sending the email. Since the message was never actually transmitted through a chain of servers, the likelihood of accidental interception was significantly reduced. Intentional interception was another matter altogether. If your digital traffic was being monitored, your access to the draft folder would be tracked and the message would no longer be private.

For that reason, the iCloud account was generally used for routine communications. When operational security was required, the Chess Board message was signed with a name August didn't know, which told him to switch to CryptoCat.

CryptoCat isn't actually an email program, but a desktop application that allows users to set up chat conversations through CryptoCat's own encrypted servers. August had done a little research about it once, just in the interest of broadening his education, and found CryptoCat described on its website this way.

CryptoCat uses a Double Ratchet-based encryption protocol that combines a forward-secure ratchet with a zero round-trip authenticated key exchange.

He never did figure out what that meant.

Regardless of how CryptoCat worked, however, it was a neat little commercial solution to establish secure communications without the need to lug around special gear like encrypted sat phones that make you look a little conspicuous. All you need is your laptop and an internet connection and you're pretty much secure wherever you are.

Of course, pretty much secure doesn't always cut it. Since all electronic communications are vulnerable in one way or another, when you need to be certain your communications are secure, *absolutely* secure, there's only one way to do it. You communicate face to face. You put a guy on an airplane and send him to deliver your message in person. Old school, sure, but that's the only way to guarantee complete security.

That was the irony about the explosion in technology. The only sure way to maintain secrecy now was to avoid technology entirely. The world had progressed a century into the past.

Of course, the message could still leak but, if it did, you could be certain that nobody had found a clever way to listen in somehow and you didn't have to run around like crazy trying to figure out how they had managed to do it. All you had to do was shoot the guy who delivered the message and the leak was plugged. Simple as that.

That was why generally the CryptoCat sessions were used only to communicate that a courier was on the way, to tell August when he would arrive, and to give him the identifying phrases they would each use to establish their bona fides.

August laid his Camel on the edge of the ashtray and opened CryptoCat on his MacBook.

It only took a few moments for him to establish a chat session with whoever it was who used the name Uncle George. August had no idea who that actually was, of course, but it didn't really matter.

CryptoCat handled the exchange of random keys in a manner which was supposed to guarantee both that you were communicating with whoever you thought you were communicating with, and that you were doing it securely. August never entirely believed that, of course, having no idea on earth what a double ratchet-based encryption protocol actually was, but he figured maintaining a healthy level of cynicism about such things was probably a good thing.

As soon as the CryptoCat server authenticated the chat session, August began typing.

This is Aunt Susie.

Uncle George, Aunt Susie. August frequently wondered who had come up with something so idiotic.

He picked up his Camel and smoked quietly while he waited to see what Uncle George had in store for him this time.

After two or three minutes the first line of the session appeared on his screen.

Expect visitor Thursday approximately 1100 Zulu.

11:00am GMT on Thursday would be 6:00pm, Thai time.

Authentication phrase: Do you think the Redskins will make it to the Super Bowl? Response phrase: They might if their passing game doesn't let them down.

Since the Redskins hadn't been in the Super Bowl in at least twenty-five years and looked like they might never go to a Super Bowl again, August figured that pass phrase was as unique as anyone could possibly come up with.

Acknowledged, he replied.

And with that Uncle George, whoever he was, terminated the chat session.

August stubbed out his cigarette and finished his coffee. It had gone cold, but he drank it anyway.

T HE ORIGINS OF the Band went all the way back to the time of Ronald Reagan, but when Bill Clinton became president the gray eminences behind it started to worry.

They decided that it would be better to move the Band entirely outside of government rather than risk exposing its workings to the scrutiny of politicians who might be unsympathetic, even ready to score political points for themselves by exposing some of the things the Band had done.

An international business consultancy was quietly organized under the wonderfully bland name of Red River Consultants and all the functions of the Band moved into it. The Band still did the same stuff, but it did it without risking attracting attention from some Congressmen who might get curious about its activities or people from the Office of Management and Budget who might wonder what those bland looking entries in the national intelligence budget were really for.

That was all quite a bit before August's time, of course. The CIA recruited him out of Delta a year or so after 9/11 and he got all fired up about joining the Agency. It felt like a chance to get right out on the edge and go face to face with the worst of the bad guys. And that was exactly what it turned out to be. He thought he had been part of some serious shit when he was Delta, but over the next twenty-two months he discovered he didn't have any idea what serious shit really was.

After a couple of years in Washington, the Agency posted August to the American Embassy in Thailand under diplomatic cover. His title was National Security Council Liaison to the Department of State. The title didn't make much sense to him, and it made even less sense to the Foreign Service Officers he knew around the embassy. The truth was that nobody at the State Department had the slightest idea what August was really doing there in their embassy, but they all had the good sense not to ask. He was glad they didn't. If they had found out, they would have had a fucking cat.

The truth was that August's job was pretty straightforward. He was the Agency's go-to guy whenever some kind of off-the-books action was needed in the Asia-Pacific region. Putting it plainly, mostly he was called on to kill people when people in Asia needed killing.

Those assignments generally fell into three distinct categories.

The first category was simply to make somebody dead, and how August did that was up to him. That was the rarest of all his assignments.

The second category was to make somebody dead, but for it to appear they died accidentally rather than on purpose. That was his most common assignment.

The third category was complicated. It was to make somebody dead in a way that would appear to be an accident to almost everyone, but to a specific and very limited audience the death would have a very different meaning and convey a very distinct message.

August quickly discovered he had a real knack for killing people and making their deaths look accidental. It's not the kind of talent your mother brags about to the neighbors maybe, but in the right hands and for the right purposes it can be very, very useful.

August killed terrorists, mostly, but also a few criminals and some money launderers and a couple of traitors, too. The people whose lives he took for his country all needed killing, as far as he knew, and he thought killing them had saved the lives of other people, perhaps a great many of them. Could he be absolutely certain of that? Of course not, but when he was a soldier he never spent a minute wondering whether the deaths for which he was responsible were really necessary. When he was with the Agency, he continued to think of himself as a soldier, and he didn't spend a minute wondering about it then either.

August used to believe the truth would set people free, but he came to understand that a bullet was a far more dependable bet.

A UGUST WAS WORKING under diplomatic cover in the embassy in Bangkok when he was recruited into the Band during the last years of Bush the Younger. He was approached by a senior Agency figure who had recently retired and taken up employment at Red River Consultants where he ostensibly offered his wisdom on world affairs to the firm's clients. The reality of it, however, was that he led the Band. And he was referred to by the few people who knew what he really did, perhaps inevitably, as the Conductor.

August had no idea the Band existed, of course, but when the Conductor read him in on it, a lot of things he had heard about during his time at the Agency started to make sense to him. He had always thought it awfully strange how from time to time certain people who meant harm to the United States committed suicide or died in accidents or simply disappeared without a trace. Since he hadn't been involved in arranging their deaths and was pretty sure the Agency hadn't been involved, he generally assumed that the operation had been carried out by another friendly intelligence organization like the Mossad. Or for all he knew they really *had* all died in accidents or committed suicide, although he doubted that.

He liked and admired the man who was the Conductor so it wasn't hard to convince him to leave the Agency and join the Band. Once he knew there was an organization so secret he had never heard the slightest whisper about it, an organization that took on the most sensitive and important operations at the personal direction of the President of the United States, he had no doubts. He wanted to be part of it.

The Conductor asked August to remain in Thailand and put together a small team to operate from there. He had built up a good deal of experience in moving through Asian cultures without making unnecessary waves, and that was something not many white guys could do. The Conductor told him they had guys who knew the Middle East, guys who knew Europe and Africa and South America, but guys who knew Asia were much rarer. August knew it was probably bullshit and the Conductor was just flattering him to get him to sign on, but he really didn't care. He wanted to be part of the Band.

And that was how August wound up owning a bar in Pattaya. A middle-aged white guy who retired early from the State Department and bought himself a bar in Pattaya as a retirement gig?

No one would think twice about why August was in Thailand or what he was doing there. He was a walking cliché.

SEVEN

ON THE SECOND floor of Secrets there was a small office where August worked when he needed to do the things required to keep the place running and as solvent as possible. That's where he was on Thursday afternoon when Woods gave the door a single sharp rap, opened it, and leaned in.

"Visitor downstairs, boss."

August looked at his watch. Ten minutes before six. The messenger was pretty much right on time.

"Bring him up here."

Woods hesitated.

"What?" August asked.

The corners of Woods' mouth twitched. It was as close as August had ever seen him come to an actual grin.

"It's not a him," he said.

That stopped August. The last half dozen times the Conductor had sent out a messenger it had been the same fellow. A young guy with dark brown hair brushed straight back who was slightly built, wore heavy black glasses, and dressed with the preppy consistency of a man whose clothes were ordered in bulk from Ralph Lauren catalogues. He told August his name was Lawrence. It probably wasn't, but August didn't care. The name fit the guy perfectly and it led August to coin the ideal nickname for him.

"You're telling me that the messenger isn't Lawrence of Princeton?"

Woods shrugged. "This is some chick."

"Maybe it isn't the messenger."

Woods shrugged again.

"Do you know her?" August asked.

Woods shook his head. "Never seen her before."

"She's a Thai?"

"Looks a little Chinese to me."

"Chinese? I don't know any Chinese chicks."

"You might want to know this one. Pretty outstanding."

Woods did the thing with the corners of his mouth again.

Sending a woman people would notice and remember as a messenger didn't sound like something the Conductor would do. The timing had to be just a coincidence, August decided. This couldn't be the messenger. It had to be somebody else.

But now he was curious. Who was this woman Woods felt compelled to describe as outstanding-looking, and why was she at Secrets asking to see him?

"Don't bring her up here," he told Woods. "I'll come down."

A UGUST STOOD IN the shadows at the bottom of the stairs and examined the woman who had asked for him. He was certain he had never seen her before.

She was slim and on the short side and her black hair was pulled tightly into a braided bun at the back of her head. She was wearing jeans and black ankle boots with low heels and a shirt buttoned at the cuffs that was so white it could have been a puff of fresh meringue. The woman's back was to him so August couldn't see her face, but her body language as she stood at the bar was confident. It radiated impatience and even disdain. She had a big dark-green leather bag hanging over her right shoulder that looked expensive. Actually, everything about her looked expensive.

Secrets wasn't very crowded since it was early. There were a couple of guys at the bar and three couples up at the front of the room had pulled two tables together and were sharing bottles of wine. August walked to a table as far away from everyone as possible, caught Woods' eye, and made a little circling motion with his forefinger. Woods leaned toward the woman and touched her on the elbow. He pointed to where August was sitting and she turned.

August saw that she was less than beautiful, but a good deal more than pretty. She had a high forehead and sculptured brows above big almond-shaped eyes that were more green than brown. Her wide cheekbones and oval face reminded him of a bust he had once seen of some ancient Egyptian queen whose name he couldn't quite remember. Chinese looking, to be sure, August thought, but with a good bit of Dutch trader or Portuguese sailor somewhere back there in her gene pool. There was a murmur of nineteenth-century Eurasia about her, a whisper of exotic aromas and spicy tastes.

The most striking thing about her was her pale complexion, so achromatic that her skin appeared almost entirely without color. Her face looked nearly translucent and seemed to glow with a formless light from somewhere within her. It gave her features the wan luminescence of an angel in a Tintoretto painting.

He rose from his chair.

"I'm John August," he said, offering his hand. "How can I help you?"

She took his hand with a slight smile and it felt just like he knew it would. Soft and firm at the same time. When she took the chair opposite him, she said nothing at first. She seemed to study him as if she was trying to remember something, then she leaned forward against the table on her forearms and spoke in a voice that was throaty, like a smoker, and surprisingly low pitched. She spoke just loudly enough for August to hear what she was saying without it carrying to anyone else.

"Do you think the Redskins will make it to the Super Bowl?"

Oh shit. Seriously?

August was badly enough wrong-footed that it took him a few seconds to dredge the confirmation phrase out of his memory. Finally, it came to him.

"They might if their passing game doesn't let them down."

Neither August nor the woman said anything else for a moment, but then she smiled. He thought it was a great smile.

"You look surprised. Did you forget when I was getting here?"

"No, I didn't forget. It's just that… well, I was expecting Lawrence of Princeton."

"Who?"

"It's the nickname we've given to the usual messenger."

"If you give me a nickname, I hope you'll come up with something more interesting than that."

August wasn't sure what to say so he didn't say anything.

"Anyway," she continued, "I trust you're not too disappointed I'm not the messenger you were expecting."

"I'm not complaining. To tell the truth, you're a lot taller than Lawrence of Princeton is. Which is good."

Since the woman wasn't very tall at all, his comment seemed to amuse her, and August felt that frisson of pleasure that every man feels whenever he manages to raise amusement in a good-looking woman. He knew he was beginning to preen a little and that annoyed him.

"Maybe we'd better take this upstairs to my office," he said quickly, covering his response. "Would you like a drink?"

"No, thank you. I don't drink."

"Coffee then, maybe? A soda?"

"Coffee would be fine. Black, no sugar."

"Just the way I drink it."

45

The moment the words were out of August's mouth, he felt like an idiot. Why had he said that? He knew that most men lose all control and start to prattle pointlessly whenever they are talking to an attractive woman, but he wanted to think he was better than that. Maybe he wasn't.

August stood up before he had to think about it anymore, walked to the bar, and asked Woods to bring two coffees up to the office. Woods raised his eyebrows, which for Woods was practically a recitation of the Gettysburg Address, and nodded.

Back at the table where the woman was waiting, August said, "This way please."

A UGUST THOUGHT OF his office as comfortable, but it was a place where he worked. It wasn't designed to impress visitors.

Along the wall opposite his desk he had one of the tables and two of the same leather chairs from downstairs so he would have a quiet place to eat. If he ate downstairs, people came over to talk or, worse, insist he join them at their table. Why did so many people think eating alone was sad, even pitiful, and that it was their duty as friends to save you from the shame of it? August liked eating alone, generally reading while he ate, but to be allowed to do that in his own place he had to hide upstairs in his office. It hardly seemed fair.

August gestured the woman toward the closer of the two chairs, then he moved some files he had stacked on the other chair and sat down opposite her.

"You have me at something of a disadvantage," he said. "You know my name, but I don't know yours."

"That's right," she said. "You don't."

August was still trying to decide what to say to that when Woods came in without knocking and served the coffee. After he finished, he left and closed the door behind himself, never having said a word.

"So, you're not going to tell me your name?"

The woman appeared to think about that briefly, then said, "No."

"Suit yourself."

"I'm just trying to make it more difficult for you to give me a nickname."

"Well then, you've failed. I already have a nickname for you."

"Really? Are you going to tell me what it is?"

August made a show of thinking about that for a moment, then said, "No."

The woman laughed, and it was heartfelt and genuine, and in spite of himself August again felt the same frisson of accomplishment he had felt the first time she had laughed at something he said.

"Maybe we should just get right down to it then." August folded his arms and shifted back in his chair. "What do you have for me?"

EIGHT

THE WOMAN PUT her dark-green shoulder bag on the table and dipped into it to remove an ordinary manila envelope.

It wasn't very thick. August knew that could be good news or it could be bad news. It might mean the assignment was something simple that wouldn't involve the risk of starting World War Three, or it could mean it was something complicated about which the Conductor knew very little and August would be mostly on his own.

The woman pulled open the flap. August noticed the envelope wasn't sealed, which was odd.

She removed an 8x10 photograph, placed it on the table, and turned it toward him.

"This is Fang Li Bao, known to his friends as Billy Fang," she said. "He works for the Hong Kong and Shanghai Bank in London where he runs a small team that does security assessments for the bank, mostly of their employees and properties they own. He is closely involved with the bank's operations in Hong Kong and China in particular. Until two years ago, Billy was an employee of the Central Intelligence Agency with a level four clearance."

The woman looked at August carefully as though she thought he might not be following everything she said.

"He was a case officer?" August asked.

She bobbed her head once, quickly, almost as if she didn't want anyone else to see her responding. Since there was no one in the office other than the two of them, however, August didn't see the point in her being so discreet.

"Beginning about a year ago," she went on before he could ask her about it, "the Agency has seen some of its most valuable assets inside China go down. And I don't mean going down in a casual sort of way. We're talking about China. They were executed. One was reportedly shot right outside the government building where he worked just to make sure his coworkers got the message. The lucky ones were imprisoned. Seventeen separate sources have been blown and five covert facilities exposed. And that's just so far. It's already been one of the most damaging counterintelligence losses in the history of the Agency, and there are concerns it could get worse. Maybe a lot worse."

"And Billy Fang was responsible?"

"Yes."

"Yet he hasn't been arrested."

"No, he hasn't. The FBI has run surveillance on him for two years, but they don't think they've got enough to extradite him from the UK, and certainly not enough to convict him even if they can get him back in the US. He's very good. Very careful."

August nodded and waited for the rest.

"Billy Fang has been drip feeding what he knows about our assets and operations in China to the Chinese government for at least a year. He will soon be making a trip to Hong Kong during which there is reason to believe he intends to defect to China and turn over to the Chinese the balance of what he knows about American assets there. It's apparently quite a lot."

"And the FBI isn't going to pick him up before that?"

"They've proposed that to the Brits and been turned down. There's nothing more they can do."

"I think I can see where this is going."

"I'm sure you can. Your assignment is to intercept Billy Fang in Hong Kong and stop him before he can defect."

"And by stop him, I gather you mean—"

"Of course that's what I mean, Mr. August."

"Do you know exactly when he's traveling from London to Hong Kong?"

"Yes. Tomorrow."

At first August wasn't certain he had heard her correctly.

"I'm sorry, when?"

The woman just looked at him.

"You didn't really say tomorrow, did you?"

She looked some more.

"You can't be serious."

"Mr. Fang is leaving London Heathrow tomorrow on a Cathay Pacific flight that arrives in Hong Kong on Saturday morning. He has a booking at the Cordis Hotel in Mongkok. We think the Chinese intend to pick him up on Sunday. Perhaps Monday at the latest."

August struggled to keep his face empty and said nothing. He just drank his coffee and looked at the woman.

After a moment she smiled slightly. Maybe, he thought, his face wasn't as empty as he would have liked.

"Do you want me to tell the Conductor you can't do it?" she asked.

"Nobody can do it. If we left for Hong Kong right now, I couldn't get my people in place until late on Friday. That would give us, at most, thirty-six hours to identify this guy, come up with a plan, and execute it."

"If you don't do it, Billy Fang is going to defect to China. American assets in place there will be killed, perhaps dozens of them, and we will go blind in China for a decade, maybe even longer."

"It doesn't matter if this guy is going to personally fire a nuclear missile at New York City. That changes nothing. This can't be done in thirty-six hours."

The woman drank some coffee and thought about that.

"What do you expect me to do now?" she asked.

"I don't expect anything," August shrugged. "Your job was to deliver a message. You've done that. I guess that means you can go home now. Unless, of course, you want to go to Hong Kong and take a crack at the assignment yourself."

"I'm just a messenger. You're the operator."

"Then maybe I ought to ask the Conductor to make me a messenger, too. Sounds like a hell of a lot better job than the one I have."

"He's not going to be happy about you refusing this assignment."

"I'm not refusing the assignment. I'm telling you it's not possible."

"You haven't even gone to Hong Kong and you're saying it's not possible. Like I said, I'm just a messenger, but even I can see there's a big difference between going and looking at the assignment and concluding it's not possible, and sitting on your ass in a bar in Thailand and saying it's not possible."

August hadn't expected to get that kind of push back from the woman. Lawrence of Princeton would have just nodded and been on his way. He didn't know whether to be annoyed or amused. He settled for a little bit of each.

"Would you like some more coffee?" he asked her.

"No, I don't want any fucking coffee! This is important! This matters! Don't you even care?"

"Look, lady, don't try to push this off on me. I wasn't the one who investigated this clown for two years and couldn't come up with enough evidence to take him. I'm not the one who let this go on until the day before everything is about to hit the fan. I'm not responsible for any of this. I just work here."

"Then do your goddamned job! You may not be responsible

for it happening, but you have the power to stop it, and if you don't, you're responsible for that."

August got up and walked over to his desk and pushed papers around until he found a half-empty pack of Camels and a box of matches. He scooped up a heavy, cut-glass ashtray, returned to where he had been sitting, and dumped the ashtray on the table in front of the woman.

"I'd prefer you don't smoke," she said.

"Really?" August asked. "And you think I look like a guy who gives a shit what you prefer?"

He shook out a cigarette and rolled it around in his fingers for a moment as if he was giving due consideration to her asking him not to smoke. He wasn't. He put it in his mouth and lit it. He started to offer the woman one just to be even more annoying, but then he decided not to bother.

"This is my office and my office is inside my bar. No one is forcing you to stay. You can leave anytime you want."

He dumped the match into the ashtray and leaned forward on his forearms. He smoked quietly and looked at the woman without saying anything else.

"Are you always like this?" she asked.

"No, sometimes I'm rude and ungracious. Occasionally I'm told I'm downright unpleasant. You must have caught me on a good day."

The woman reached out and rolled her coffee cup around in its saucer. August's eyes went to her hand and he couldn't help but notice how long and graceful her fingers were.

"You have to try to do this, Mr. August. It matters. You're the last hope of stopping this guy before he does more damage than you can possibly imagine."

August smoked. He said nothing.

"For God's sake, at least go to Hong Kong and have a look. Check out the circumstances. Maybe there's some way to get it done you haven't thought about."

He smoked. He continued to say nothing.

"Why won't you even do that?"

August finished his cigarette without answering the woman. Stubbing it out in the ashtray, he leaned back in the chair and folded his arms.

"You don't sound like you're just a messenger."

"What do you mean?"

"Messengers deliver messages, and then they go home. They don't sit around and argue with me about the assignment that's in the message."

"I'm not Lawrence of Princeton."

"I can see that, but it still sounds to me like you are personally invested in this assignment somehow. What are you not telling me?"

"I'm not interested in answering your questions. My job was to deliver this assignment to you and I've done that."

She picked up the manila envelope and dumped it on top of the photograph. She neatly squared up the edges of the two and pushed the small stack across the table to August. He wondered what else was in the envelope, but he didn't pick it up.

"This is what I was instructed to give you, and I have done that. I hope you will carry out your assignment. At the very least, I hope you will go to Hong Kong and look over the circumstances before you decide that you cannot carry out your assignment."

The woman stood and picked up her shoulder bag.

"I apologize if I have spoken out of turn. I was simply surprised when you said you wouldn't do it, and I spoke my mind without thinking. I have completed my assignment. Now it's up to you whether or not you complete yours."

"Are you headed straight back to Washington or are you staying in Pattaya tonight?"

The woman hesitated. "I don't see why that's relevant."

"I guess it isn't," August shrugged. "Unless you want to have dinner."

The woman looked at August and a half smile flickered at the corners of her mouth.

"Seriously?"

"Sure. Why not?"

"I can think of a half dozen reasons off the top of my head, and if you give me a minute or two I can probably come up with a dozen more."

"Is that a no?"

"Why would you even ask, Mr. August?"

"Well, hell, I had to try. If I hadn't, just think how disappointed you would be."

She shook her head slowly. "I would like to tell you that you're the most arrogant man I have ever met, but you're not."

"You mean you know men worse than me?"

"Oh yes, quite a few actually."

"Shit, I've got to up my game."

The woman laughed out loud, and it was throaty and apparently genuine and filled with promises August knew she would never keep.

"Good night, John August. I know you'll do the right thing."

Then she turned, opened the door, and was gone.

NINE

UGUST PICKED UP the envelope the woman left behind and slid out the small stack of paper inside. There was a sheet with a few of the usual details about the target's personal habits, the sort of thing that might be helpful in planning an operation, and a couple more photographs, but there was nothing else.

Now he knew Billy Fang was intelligent, punctual to a fault, liked western women, and ate a lot of cheeseburgers. August wondered what good any of that did him. He also wondered how many blonds eating cheeseburgers Billy Fang would be likely to find in Beijing.

August decided to stop thinking about Billy Fang. The operation the messenger had described was impossible in the time they were being given to do it. It was as simple as that. A complete non-starter.

He stuffed everything back into the envelope and went downstairs.

. . .

C LAIRE WAS WAITING for him at the same table where he had been sitting with the messenger.

"I gather this isn't a coincidence," August said as he sat down.

"There are no coincidences, Bossman. You taught me that."

August nodded and waited for what he knew would be coming. She didn't make him wait very long.

"What did the messenger have for us?" she asked.

August hadn't told her he was expecting a messenger, but they hadn't had an assignment in a while and he wasn't silly enough to think that Woods and Claire didn't talk about things like that.

"You must be bored," he told Claire. She didn't answer. She just looked at him and waited.

Claire wasn't her real name, of course, but it was the one she used now. She was tall for a woman, lean and fit looking, and her long hair was pulled back into a ponytail. She looked like a girl who hadn't been out of college all that long and had probably played on the volleyball team when she was there. August didn't know where Claire had gone to college, but he doubted she had played on a volleyball team wherever it was.

She had been an operator at the Agency at the same time he was and had joined the Band a few years later. Now she was generally thought of by most everyone as August's second-in-command in Asia. He was pretty sure he had never said anything like that officially, but sometimes he thought perhaps he should have.

August glanced around to make certain there was no one within earshot. It wasn't even seven yet, and on Pattaya time that was pretty much first thing in the morning so the place was mostly empty. Woods was playing one of his favorite remastered Bessie Smith cuts, 'Nobody Knows You When You're Down and Out'. If Pattaya ever had to designate a national anthem, August thought, that song would be the perfect choice.

"I told her we wouldn't take the assignment."

"Really? You've never refused one before."

Then Claire realized what else August had just said. She leaned forward and lowered her voice.

"*Her*? The messenger wasn't Lawrence of Princeton?"

August shook his head and looked around again. He knew no one but Claire could hear anything he said, but he still felt uncomfortable having a public conversation about an assignment.

"Maybe we'd better take this upstairs," he said.

"WHO WAS SHE?" Claire asked.

August was sitting exactly where he had been with the messenger a half hour or so before and Claire was sitting exactly where the messenger had been. He knew it didn't matter, but there was something about it that bothered him anyway.

"No idea. Never seen her before."

"Then how can you be sure—"

"She had the correct recognition phrase. Everything else fit. I have no reason to doubt she was who she said she was."

"Okay, so what was the assignment and why did you turn it down?"

"I'm going to call down and ask Woods to bring me a beer," he said. "How about one for you?"

When Claire nodded, he walked over to the desk, picked up the telephone, and told Woods to bring up a couple of Beerlao's. He put the phone down, but almost immediately picked it up again.

"Make that three, Woods, and get somebody to cover the bar for you. You need to hear this, too."

· · ·

A FTER WOODS PASSED the beers around, he pulled a chair over and sat down. He and Claire looked at August and waited.

"The problem with the assignment," August said, "is that it's in Hong Kong and has to be completed in less than forty-eight hours. There's simply not enough time to get where we need to be, develop a plan, and implement it without taking unacceptable risks. I'm not going to do that."

"Who's the target?" Claire asked.

August pointed to the envelope lying on the table between Claire and Woods, and picked up his beer. "It's all in there," he said. "Knock yourself out."

Claire slid the pages from the envelope. Everyone sipped their beers in silence while she examined the photos, passed them to Woods, and then read the notes that were in the envelope with them. She passed those to Woods as well and then looked at August, waiting for the rest.

"He's a former CIA employee who has been under investigation by the FBI," he said. "They think he's been leaking the identities of American assets in China to the Chinese, but they don't have enough to charge him or arrest him. They also think he's about to defect. He leaves London tomorrow on a flight to Hong Kong that arrives on Saturday morning, and their information is that the Chinese are picking him up there in Hong Kong on Sunday. You see the problem."

"The Conductor is giving us forty-eight hours to find this guy, scout out the location, develop a plan, and implement it?"

August nodded at Claire. "In a nutshell."

"Wow," she said.

"Exactly."

T HE THREE OF them drank their beers quietly for a few minutes and thought about that. Nobody said anything.

August figured that was because there really wasn't anything to say. He was just about to declare the meeting closed when, to his surprise, Woods spoke up.

"How much damage could this guy do if he makes it to China?"

"All I know is what the messenger said. And she said it could cause a lot."

"Do you know about the American assets in China who've been executed over the last year or so?"

August nodded.

"There've been five or six that I know of. They even shot one of them right in the middle of the office where he was working as a lesson to everyone else there."

August nodded again.

"Was this guy responsible?"

"That's what the messenger said."

"And you believe her?"

"I have no reason not to."

Woods took that in while he finished his beer. He thought about it some more, and then suddenly rapped the bottom of the empty bottle sharply against the table.

"Well, fuck," he said. "That's a big goddamn deal. I think we ought to at least check this out."

"That's what I think, too," Claire quickly added.

"Whoa," August said. He leaned back in his chair and folded his arms. "This isn't exactly a democracy, you know. We don't take a vote on this stuff."

"Maybe not, Bossman," Claire said, "but Woods has a good point. We're just asking you to take another look at this."

"You can't seriously believe that we have enough time to find this guy and put together a feasible plan before he takes the big leap, do you?"

"Do you know where he's staying?" she asked.

"The Cordis in Mongkok."

59

"Never heard of it."

"It used to be called—"

"I remember now," Claire interrupted. "Langham Place. That's that big hotel they built in Mongkok a few years ago thinking it would revive the neighborhood."

August nodded.

"Mongkok's a good choice as a place to stash him if the Chinese are going to pull him out. Every street mobbed with locals and not a tourist in sight." Claire tapped her forefinger on the stack of photographs that Woods had dropped back on the table while he read the brief. "With a face like his he's not going to stand out in Mongkok, and there's not much chance of him running into anyone he knows around there."

"Look, all I'm saying," Woods jumped in, "is that we ought to go to Hong Kong and look around. My guess is it will turn out you're right. There's simply not enough time for us to get it done."

"Then why go at all?" August asked.

"Well, who knows? Funny shit happens all the time. Maybe we'll find ourselves standing behind this guy on Nathan Road and just push him in front of a bus. There's a lot at stake here. I think we ought to at least take a look."

August had known Woods for over a decade and that was the longest speech he had ever heard him make. He might have used up his quota of words for at least the next six months, but he had gotten August's attention by doing it. Just as he no doubt expected to.

August looked at Claire. "And that's what you think, too?"

"Hong Kong's a cool place," she said. "We go, spend a couple of days, have some good Cantonese food, and come home if an opportunity to deal with the target doesn't come up. Come on, Bossman. In and out, quick and clean. No footprints. What have we got to lose?"

August looked from Claire to Woods and back again.

"You guys seriously want to check this out? Really?"

Claire and Woods both nodded.

"Well, shit," August sighed.

TEN

AUGUST HADN'T CHANGED his mind about whether they could do it, but Claire and Woods were right about one thing. There was a lot at stake and it was at least worth taking a look.

There was almost certainly no way they could develop and execute a plan in the time available to them without being downright reckless. Strange things did occasionally happen, however. Maybe there was only one chance in a hundred they would stumble over some way to get to the target within the very small window they had, but it was a short trip up to Hong Kong and just taking a look didn't really create any risks, did it?

At least that's what August told himself at the time.

Later, looking back, he wished he had told himself something else.

AUGUST AND HIS team generally moved around the region using a charter company that flew a couple of Dassault Falcons and a Gulfstream out of Manila.

Red River Consultants paid all the bills, of course, but the lunatic German who ran the charter company thought he had figured out that they were really CIA so he never argued with any strange requests they might have and gave them priority service in getting aircraft where they were needed. August liked that. He figured it made them the only operators in the entire world who used the Central Intelligence Agency for a cover.

But, if they were going to do this, they needed to keep a far lower profile than flying into Hong Kong on a sixty-five-million-dollar private jet would afford them. They needed to slip quietly into town, take a look around, confirm what he already thought — that the assignment was impossible — then slip quietly right back out of town again. No muss, no fuss. Like they were never even there.

"I want to keep this strictly low profile," August told Claire and Woods. "Just the three of us. We travel separately on three different commercial flights and use different credit cards to keep the reservations from being linked together."

"If we do all three bookings at once and anyone checks the booking times," Claire said, "the connection will still be obvious."

"If anyone goes to that much trouble, it'll probably be because we're already screwed anyway."

Claire moved over to August's desk, woke up his laptop, and checked the Friday flights from Bangkok to Hong Kong. The early morning flights were all full, but there were seats available on a Thai Airways flight at 12:30pm, a Cathay Pacific flight at 1:30pm, and another Thai Airways flight at 2:00pm.

August might be willing to take a little punishment every now and then for his country, but flying Thai Airways was beyond his tolerance for pain. He told Claire to book the 1:30pm Cathay Pacific flight for him and she and Woods could divide themselves up on the two Thai flights. That would get him to Hong Kong on Friday at about 5:00pm local time, with one of the others arriving just before him and the other just after.

"What identities do you want to use?" Claire asked.

"Mix them up. Maybe one Canadian, one Australian, and one Brit. Pick some identities we haven't used in a while. Other than that, surprise me."

Claire nodded and bent back to the laptop's keyboard.

"One other thing," August said. "Get us rooms at the Cordis so we can stick close to this guy. And we'll all use public taxis to get to the hotel from the airport. No hotel cars. Too conspicuous and easy to keep track of."

"You don't want to stay at the safe house?"

The Band kept an apartment in a big building high in the Mid-Levels above Hong Kong Harbor. It was a nice apartment and August liked it, but it was a long slog from the Mid-Levels across the harbor and all the way up the Kowloon Peninsula to Mongkok. Even using the MTR and doing most of the trip underground, it would take them close to forty-five minutes every time they went back and forth, longer during busy periods, and Hong Kong had a lot of busy periods.

"If the information they're giving us is good, we'll probably have thirty-six hours between the time this guy gets to Hong Kong and the Chinese pick him up. I don't want to use up most of that traveling from the Mid-Levels to Mongkok and back."

"You sound like you're changing your mind about whether we can do this, Bossman."

He did sound like that, it occurred to August. Force of habit, he supposed. When you work an assignment, you think about handling it, not reasons you can't do it. He had looked at assignments like that for a long time. It was hard to think about them any other way.

"What do you want to do about gear?" Woods asked.

That was a good question. The safe house had a cache of weapons and other gear that was difficult to carry when they traveled and it wouldn't take too much time for one person to make a single quick trip to the safe house to grab some of it, but what would they need? Since August had no plan, and not the slightest idea there was even any way they could do this much less *how* they might be able to do it, he had no idea what gear they might need. None.

When August hesitated, Woods said, "Never mind. I'll take care of it. I'll just use my imagination and surprise you."

August nodded. Normally the way they geared up would be his call, but this wasn't really going to happen anyway, was it? So why should he care what gear they had? He quietly congratulated himself on his indifference and saw that as solid proof that his feet remained planted firmly on a road that would take them on to reality.

August told Woods and Claire he would see them in Hong Kong. Later that night, he rode the Norton up to Bangkok.

B ANGKOK HAS TWO airports, but the primary one used by most international flights is called Suvarnabhumi.

The construction of Suvarnabhumi began in 1973 in an unpromising marshy area south of Bangkok that most people called the Cobra Swamp, but the airport didn't actually open until the end of 2006. If you can figure out how it took the Thais thirty-three years to build a new airport, you will understand exactly how the entire country works.

Cobra Swamp lies just off the main highway between Pattaya and Bangkok. It's normally about an hour north of Pattaya, or maybe twice that if the traffic is awful, and it can be reached from most parts of Bangkok in about the same amount of time. August didn't really need to go up to Bangkok the night before they left in order to make his flight. He just wanted to.

August had a bolt hole apartment in Bangkok in a building just off Soi Thonglor that was on the south side of the city. The location gave him easy access from Pattaya without having to cross the city and endure its internationally famous traffic jams. No one else knew about his apartment and he had gone to considerable lengths to keep it that way. The Conductor didn't know about it. Even Claire and Woods didn't know about it. August's guess was that Claire and Woods had bolt holes of their own that he didn't know about either.

It wasn't that you didn't trust the people you worked with, although he supposed sometimes you probably didn't, but you still needed a place to go to ground where you were absolutely positive no one could find you for at least a few days. There were too many ways they could all end up in the shit. There had to be a safe place where you could go to clean up and regroup and figure a way forward.

August's apartment was in an older building in a quiet area off the main road. It wasn't the sort of flashy new building that had sprung up recently all over Bangkok to attract foreigners who were too dumb to know the prices real estate developers were asking them were outrageously inflated. There were a couple of Japanese tenants in the building and some Indians, but no westerners he had ever seen. Certainly, no Americans.

August habitually avoided other Americans in Thailand and most Europeans as well. There was an Australian girl in Bangkok who worked at the embassy whom he slept with occasionally. He'd had her checked out, of course, but she came up clean. If you had to take a risk with somebody, he thought Australians were generally a good choice because no one believed Australians were important enough to bother to compromise them. New Zealanders were okay, too, but then they were almost the same as Australians anyway.

The staff at his building knew him as Francis X. Bushman, which he thought was rather droll. Bushman was presumably a Canadian investor who lived somewhere in North America and only used his apartment in Bangkok occasionally.

August wasn't certain how showing up on a lovingly restored 1971 Norton Commando fit the image of a Canadian investor looking for business opportunities in Southeast Asia, but he didn't worry about it. His guess was that the Thais just shrugged off his bike as nothing more than one more piece of evidence of something they already knew perfectly well: all white guys really were nuts.

F OR A FOREIGNER, life in Thailand can be pretty good. It's a little like being in a kindergarten class where the teacher doesn't bother to show up very often.

That was one of the reasons August particularly liked riding the Norton at night. The Norton had a reputation as one of the fastest production bikes ever built and August thought it was only right to let it strut its stuff every now and again. There was no better time to do that than a late-night ride from Pattaya up to Bangkok.

Bikes weren't allowed on the motorway, so when August flew by on the Norton at ninety miles an hour any cop who wasn't asleep or drunk would quickly look the other way. Thai policemen instinctively understand that no good can possibly come from messing with a foreigner doing ninety on a big, expensive bike and riding on a road where he isn't allowed.

Anybody with the balls to do that had some serious juice. The foreigner knew somebody, he had to, and the somebody he knew would be a long way above a traffic cop in status and authority. There's an old saying about pilots. There are old pilots, and there are bold pilots, but there are no old, bold pilots. The same could be said of Thai cops. There were no old, bold Thai coppers. Not a one.

The other reason August liked riding the Norton at night was that the tropics only truly come alive in darkness. An elevated expressway runs most of the way from Pattaya to Bangkok, but there is also an older highway a bit to the east and that was the route he usually took. That road ran through some of the flattest and most unpromising countryside August had ever ridden in anywhere, but it also cut a swath through the reality of life in Thailand. The sights, the sounds, and the smells of it were all right there on the surface. When you're sealed up in an air-conditioned car, you encounter little or nothing of them. But when you're on a bike, you don't just encounter them, you become part of them.

Yellow vapor lights on tall aluminum poles dotted both sides of the road in locations so random that their layout defied rational analysis, their lamps throwing sulfurous-looking stripes across the highway. Near Pattaya, the roadside was crowded with street vendors, their metal cooking carts strung with fluorescent tubes and their charcoal fires painting the air with a streaky haze. A barefoot boy in dark shorts and a t-shirt who looked to be not much more than ten sat on a rock next to one of the carts eating some kind of meat off a wooden stick and following August's bike with his eyes. When he saw August looking at him, he broke into a grin and waved. August waved back.

A little further on, the vendors thinned out and a few scattered, doll-sized houses appeared. They were built largely of concrete blocks and most of the windows and doors were cut directly into the blocks causing the lights inside to give them the look of giant jack-o-lanterns.

Wide porches sheltered motorbikes propped against front walls, but there were no driveways and no cars. Patches of scrawny brush and thin clumps of unidentifiable vegetation freckled the sandy ground between the houses. Occasionally the blue-white glow of a television flickered from a window, but you only felt rather than saw people moving in the darkness. It was as bleak as any place August could ever remember seeing.

Suddenly the road was engulfed in a dense grove of palm trees and crossed a muddy river on a narrow bridge that rattled underneath the Norton. On the opposite bank a Thai temple, bathed in light, loomed white against the black sky. It glittered like fire from red and yellow glass embedded in its masonry.

Then the temple was gone as abruptly as it had appeared and August was in darkness again, riding through the swampy, featureless scrubland.

A little further along the concrete skeleton of a huge building appeared out of the night. It was completely dark, unfinished and abandoned, and it rose thirty or forty floors over absolutely nowhere at all. Beyond it were yards filled with wrecked cars and huge metal warehouses with signs in Thai script. Two old cargo airplanes in fading camouflage paint appeared like ghostly apparitions in an empty field just past the abandoned building. And around them a handful of scrawny cows grazed silently.

A half hour or so later a bridge lifted the road in a long hump over a spider web of creeks and canals and at the crest the lights of Bangkok rose out of the distant blackness. Bangkok was like most cities. The further you got from it, the better it looked, and floating in the darkness twenty miles away it looked to August like a beguiling hallucination. The city sprawled from horizon to horizon, an open-legged trollop beckoning him forward.

A million lights glittered triumphantly from a thousand soaring towers and for a moment August could almost forget the despair hiding in the valleys of darkness between those buildings. There were people who passed their lives in that darkness, millions of them, and they were people who lived on little more than perseverance. They were like the boy sitting on the rock at the side of the road who had waved at August when he passed. They took life as it came, a moment at a time, and they simply got on with it.

There was dignity in that, August thought, even a little hope for the rest of us, if we were willing to see it.

There were times when, God help him, August loved Thailand. Riding up from Pattaya, the Norton slashing the heavy air like a straight razor as the lights of Bangkok reached out of the darkness to embrace him, was one of those times.

ELEVEN

WHEN AUGUST GOT to Hong Kong, he took a taxi to the Cordis Hotel in Mongkok,

A slightly chubby Chinese woman greeted him from behind the reception desk. She was wearing a gray suit and black glasses that were far too large for her face, and her shiny black hair was pulled back so tightly into a bun that it very nearly constituted a do-it-yourself face lift.

With a smile that made August think of a night nurse preparing to take a rectal temperature reading, she asked for his passport and a credit card. Her English had a pronounced Australian accent, which worked out well for August since he was now Lawrence Silver from Sydney. Her smile warmed up considerably when she saw the Australian passport Claire had used to book the hotel. She even upgraded him to an executive suite.

The suite was L-shaped and occupied the whole northeast corner of the the forty-first floor. The living room had a couch upholstered in white canvas and two dark brown leather chairs grouped around a glass coffee table. The king-size bed was tucked away behind a blond wood half-wall on both sides of which hung extremely large flat screen televisions.

But the suite's most striking feature was its view. Both exterior walls were floor-to-ceiling glass curtains. From the living room, August had an unobstructed view over the hundreds of wooden junks tied up in the Yau Ma Tei typhoon shelter and all the way out to the immense modern container port at Stonecutters Island through which passed a considerable portion of the manufacturing output of China.

From the bedroom he looked out over the teeming jumble of Mongkok and north into the New Territories. Deep in the haze he could see the low range of hills that marked the beginning of mainland China, once a land as closed and mysterious as any on earth, but now the seat of a manufacturing empire threatening to submerge the whole world under the flood tide of goods pouring out of its factories.

He was still staring off to the north and contemplating the future when the doorbell rang. It was Woods.

"How did you find me so fast?" August asked him.

"Spike hacked into the hotel's reservation system. He called me as soon as you checked in."

"I should have guessed."

"He's into the Cathay Pacific system, too. Billy Fang is on Cathay Pacific 238 which is scheduled into Hong Kong tomorrow at 12:55pm, and he's booked a hotel limousine to bring him straight here from the airport."

"Not much traffic on a Saturday. Even allowing for clearing Immigration at the airport, that would put him here somewhere around 2:00pm if the flight is on time."

Woods nodded.

"Spike is going to keep us posted?"

Woods nodded again.

Spike was a Chinese guy who served for a decade in the famed Snow Leopards anti-terrorism unit of the People's Armed Police in Beijing, but they made the mistake of sending him to Hong Kong on special assignment and he quickly decided Hong Kong was a lot cooler than Beijing. He promptly resigned from his unit, informally of course, and disappeared into the mass of the Chinese population in Hong Kong.

Eventually he met a guy who knew a guy who knew another guy who sent him to August. That's how things usually worked in Hong Kong. There was always a guy who knew a guy who knew somebody else. Because of the skills Spike had developed working for the Chinese police as a computer hacker, August promptly signed him on, sent him to Pattaya, and set him up with all the gear he could think of.

Spike's real name was Dong Shui, which is probably why he chose a nickname for himself. When everyone was speaking English, who the hell wants to be called Dong? He claimed to have come up with Spike as a nickname from watching American cartoons to improve his English. August had no trouble believing that since when Spike spoke English he sounded a little like Scooby-Doo, although August didn't really care how Spike sounded. He was an artist with a laptop. Spike had yet to meet a computer system he couldn't access. With Spike back in Pattaya using his keyboard to tap into the known universe, and for all August knew maybe parts of the unknown one too, August felt like he had a direct line to the Almighty.

"WHY DON'T YOU check the minibar?" August said to Woods as he closed the door behind him. "We both could use a beer."

Woods dropped the small leather duffel bag he was carrying on the coffee table and rooted around in the minibar until he found two bottles of Tsingtao which he regarded doubtfully. Tsingtao claimed to be the best-selling beer in the world. If it really was, Woods figured that had to be just because there were a couple of billion Chinese without all that many choices as to what beer they drank.

Woods found an opener, popped the caps on both bottles, and brought them back to the coffee table. He and August clicked bottles, each of them took a long pull, and then Woods put his bottle down and unzipped the little leather duffle he had brought with him. He took out two Samsung Galaxy S4's and set them on the table in front of August.

"I went to Sin Tat Plaza as soon as I got here and bought six phones. All the same model. Decent batteries and good screens. The camera's okay, too, but I guess that doesn't matter. I've loaded all six phones with prepaid SIMs that have enough air time for all the talking and texting we're going to want to do in thirty-six hours."

Mongkok was notorious as a market for fake and hot goods, and Sin Tat Plaza on Argyle Street was where you went if you were looking for cell phones that might still be slightly warm. Picking up a stash of local burner phones was the starting point for every operation, and recently stolen phones were the Dom Pérignon of burners.

Woods reached out and turned the two phones over. On the back of one was a piece of tape with the numeral 1 written on it, and on the back of the other another piece of tape that said 2.

"We use the set marked 1 for communications and save the set marked 2 as a backup if we have to ditch the first set for any reason. I've programmed all the numbers for each set into the other two phones in that set."

August pulled up the directory for the phone with the numeral 1 on it. Sure enough, there were only two entries: one for Woods and one for Claire, labeled as W and C respectively. An impenetrable cypher if he had ever seen one.

"You got any ideas how we can do this yet, boss?"

"Not a fucking clue."

The doorbell rang and that took August off the hook from having to expand on his pronouncement, which he couldn't have anyway. Woods got up and let Claire in.

"THAT LOOKS GOOD," Claire said, flopping down in a chair and pointing at one of the half-empty bottles of Tsingtao on the coffee table. "I'll have one, too."

August looked at Woods. He gave a little shrug.

"You're kidding me," Claire said, looking back and forth between August and Woods. "You drank all the beer?"

"There were only two," Woods said. "Have something else."

"I don't want something else. I want a beer."

Woods shrugged again.

"Why don't you look in the minibar?" August said, pointing toward it. "Maybe there's another brand."

Claire walked over and opened the door. August glanced at Woods and saw him frown slightly. August was still trying to figure out what that meant when Claire stood up and turned around. She was holding up a bottle of Miller Lite.

"A couple of real gentlemen, aren't you? You leave nothing for me but cat piss."

"First come first served," August shrugged. "Sexual equality is our guiding credo here."

"One for all and all for one," Woods contributed.

"Well, fuck you both very much, too."

Claire opened the Miller Lite anyway, and then walked over and sat down with August and Woods.

Woods dipped into his leather bag, pulled out two more Samsung phones, and went through the same explanation with Claire that he had with August. Claire did exactly the same thing August had done. She picked up the phone marked 1 and checked the directory.

"Brilliant code," she said. "Fucking brilliant."

She put the phone back on the table, drank some Miller Lite, and made a face.

"So now what?" she asked.

"I got no idea," August said. "None. Billy Fang is getting here about two tomorrow and we're being told the Chinese are going to pick him up sometime the following day. That leaves us less than twenty-four hours either to take him or forget it. I still just can't see it."

"We got to try, Bossman. If he goes over to the Chinese, he'll take enough with him to get a lot of people killed."

"I understand that, Claire, but it doesn't change what we're looking at here. I don't care if he's turning over all our stealth fighter technology, we've still got less than twenty-four hours to take him."

"So, we just shoot the bastard. That won't take twenty-four hours."

"Here's the thing. In order to do this and get ourselves out of Hong Kong, we've got to make it look enough like either an accident or natural causes to buy us at least twelve hours. We're surrounded by China here, and under the circumstances I'm sure you will agree that crossing the border into China is a truly shitty idea. There are only two ways out of Hong Kong for us. One is by sea and the other is by air, and they are both pretty damned conspicuous."

"What's the big deal?" Claire asked. "We shoot him and then we go to the airport and fly home. End of story."

"Not quite. There's only one airport here. If the Hong Kong police know this guy has been killed and they have anything to go on at all, they'll flood the airport looking for us before we can even get there."

"Then we're just going to give up?"

"Give me a break here. I'm not giving up. I'm just telling you that I don't see how we can do it. In order to pull this off and get out of Hong Kong, we need to find a way to make it look either natural or accidental long enough for us to get on an airplane and back to Thailand, and I don't see how we can do that in the time we have available."

A small silence fell after that. They each drank their beer and peered off into the distance as if they were thinking through possible courses of action, but mostly they were all just feeling frustrated.

"Maybe we'll get lucky," Claire said after a while.

"Yeah," August said, "maybe he'll be hit by a bus out on Shanghai Street before he can get inside. That would do it."

Claire finished her Miller Lite and plunked the bottle down on the coffee table. "I don't know about you guys, but I'm going downstairs and look for a bar that has real beer. Anybody coming with me?"

"You two go ahead," August said. "I'm going to go out and walk the area. Maybe I'll get a bright idea."

"You want us to come with you?" Woods asked.

"No, I just need to think. You two find some decent beer and have a good dinner." He scooped up one of the phones Woods had distributed and wiggled it. "I'll call you if I need you."

"So where and when do you want us next?" Claire asked.

"Right here. Ten o'clock tomorrow morning. That will give us four hours before the target gets to the hotel. If we can't be brilliant in four hours, we're not going to be brilliant at all."

TWELVE

AUGUST LIKED Hong Kong. He liked the way the city throbbed with energy. No matter who you are or how old you might be, some of that energy seeps into you and makes the world feel more intense there.

The colors are brighter, the sounds louder, and the odors more powerful. Usually that's a good thing, but not always. Particularly that part about the odors. Hong Kong stinks of a mix of carbon monoxide, raw sewage, rotting garbage, and duck mess. It smells like no other place on earth.

Tourists absolutely love Hong Kong. They ride the Star Ferry back and forth across the harbor, shop at the designer boutiques in Central, and take the tram up to the Peak to gape at the city spread out below them. And there is much to gape at.

Between Victoria Island and the Kowloon Peninsula lies one of the most perfect natural harbors in the world. On the green slopes that surround it, glittering skyscrapers are crammed like toy buildings flung around by an unruly child. It is a lot to absorb. It is a spectacle of splendor and wealth. Hong Kong, the tourists tell each other, is truly the future.

Mongkok is just a few stops north up the Kowloon Peninsula on Hong Kong's ferociously efficient Mass Transit Railway, a couple of miles away from all that. Tourists don't come to Mongkok. There is no splendor there, no spectacular harbor, no green clad hills, no designer boutiques. What is there instead is organized crime, the sex trade, and a couple of centuries' accumulation of people who are hanging on to life by their fingernails.

Block after block of grimy concrete buildings line the streets, cracked and pitted by the bad air, and rusted air-conditioner compressors dribble yet more dirty water down their walls. Black, Rorschach-like stains are smeared over walls that probably once, a very long time ago, were white.

And then there are the people, more people than you have ever seen anywhere before. They say Mongkok is the most densely populated urban area in the world, and after a few minutes on the streets you can believe it. The crowds are so great that they have spilled off the sidewalks and taken over the roadways. There isn't very much motorized traffic in Mongkok. There is no room left in the streets for it to drive.

The Cordis hotel is in Langham Place which sits smack in the middle of it all. Two soaring towers of green glass house the hotel, a massive shopping mall, and a whole lot of offices. The two sleek skyscrapers rising out of all that cracked and dirty concrete look like a mirage, as if two gigantic rocket ships had arrived from outer space and somehow unaccountably picked Mongkok as the best place to land.

August liked Mongkok at night, when the darkness smoothed away the sharp edges and softened the misery. Some of the streets turned into night markets then and the business of living sat very close to the surface. Old men, some shirtless in the sticky heat, gathered in knots at the foot of greasy staircases, smoked foul-smelling Chinese cigarettes, and shouted to each other about the wrongs they had suffered that day, some imaginary, but others achingly real.

.   .   .

UGUST LEFT THE hotel through the main entrance, turned left on Shanghai Street, and strolled north between the tower housing the hotel and the one containing the shopping mall.

At Argyle Street, the main artery through the heart of Mongkok, he turned right and shouldered his way through the crowds as far as Nathan Road, then he turned right again and circled back around the two towers until he had made a full circuit of them. Nothing he saw was encouraging.

The towers were connected by two glassed-in walkways over Shanghai Street through which hotel guests could access the shopping mall. The hotel had half a dozen entrances and exits. Cross over to the shopping mall and there were a dozen more. It would take an army to keep a target in the hotel under surveillance. Three people had no chance at all other than blind luck, which he had never figured for a winning strategy.

August entered the mall from Portland Street and took an escalator up to the second level. At the top he saw a Starbucks on a raised platform in the middle of a gigantic domed space where half a dozen major walkways intersected. He bought a coffee and sat down for a while to watch and think.

The crowds surging back and forth around him made him feel like he was drinking coffee on a pier over the ocean and watching the surf wash in and out. Directly in front of him, right between the entrances to the two glass bridges that crossed over Shanghai Street to the hotel, stood a huge paper mache statue of a black and white panda bear. The thing must have been fifteen feet tall and it was surrounded by at least a dozen low tables on which rested red Chinese lanterns with bright lights inside.

August couldn't really see what the significance of the panda was, but nevertheless a couple of dozen Chinese families were lined up before it, each group stepping forward and organizing a photograph in front of the panda when their turn came.

Perhaps, August thought to himself, some mysterious Chinese holiday was approaching that he had never heard of.

While he drank his coffee and watched the Chinese families posing happily with the giant panda, August thought about Billy Fang. He wondered if Fang would be expecting surveillance here. The briefing material offered no indication Fang knew he had been outed but, if he thought he was safe, then why was he running?

Surely, he didn't just wake up one morning and decide that spending the rest of his life in Beijing would be cool. He must have had some indication, at the very least a suspicion, that he had been burned. If he had, he would be on his guard, or he might be on his guard anyway. After all, he was a former intelligence officer with experience in the field. Counter-surveillance was probably second nature to him.

August finished his coffee and strolled across the right-hand bridge back into the lobby of the hotel. The lobby was big and busy and had a lot of places to hang out. Maybe that was the answer. Woods and Claire could split time in the lobby and somehow find a way to take Fang when he was passing through.

He looked around the lobby again. Who was he kidding? He didn't see a single face anywhere that wasn't Chinese. Woods and Claire would be about as inconspicuous hanging around the lobby as a Rose Parade float in a Walmart parking lot. But if they couldn't cut Billy Fang off in the lobby, and they couldn't cover all the exits, how in the world would they manage to get close enough to him to kill him, even if they could find an inconspicuous way to do that?

August had no idea how he could possibly carry out the assignment to take Fang down before he defected. None at all. He was more convinced than ever that it couldn't be done in the time they had been given to do it.

An elevator opened and August quickly jumped inside before it closed again. He was annoyed and tired and hungry. All he wanted now was to go upstairs to his room, order a burger and a beer from room service, and get to bed early. Surely everything would look better in the morning but, even if it didn't, he figured it probably wouldn't look any worse.

A UGUST HAD HOPED to have an idea of some kind by the time Claire and Woods got to his room at ten the next morning.

A lame one would have been okay, even a dumb one would have been a start, but he had nothing, so he ordered a fresh pot of coffee from room service and told them about his scouting trip around the area the night before. They asked him some questions about the exits and the sight lines around the hotel, but he could see their hearts weren't in it. When the doorbell rang and he let the waiter in to serve coffee, everyone seemed glad of the interruption and fell silent until he was gone.

"Okay," August said when the door clicked shut behind the waiter, "I officially open the floor for suggestions."

Claire cleared her throat. "Maybe you're right, Bossman. We don't know enough about this guy to put together any kind of a plan, and we don't have enough time to execute a plan even if we had one. We don't even know for sure what he looks like. He may have changed his appearance since those photos were taken."

"If we can find him, maybe we can take him in the hotel," Woods said. "I brought the insulin kit."

The insulin kit was a plastic case that held two hypodermics and two glass vials with labels proclaiming the contents of the vials to be insulin. The plan had always been for whoever was carrying it to explain that they were a diabetic should their possession of it ever be questioned by customs somewhere, but they had never had to put that little subterfuge to the test since no one had ever said a word about it. Customs was so lax almost everywhere in Asia that sometimes August thought he could walk into almost any country with a bazooka under one arm and no one would say a word.

"What did you put in it?"

"The usual. Sodium thiopental and pentobarbital."

They saw what Woods was thinking, of course. If they could get into Billy Fang's room and hit him with a heavy dose of sodium thiopental, he would be out cold in ten seconds. Then they would give him another injection of pentobarbital, tuck him up in bed, and put out the *Do Not Disturb* sign. It would probably be twelve hours before anyone got suspicious enough to check on him. Even then, they would find nothing disturbed in his room, no sign of violence. Billy Fang would just look exactly like he had died peacefully in his sleep.

When they did an autopsy and ran the lab work, they would figure out what really happened, of course, but how long would that take? A few days? Maybe even a few weeks? August and his crew would be safely back in Pattaya having a beer at Secrets long before anyone even knew Billy Fang was dead, let alone before they found out how he had gotten that way.

"You got a way to get us into his room in the middle of the night?" August asked.

Woods shrugged.

"You think maybe we can knock and he'll just invite us in? Maybe he'd enjoy having a chat with three fellow Americans before he defects to China the next day."

"Must be some way in." Woods shrugged again. "Best idea I got."

"Maybe we should have brought Spike," Claire put in.

It would doubtless have been useful to have a Chinese face to help with the surveillance, but August needed Spike at his keyboard watching the airline arrivals and the hotel's reservation system. He was far more valuable where he was than he would have been on the streets of Hong Kong.

"Regardless of everything else, the first thing we have to do is pick up Billy Fang when he checks in and make a positive ID.

We've got to be absolutely sure we've got the right guy. I want the two of you together in the lobby somewhere you can see the front desk. A couple will be less suspicious than a lone male trying to hide behind a newspaper."

"We could take a bag down. Look like we'd had to check out because of the hotel's check out time and are waiting around to go to the airport."

"Good idea. When Spike tells us the Cathay Pacific flight has landed, get in place about a half hour later. He can't possibly get here any sooner than that, and I don't want you hanging around the lobby any longer than you have to. I'm sure it's all covered by cameras and you don't want to attract unnecessary attention."

"Where are you going to be, Bossman?"

"I'm going to try to find a way to cover the hotel's entrance from outside. Billy Fang is supposed to be coming in from the airport in a hotel limousine which means he'll be brought straight to the main entrance. How many people could possibly be arriving by limo in the time frame we have? Six or eight? A dozen? I ought to be able to pick him up easily enough. When I do, I'll give you a heads-up by telephone and follow him inside."

"Maybe I can get close enough to take a selfie with my phone and get him in the picture behind me."

"Don't do anything to spook him, Claire. A picture would be nice, but it's not worth blowing everything to have it. Unless we're not certain about the ID, we don't really need it."

Claire nodded, but she said nothing.

"Okay," August said, standing up. "Anybody got anything else?"

He looked from Claire to Woods and they both shook their heads.

"Okay, text me when you hear from Spike. And be careful out there."

THIRTEEN

AUGUST FIGURED THAT surveillance operations were one time when you could claim smoking offered real benefits.

People just standing in the same place doing nothing look suspicious as hell, but people with cigarettes in their hands can loiter as long as they like staring off into space and nobody gives them a second thought.

In most big cities these days, crowds of smokers gather around doorways on every block and we walk past them without a glance. That was especially true in Mongkok. Half the men on the sidewalks had cigarettes dangling from their lips. Join them and nobody sees you anymore, even if you're a foreigner.

A cell phone up against the ear isn't bad, but most people talking on cell phones seem to be striding along at a purposeful clip, which doesn't work very well for surveillance. A cigarette is the perfect beard. Cigarettes smokers dawdle, they meander, mostly they just stand and look at nothing, and nobody cares.

The burner phone that Woods gave August buzzed at 12:45pm and he checked the text message.

Flight at gate.

Billy Fang was slightly early, but August still didn't see any way he could make it through immigration, get to the hotel limo, and be driven in from the airport to Mongkok before 2:00pm at the earliest. More like 2:30pm probably or a little after, even allowing for a little less traffic congestion than normal since it was a Saturday afternoon. But August was down on Reclamation Street outside the hotel's main entrance by a little after 1:00pm anyway, just in case.

It was hot on the sidewalk. It was hot in Hong Kong most of the time. Not the heavy, intense, unyielding heat of Thailand perhaps, but in some ways the heat felt more brutal there.

There was almost no vegetation anywhere in the city. Parks didn't make money so there were few of them in Hong Kong. The unchanging landscape of concrete, glass, and steel sucked in the heat like a vacuum, bounced it around, and amplified it until the entire city became a gigantic convection oven and people braving the sidewalk became the dry-roast.

August lit up a Camel and dawdled near another smoker who had also taken up a post there on the sidewalk to satisfy his nicotine cravings. He looked like a Frenchman to August. He had a long, thin face and was wearing a dark suit with a white shirt and a blue tie that looked expensive. They didn't speak, but they exchanged those nods of mutual recognition and sympathy that smokers exiled to sidewalks exchange the world over.

The hotel's main entrance faced onto a wide driveway that was actually a two-lane road paved in brown brick that ran through an open portico underneath the building. It went from where August stood on the sidewalk along Reclamation Street all the way through to Shanghai Street on the other side. The whole thing was more attractive than it sounded, interestingly designed and adorned with bright orange awnings on both ends. Two of the hotel's limos were waiting for passengers in a parking area at the right side of the driveway, and August smiled. They were both stretched Mercedes sedans painted bright red. Billy Fang couldn't be any more conspicuous if he arrived riding on the back of a fire truck.

The one-way street system in the area meant there was only one direction in which Fang's limo could approach the hotel: north up Reclamation Street. When August finished his cigarette, he stubbed it out in a standing ashtray the hotel had thoughtfully provided for its guests and strolled slowly up Reclamation Street in the direction from which Fang would approach. He was looking for a Starbucks or some other similar place where he could settle down for a while and watch the hotel without being obvious about it, but he didn't see anything that worked.

This was Mongkok, after all. Instead of a Starbucks, August passed the Shing Wai Electrical Supplies Company, two open storefronts selling power tools, one space mounded high with piles of truck tires, something called Yen Fung Electric, and the Nam Sam Hardware and Machinery Company. None of those places held much promise as a location for setting up an inconspicuous surveillance post so he turned and walked slowly back up the street to his previous post outside the hotel's entrance.

His smoking companion had moved on and August was left to smoke his second cigarette all alone. Right after he lit it, he saw a red, stretched Mercedes approaching the hotel up Reclamation Street. Sure enough, it turned into the driveway and the gray-suited driver jumped out and opened the rear passenger door. August took a quick glance at his watch. Not even 1:30pm. Couldn't be Billy Fang.

And, unless Billy Fang was cleverly disguised as a very fat, very black man wearing a purple dashiki, it wasn't.

August watched as the doorman gathered three matching Louis Vuitton suitcases from the truck of the Mercedes, piled them onto a gold-colored luggage cart, and followed Mr. Purple Dashiki inside.

When August finished his second cigarette, things got awkward. He had no other smokers to stand with to make himself less conspicuous while he waited for Billy Fang, and he couldn't find a place to drink a cup of unwanted coffee. August shook out another Camel and put it in his mouth without lighting it, but after a few minutes he felt so silly that he put it back in the pack.

He let his eyes track the other side of Reclamation Street north of the hotel. He would rather stay to the south since that would be the direction from which Billy Fang would arrive, but he had to go somewhere.

That was when he spotted the Chan Kee Roasted Goose Company. It was a little beyond the turn-in to the hotel's entrance, but it had a big window in front and he could see a couple of empty tables just beyond the glass. August doubted he could see the main entrance doors from there, but he could see at least the first twenty feet or so of the driveway and a bright red stretched Mercedes turning into it would be hard to miss.

He glanced at his watch. Just before 1:45pm. Surely it would take Billy Fang at least another half hour to get there, perhaps even longer. There was nothing remotely appealing to August right then about a plate of roast goose, but the only alternative seemed to be pacing around on the sidewalk smoking Camels and becoming more and more conspicuous. Not a good alternative.

T HE CHAN KEE Roasted Goose Company was slightly scruffy in the same way that a lot of neighborhood restaurants in Hong Kong are.

Black plastic chairs pushed randomly here and there, cracked Formica tables cleaned only in the most general sense of the word, and a jar of colored plastic chopsticks in the middle of every table for diners to help themselves.

August walked in and looked around. The place wasn't very crowded. It was late for lunch in Hong Kong and, besides, a local restaurant in Mongkok wasn't a place people went for a leisurely meal or to hang out with their friends.

In Hong Kong, people went to local restaurants to eat. They ate and they left. They didn't hang around late into the afternoon chatting with their friends, and that suited August just fine. He took the table next to the front window that gave him the best angle to the front of the hotel without waiting for it to be offered to him.

His was the only white face in the place, of course. Mongkok isn't a place where round-eyes eat lunch in local restaurants. A dumpy Chinese woman of indeterminate age wearing a shapeless green dress shuffled over, dropped a stained plastic menu in front of him and shuffled away again without speaking a word. Keeping one eye on the hotel driveway, August opened the menu and glanced at it. It was entirely in Chinese. Wonderful.

After he had gone through the entire menu and found not a word of English, he looked up. The woman apparently thought that meant he was ready to order and she shuffled back over.

August pointed at the menu. "English?"

The woman shook her head and stood there looking at him. "Do you speak English?"

This time the woman didn't even bother to shake her head.

August shot a quick glance back out at the driveway.

Nothing happening.

He knew he had to order something to justify occupying the table, and the menu obviously wasn't going to be of any help, so he glanced around the restaurant while the woman stood there and waited him out.

Finally, as much to get rid of her as anything, he pointed to a table across the room where two Chinese men faced each other over a pink plastic plate that had some green stuff and some brown stuff on it. They were energetically shoveling whatever it was into their mouths with chopsticks and neither appeared seriously ill so August took that as the best recommendation he was likely to get. The woman looked where he was pointing, then she turned and walked away without a word.

August wondered if he had ordered goose. He wondered if the restaurant even sold anything other than goose. Surely it did. The menu was four pages long even if he couldn't read a word of it. There couldn't possibly be that many different ways to prepare goose, could there?

Looking back out the window he saw a white panel van turn into the hotel driveway, but there was no sign of another stretched red Mercedes.

In a few minutes the woman shuffled back to the table and placed a blue plastic bowl containing a heap of rice in front of August.

"Do you have beer?" he asked her.

She didn't answer, but after a bit she returned with a bottle of San Miguel. Apparently, the word *beer* worked equally well in both English and Chinese. Good to know.

August sat looking out the window, sipping his beer, listening to the other half dozen or so customers in the place all shouting at once. Chinese isn't a spoken language, someone had once told him, it's a screamed language. Over the noise of plastic plates banging on the Formica tables and the legs of chairs scratching on the concrete floor, he listened as several different Chinese dialects went to war with each other.

About ten minutes later, the woman returned with whatever it was he had ordered. Thick slices of something he took to be goose were arrayed with large chunks of bok choy on a white plastic plate. The crispy brown skin of the goose glistened with fat. After another quick glance out the window, he pulled a pair of plastic chopsticks out of the jar in the middle of the table, picked up the pink bowl with the rice in it, and placed a slice of goose that looked a little less fatty than the others on top of the rice.

Hong Kong people eat by holding their rice bowl in the palm of one hand, putting morsels from the table on top of the rice, and then lifting the bowl and shoveling both the food and the rice into their mouths using energetic scooping motions of their chopsticks. August had learned to eat Chinese food that way himself a long time back. It was a little indelicate perhaps, and it certainly fell far short of western norms of what most people considered good table manners, but he had come to admire the technique for its sheer efficiency.

He wasn't particularly hungry, but he had to do something until Billy Fang showed up, so he ate slowly and watched the hotel's driveway for a red Mercedes. He didn't see one, but the goose tasted better than it looked and he had finished most of it when the burner phone buzzed in his pocket.

He pulled out the phone and looked at the screen.

Spike says target checked in. Room 1121.

What the hell?

August was absolutely certain he couldn't have missed Billy Fang entering the hotel, not unless he had gone in through some entrance other than the main one, and why would he have done that?

He tapped out a response.

You spot him?

A pause.

No. You?

That didn't make any sense.

How could Billy Fang have ridden a hotel limo in from the airport and checked into the hotel without coming in through the main entrance or being seen by Claire and Woods at the front desk?

For just a moment August thought back to the fat black guy

in the purple dashiki, but he quickly dismissed the thought. That was ridiculous.

He texted back.

Meet me at Chan Kee
Roasted Goose Company.

That brought a pause.

Where?

August sighed and pushed at the telephone's keys again.

Across Reclamation Street from the hotel.
Come out main entrance. You'll see it.

Another pause. Then…

OK.

FOURTEEN

THE DUMPY CHINESE woman didn't look all that happy when Woods and Claire came in and sat down with him. August gathered that dealing with one foreigner a day was pretty much her limit.

He held up his half-empty bottle of San Miguel and wiggled it at her, pointing first to Claire and then to Woods. The woman stared back expressionlessly for a moment, then shuffled away. Maybe she was bringing two more beers. Or maybe not.

"Did you actually eat whatever that was?"

Claire pointed to the white plastic plate on which August's goose had been served. It was empty now, except for a thin coat of congealed grease that glistened yellow in the wan light.

August just smiled.

"Oh, man," Claire said, "it's a good thing I'm not hungry."

The Chinese woman reappeared carrying two bottles of San Miguel and banged them down in the middle of the table with perhaps a little more energy than was strictly speaking required. Claire took one and pushed the other over to Woods.

She inspected the neck of the bottle with some suspicion and then pulled a tissue out of her pocket and wiped it carefully all the way around. Woods watched her without expression, gave August a look he couldn't quite interpret, and took a long pull from his own bottle without even looking at it.

"Okay," August said, "let's get to it. How did he get by you?"

"How did he get by *you*, Bossman?"

"He didn't get by me. He didn't come in through the main entrance. The only guy who arrived in a hotel car was a fellow in a purple dashiki who looked like an African."

"Maybe wearing a purple dashiki makes you look African."

"It wasn't Billy Fang, Claire. This guy must have gone 250, 280 if he weighed a pound."

"Yeah, we saw him at the reception desk. He looked like a check-in. Had a pile of luggage. But Billy Fang didn't come to the reception desk. You can take that to the bank."

"Maybe he didn't check in. Maybe Spike made a mistake."

"No way." Woods shook his head. "No fucking way."

"So, if he is checked in, and he didn't come in through the main entry and he didn't go to the reception desk—"

"Someone else must have checked in for him," Claire interrupted.

"You see anybody who could have done that?"

Claire hesitated, looked at Woods. He shrugged.

"There were a lot of people at the reception desk," Claire said. "It's a busy hotel. It could have been anybody."

August drank some beer he didn't particularly want and thought about that.

"It seems pretty obvious Billy Fang must know he's under surveillance," he said after a moment. "He's being careful."

"Maybe he doesn't know," Claire said. "Maybe he's just covering himself out of habit."

"Maybe," August said, but there was a doubtful tone in his voice.

"Or maybe it's the Chinese being careful with him," Claire went on. "If I were pulling in a defector as valuable as they claim this guy is, I'd sure as hell be careful about how I did it."

That made sense to August, but whatever the explanation it

looked like getting to Fang would be more difficult than they thought. Who was he kidding? Getting to this guy was already impossible. How could it have become harder than impossible?

August studied the table top, Claire looked out the window, and Woods seemed lost in picking at the label on his beer bottle.

"Look," August finally said, spreading his hands. "We can't even be sure Fang is really in the hotel, much less what room he's in. The room they have in his name might be just a decoy. If somebody else checked him in, he could be anywhere."

Nobody said anything.

"All we even think we know for sure," August went on, "is that the Chinese are picking him up tomorrow. That gives us twenty-four hours to figure all this out, maybe less. I've got to be honest with you. I've got nothing here, but I'm open for ideas."

Slowly, with obvious reluctance, Claire shook her head. "Nothing from me."

"I may have something," Woods said, and both Claire and August looked at him.

Woods pulled his phone out of his shirt pocket. He touched the screen, turned it around, and pushed it out into the middle of the table. August looked down, but all he saw was a column of eight-digit numbers that ran off the bottom of the screen.

"What is this supposed to be?"

"It's an app," Woods said. "It's for opening magnetic card key locks."

August just looked at him.

"Yeah, really," Woods nodded. "Spike has been playing with it for a while. He asked me to try it out around the hotel to test it for him."

"And it works?"

"It worked on my door, but that's the only one I've tried it on."

"Let me get this straight," August said. "You mean you put your phone up against a door, use this app, and it opens the door?"

Woods gave him a look. "You don't think I'm serious, do you?"

August made a rolling motion with one hand, leaned back in his chair, and folded his arms.

"Most magnetic key locks have a USB port so the hotel can reset the lock in case there's some kind of problem. I checked the lock on my door and found the port on the bottom of the lock plate."

August waited, but Woods appeared to be done.

"Am I going to have to pull this out of you one sentence at a time?" he asked.

Woods grunted. "I thought the rest would be obvious."

"It's not."

"Look, you just use a USB cable to plug the phone into the port. It reads the code that's been assigned to the lock, then sends the code and unlocks the door."

"And you tried this out on your door and it worked?"

Woods nodded.

"This I got to see," August said.

He stood up, dropped a couple of hundred Hong Kong dollars on the table, and pointed across the street to the hotel.

CLAIRE AND AUGUST stood in the hallway in front of Woods' room and watched him open the door with his phone. August still found it hard to believe it was that easy, so he asked Woods to do it again.

Just like he had the first time, Woods plugged a short cable running from his phone into a USB port underneath the bottom edge of the brass plate that surrounded the handle and the lock. He selected the app and hit a key on the phone. A few seconds later everyone heard a CLICK, Woods pushed down on the handle, and the door opened.

A heavy-set Chinese woman wearing a maid's uniform and large black eyeglasses emerged from a room three or four doors down and began gathering up fresh towels from a housekeeping cart. She took a long time doing it and August glanced over to see her watching them with a suspicious expression. He gave her a cheery wave, nudged Claire and Woods inside the room, and quickly closed the door behind them.

"How long has Spike had this?" he asked when they were inside.

"He's been working on it for a while, but he didn't want to say anything until he was sure it worked."

"And, apparently, it does."

Woods shrugged. "At least on my door."

"Before you get too carried away here," Claire put in, "I don't see what good this does us."

Woods and August both looked at her.

"We don't even know for sure that the target is in the room Spike says he checked into," she said. "Right?"

August nodded.

"And even if he is in that room," she went on, "I don't see how it does us much good just to be able to open his door."

Claire walked back to the door that led into Woods' room from the hallway and pointed up the short hallway, past the bathroom, and across the room to the desk that stood in front of the windows.

"Assuming his room is pretty much like this one," she said, "if he's in the room at all, he's going to be in one of three places. On the bed, sitting at this desk, or sitting in that easy chair."

"He might be on the toilet," Woods said.

Claire looked at Woods, but she went on as if he hadn't spoken.

"Now I make it at least twenty-five feet from here to any of those three spots. Wherever this guy is, he isn't going to just hang around while the three of us stumble through the door to his room, rush across those twenty-five feet, and take him down.

We already think he may be on alert and there's no doubt he's nervous."

"Yeah," Woods began, "but—"

"Either he's going to be armed, in which case we're fucked immediately, or he's not going to be armed and he raises a ruckus, in which case we're fucked later. The only thing getting through his door does for us is guarantee a mess."

"It might if we went in through his front door, but we're not."

Claire and August both looked at Woods. He didn't say anything. He just walked toward where Claire was standing by the door from the hallway, but he stopped before he reached the bathroom and pointed to his left.

"We're going to go through here."

"The connecting door," August said.

Claire was still skeptical. "How do you know the target's room even has a connecting door?"

"Spike checked. It does. And the room that connects to it is empty. He checked that, too."

Claire gestured at the connecting door. "Try it."

"I already have," Woods said. "The connecting door is really two doors. The one on this side opens toward us. It isn't locked from our side, only from the other side."

Woods swung the handle of the connecting door down and pulled it toward them. Sure enough, they were looking at the front of another door. Woods took the cable from his telephone and felt underneath the brass plate around the handle. When he found the USB port, he plugged the cable in and started the app. After a few seconds, the lock clicked. He pulled down on the handle and pushed the door open. The room beyond was dark and empty.

"I already knew there was nobody in there," Woods said. "I'm not just a pretty face."

Claire and Woods looked at August. He scratched at his ear and thought about it.

"Okay," he said, "it might work."

He walked over to the window and stood there for a moment looking down at the street.

"We'll wait until three or four in the morning," he said when he turned back around. "If the target is going to be asleep at all, he'll be asleep then. Coming in from the hallway would probably wake him up since there wouldn't be anything we could do about the hallway lights. But if we keep the connecting room dark and open the connecting door very quietly, we ought to be able to slip in without spooking him."

August walked through the connecting door and looked around the other room.

"It's no more than ten feet from the connecting door to the bed. If the target's room is like this one, we should have no trouble getting control of him before he wakes up. We hit him with some sodium thiopental, then when he's out we give him the phenobarbital and tuck him up in bed. We close the connecting doors, exit through his door into the hallway, and put out the *Do Not Disturb* sign. By the time anybody gets suspicious enough to check on him, we'll be back in Pattaya."

"Sounds like a plan," Woods said. "Want me to go to the safe house and bring back weapons just in case everything goes to shit?"

"Three handguns with suppressors," August said. "One spare magazine for each. But that's it. Nothing bigger. We're not going to shoot our way out of Hong Kong."

August looked from Woods to Claire and back again.

"Are both of you okay with this?"

Woods nodded quickly. Claire took a little longer, but eventually she nodded, too.

"Okay," he said. "Woods, head over to the safe house now and get the handguns. While you're there, see if we have a fiber-optic snake that will fit under the connecting door. I'd like to see what we're getting into before we go in."

Woods nodded again.

"You talk to Spike, Claire, and get him to keep an eye on… what room is it?"

"The target is in 1121," Woods said. "The connecting room is 1119."

"Then tell Spike to keep an eye on the hotel system and make sure no one checks into 1119. I don't want to walk in there in the middle of the night and have to shoot a couple of tourists from Cleveland."

"Maybe Spike can find a way to block up the room in the hotel's inventory," Claire said. "Log it as having a maintenance problem or something."

"Good idea. Tell him to try that."

August looked back and forth between Claire and Woods.

"We'll meet back here at midnight, run through everything again, and go down to 1119. Unless we see a reason not to, we'll go into 1121 about four. Get some sleep. You'll probably need it. Any questions?"

Nobody had any.

"One other thing," he added. "Bring your passports and your gear just in case we have to make a fast exit. Don't leave anything behind. If this all goes to shit, I don't want to be standing around with my dick in my hand while you two get your stuff. Got that?"

This time both Claire and Woods nodded in almost perfect synchronization.

FIFTEEN

JUST BEFORE MIDNIGHT, they all regrouped in August's room and Woods handed August the fiber-optic snake he brought from the safe house.

"I thought we had one there," August said. "Have you checked that it's functioning right?"

Woods nodded.

"And you've tried it under the connecting door?"

Woods nodded again. "Fits fine."

August handed the snake back and Woods tucked it away in his backpack.

"Spike put a maintenance block on 1119," Claire said. "But he's watching the hotel system just to be sure nothing gets changed."

"We're sure that 1119 is still unoccupied?"

"Positive."

"And Billy Fang is still in 1121?"

"He is according to the hotel inventory system," Claire said, "but Spike says no charges have been posted to the account other than the room charge. No telephone calls, no room service, no movie charges."

"So now at least we know he's not in there drinking and watching porno?"

Nobody bothered to respond. August didn't blame them.

He looked at Woods. "The insulin kit?"

Woods nodded and patted his backpack.

"Both syringes filled?"

Woods nodded again.

"Okay, let's gear up."

August picked up one of the Sig Sauer 9mm's that Woods had laid out on the coffee table and Claire and Woods collected the other two. August ejected the magazine from his, checked the action, then reseated the magazine. He holstered the Sig and slid the paddle holster onto his belt at the four o'clock position so that his lightweight blazer would cover it. The extra magazine and the suppressor went into his backpack along with his passport, the burner phones, his own iPhone, and the few other things he had brought with him.

"Okay, then. Everybody ready?"

"Let's go, Bossman."

WHEN THEY LEFT the elevator on the eleventh floor, the corridor was quiet and empty.

August figured the odds favored that after midnight, of course, but you never know. Murphy's Law had taken over operations more often than he wanted to remember. He wouldn't have been all that surprised to discover the Texas A&M Marching Band doing drills in the hallway right outside of 1119.

August looked both ways, checking for cameras. Other than two that covered the elevators, he didn't see any. That didn't mean there weren't any, of course, but it seemed unlikely the cameras covering the elevators would be left visible and hidden cameras installed in the corridors. He had checked his own floor and Woods' floor earlier and the set-up was the same so he was reasonably sure they weren't being watched by some rent-a-cop slurping noodles in the basement. Regardless, by reflex he was still checking for cameras when they stopped in front of 1119.

"Let's use the viewer before you pop the lock," August said to Woods. "Just to be on the safe side."

Woods put his backpack against the wall, pulled out the fiber-optic viewer, and began unrolling the snake.

"I'll wait at the elevators," Claire said. "If anyone gets out, I'll push in and bump into them to give you time to cover yourselves."

As Claire walked toward the elevators, Woods pushed the snake into the narrow gap between the hallway carpet and the bottom of the door. He moved it slowly back and forth with one hand and held the small screen of the viewer with the other. It was too close to Woods' face for August to make out what it showed.

"Room's completely dark," Woods said. "Can't see anything at all. What do you want to do?"

"Go ahead and pop the lock. I'll take point."

Woods withdrew the snake and put the viewer away in his backpack, then he pulled out his iPhone and a cable. He squatted down and ran his finger under the lock plate, looking for the USB port.

DING.

At the sound of the chime announcing the arrival of an elevator, August swiveled his head toward Claire. He saw her moving directly up in front of the doors of the elevator closest to them and blocking it with her body.

Woods found the port and plugged in the cable, then he opened Spike's app.

"Oh, I'm so terribly sorry," August heard Claire saying. "I'm not thinking clearly. Jet-lag I suppose. Are you okay? I really am so sorry. Can I help you up?"

CLICK.

"We're in," Woods announced and pushed the door open.

August went through the door in front of Woods, staying low. The backpack was looped over his left shoulder and his right hand was under his jacket resting on the butt of his Sig. Woods jerked the USB cable away with one hand, held the door open with the other, and slipped through right behind him.

The room was empty. Bed made, no luggage or personal items. Empty. Exactly as Spike had promised. Wonderful, August thought. He wouldn't have to shoot two tourists from Cleveland after all.

He and Woods dumped their gear on the bed and August's burner phone started to vibrate. He hit the button to answer the call.

"Everything cool?" Claire asked.

"As the proverbial cucumber."

"I went back up to my floor when I got on the elevator, just to make it look good if anyone was watching. I'm on my way back down now."

"Roger," August said and disconnected the call.

He opened the drapes to let in the ambient light from the city and killed the room lights. Woods opened the inside connecting door and got down on his knees to examine the lock on the other door.

"The same," he whispered. "No problem."

Woods smoothed out the fiber-optic snake and slid it under the door very slowly. With his free hand, he flicked on the viewer.

"Some light, but no lights turned on. Drapes must be open a little."

He slid the snake all the way to one side of the door and pushed it a little further into the room.

"I can't really see up onto the bed, but it doesn't look completely flat. Could be somebody under the comforter."

August went down on one knee and looked over Woods' shoulder at the screen of the viewer. The bed was too close to the door and the angle was too steep to make much out, but it looked like there was something in the bed. It was obvious enough that the surface was lumpy rather than flat and smooth. Still, it was impossible to tell for sure if there was anyone in it, let alone whether or not they were asleep.

"Maybe," August said, "but who sleeps with the drapes open?"

There was a soft knock at the door and he walked over and let Claire in, which saved him from having to answer his own question.

T HEY WERE ALL in place now and, as far as they could tell, the target was in the room next to them.

All that was left for them to do was watch and listen to see if anything changed, wait until the early hours of the morning when the target was likely to be at his weakest, and then go in fast and hard.

August had spent most of his life waiting. School, army, the Agency. Hurry up and wait. He had gotten pretty good at it. Claire and Woods were almost as good. They just had a little less experience.

Woods leaned back against the headboard on one side of the room's king-sized bed, turned on the reading lamp, and opened a paperback he pulled out of his backpack. Claire sat in the room's easy chair, fiddled idly with her phone, and stared out the windows at the lights of Hong Kong. August stretched out on the bed next to Woods and closed his eyes. It was a soldier's habit. Eat when you can, sleep when you can, and never pass up an opportunity to do either.

When his eyes opened, he looked at his watch. 1:40am.

He turned his head toward Woods who was still reading. "Hear anything?"

Woods didn't look up from his book, but he shook his head.

August swung his feet to the floor, stood up, and stretched.

"Let's take another look," he said.

Woods closed his book, retrieved the viewer and the fiber-optic snake from his backpack, and went over to the connecting door. He looked back over his shoulder at August and pointed to the reading light he had been using. August flipped it off and the room went almost completely dark. Woods waited a minute or two for his eyes to adjust, then he opened the inside half of the connecting door.

After he extended the snake under the other side of the door and flipped on the viewer, August stood behind him and looked at the screen over his shoulder. Woods manipulated the snake, moving it slowly into the room and then sliding it side to side.

Nothing. No clear view of the target. No movement. Only the same dim, gray light and the same lump in the bed they had seen before. Woods looked back over his shoulder at August and raised his eyebrows in a silent question. When August nodded, Woods slowly withdrew the snake, stood up, and quietly closed the inside half of the connecting door.

"I don't feel good about how little we know," August said.

Woods hesitated. "I could try it from out in the hallway," he said. "I think we'd get a better look at the bed from there."

"Yeah, but if somebody comes out—"

Claire jumped to her feet. "I'll cover you with my elevator bit. It worked last time."

"That won't get it done if somebody comes out of another room."

"It's 1:30am," Woods said. "The chances of somebody leaving their room now have got to be pretty small. I'll be quick, boss. Let me give it a shot."

August hesitated, mostly just making a show of it, then nodded his head.

SIXTEEN

WHEN AUGUST OPENED the room's front door and looked up and down the hallway, he saw no one.

He stepped out into the corridor and gestured to Woods and Claire to follow. Claire positioned herself in front of the elevators to intercept anyone who might emerge. By the time she was in place, Woods was already on his knees sliding the fiber-optic snake under the door of room 1121.

August bent down and looked at the monitor. He struggled to understand what he was seeing from the worm's-eye perspective it gave him.

"I'm pretty sure I see someone in bed," Woods said. "And the drapes are closed. The light we saw was just ambient light from out here seeping under the door."

Woods adjusted the snake a little to one side and August saw the lumpy form under the duvet. It was probably a human being, and probably the target, but it could have just been a stack of pillows and it could have been somebody else entirely. Woods continued adjusting the snake trying to get them a better view, but nothing seemed to help. The angle was simply too steep to be certain of anything.

"Can you get us a better look at that?" August asked, touching the screen of the viewer where a dark lump stood a little off to one side between the door and the bed.

Woods pulled the snake back and turned it as far to the side as it would go.

"Looks to me like luggage," he said.

August peered hard at the monitor, willing it to resolve the image with greater clarity, but of course it ignored him. Still, he thought there was something weird about the dark lump. It seemed almost pyramid shaped and it looked like it was covered in some kind of recurring pattern of light and dark shapes. Could that really be a stack of luggage? Maybe. But if it wasn't, he didn't know what the hell it was.

"That it?" Woods asked.

"Yeah."

He smoothly withdrew the snake and came quickly to his feet, looping the flat cable around his forearm. Claire had been watching them from in front of the elevators and immediately turned and walked back. A few seconds later they were all back in 1119 with the door closed.

"I didn't see anything that bothered me," August said. "It does appear there's somebody asleep in the bed, but we're not going to be able to identify who it is until we get inside. Let's give it another couple of hours. Then I want Woods to check the room once more from the connecting door. If nothing has changed, we'll go in."

But August *had* seen something that worked at him. Something that wasn't entirely right. He just couldn't figure out what it was.

They all resumed their prior positions.

Woods went back to his book, Claire went back to staring out the window, and August stretched out again and closed his eyes.

A little over an hour later, August opened his eyes. When he did, he knew exactly what he had seen that bothered him.

. . .

"IT'S THE LUGGAGE," August said, sitting up.

Woods and Claire looked at him.

"The shape we saw from the hallway. I think it's a stack of luggage and the pattern on it is the Louis Vuitton logo."

"So, it was Louis Vuitton luggage," Claire said. "Why does that matter?"

"Remember I told you about the guy in the purple dashiki? He had a pile of Louis Vuitton luggage."

"A lot of people have Louis Vuitton luggage."

"A lot of people who checked in to this hotel at exactly the same time Billy Fang is supposed to have checked in?"

"What are you saying, Bossman?" Claire asked. "That Billy Fang was disguised as an African with a pile of Louis Vuitton luggage?"

"Probably not, but it looks likely the luggage our African pal brought into the hotel ended up in the room registered to Billy Fang. Maybe he checked Billy in and delivered some stuff he's going to take with him to Beijing. Then, after that, Billy slipped in through another entrance so he wouldn't have to go through the lobby."

"That makes sense," Claire said.

"I'm not so sure it does, but at least it's one explanation."

"Another explanation is that it's a coincidence."

"And a third is that there's something happening here that we don't understand and we're about to walk right into it."

They all thought about that for a moment.

"Then what do you want to do?" Claire eventually asked.

"What I *want* to do is go back to Pattaya and forget about all this. But what we're *going* to do is check the room from the connecting door again in an hour and, unless we see something that's out of line, we'll go in."

Woods nodded and went back to reading his book. Claire

nodded and went back to looking out the window. August lay back down, but this time he didn't close his eyes.

T IME CRAWLED BY.
    The waiting reminded August of Christmas mornings when he was a child, those mornings when he would wake very early and have to lie quietly and wait until his mother and father also woke up and let him go downstairs to see what Santa Claus had brought him. He figured this was pretty much the same thing, only he wouldn't have his mother's shoulder to cry on if it turned out that Santa had left him nothing but lumps of coal.

August was sure he looked at his watch every five minutes, but Claire and Woods were polite enough not to mention it. When the hands finally crept slowly past 3:45am he decided he'd had enough of waiting. It was time to get in there and open up whatever Santa Claus had for him.

"Get the viewer, Woods. Let's take one more look."

Woods pulled out the fiber-optic viewer and they looked under the connecting door again. Nothing had changed. There was still just that glimmer of gray light from the hallway, a lump on the bed that could be Billy Fang, and nothing else.

"Okay," August said when Woods had pulled the snake back and closed the connecting door on their side, "that's enough of this bullshit. Here's how this is going to go. Woods will pop the door and push it open. It opens inward and to the left covering the bed. I'll take a pillow in with me and go in first when the door swings open. Then I'll use the pillow to press Fang's head down on the bed and muffle any noise he makes as he wakes up."

August looked first at Woods and then at Claire, and they both nodded.

"Woods will come in right behind me, go right to clear the bathroom and closet, then help me by securing the target's feet against the bed. Claire will come in third with the insulin kit.

Woods and I will have the target's head and feet pinned so he ought to be fairly still. Claire grabs whichever arm is easiest for her to access and injects him with the sodium thiopental. When he goes under and stops moving entirely, which shouldn't be more than ten seconds, I'll take the pillow off his face and make certain it's really Billy Fang we've got."

More nods.

"Assuming it is, Claire will inject him with the phenobarbital and we'll tuck him up in bed, then straighten up the room. We'll grab our gear, and close and secure both halves of the connecting door. Then we'll leave through the hallway door and put out the *Do Not Disturb* sign."

"What if it isn't Billy Fang?" Claire asked.

"Then we leave whoever the poor bastard is right there, grab our gear, and get the fuck out of Dodge. We'll have forty-five minutes to an hour before he comes out of the sodium thiopental. That ought to give us plenty of time to be well on our way to the airport before he can wake up and make enough sense out of what happened to him to tell anyone."

August looked from Claire to Woods and back again.

"Any questions?"

No one said anything.

"Okay, then. Weapons check."

All three of them took out their handguns, screwed the suppressers onto the muzzles, and worked the slides to chamber a round.

"No shooting unless I shoot first," August said. "No matter what happens. Got it?"

"Got it," Claire said.

Woods nodded.

August pulled a pillow off the bed and held it against his chest with one hand.

"Somebody kill the lights."

Woods hit the master switch next to the bed and the room went dark. The glow of the city out beyond the open drapes provided enough light for them to move around without bumping into things. They all stood in silence, letting their eyes adjust to the near darkness.

"Okay," August said after a minute or two. "Let's do this."

W OODS PULLED OPEN the connecting door on their side and squatted down with his face close to the lock of the other room's connecting door. August moved in behind Woods and felt rather than saw Claire falling in behind him.

Woods ran his fingers along the base of the lock plate until he found the USB port, plugged in the cable, and touched the icon on his iPhone for the app Spike had built. When the phone's screen suddenly lit up, it looked like a searchlight in the dark room. Woods paused as their eyes adjusted to the additional light, then activated the app.

August watched over his shoulder as columns of numbers rolled up the phone's screen. After no more than twenty seconds, the numbers stopped, the lock gave a whirring sound, and there was a soft *clunk* as it snapped open. The connecting door drifted open about an inch. All three of them stared at the narrow crack that had opened between the door and the frame and felt the same relief that no light showed through it. The target's room was at least in darkness. It was a start.

Woods pulled the USB cord loose and rose to his feet. He placed his right palm against the door and pressed it gently back. When it was open almost far enough for August to slip through, something that seemed to be a sound came to them and everyone froze.

It was so faint that they weren't absolutely certain they had really heard anything at all. August and Claire watched Woods carefully as he rotated his head slowly side to side, listening. It made August think of a dog sniffing the air for danger when he can't figure out what the danger is or where it is coming from or even if it is really there at all.

Woods leaned forward very slowly and poked his head a few inches into the target's room. When he did, the sound came again, and this time they all heard it clearly.

Click.

Woods instantly stood up straight and pushed back against August.

"Exfil! Exfil! Exfil!" he bellowed. *"Move!"*

Neither August nor Claire asked any questions. They moved.

Quickly and smoothly both of them turned away from the connecting door, scooped up their backpacks from where they had left them against the wall near the room's entrance, opened the door, and walked into the hall. Behind them, they heard Woods slam first the inner connecting door, then the outer connecting door. They had started for the elevators when he bolted into the hallway just behind them.

"No," Woods barked when he saw where they were going. He pointed down the hallway in the opposite direction. "Stairs."

He jogged about twenty feet down the hallway and pushed open a black metal door marked Emergency Exit in red letters. August and Claire followed him and found themselves in a concrete fire stair with emergency lighting fixtures bolted to the wall at one-floor intervals.

Woods jogged down the stairs and they broke into a trot behind him, following blindly without understanding why he was leading them as quickly as he could away from the room where Billy Fang was supposed to be.

Then they did understand.

They had made it down only two flights when they felt more than heard the massive explosion rip through the floors above them.

SEVENTEEN

THE STAIRWELL'S emergency lights flashed on and fire bells began to ring. Each emergency light box had a rotating beacon on top that activated when the light came on and the swirling streaks of red the beacons threw across the stairs gave the whole scene a lurid, surreal feel.

The echo in the stairwell made the fire bells sound as if they were coming from everywhere at once and the cacophony ramped up a further notch when loudspeakers began blaring recorded evacuation instructions in several languages.

As the three of them jogged steadily on down the stairs, doors began to slam open on first one floor and then another, and the stairwell filled with a growing stream of guests in a variety of states of dress and undress hastily evacuating the hotel. Down here on the lower floors, they probably hadn't heard the explosion, only the sound of the fire bells and the evacuation orders coming over the loudspeakers, but August had heard the sound of the explosion, and he had felt it.

He couldn't help but think of September 11 and the towers of the World Trade Center pancaking down, each floor falling on the one below until a hundred floors had fallen and nothing was left of the towers but a massive pile of rubble. The people unlucky enough to be left inside when the towers collapsed didn't just die, they were crushed into powder.

August shot a look over his shoulder at Claire, saw that she was keeping up with him, and jogged faster.

A thick-bodied Chinese woman wearing green pajamas pushed into the stairwell through a door directly in front of August and he put out his hands to keep from running over her. He had just registered that there was something odd about the way she was standing when he realized she was pressing a small white dog to her chest and the dog was trembling in fright. Suddenly the woman turned toward August and inexplicably thrust the dog directly at him as if she expected him to relieve her of her burden. August pushed past her and jogged on down behind Woods.

By the time they made it to the lobby, rivers of people were pushing out of the doors of every emergency stairwell. The crowds wrapped them in a blanket of anonymity for which they were grateful.

A few uniformed hotel personnel stood in the lobby directing the crowds emerging from the stairwells toward the exits. Under the circumstances the sight of any uniform, even that of a bellboy, was a calming influence and the crowds were moving outside in an orderly fashion.

August was shoulder to shoulder with Woods as they passed through the lobby and Claire was right behind them.

T HEY EMERGED ON Reclamation Street.

The people leaving the hotel had mostly stopped walking the moment they got outside and the areas just beyond the exits were quickly jamming up. August pushed his way through the crowd with Claire and Woods right behind him and moved away up Reclamation Street to put some distance between them and the hotel. He felt himself crunching over glass shattered so finely it was like walking on beach sand.

When they found a space on the sidewalk that was less crowded, they stopped and looked around. Most of the people along Reclamation Street were staring up at the hotel building with stunned and frightened faces.

The three of them looked up, too.

"Holy shit," Claire murmured.

Neither August nor Woods said anything at all.

U P ON WHAT they assumed was the eleventh floor, and for two or three floors both above and below it, a hole had been punched in the hotel that made August think again of 9/11.

A huge chunk of the building was simply gone, and all around the void draperies that were never meant to see the outside world fluttered desperately through shattered glass as if they were trying to escape the carnage. Who could blame them? From one pair of broken windows a bed teetered half in and half out of what was left of the room, and in another a green chair looked as if it was trying to decide whether or not to jump. Strangely there was no sign of flames or smoke, no fire at all. Just immense and total destruction.

It looked as if a bomb had gone off.

It certainly did.

"What the fuck just happened?" Claire murmured.

"Woods saved our lives," August said.

"You mean the Chinese tried to kill their own defector and we walked right into it?"

August said nothing. He just shook his head. Then he looked at Woods, and Woods shook his head, too.

August glanced at his watch.

4:30. It wouldn't be dawn for another hour or so.

He pointed north on Reclamation Street.

"There's a twenty-four-hour McDonald's around the corner on Argyle Street. Let's get some coffee and figure out what to do now."

W HEN THEY GOT to the McDonald's, it looked as if all of the customers and most of the employees had rushed outside at the sound of the explosion and were now standing together in little groups babbling to each other in Cantonese and pointing up at the side of the Cordis Hotel.

August, Woods, and Claire went inside anyway, found some-body to wait on them, and got coffee. They took their cups over to a red and yellow booth that was well away from everyone else and sat drinking in silence while they each contemplated sepa-rately what had just almost happened to them.

"Anybody else hungry?" Woods asked all of a sudden.

Claire and August just looked at him.

"Personally," he said, "I could go for a Big Mac right about now."

When nobody said anything, Woods looked back and forth between August and Claire. "Okay, well… suit yourselves."

He shrugged, slid out of the booth, and walked back to the counter.

"He's going to *eat?*" Claire asked August. "*Now?*"

August thought about that for a moment.

"I've changed my mind," August said and slid out of the booth. "You sure I can't get you something, Claire?"

"More coffee," Claire muttered. "And… uh, maybe an Egg McMuffin if they have them here."

August smiled, but he didn't say anything else.

·   ·   ·

A UGUST PUT A fresh coffee in front of Claire and handed her an Egg McMuffin. She unwrapped it slowly, her eyes fixed on Woods.

"How did you know about the bomb?" she asked.

"I heard the trigger when the door opened. I'm guessing it was a proximity device of some kind, and the movement of the door into the room tripped it."

"But the bomb didn't go off when you opened the door. It didn't go off for two or three minutes after that."

"The proximity detector must have activated a time delay mechanism."

"But why a proximity trigger *and* a time delay? What's the point of that?"

"Probably to make sure all three of us had time to get inside the room."

"Wait. You're saying the bomb was meant for *us*? Not for Billy Fang?"

When Woods didn't respond, Claire glanced at August. He didn't say anything either, but it was clear he was thinking the same thing.

"Somebody just tried to kill *us*? You're telling me the Chinese were willing to murder a valuable defector like Billy Fang just to get us? I don't believe it."

Woods and August exchanged looks.

"I doubt Billy Fang even exists," August said. "I think this was a set-up from the beginning. The whole idea was to get us into that room and kill us."

"*Whoa*," Claire breathed out.

"Those Louis Vuitton suitcases delivered by our chubby friend in the purple dashiki probably contained the bomb and the trigger. Maybe he set the trigger, maybe somebody else came in later and set it. Either way, the plan was to kill us."

"The Chinese wanted to kill us?"

"I don't think so. Too messy, and too obvious for them to do something like that here in Hong Kong. The location immediately throws the suspicion on them. If the Chinese wanted to kill us, they'd do it in a third country."

"But if it wasn't the Chinese, then who the hell was it?'

"I've got no idea."

"Who even knows we're here?" Claire asked.

"The three of us, of course, and Spike and the messenger."

"And the Conductor," Claire added.

"And the Conductor."

"Well, it sure as hell wasn't any of us who were responsible and I'd bet my life it wasn't Spike either." Claire looked from August to Woods and neither of them appeared to disagree with her. "That leaves the messenger and the Conductor."

"Unless we have a mole," August said.

Woods and Claire just looked at him.

"You think the Band has been compromised?"

August looked down at the yellow Formica table top and slowly shook his head.

"Look," he said, "here's what I *do* know. Somebody wanted the three of us dead. And that has to be somebody who knew we had instructions to take down Billy Fang here in Hong Kong. They also had to know we had a limited window of time, and that was what allowed them to focus down to an exact time and place to go after us. Whoever it was, they knew everything."

"You think somebody is trying to shut down the Band?"

"That's my guess right now."

"Maybe the Conductor is pulling the plug," Woods said, "and he's tying up loose ends."

"Oh, come on," Claire snapped. "That's not possible."

She looked at August.

"It isn't, is it?"

"Look, Claire, I don't know what to think yet. But right at this moment I don't trust anybody other than the two of you."

"And Spike."

August hesitated. "Probably."

"You're scaring me, Bossman."

August said nothing and Claire and Woods looked at each other.

"Here's what I want you to do," August continued. "Whoever set that bomb almost certainly thinks the three of us are dead. Maybe they were watching the hotel, but as many exits as there are and as big as the crowd coming out was, I think it's a long shot that they would have seen us. Right now, odds are we're dead as far as they're concerned and that gives us some short-term cover. I want to protect that as long as I can. We need to go to ground until we get a clear fix on this. You've both got bolt holes, don't you?"

In their line of work, they had to have lifelines in case everything went sideways. Bolt holes weren't just a place to hide, they were equipped with emergency IDs, virgin passports, unused credit cards, and a pile of cash. Survival stashes.

August looked at Claire, who nodded, then he looked at Woods, who nodded too.

"How about Spike?"

Another nod from Woods.

"Okay, use them. Don't let anyone know where you are. Not each other, not even me."

"How do we find out who did this if we all go off and hide in holes?"

"Leave that to me."

"You mean you're not—"

"Dump your guns and the burner phones we've been using. The second set of burners has got to be clean. Keep those. Tell Spike to get a clean burner, too, and then text the number to one of you. When I find out what's happening and decide what we're going to do about it, I'll be in touch with Claire and she can get in touch with everyone else. Until then, stay silent and stay invisible."

"Look, Bossman, wouldn't it be better if—"

"I want both of you to get out of here right now," August

interrupted. "Get yourselves on the first flight out of Hong Kong that takes you to wherever you're going. Travel separately to the airport and change cabs a couple of times just in case you've been spotted."

"What are you going to do?" Claire asked.

"I don't know."

But that wasn't true.

August knew exactly what he was going to do.

EIGHTEEN

AUGUST CAUGHT THE early morning Cathay Pacific nonstop flight from Hong Kong to New York and took a cab into Manhattan.

He had dropped off their gear and picked up an identity package from the Hong Kong safe house on his way to the airport and he was traveling under an Australian passport with a driver's license and credit cards to match.

The package also included a couple of Australian SIMs for his telephone so, while the cab was still on the Van Wyck Expressway, he inserted one of them and used his phone to pick out a middle-market hotel on the northern fringe of Chelsea where he had never stayed before. He booked a room using a popular booking app without ever speaking to a soul, which was his favorite way to do everything.

It was almost five in the afternoon when August got to the hotel, a pleasant enough looking place on 25th Street just off Eighth Avenue. He had dozed briefly on the long flight in from Hong Kong, but he never slept well on airplanes. Some part of him always remained on alert just in case the pilots needed his help.

August asked for a quiet room on a high floor in the back

away from the street. The worst thing about flying into New York, he always thought, was plunging straight into the noise of the city. Some people called New York *the city that never sleeps.* August called it *the city that never shuts up.* He took a shower, ordered an early dinner from room service, and slept for nearly twelve hours.

The next morning, he checked out just after nine and walked north on Eighth Avenue carrying his small leather duffle bag. A block or two up he stopped at a deli and had a bagel with cream cheese and two cups of coffee, then he walked four more blocks to Penn Station. By ten, he had an Amtrak ticket on the ten-thirty Acela Express to Washington D.C. and was on his way out to board the train.

The train encountered the usual delays around Philadelphia and it wasn't until a little after three in the afternoon that August got to Union Station. He walked out through the main entrance and stood for a moment facing the big traffic circle in front of the station. Across on the other side, the dome of the United States Capitol loomed huge and somehow a little unreal. It gleamed in the afternoon sun like a field of virgin snow.

August walked to the taxi stand where he stood to the side and allowed several people to go in front of him. Eventually, he fell into line behind a woman with two small children and when it came his turn he got into the next taxi on the rank. The driver was an elderly black man, bald except for wisps of gray hair above each ear.

The old man half turned and looked back over his shoulder without making eye contact. August noticed his eyes looked rheumy and unfocused. He hoped the man could see well enough to drive.

"Where to?"

"National Airport," August said.

"You mean Reagan, don't you?"

August hated it when the traditional names of airports or roads or buildings were changed as a gesture to the fashion of the day. Out of sheer stubbornness, he steadfastly refused to use whatever the new name might be and stuck with whatever name he had always used.

He had no doubt the driver knew exactly where he wanted to go so he didn't bother to reply. The driver only grunted and pulled away.

After a bit, not bothering to look back again, the driver asked, "What airline?"

August picked one at random.

"United."

Another grunt.

August leaned back in the seat and crossed his legs. National was just on the other side of the Potomac River in Northern Virginia. The ride wouldn't take more than fifteen or twenty minutes across the Fourteenth Street Bridge and south on the George Washington Memorial Parkway unless they ran into one of the random, haphazard traffic snarls for which Washington was justly famed. They didn't.

A little over fifteen minutes later, August paid the driver and walked into the United terminal at National, or Reagan, depending on your point of view. He took an escalator down one floor to the baggage claim area, walked outside to the curb, and randomly got on the first car rental shuttle bus that came by. No one got on with him.

When the shuttle arrived at the Avis garage, August used his Australian passport and credit card to rent a white Honda Accord. Driving an Accord, particularly a white one, made him as close to invisible on an American road as it was possible to be. He threw his leather duffle on the back seat, pulled out of the airport onto the parkway, and headed south.

He had watched carefully throughout all of the zig-zags on the trip from Hong Kong to New York and on to Washington and nothing he had seen yet caused him to twitch. Of course, if there was a full team of professionals on him, he wouldn't have caught any sign of them. He had no illusions about that. If they wanted to keep him boxed, they would, and he wouldn't get a glimpse of them until it was too late.

But still, he figured the odds were in his favor. He was dead, wasn't he? Who would deploy a large and very expensive team of watchers, then spread them around half the globe just in case he suddenly popped back to life? No, that was too unlikely to be realistic. Not impossible, of course, but unlikely. August liked his chances.

The more he thought about it, the surer he was.

Nobody knew he was coming.

R ED RIVER CONSULTANTS operated out of a small, two-story brick building on a quiet side street in Alexandria, Virginia, a peaceful and dignified community a few miles south of National Airport on the west bank of the Potomac River.

Alexandria was the sort of place where two-hundred-year-old houses shared the brick and cobblestone streets with small commercial buildings carefully designed to fit into the area's historical tone.

Red River's neighbors were accountants and lawyers and investment managers, people who could have their offices in the civilized climate of Alexandria rather than in one of the bland K Street buildings in downtown Washington because they had the sort of clients who didn't care where they were. Red River Consultants didn't just have clients that didn't care where they were. Most of them didn't *know* where they were, or even particularly want to know.

The front of the house, as everyone called it, consisted of about a dozen people who kept up the façade that Red River was an international business consulting group. As far as August knew, Red River really did have a few legitimate clients, but he had always suspected that claim required using a rather elastic definition of the word *legitimate*. The intelligence establishment in Washington was everywhere, and it was ferocious. It protected its own. If Red River needed some legitimate clients to maintain an acceptable front, August was sure it had been provided a few by the Conductor's friends.

The back of the house was composed of a much smaller group, perhaps six or eight people, although exactly how many there were even August wasn't certain. He recognized most of those people when he saw them, which was seldom, but he couldn't really say that he knew any of them. He had spoken a few times to a woman who said her name was Sally on those occasions when he had tried to reach the Conductor and he hadn't been available. She sounded like a woman in late middle age, but there were three or four women there who met that description. Maybe Sally was one of them, maybe she wasn't.

August and his people in Pattaya were more or less completely isolated from Red River, which naturally was the whole idea. He knew there were other operators out there who worked the same way, but he wasn't even certain where they were and he was pretty sure they didn't know where he was. *Secret* was a word tossed around in all sorts of ways to describe various government operations that really weren't. To call a government operation secret usually meant little more than that it hadn't been on the front page of *The New York Times*. At least, not yet. The Band really *was* secret.

So, what the hell was that set-up in Hong Kong all about?

August had been thinking about that for the last thirty-six hours while he sat on airplanes, on trains, and in a succession of motor vehicles. He had run through the possibilities backward and forward, but he was no closer to an explanation now than when he had been standing on Reclamation Street in those first moments staring up at that gaping hole in the side of the Cordis Hotel.

Somebody had gone to a lot of trouble to make him dead and to take two members of his operating team down with him. The question was *why*?

Maybe some foreign intelligence service had a mole in the Band, it had of course occurred to August. But even if they did, what would be the point of blowing their penetration just to kill him and a couple of people who worked with him?

He wasn't overly modest about his skills and his accomplishments, but surely a successful penetration of an organization as secret as the Band was worth far too much to trade it for the death of any operator, no matter who he was. Penetrations like that took years, sometimes decades to build. They were gold. You didn't throw them away unless it was for something big, really big. August knew he had made some important contributions, but he wasn't worth that. Not even close.

Then what did that leave? It left the decidedly nasty possibility, that the source of the action was domestic, not foreign. Perhaps the Band was being shut down and the pink slips being sent out were of the permanent variety. August didn't see how that could be done without the consent and the participation of the Conductor so that was why he had traveled from Hong Kong to Washington and was now driving toward Alexandria.

It wasn't that he didn't trust the Conductor, he always had, but part of the business he was in was understanding that your trust could still sometimes be misused.

Trust your friends, but cut the cards.

Either the Conductor knew what had happened in Hong Kong or he didn't. August had to be certain which it was.

Time to cut the cards.

NINETEEN

THE CONDUCTOR LIVED in a three-story brick row house that was built around the time of the Revolutionary War and had somehow survived ever since. It was on a cobblestoned block shaded by huge trees that was a pleasant stroll from the office building that housed the Band.

August had never been to the Conductor's house, but the Conductor had once pointed it out to him when they were taking a walk through Alexandria during a break from a long and frustrating operational planning session, back in the days when he did visit the office on occasion. He had told August that the plot on which the house was built had been originally surveyed by George Washington. It was a story that seemed far too fanciful to August to be true, so he had only nodded, passed on by, and not asked any questions.

August had a way of filing away facts that had no immediate value to him but might somehow have value in the future, and now he had two facts that would make it possible for him to do what he needed to do.

Take the Conductor by surprise and read his reaction to August's sudden appearance right in front of him.

He would probably see only a fleeting moment of truth

before the Conductor was able to adjust his reaction to whatever
he thought it should be, but taking him completely unaware
ought to give him that moment. If he thought August was dead,
August was certain he would see it in his eyes.

Setting up the surprise wouldn't be difficult. He knew where
the Conductor lived, and he knew that he usually walked back
and forth between his house and Red River's offices. He didn't
know if the Conductor was even in town, of course, or had
perhaps left the office early to meet his mistress — well, probably not that — but he could hardly telephone that nice middle-
aged woman who took the Conductor's messages and ask, could
he? Sometimes there were things that just had to be left to
fortune.

A UGUST DROVE THROUGH Alexandria passing
within a block of Red River's office, then he circled
around and passed by a block on the other side going in the
opposite direction.

He wasn't looking for anything in particular other than some
reassurance that nothing big had changed. He was pleased to
see that everything looked exactly as it had the last time he had
been there. It was what he expected, of course. Alexandria
didn't change much in a year. A lot of it hadn't changed much
in two hundred years.

He parked the Accord in a public garage just off King
Street, the major commercial artery that bisects Alexandria
from east to west. King Street is Bourbon Street without the
Dixieland bands. It's lined with bars and restaurants and
thronged year-round with tourists who come to Alexandria in
search of America's past. August thought every passing year was
making it harder and harder for anybody to find even the
slightest trace of America's past, but the tourists keep coming
anyway.

August walked a couple of blocks down King toward the

river and sat at a sidewalk table in front of an Italian restaurant where he vaguely remembered eating once or twice. From there, he had a clear view along King to the two cross streets that offered the Conductor the most direct route to walk from Red River's offices to his house.

There were fifty different routes the Conductor could choose to walk through the blocks of this small-scale neighborhood of historic homes, cobblestone streets, and big trees, but August couldn't cover them all so he chose to cover the most likely ones. It was that fortune thing again. Sometimes August thought the most important element in the success of every operation was having a little good luck.

He asked the waiter for a beer and put him off about ordering dinner. He glanced at his watch. A little after five. Who ate dinner at a little after five anyway? Obviously middle-aged and elderly tourists in Alexandria did because all up and down King he could see them seated at tables doing exactly that. August wondered briefly whether he would ever be old enough to seriously consider ordering dinner at five o'clock. That seemed extraordinarily unlikely.

August ignored the glass the waiter brought with the beer and sipped it straight from the bottle. He liked the feel of a beer bottle in his hands. It felt solid, substantial, and given the shaky underpinnings of his hastily organized operation in Alexandria, a little feeling of solid and substantial was particularly welcome right then.

August had finished most of the beer when, about half an hour later, he had some of that good luck he had been banking on. The Conductor crossed King Street about half a block down from where he was sitting.

He was an unremarkable looking man of somewhere around seventy. He was of average height and average weight, and he dressed and cut his hair in an entirely average way. He looked like everybody. No one who encountered him would be able to give you a description five minutes after he had gone.

August supposed that was one thing that had made him such a good spy.

The Conductor was walking south at a relaxed pace. August was certain he was on his way home.

A UGUST STOOD UP and dropped a twenty-dollar bill on the table. Beer was expensive in Alexandria.

He walked quickly up King away from the intersection where the Conductor had just crossed and turned left at the next street to circle the block. That would put him in position to walk directly toward the Conductor as he approached his house. August needed to see the Conductor's face when he realized it was August coming toward him.

Would the Conductor merely be surprised to see August here in Alexandria, ten thousand miles away from where he was supposed to be? Or would he be surprised in the way someone would if they suddenly found a dead man walking toward them?

Whatever the Conductor's reaction, it would only be there for a moment before he covered it with the professionally unruffled façade he had practiced for nearly half a century. August was betting he could catch the real reaction. If he didn't, he wasn't sure where that left him.

August moved fast. He turned the corner and walked east at almost exactly the same moment the Conductor turned the corner a block down and walked west.

It was a quiet and distinguished residential block. No one else was on the brick-paved sidewalks that ran between the cobblestone streets and the three and four-story row houses that had been standing there for hundreds of years.

August and the Conductor walked directly toward each other there on that empty sidewalk. They drew closer and closer and August could almost believe he heard their footsteps echoing hollowly on those brick pavers, but he knew that was just his imagination.

He felt like he and the Conductor were reenacting the climactic gunfight scene from *High Noon*. When August thought about it that way, it occurred to him that maybe that was exactly what they *were* doing.

At first the Conductor didn't appear to pay any particular attention to the man walking toward him. Then, as the distance between them closed, August saw the Conductor's eyes sweep over him, stop, and immediately come back.

The Conductor slowed his pace and tilted his head slightly to one side.

And then something happened that August hadn't anticipated.

The Conductor's face lit up in an enormous smile.

"Damn, it *is* you, isn't it, John? What in God's name are you doing here?"

August said nothing until he got within an arm's length of the Conductor. When he did, they both lifted their hands by reflex and they shook.

"There's something we need to talk about."

"Uh-oh." The Conductor looked to August to be more bemused than alarmed. "Sounds ominous."

"It is. Somebody tried to kill me."

The Conductor stopped smiling.

"You're being serious?"

August nodded. "Together with two of my people. Claire and Woods."

"Well." The Conductor thought about that for a moment. "Maybe it would be better if we took this inside."

He pointed to his house which was only a couple of doors up from where they were standing. August nodded and followed the Conductor as he walked to his front door, opened it, and ushered him inside.

August was certain now that the Conductor knew nothing about what had happened in Hong Kong. He had watched the movement of every muscle in the Conductor's face, every shift of his eyes when he had realized August was walking toward him there on the sidewalk. And he saw… nothing. Nothing at all.

Nobody who thought August was dead could disguise his shock that completely. Nobody was that good. The Conductor didn't know what had happened in Hong Kong. August would bet his life on it.

Which, he supposed when he thought about it as he walked through the Conductor's front door, was exactly what he was about to do.

A UGUST HAD NEVER been inside the Conductor's house before this and he had never really thought about what it might look like.

Since the exterior was a brick row house with small-paned, shuttered windows that was a couple of hundred years old, he had naturally assumed the interior would reflect the same general sensibility. Probably a lot of dark-framed period furniture, perhaps shelves of leather-bound books, and maybe a few portraits of presidents that looked like they had been painted by Gilbert Stuart but probably hadn't been.

Looking around as the Conductor closed the door behind them, August reminded himself, not for the first time, that assumptions were dangerous things. He and the Conductor weren't exactly drinking buddies, not the kind of men who headed for a bar together after a long day of work and downed a few beers while they talked football, but August still thought he knew his boss reasonably well. At least he had assumed he did. There was that word again.

The Conductor hit the lights and crossed the room to a narrow Plexiglas table that held a collection of bottles and glasses. August looked around while the Conductor poured drinks.

The room was a gallery of contemporary art. The furniture

was minimalist. Four black-leather Corbusier armchairs were grouped in the middle with a low round table that looked like marble. The table was so white that it appeared almost luminescent, as if it was lighted from within by some otherworldly source of power.

On the wall directly in front of him was a single giant canvas lighted by hidden spots in the ceiling. The painting was comprised of a series of rough red and orange bands shot through with streaks of yellow that looked like heat lightning dancing across a summer afternoon. It must have been at least ten feet long and eight feet high and it made August think of Robert Rauschenberg. But he immediately dismissed the idea. If it was really a Rauschenberg it would have to be worth enough to clear a significant chunk of the national debt.

On another wall were two paintings that August was pretty sure he did recognize. They were Warhol's, one from his series of Marilyn Monroe portraits and one from his series of portraits of Mao.

"Single malt okay?" the Conductor asked as he handed August a glass.

"Fine, sir." August took the glass and tipped it toward the large painting that looked like Rauschenberg. "Is that—"

"Let's talk out in the garden," the Conductor interrupted. "It's too nice an afternoon to stay inside."

And there was more privacy out there, August thought to himself, in the event there was some form of surveillance operating inside the Conductor's house.

The Conductor led August down a short hallway and into a smaller room that looked less like a gallery and more like a space in which someone actually lived. A comfortable looking brown leather couch flanked by two matching chairs faced a large flat screen television mounted on one wall. The Conductor took a small ring of keys from his pocket and unlocked a glass-paned door which led outside to a small bricked garden surrounded by a high wall.

As August followed, he glanced at a collection of pictures in silver frames arranged on a console table behind the couch. Most of the pictures were of an attractive blond woman in different places and at what appeared to be different ages and periods in her life. In some of the pictures she was with small children and in others she was alone. Was she the Conductor's wife? His former wife? August had no idea. The Conductor did not live in a world in which you shared domestic details with your acquaintances. And August did not live in the sort of world in which you showed any interest in such things.

Out in the garden several high-backed rattan chairs with bright orange cushions were arranged around a square black metal table. The Conductor settled himself in one chair and gestured August toward another.

It was remarkably quiet, August thought, particularly when you realized they were in the middle of the city and only a few miles from the White House. They sat in silence for a moment and sipped at their drinks. August listened to the birds and waited for the Conductor to speak first.

"Tell me," the Conductor eventually said.

So, August did.

TWENTY

AUGUST FINISHED THE story of their assignment and the bomb that had been waiting for them in Billy Fang's room at the Cordis Hotel in Hong Kong about the same time he and the Conductor both finished the last sips of their whiskeys.

"You have a leak somewhere in the Band, sir. There's no other way this could have been set up. Whoever laid this trap for us must have known we were going to that room before we knew. There's no other way they would have been able to make the preparations that were required."

The Conductor kept his face empty and said nothing, then after a moment he rose slowly from his chair and reached for August's glass.

"No more for me, sir."

The Conductor took August's glass anyway.

"You'll change your mind when you hear what I'm about to tell you," he said.

· · ·

H E DISAPPEARED INTO the house and August listened to the birds some more and wondered if he had made a mistake with his absolute faith that the Conductor was not responsible for what had happened.

Perhaps the Conductor was inside right at that moment making a telephone call and arranging for people to come and take August down. He didn't really believe that was true, but the thought occurred to him nevertheless. How could it not?

The Conductor returned almost immediately and handed August's refreshed drink to him, then settled heavily into the chair where he had been sitting before and took a long pull from his own drink. He cleared his throat and pretty much put an end to any lingering doubts August might have had.

"Here's the thing," he said. "I never heard of Billy Fang."

"I don't understand, sir."

"Neither do I. I don't know who Billy Fang is or even if he really exists. There was no leak at the Band. There was nothing *to* leak. I didn't give you an assignment. I didn't send a messenger to you."

August thought about that for a moment.

"Ah shit," he said.

"Exactly," the Conductor agreed.

T HEY SIPPED THEIR whiskeys and weighed the implications of what they both now knew that they had not known a few moments before.

"Everything about the assignment was exactly as it always has been," August said. "The post on the Chess Board. The CryptoCat messages about the messenger's schedule. And the messenger's arrival. Nothing was any different except that the messenger was a woman I didn't know."

"That didn't make you suspicious?"

"Why should it? I don't know all the Band's personnel. I know almost none of them. And that's as it should be."

"The Band doesn't have a woman messenger, John. Lawrence of Princeton delivers all the assignments for me."

In spite of himself, August smiled. "How did you know I call him that?"

"Because we all call him that."

August chuckled, but his amusement faded quickly.

"Well, fuck," he said. "Somebody has our communications protocols and used them to set me up."

"It would seem so."

"That's worse than a leak, Conductor. The Band has been completely compromised."

The Conductor nodded thoughtfully, but he didn't say anything.

Suddenly a limb of the tree in the middle of the Conductor's garden rattled and shook, and when August glanced over he saw a red-brown squirrel with a sprinkling of white on his bushy tail leap from the tree limb to the top of the brick wall that surrounded the garden.

The squirrel edged toward them along the wall, taking a few steps forward, freezing to see what would happen, and then taking a few more. After a bit, the squirrel apparently decided the two men posed no threat to him and he strode confidently along the wall until he came to the point that was close to where they sat. Then he settled back on his haunches, sat down, and examined them with evident curiosity. He clearly couldn't understand what the two men were doing, sitting there together silent and unmoving, and the squirrel turned his head first to one side and then to the other as if that might somehow improve his comprehension.

August could easily understand why the squirrel was having difficulty deciding what the two men were likely to do next, since August himself had no fucking clue.

"Maybe this was personal," the Conductor suddenly spoke up. "Maybe someone was targeting you and this has nothing to do with the Band."

At the sound of the Conductor's voice the squirrel started in alarm. He leaped off the wall into the neighbor's garden and disappeared. August wished he could do exactly the same thing.

"I don't think so, sir. The bomb was evidently triggered by a proximity detector, but then there was a time delay built in as well. We think the purpose of the delay had to have been to make certain all of us had time to enter the room before the bomb detonated. Whoever set it to trigger that way intended to kill us all, not just me."

"It's possible they just wanted to make certain you were in the room and they didn't know how many people would enter or in what order so they allowed a little extra time, to be sure they'd get you."

August nodded. Maybe. He supposed that was at least possible, but it didn't feel right to him. If somebody wanted to kill him, there were an awful lot of far easier ways to do it. Why go through the elaborate set-up of faking an assignment that would pull his entire crew into that hotel room in Hong Kong and then rigging the room to blow up? You would only do something like that if you were trying to land a knock-out blow on the Band, not simply kill John August.

"Are the other teams all secure?" August asked the Conductor.

"Yes, as far as I know. On the other hand, twenty minutes ago I would have said your team was secure, too."

"Perhaps you should stand everyone down for a while."

The Conductor looked distinctly unenthusiastic about that, and August could easily understand why. It would doubtless cause all sorts of disruptions in ongoing operations that August didn't know a thing about. And he wasn't about to ask.

"Any ideas about who it could be, sir?"

"Not unless it's one of your old girlfriends, John."

August didn't bother to laugh and the Conductor didn't look like he expected him to.

"Have there been any recent operations that might have triggered someone to look for revenge against the Band?"

The Conductor shook his head.

"Any threats? Problems? Blown operations?"

The Conductor was silent for a long while. After a bit he lifted his whiskey glass automatically and seemed surprised when he put it to his lips and found it was empty.

"Almost no one even knows the Band exists, John. You know that."

"But there are some people in the government who know it exists, and some of them don't like what we do."

"Enough to start killing my people? They don't do that."

"We do that, sir." August thought of Billy Fang, assuming he existed, and he thought of some of the others who had posed a danger to the country and whose danger the Band had put an end to. "We kill people when they're a threat. If someone thought we were a threat, why wouldn't they do the same thing?"

The Conductor shook his head, but he said nothing.

Out of the corner of his eye August caught a sudden flash of movement and turned his head in time to see that the squirrel with the white sprinkled tail had returned. It sat motion-lessly on its haunches on top of the garden wall and silently watched the two men. After a minute or two, it scampered down the wall, built up its momentum, and launched itself into a graceful bound back into the tree in the middle of the garden. A limb shook, then another and another, until finally silence returned and the squirrel was gone.

August watched it disappear and he envied its complete freedom and its utter autonomy. If the Buddhists were right, and our souls lived endless cycles of life in different forms, August decided he could do worse the next time around than put up his hand to come back as a squirrel.

"I F SOMEONE IS trying to take down the Band, sir, this doesn't end here. We may not have much time before they hit us again."

"But surely, since they failed in their first try—"

"They don't know that. They think they succeeded."

A quizzical expression crossed the Conductor's face. August realized he hadn't really focused on that part of the story yet.

"They missed getting us only because of Woods' instincts and a bit of sheer luck," August continued quickly. "Even if they were watching the hotel, they almost certainly don't know we survived and slipped away in the chaos. I doubt they know they failed. They think they succeeded."

"It is then your conviction that they'll feel emboldened by that perception of success and keep coming."

"Yes, sir. If it were me, and I wanted to destroy the Band, I'd finish the job before you figured out what was really happening."

The Conductor folded his arms and looked away. August imagined he was seeing sights he would rather not.

"Maybe I'm wrong, sir. Maybe there's another explanation."

"Do you have one?"

"No."

"Neither do I."

They sat quietly after that for a bit, each teasing out his own thoughts. When the Conductor finally spoke again, it was in a voice so soft that August might almost have missed it.

"What do you think we ought to do, John?"

"We need to fix this quickly. I'm going to do that the way I usually fix things. I'm going to find the threat and eliminate it."

"You're going to kill whoever is behind this."

It wasn't a question so August didn't give the Conductor an answer.

"It may not be easy this time," the Conductor said.

"It's never easy, sir. I don't do it because it's easy."

"If you're right, if somebody really is trying to destroy the Band, how are you going to find who it is? You've got nothing to work with. You've got no place to start looking for them."

"But I do. That woman who came to Secrets posing as a messenger from you set us up. That's where I start. With her."

The Conductor nodded slowly, but he didn't say anything.

"How many people know about our security protocols, sir? How many people know about leaving a message on the Chess Board and then communicating the messenger's schedule through CryptoCat?"

"Maybe ten."

"And how many people know about me and about Secrets?"

"Fewer. Perhaps four or five."

"That's why the messenger is the place to start. She's got to be connected somehow to someone who knows about Secrets."

"I'm one of those four or five people, John."

"Yes, you are. That's why I'm here. I needed to eliminate you first."

"You thought I might have betrayed you."

There was no anger in the Conductor's tone, no resentment. He was simply stating a fact.

"It wasn't personal, sir. It was just math. The number of people who know about me is small. They each have to be eliminated no matter who they are."

The Conductor nodded and thought for a moment.

"You're not an investigator, John. Your strength is—"

"I know what my strength is, sir. When you give me an assignment, you always leave the details to me. That's what you need to do here, too."

The Conductor nodded slowly again and thought about it. He didn't have to think for very long.

"Okay," he said, "I'll give you a week. But that's it. If you don't get to the bottom of this by then, I'm going to have to get at it another way. What do you need from me?"

"First, stand down the other teams so that they can't be pulled into a set-up the way we were. And do nothing at all to suggest you have the slightest interest in the explosion that occurred at the Cordis Hotel in Hong Kong."

"All right."

"And I'll need a list of all the people who know about Secrets and about me, and I need a list of everyone who knows what our communications protocols are."

"I can give you that now."

"You have some burner phones, don't you?"

"Of course."

"Here?"

The Conductor nodded again.

"Give me a number that's never been used and that will only be used for communication between us."

"Fine. Do you need any logistics support?"

"I'm dead, sir. How could I possibly need any logistics support?"

The Conductor chuckled slightly. "John," he said, "I'm beginning to get the idea you *like* being dead."

"You have to admit there is a certain sense of freedom to it, sir."

August thought for a moment of telling the Conductor about the squirrel, but then he thought better of it and let it go.

A UGUST FELT LIKE he was right in the eye of a storm and he couldn't see the whole of it yet.

He knew the Conductor was right to say he wasn't much of an investigator. He did the down-low stuff when it needed to be done, not the visible stuff.

The painstaking rooting out of facts and their transubstanti-

ation into something like awareness was a different affair altogether. He would need help for that. He would need help to
grasp the dimensions and depth of the storm, to determine
where it originated and where it was going.

And August knew just the guy who could do that.

PART 3
PROGRESSIO

TWENTY-ONE

I T WAS A few minutes before sunrise and Tay watched
Singapore slide by outside the windows of the taxi taking
him to Changi Airport.

In the gray half-light of a false dawn, he saw heat lightning
flashing silently behind banks of clouds massed to the south over
the Singapore Strait. It looked as if a naval duel was being
fought far out on the ocean, some place too far away for him to
hear the sound of the guns.

August must have been confident Tay would help him
because he already had everything organized. A ticket on Singapore Airlines, a booking at the Pattaya Hilton, a pile of Thai
currency, and a local contact Tay could trust if he needed him.
August had also given Tay a prepaid phone which he insisted on
calling a burner.

Tay was familiar with the term, of course, but only from spy
novels and the movies. The kind of villains he had dealt with in
Singapore just made do with their own phones and didn't seem
to be overly worried about being tracked by sophisticated elec-
tronics. Singapore was a small place. You didn't need to track a
phone to find somebody. You just asked around among the

uncles and aunties, and somebody could tell you where to find almost anybody.

August was leaving it to Tay to find out who had tried to kill him in Hong Kong. He told Tay he figured it was better for him to stay dead for a while so he had gone completely dark. He thought that whoever was responsible for the bomb in Hong Kong would doubtless be less wary if they believed the operation had been successful and that August and his team were dead.

That made sense to Tay, so he hadn't argued. Besides, truth be known, he really preferred going it alone.

Besides, how hard could it be? August had told him what he knew about the woman who had come to him pretending to be a messenger for the Band, and that sounded to Tay like as good a starting point as any. If he could identify her, then everything else would fall into place from there. Well… probably it would.

Pattaya wasn't a very big town, and Tay's guess was that not a great many women traveled there, certainly not attractive ones who were on their own. The way August had described this woman, his guess was she would have been noticed by a fair number of people. What he had to do was find some of them.

Having the exact date and time she had gone to Secrets was a good start. That gave Tay a nice, tight little window to work with. If he could pinpoint the woman somewhere in that window, he could begin to trace her movements around Pattaya, maybe find out how she had gotten there and how she had left, and where she had gone other than to Secrets to meet August.

If she had stayed in a hotel, that meant a registration, and a registration meant a passport and a credit card. They both might well be fakes, of course, but even fakes told you something about the user's identity, and something was more than they had now.

Naturally, the big win would be to find the woman had been caught somewhere on CCTV and get a picture of her. With a picture and some minimal information about her, he was sure

August could use his intelligence contacts to ID the woman, and once they knew who she was then everything would begin to unravel.

It would be simple, Tay told himself. He really hoped he was right about that. He wanted this over as soon as possible so he could go home. He had never been a keen traveler. He thought all that business about how you broadened your mind when you visited other countries was nonsense.

When you visited other countries mostly what you discovered was how good you had it at home.

I N THE PREDAWN gloom, Singapore felt empty, desolate. The darkened buildings and the metal grates pulled down over the shop fronts made it seem as if he and the cab driver were the last two people left alive on earth.

For just a moment, Tay found himself wondering if he might be seeing Singapore for the last time. He wasn't sure why that thought occurred to him right out of nowhere, but once it had, he wished it hadn't. Singapore was his home, the only one he had ever known. He did not know what would become of him without it.

Yet, if he was being entirely honest with himself, he had to admit he had developed strangely mixed feelings about the city. Singapore had been a place he had loved unconditionally once, but that was a long time ago. He didn't really love Singapore like that anymore. He wished he did, but he didn't.

When he was a child, Singapore had been a place of wonder for him. It had been a paradise then, a serene and sweet-tempered place where the warm breezes rattled the palm trees with a sound that came back to him with absolute clarity now, even after almost forty years.

Sometimes Tay thought he could close his eyes and see everything again just as it had been then, back when he was eight years old and Singapore was thrilling to him, but he wasn't absolutely sure anymore he really could. Was he seeing something he actually remembered, or was he only seeing something he wanted to remember? The older Tay got, the harder it was for him to tell.

As the years had passed, his city had begun to break his heart. Singapore had become a place he hardly knew anymore, a place he really didn't want to know. The city in which he grew up, the city of shaded laneways warmed by the tropical sun and cooled by the ocean breezes, was gone, as gone as if it had never existed at all. It had been fed by mindless bureaucrats into the merciless grinders of progress, and it had emerged without its soul.

Somewhere along the way, the city he had loved for the whole of his life had turned fat, ugly, and mean. Maybe it wasn't just Singapore. Maybe the whole world had turned fat, ugly, and mean, but Tay only lived in one small part of it so he couldn't be sure whether it had or not.

Perhaps, he sometimes thought, it wasn't the city or the world that had changed so much. Perhaps it was just him. As he had grown older, Tay had noticed time beginning to fold back on itself. His oldest memories had become brighter and more vivid than his newest. Perhaps it was only natural when one had no future that the past came alive with newfound intensity. If he could live in that past again, he thought he probably would.

Tay saw the headlights of another car crossing the road somewhere far in front of the taxi and he felt a sudden rush of relief. He and the driver were not the only two people still alive in a landscape of desolation. There were other people out there.

But then abruptly the lights vanished and the other car was gone, as gone as if it had never existed at all, and he and the cab driver were alone in the darkness again.

· · ·

T AY HADN'T REALIZED his ticket was first class until he got to the airport.

It was a nice surprise to be conducted past the long line of people waiting to check in and taken into a private area furnished with comfortable couches and chairs where neatly uniformed women waited behind desks to make his life as easy as possible. Still, he felt a little bit guilty relaxing in an over-stuffed chair with a cup of coffee while someone else took his ticket and passport and dealt with the minutiae of sorting them out and checking his bag. He hadn't finished even half the cup when a smiling woman returned, gave him his boarding pass and luggage check, directed him to the private immigration desks, and told him how to find the first-class lounge.

The lounge offered an elaborate breakfast buffet, but Tay took only a single Danish pastry, got another cup of coffee, and settled himself in a deeply cushioned club chair with a matching ottoman that was off in a deserted part of the lounge. When he saw the copy of the *Financial Times* folded neatly and waiting on the side table it occurred to him that he had no idea what the exchange rate was for the Thai baht so he flipped to the back and scanned the foreign-exchange table until he found it.

He took out the money August had given him, counted it, and did the math in his head. His first thought was to be impressed that August had provided him with almost $5,000. His second thought was less cheerful.

Why would he need $5,000 for just a couple of days?

Clearly August expected this to take longer than that. Did August know something he hadn't yet shared with Tay? Of course he did. August knew all kinds of things he hadn't yet shared with Tay and never would. That wasn't really the question. The question was whether August knew a little thing that was likely to turn into a headache for Tay, or if he knew a big thing that was likely to dump him straight in the shit.

The large amount of money August had provided him

didn't seem like a good sign. That probably meant it was a big thing that August was holding back. Maybe a really big thing.

Tay thought about all that while he ate his Danish pastry and finished his coffee, but he came to no useful conclusions. He was venturing into unknown territory, that was obvious enough, but he supposed regardless of that he would simply do what he always did in any investigation. He would take whatever problems arose head on and solve them one by one as they appeared. What else could he do?

He looked up at the video screen which displayed departing flight information and checked the boarding time for his flight. It was still forty-five minutes away, but he wiped his hands on a napkin, stood up, and collected his things anyway. Better to leave the lounge early and take the walk to the gate at a leisurely pace.

Tay had learned a long time ago that nothing good ever happened to him when he had to hurry.

TWENTY-TWO

THE FLIGHT WAS a short one, only a couple of hours.

Throughout it identically smiling flight attendants with perfectly matched uniforms, hairstyles, and body types made Tay feel like he was surrounded by a squad of androids. Had artificial intelligence progressed to the point that robots had replaced human beings as flight attendants? He didn't think so, but before the flight was over he had begun to wonder. The droids implored him to eat an elaborate breakfast. Tay stuck to coffee. It tasted real. More or less.

Arrival in Bangkok wasn't nearly as pleasant and trouble-free as his departure from Singapore had been. The immigration hall was a heaving mess of bodies, most of whom appeared unimpressed by the frantic efforts of a few uniformed personnel to direct them into recognizable lines. It took Tay nearly an hour to fight his way through the masses of Chinese tour groups led by flag-waving minders, get his passport stamped, and find his suitcase.

When Tay left the terminal building to search for the taxi queue, he felt like he had walked into a wall. Singapore was hot and humid, but Bangkok was in a class of its own. The air was gelatinous, so heavy it was as if it had congealed. Tay felt like he was breathing Jell-O.

The line of people waiting for taxis was long and it moved slowly. Tay finally made it to the front, got into a cab, and told the driver he was going to the Hilton in Pattaya.

The man grinned and named a fare for the ninety-minute drive that Tay had no doubt was extortionate, probably by a factor of at least five, but he was tired and he was hot and he didn't have the energy to argue about it. He hated the driver thinking of him as a mark to be swindled, but the air-conditioning in the taxi was on high and blowing cold, dry air and Tay decided that was far more important than what the man thought of him. Whatever amount he paid, it would be worth it just to regain his humanity.

Tay leaned back in his seat and waved the driver on. The man grinned even more widely. He looked as if he couldn't believe his luck.

TAY HAD BEEN to Pattaya a couple of times before and had decidedly mixed feelings about the place.

He had to admit that both of those trips had been pleasant enough, possibly because they were short, but Pattaya simply wasn't a town that appealed to him very much. Too coarse, too crude, too blatant. "There always has to be some place where the world sweeps its dirt," someone once said. They had been describing Shanghai before World War Two, Tay knew, and he had no idea if that had been an accurate characterization of Shanghai back then or not, but he thought it certainly would be a good description of Pattaya today.

The Pattaya Hilton stood well above the rest of the place, both figuratively and literally. A thirty-five-story glass tower resting on top of Central Festival, Pattaya's classiest retail mall, the Hilton was doubtless the best hotel within at least a hundred miles.

When Tay checked in, he was given a very nice room on the thirty-first floor with a view across the bay to a narrow headland where huge orange letters on a tree-covered slope spelled out PATTAYA CITY. The sign was no doubt supposed to put people in mind of the famous white letters spelling out HOLLYWOOD against the Santa Monica Mountains in Los Angeles, but the comparison really wasn't working for Tay.

It was only a little after mid-day so Tay went down into the mall and wandered around until he found a Japanese restaurant that looked okay and had a lunch of shrimp tempura and tuna sashimi. While he ate, he thought about how he ought to proceed.

According to August, the woman had come to Secrets at exactly six o'clock on a Thursday evening, not exactly a peak time in the warren of tiny laneways around August's bar, but still busy enough. Tay had been to Secrets a year or so back to meet August and he remembered that there were no roadways anywhere close to it that carried automobile traffic. You could only get to the place on foot or by motorcycle.

If the woman who had come to August posing as a messenger from the Band was nearly as attractive as August had said she was, she would have been noticed by a lot of people. There would have been people in the area on foot, perhaps even a lot of people, and few if any of them would have been attractive women who were not Thai. Somebody would have noticed this woman.

All Tay had to do was to locate a few of those people, find out from them the direction the woman had come from or the direction she went when she left Secrets, and he would be on his way to working out her movements both before and after her meeting with August. Those movements ought to lead him to a hotel or maybe to an airline flight, and a hotel or an airline flight would lead him to a name and some kind of identification, maybe a credit card, and he would be close to finding out who the woman was.

People in Tay's profession didn't like to admit it, but the hard truth of every investigation was that you needed a break. Sometimes you made your own break, but more often than not the break was simply a fluke. Tay had learned a long time ago that the difference between a detective with a reputation for success and one with a reputation for failure was that the successful detective recognized the fluke when it came along.

August had told him that Secrets didn't have a CCTV system. That was a shame, but it was easy to understand why it didn't. With the kind of things that August got up to there, it was no wonder he didn't want any of it recorded.

Still, the thought gave Tay an idea.

Maybe some of the other bars and shops in the area did have CCTV. If he could begin to work out the woman's movements, then maybe one of the businesses she walked past had an exterior camera that had caught her. A decent picture could well make this thing game over. That might be enough for August's intelligence contacts to identify the woman without Tay having to track down a hotel registration or airline trip.

Either way, the starting point was the same. He had to get out on the streets at about the same time of evening as the woman had come and gone from Secrets and see what he could put together. Street vendors operating from fixed locations, doormen at bars, and even waiters in outdoor cafés could have seen her. Then once he at least knew the direction from which the woman had come and gone, he could walk the routes she might have taken and look for CCTV coverage.

All that made sense conceptually, but it raised a glaring problem. Tay didn't speak a word of Thai, so how was he going to approach people who might be able to help him?

He did have one thing going for him. When he retired, he had kept his warrant card identifying him as a detective in the Criminal Investigation Department of the Singapore Police. At the time he wasn't absolutely sure why he had done that. Mostly, he supposed, he had simply been so angry at being forced out that he didn't want to be even remotely cooperative. He had returned his service weapon, but when they asked for his warrant card he said that he had lost it. They didn't believe him, of course, but nobody wanted the embarrassment of making an issue out of it so they had let it go.

He had brought his old warrant card to Pattaya with him without even really thinking about it, but he saw now that there could be an advantage in identifying himself as a detective from Singapore CID. He had been a detective in the Criminal Investigation Department for almost two decades and he would still be a CID detective if they hadn't forced him out, so saying that he was one now only stretched the truth a little bit.

Tay thought that was a perfectly adequate justification. Good enough for him anyway.

On the other hand, there was something else to consider. He doubted Pattaya was a particularly friendly town for a cop to go around asking questions. Singapore was a place where everyone respected official authority, whether that authority was worthy of respect or not, but Pattaya was world famous as a haven for international criminals on the hustle and villains on the lam. Official authority probably didn't translate into respect here quite the way it did in Singapore. He might need somebody to vouch for him.

Fortunately, August had provided him with a local contact, a fellow bar owner who ran a place called Babydolls. As soon he got some ideas about where to start looking for traces of the mystery woman, he would look the guy up. August had told Tay that he could trust him, but Tay was going to make up his own mind about that. It didn't help that August had told him to go to Babydolls and ask for Mad Max. While Tay had a lot of confidence in August's judgment, putting his trust in someone called Mad Max bothered him. Pattaya was a long way from Singapore. Tay understood that. But he wasn't sure it was *that* far.

He looked at his watch. Just after two o'clock. Enough time

to go up to his room, take a little nap to make up for the lack of sleep last night, and then hit the streets.

TAY LEFT THE Hilton at a little after six, crossed over Beach Road, and turned south on the walkway along the beach.

The atmosphere was so dense with humidity it felt as if the air itself was sweating. The sun was a red orb sitting on the horizon, too tired to give any heat, too lazy to take its leave. The last of its light had turned the sea to pewter and a soft mango-colored haze was filtering over Pattaya. A gentle breeze off the ocean brought odors of salt and fish and made Tay think of places he would rather be.

Out on the bay, neon lights sparkled from the anchored party boats gearing up for another night of riot and debauchery. The boats scattered here and there across the bay looked like floating Times Squares or Piccadilly Circuses. One boat even sported a huge cross on top. It was bathed in white light and gave the party boat a resemblance to a floating church. Or maybe the boat *was* a floating church. Surely not, Tay thought. Not in Pattaya.

In Tay's view, calling the narrow mud flat that lay between the walkway and the ocean a beach was stretching the word beyond all reason. Even the waves that washed up on it were flat and gray-brown. It wasn't exactly Hawaii, was it? Tay had never actually been to Hawaii, of course, but he had seen pictures, and he had once a long time ago watched an episode of *Hawaii Five-0* on television.

Still, the walkway was very nice. It was about fifteen feet wide and paved in ceramic tile formed into a wavy cream and white pattern. The walk was lined along both sides with tall coconut palms, their leaves slapping together in the warm ocean breeze like ranks of snare drummers each of whom was drumming a separate rhythm.

The other thing lining both sides of the walkway was street-walkers, although in this case Tay thought perhaps beach-walkers might be the more appropriate term. The girls stood quietly all along the walkway in ones and twos, in some places almost shoulder to shoulder, and waited for passing males to show signs of interest.

To fill the time until they were approached, they were all, every single one of them, utterly absorbed in staring at their telephones. The cool gray-blue light from the telephone screens imbued their features with an otherworldly luminescence that made their faces look eerily disembodied, each of them floating independently there in the darkness. It made Tay think of a race of aliens just emerged from the sea and looking for just the right moment to step forward and announce its arrival.

The girls' most enthusiastic suitors were packs of men who appeared to be Indians, eight or ten to a group, roaming up and down the beach walk leering at all the girls uniformly: young or old, tall or short, fat or thin. It struck Tay as strange that very few of the men in those little bands ever seemed to approach any of the girls directly. Perhaps they were too shy and seeking protection in their packs, or perhaps they were looking for a girl who advertised a group rate. The girls, however, didn't seem to notice or care. They only had eyes for only one thing: their telephones.

About a hundred yards along, a frail, elderly woman suddenly appeared from somewhere and flung herself prostrate at Tay's feet. She thrust a grimy plastic cup at him and Tay recoiled. When the woman remained stretched out in front of him, unmoving, cup thrust upward, Tay fumbled in his trouser pocket, but he couldn't find any change. Finally, in desperation, his hand closed around the first bill it touched. He shoved it into the woman's cup and sidestepped quickly around her. He had been taken, of course, and he knew it.

He wondered how much he had given her, but as in the case of the taxi driver he didn't much care. He had gotten what he wanted, which was to be away from the woman, and how much it had cost him didn't really matter.

A little further along the walkway the line of girls thinned out a bit and Tay found himself glancing at them as he passed. He was surprised to see that most of the girls looked young, most were conservatively dressed, and a few were downright attractive. He noticed one girl dressed in heels and what appeared to be a tan business suit. She could have been on her way to the office where she worked, he supposed, but of course it was pretty obvious she wasn't.

Then he noticed something even odder. The girl was holding a dog's leash with what he thought was probably a beagle on the end. A streetwalker with a dog? For a moment Tay flashed on an image so disgusting he felt nauseous. Surely not, he told himself. Not even in Pattaya.

Tay increased his pace and was relieved when the walkway along the beach petered out and he found himself in the upheaval of Walking Street where the packs of Indians and loitering hookers were replaced by Chinese tour groups and go-go bars. He spotted Babydolls, but he wasn't ready to talk to Mad Max yet. Besides, it was almost certainly too early to expect any self-respecting Pattaya saloonkeeper to be at work anyway.

The first few hours of any investigation were always the best hours for Tay. His mind was uncluttered by half-formed theories and assumptions, and his energy was at its peak. After that, the confusion and tedium settled in soon enough. That was why he always tried to make the most of the magic hours at the beginning.

Secrets was only a few hundred yards away and taking a careful look at the area around Secrets was what Tay wanted to do first.

It was time to go to work.

TWENTY-THREE

THE FIRST TIME Tay had ever been in Pattaya was when he was taken there to meet August by a United States diplomatic security agent.

He and the woman were jointly investigating the murder of the wife of the American ambassador in Singapore and she thought August could help them. She described August as a retired State Department employee who had bought a Pattaya go-go bar for a retirement gig. The bar August owned then was called Babydolls, the same bar where August told him he could find Mad Max now if he needed a local he could trust. Not a coincidence, obviously.

The second time Tay was in Pattaya had been when he got a cryptic summons from August concerning a different case. He met August that time at Secrets, and August told him he had sold Babydolls.

Babydolls had been typical of Pattaya. It was a raucous go-go bar filled with half-naked Thai girls and loud, mostly white tourists swilling beer and ogling the women. Secrets was anything but typical of Pattaya. It was more of an old-school gentlemen's club, one that smelled of fine leather, expensive whiskey, and good cigars.

Tay had been uncomfortable in Babydolls. He hated admitting that, even to himself, because it made him feel like a bit of a
wimp. Oddly, he had the sense that August didn't much like
Babydolls either. He may have been wrong about that, but
August's abrupt change in style caused him to believe he probably wasn't.

T AY RECOGNIZED THE laneway off Walking Street
that led to Secrets when he came to it.

It was a narrow alley paved in cracked concrete and over-
hung with big signboards promoting the bars, restaurants, and
modest hotels to be found along it. The wall of the building on
the corner had probably been tiled one day long ago but, if it
had been, the tiles had all cracked and fallen away leaving
nothing but a rough masonry wall on which someone had inexplicably painted a wide red stripe about head high.

A hundred feet or so along, Tay passed the Grand Hotel,
which didn't look particularly grand, and next to it a shophouse
with a tattoo parlor on the ground floor. There was a metal
grating pulled down over the tattoo parlor and Tay glanced at
his watch. A little after six. Either the tattoo business wasn't very
good these days, or maybe in Pattaya tattooing was strictly a
late-night pursuit.

Tay walked past a bar called the Dollhouse and another
called Annabelle's and continued on until he came to Secrets,
which was a hundred feet or so further along on the right. It was
a simple whitewashed building with an oversized polished wood
door and a small brass plaque next to the door that said *Secrets*.
There were no flashing lights and no garish signboards. It
looked almost out of place.

He was disappointed to find the little lane outside Secrets
was almost deserted. He thought he could remember from
before that there had been some food vendors with carts parked
here and there as well as doormen hovering in front of the other

bars, but now there was virtually no one in sight. Was it because it was early, or had trade in the area fallen on hard times?

Tay walked past Secrets and continued on until he came to where the laneway forked. Going left would take him generally back in the direction of the Hilton, while going right looked like it led into a warren of tiny alleys lined with a motley collection of second-rate bars and cheap hotels. He had taken a few hesitant steps up the alley to the right when a dumpy woman of indeterminate age wearing wrinkled yellow shorts, a stained t-shirt, and red flip-flops leaned out of a doorway and flapped her hand at Tay.

"Hey, handsome man!" she called.

Tay shook his head and turned away. He didn't want to be too hard on the woman. After all, she was just trying to earn a living by offering the promise of sex to lonely males, although in her case it seemed to Tay like more of a threat than a promise.

He walked back to the fork in the laneway and spotted an elderly woman a little way up the other alley. She was wearing an orange t-shirt and a white cap and she stood behind a metal-wheeled cart that was piled high with bananas and other fruit he couldn't begin to identify.

"Good evening," Tay said to her.

The woman offered an uncertain smile.

"Do you speak English?"

The woman kept smiling, but her eyes darted side to side as if she was evaluating her escape routes.

Tay didn't claim to be any kind of an expert on Thais and Thai culture, but he recognized that smile readily enough. It was the smile all Thais offered up when they were confronted by some crazy foreigner and had no idea what he was talking about.

Tay had hoped to find a dozen street vendors and perhaps another dozen doormen hanging around in front of bars. With enough people in static positions on both sides of Secrets, he was confident that somebody would have seen the woman pass and would remember what direction she had come from. He had not expected to find only a single vendor in the little lane. Usually the streets and alleys of Thailand were alive with vendors selling everything from exotic fruit to sex toys. The vague plan he had formulated for identifying August's messenger began to seem a little bit naïve, maybe even down-right stupid.

Tay walked back in the direction from which he had come and examined the businesses that lined both sides of the alley-way. A hairdresser, a motorcycle repair shop, a tiny pharmacy, a narrow beer bar open to the street, and another tattoo parlor. This one was open for business but without a single customer.

He kept walking and passed a travel agency, a café simply enough called Eat Here, a small grocery store with unopened cases of soft drinks stacked in front of it, and a closed-up shop front with a sign out front that said Hair Man Cut. Tay assumed that meant it was a barbershop. At least he hoped it did.

When Tay reached Walking Street, he turned around and strolled back toward Secrets again, this time searching for secu-rity cameras on the buildings along the lane. The Grand Hotel was a possibility. Tay stopped and scanned the front of the building. Nothing. No cameras at all that he could see. Contin-uing on, he examined all the buildings on both sides of the little lane without finding a single camera anywhere.

When he got all the way back to the fork at the end, he stopped, turned around, and thought about what to do next. The woman with the fruit cart was still in the same place she had been before, but when she saw Tay had returned she looked as if she might be considering making a break for it.

Only one vendor who might have seen the woman going and coming from Secrets, no hovering doormen, and no secu-rity cameras at all? Tay thought about going inside some of the shops along the lane and trying to talk to whoever he found there, but that seemed pretty desperate. Besides, who was he kidding? What were the chances that he could communicate well enough with some random Thai working in a tattoo parlor for him to describe the woman he was looking for and ask if they remembered seeing her?

Tay felt like a complete idiot. Had he already lost his touch as a detective, or had he simply spent so much of his life in Singapore that he had no real grasp of how differently things worked in other places? He was certainly no fan of surveillance cameras when he looked at them strictly from a personal standpoint, but cameras had become indispensable tools in investigations when it was necessary to track someone's movements. Their near total absence in Pattaya was both surprising and a little disconcerting.

So much for Plan A. If there was any realistic chance of keeping this whole thing from turning into an embarrassing fiasco, he had better trot out Plan B pretty damn quick.

And Plan B was to look up Mad Max.

B ABYDOLLS WAS ON Walking Street, not more than a couple of hundred feet from Secrets in distance but a universe away in sensibility.

The front of the building was painted purple, and the entrance was an open space covered by heavy green drapes that looked like velvet but probably weren't. Just in case that wasn't eye-catching enough, an arch made up of thick layers of red, white, and blue balloons rose at least twenty feet up the front of the building.

Two boys in shorts who were stripped to the waist and covered in sweat were unloading metal beer kegs from a pickup truck, and Tay waited while they each rolled a keg through the drapes and disappeared inside. Then he followed.

When the drapes fell closed behind him, Tay stopped and looked around. The place was more or less as he remembered it from the first time he met August there. The lights were up because the bar was still being made ready for the night's customers and Tay thought it looked bleak and shabby. The odor of spilled beer and disinfectant mingled with stale cigarette smoke, and Tay perked up. The place might be a shithole, but at least it was a shithole where he could smoke.

To the left of the entrance there was a staircase leading up to a balcony with a couple of dozen small tables and a raised platform with stools all around it. A forest of chrome poles rose from the platform all the way up to the ceiling. The platform was empty now, but Tay knew that later in the evening an army of lithe young girls, each wearing a number pinned to whatever tiny bit of clothing she might have on, would be swinging from those poles in a vague imitation of dancing to the music booming through the bar.

To the right of the entrance was a short L-shaped bar. Behind it was a short L-shaped bartender.

The middle-aged woman was wearing a shapeless dress that might once have been green, and stacking glasses behind the bar. She didn't look particularly Thai to Tay, more Korean or possibly even Chinese, but what would a Korean or a Chinese woman be doing working behind a bar in Pattaya with so much cheap local labor available?

When Tay walked over, the woman barely bothered to glance up.

"We closed. Open later. Come back."

In a reflex honed over decades of talking to people who didn't want to be talked to, Tay took out his wallet, opened it, and held it up to display his warrant card from Singapore.

"Police," he said. "I want to talk to Mad Max."

The woman's head snapped up as if Tay had struck her. She stared for a moment, eyes flicking back and forth between Tay's face and his warrant card, then she clapped her hands to her breast and backed slowly away from him.

"Mad Max," Tay repeated in a tone that he tried to make firm but unthreatening. "Is he here?"

The woman backed off another step, bobbed her head quickly, and then turned and scurried away.

Tay smiled, shook out a Marlboro, and lit it. Maybe, he thought to himself, this authority thing was going to play better here than he had first imagined.

T AY RESTED HIS hands on the bar and watched the door at the back of the room through which the woman had disappeared.

After a few moments, it opened a crack and a single eye set in a lumpy, unshaven face peered out through the opening. Tay stood still and waited, a neutral expression on his face. After a few more moments, the door opened the rest of the way as he had been certain it would. A man appeared in the doorway and began to move slowly toward Tay. He kept his body turned to one side and walked with an odd, crab-like gait as if he was trying to minimize his profile should Tay suddenly decide to pull a gun and open fire.

The man was a stocky Caucasian with a deep tan that didn't look as if it had come from a sunlamp, muscles that appeared to be from hard work rather than a gym, and gold chains around both of his wrists that clanked when he moved. He wore a red and yellow Hawaiian shirt hanging over baggy khaki shorts with a beaten-up pair of brown Topsiders on his feet.

He looked like he could have just stepped off a boat in Miami Beach, but he hadn't. He was in a go-go bar in Pattaya, Thailand, and that made him a pimp as far as Tay was concerned no matter what he looked like.

As the man drew closer and turned his head a bit more, Tay realized that he wore a black patch over his left eye with the band holding it in place tilted rakishly over his forehead. The whole effect was to make him look vaguely like John Wayne in *Rooster Cogburn*, a Western movie Tay was certain no one under forty had seen or even heard of. Tay had seen it, of course, twice in fact, but that didn't really matter. The guy's vague resemblance to John Wayne did nothing to improve Tay's opinion of him. He was still a pimp.

The man stayed on the other side of the bar, using it to keep himself separated from Tay, and stopped about six feet away.

"Are you Mad Max?" Tay asked.

The man nodded, a single jerk of his head, but he didn't say anything.

"I'm Samuel Tay. John August asked me to talk to you."

Tay produced his warrant card again and held it up, although the man was probably too far away to read it.

"You told my girl you were a cop."

"I *am* a cop," Tay said. It appeared that August hadn't gone into the details so he figured he wouldn't either.

"Oh shit," the man muttered. "You scared the piss out of me. August didn't tell me the guy he was sending was a cop."

Tay put his warrant card away. He could see the tension abruptly draining from the man's body, his muscles loosening to the point that he actually began to sag toward the floor.

Tay glanced around the bar. The woman he had originally spoken to had reappeared and was hovering at a distance. She still looked absolutely terrified. He also spotted a couple of other women back in a dim corner watching him warily.

"Is there someplace else—"

"Yeah sure," the man interrupted. "Better we go back to my office. You're scaring the fuck out of everybody, man."

TWENTY-FOUR

M AX'S OFFICE WAS a tiny, windowless room barely big enough to hold a scarred wooden desk and two folding metal chairs.

The furniture looked to Tay like stuff that had been bought surplus when a not particularly prosperous school somewhere had closed down. Max gestured Tay toward the chairs, one of which was presently occupied by a large cardboard box and the other by a stack of a half-dozen or so rolls of toilet paper. Tay chose the chair with the box, put the box on the floor, and sat down.

Max started to take the chair behind the desk, but stopped.

"You want a drink? A beer or something?"

"You have some bottled water?"

Max looked at Tay for a moment without expression, then shook his head. He opened the door, shouted through it in a language Tay did not understand, and closed it again. Tay was pretty sure the language hadn't been Thai. Japanese maybe? But why would Max be speaking Japanese in a Thai go-go bar?

"You need to be more careful with that cop stuff, Tay. You're scaring my people to death."

Right at that moment, as if to illustrate what Max had just

said, the bartender opened the door without knocking and came in with a bottle of water. She stood as far away from Tay as the small room would permit her to and placed the bottle and a straw on Max's desk within Tay's reach. Then she scurried quickly away and slammed the door behind her.

Max saw the puzzlement on Tay's face.

"John didn't tell you?"

"Tell me what?"

Max waved vaguely toward the bar outside his door. "The ratline."

"What in the world are you talking about?"

"These people are mostly Koreans. North Koreans. They escape North Korea over the border into China. Then they're smuggled all the way south through Laos and into Thailand. Their ratline ends here. I keep them until we can get them on a boat to South Korea."

Tay was dumbstruck.

"You're smuggling people who have escaped from North Korea?"

"Most of these folks are Christians. So am I. I do what I can to help them, but I'm just part of a much larger group."

Tay didn't know what to say. A moment before he had pegged Max as nothing but a lowlife westerner living off the Thai prostitutes he pimped out of his bar. Now Max was telling him he was part of a Christian group helping North Koreans escape to the south. Could someone be both a pimp and Christian?

Tay knew the world was a subtle and contradictory place, but he had never realized it was *that* contradictory. This was obviously neither the time nor the place to enter into a meta-physical dialogue on that subject so Tay busied himself with opening the water bottle, ripping the paper covering off the straw, and taking a long pull on the water.

After he put the bottle down, Tay said, "August didn't tell me."

"Huh," Max grunted. "Figures."

Max opened the bottom drawer of his desk and rooted around in it for a moment with both hands. When they emerged, one of them held a Kydex holster with some kind of a revolver in it and the other held a box of ammunition. Max slapped the box of ammunition down on the desk in front of Tay and then slipped the revolver out of the holster and held it with the barrel pointing up, turning it first one way and then another.

"Smith and Wesson J Frame .38. Not new, but in pretty good shape. It's a solid weapon. You can rely on it."

A gun? Tay was too surprised to know what to say.

"John said to get you a wheel gun because you were a little old fashioned," Max said, raising his eyebrows at the stupefied expression on Tay's face. "But I can get you a semi-automatic if you'd prefer."

"August told you to get me a gun?"

Max nodded.

"What for?"

"I didn't ask him. I didn't really have to."

"What does that mean?"

"Look, Tay, I don't know you, but I do know this place. John said you were looking for somebody. I'm guessing that means you'll be going around asking a lot of questions and that's going to attract attention. Most of that attention is likely to be unwelcome. Some of it may even be *very* unwelcome."

Max shoved the revolver back in the holster, snapped the retention strap, and laid the rig on the desk next to the box of ammunition.

"You keep that baby handy. You probably won't need it, but you might have to show it a few times. Now, you want to wear it out, or do you need a bag?"

Max made it sound like Tay was shopping at Marks & Spencer. Tay didn't want a gun. He certainly had no intention of carrying a gun in a country where he had no authority to carry one, but he thought refusing it might make Max doubt him. He needed Max and he needed his help. Better to take the gun without arguing and just stuff it in his room safe.

"A bag, please. If it's not too much trouble."

Max produced a plastic carrier bag from the still-open drawer, dumped the revolver and ammunition inside, and then rolled it up. He placed the rolled-up bag inside a second plastic carrier bag and plunked that bag on the desk in front of Tay.

"Use it in good health."

"I'll try not to use it at all."

Max nodded and slammed the desk drawer shut with his foot.

"Good luck with that, Tay. So, when are you going to tell me what this is really all about?"

Tay told Max what he knew about the woman he was trying to identify, which wasn't much.

"Why does John want to find this broad so badly?"

Tay was pretty sure he hadn't heard anyone refer to a woman as a broad since Frank Sinatra died, but somehow the expression went nicely with Max's Hawaiian shirt and gold bracelets so he made no mention of that.

"August didn't tell you?"

Max shook his head.

"He didn't tell me about the North Koreans, and he didn't tell you about why he needs to find this woman. I guess that makes us even."

Max shook his head again and chuckled.

"Okay," he said, "I get it. I've always figured John was involved in all kind of shit I didn't want to know about so I'm not going to start getting curious now. He's really CIA, isn't he?"

Tay said nothing.

"Well, he does something other than run a bar in this shit-hole, doesn't he?"

Tay still said nothing.

"Fair enough," Max shrugged. "You're absolutely right. None of my business."

"So now can we talk about finding this woman?" Tay asked.

Max nodded, leaned back, and folded his arms.

"You have the floor."

T AY RELATED THE woman's description in as much detail as he could and told Max exactly when she had been at Secrets.

"I figured there couldn't be that many attractive white women who come to Pattaya, and knowing the exact time she was here I thought I could find people who had seen her, maybe even pictures from surveillance cameras. I thought if I could figure out where she had stayed or how she had gotten here or left, that would lead to some kind of identification. She didn't just materialize and then dematerialize. Some kind of transportation was involved and she almost certainly stayed in a hotel somewhere."

"She could be a local."

"August doesn't think so. He seems certain she came here just for that meeting with him and then left again."

"What was the meeting about?"

Tay just looked at Max.

"Okay, okay," Max shrugged. "You can't blame a guy for trying."

"There aren't a lot of ways to get in and out of Secrets," Tay continued. "I thought I would find some street vendors who had seen her or at least some cameras that might have caught her walking by. But I checked the area this evening at exactly the time she would have been there and it was a lot quieter than I remembered it."

"Business sucks now. The military takeover has scared off the tourists. We're all hurting, man."

"I couldn't find any surveillance cameras in the area either."

"John doesn't have any cameras at Secrets?"

"No."

"Fuck, I got them all over the place here. Most bars have them even if they won't admit it. A lot of people come to Pattaya who don't really want anyone to know they're here. Being on camera isn't something they'd be too happy about."

"But you're telling me most bars have cameras anyway?"

"Sure. We cover our ass. If some punter finds out and gets pissed off, so what? There are always more where he came from. Sure as shit John must've been up to some flaky shit at Secrets if he didn't want any cameras around."

"You have cameras out front?"

"Nope, all inside. I honestly can't think of any bars that have outside cameras. There are a few webcams around in Walking Street, but I think they're just live feeds. As far as I know, those feeds aren't recorded anywhere."

"So, the chances of finding a picture of her aren't very good?"

"Unless she made the rounds of the go-go bars and hustled a few broads, I'd say there is no chance at all."

"Then I guess it's back to finding people who saw her when she came to Secrets. Street vendors, doormen, maybe waiters or store clerks. And there was damn near nobody around when I walked the area around Secrets tonight. That's not very encouraging."

Max chuckled. "Don't give up so fast, my little friend. You're looking for the wrong people."

"Really? Then who should I be looking for?"

Max got up and opened the office door. He shouted something into the bar and waited until a skinny young boy Tay hadn't seen before appeared and stood deferentially in the doorway with his hands folded. Max rattled off something in the language Tay had heard before and now gathered must be Korean. The boy nodded quickly, turned, and trotted away.

"Drink your water, Tay. This shouldn't take but a few minutes."

S URE ENOUGH, NOT more than five minutes later there was a sharp rap on the office door and Max bellowed, "Enter!"

The door opened and Tay looked at the slightly tubby middle-aged Thai standing there. He wore a light blue t-shirt with dark blue jeans and white sneakers, but over his clothes was a bright orange visibility vest with the number 1 in black on one side of the vest and a few words in Thai lettering on the other.

Tay had seen motorcycle taxi riders all over Pattaya waiting patiently for passengers in queues at busy locations around town or, not infrequently, stretched out on top of the bikes fast asleep. Tay had never ridden a motorcycle taxi. Being stuck in traffic sucking on the exhaust from a clapped-out Chinese bus didn't particularly appeal to him, but he knew that motorcycle taxis were a mainstay of the urban transportation system all over Thailand.

Max spoke several sentences to the man in the orange vest in rapid-fire Thai and he nodded without saying anything.

"Give me that woman's description again, Tay."

"Somewhat Chinese looking, but more western than Chinese. Slim and on the short side. Black hair pulled back into a braided bun. She was wearing jeans and black ankle boots with low heels and a white shirt buttoned at the cuffs. She had a big green leather shoulder bag hanging over her shoulder that looked expensive. Actually, August described her as looking expensive in general. He said the most striking thing about her was her pale complexion. He said she was so pale she glowed like an angel stepping out of a Tintoretto painting."

"*Glowed?*"

"Glowed."

"Huh."

Max scratched his ear and considered that.

"And just remind me exactly when would she have been walking back and forth to Secrets," he said after a moment.

Tay told him.

Max thought for a moment, then looked back at the man in the orange vest and rattled at him in Thai for a minute or two. The man listened, but he said nothing. He just responded with a *wai*, a gracious gesture of respect common in Thailand in which the palms of both hands are brought together just below the chin in a way that looks rather like the Christian sign of prayer, then he closed the door and disappeared.

"Where are you staying, Tay?"

"At the Hilton."

"Huh," Max grunted. "I should have guessed."

"What's that supposed to mean?"

"It's a nice hotel. You look like a man who stays in nice hotels."

Tay wasn't sure what to say to that, so he said nothing.

"These motorcycle taxi guys see everything. Somchai is the big boss around this area. He'll put out the word to the boys and, if she was here, we'll get some sightings. Maybe enough to map out her movements around town. By the way, each sighting Somchai comes up with is going to cost a thousand baht for whoever saw this woman plus another five hundred baht for Somchai. I assume you can cover that."

Tay nodded. That was less than $50 for each sighting. A bargain.

"Then go back to the Hilton," Max said. "Order yourself a nice dinner from room service and wait for me to call. I'll bet I have something for you in a couple of hours."

As it turned out, it only took one hour and thirty-seven minutes.

TWENTY-FIVE

FTER TAY GOT back to the Hilton, the first thing he did was lock the gun Max had given him in the room safe. The second thing he did was find the room service menu.

He wasn't looking for a dining experience, he just wanted not to feel hungry, and the club sandwich was the first thing that caught his eye that didn't look like it would be more effort to eat than it was worth. He would wager hotels sold a lot of club sandwiches to a lot of people for exactly that reason.

When the telephone in Tay's room rang, he was just finishing the last quarter of his sandwich.

"Hello?"

"Take the elevator to the ground floor lobby, go outside, and turn right. Walk toward Beach Road. There's a Starbucks about fifty feet down that way. I'll meet you there in fifteen minutes."

"Max?"

"Who the fuck you expecting? Donald Trump? Fifteen minutes."

And with that Max hung up.

* * *

W HEN TAY FOUND the Starbucks, Max was already
sitting at an outside table with a tourist map of Pattaya
spread open in front of him.

It was late enough that the place was half empty so no one
else was near enough to overhear their conversation, and there
was enough breeze off the ocean that Tay wasn't actually drip-
ping sweat so he didn't mind the lack of air conditioning.

"What have you got?" Tay asked as he sat down.

"Nine motorcycle taxi guys who think they saw her and are
sure they have the right period of time, and three more who are
sure they saw her but aren't positive about the time."

Max pointed to the map.

"The red x's are the ones who are sure about the time, and
the black x's are the others."

Tay looked at the map in the dim light, but it was a bit
blurry no matter how much he squinted. Damn it all, he *was*
going to have to get glasses.

Eventually he was able to pick out the ocean, and that was a
start. Then he found what he thought was Beach Road, but
after that he was pretty well lost.

It didn't really matter. Lost or not, he saw immediately that
the x's were sprinkled all around the map in no discernible
pattern. Either some or all of the sightings were wrong, or the
woman had been pretty much everywhere in town.

"When you offer money for information, some of it is bullshit," Max said, "but some of it is good."

"How do you tell the difference?"

"Why ask me? You're the fucking detective."

Tay glanced at Max without responding, then pulled the
map closer and squinted at it some more.

"Where is Secrets?" he asked.

Max took a ballpoint pen out of his pocket, studied the map
for a moment, and then drew a small circle on it.

"And where are we now?"

Max drew a second circle.

With the locations of Secrets and the Hilton marked, the sightings began to look a little more orderly. There were a few outliers, three in particular off to themselves near the top of the map, but most of the sightings were strung out roughly in a straight line between the two locations.

Max put his finger on two sightings that were close together at the end of the line closest to the Hilton.

"Somchai thinks these are the most reliable reports. He says he's pretty sure neither of these riders were drunk or high on paint thinner that day."

Tay glanced up and saw Max wasn't smiling. He made a mental note to renew his policy of not riding on a motorcycle taxi in Thailand no matter how tempted he might become.

Looking back at the map, Tay tried to work out where the sightings had occurred that Max was pointing to, but he wasn't familiar enough with Pattaya for the map to make immediate sense to him.

"Where were those sightings, Max?" he asked. "Give me some kind of landmark."

When Max didn't respond, Tay glanced up again and saw Max was just sitting there pointing toward the street. Looking in the direction Max indicated with his index finger, Tay took in the line of orange-vested motorcycle taxi drivers lined up with their bikes in front of Starbucks waiting for passengers.

"*Here?*"

Max nodded. "Maybe she was meeting someone, or maybe she just drank a lot of coffee."

"Or maybe she was staying at the Hilton."

"See?" Max said spreading his hands, "I knew you were a fucking detective."

Tay left Max enough money to take care of the tipsters and a bit of extra for his trouble, then he took the map upstairs to his room and called room service for a pot of coffee. He hadn't bothered to order any when he was downstairs in Starbucks. He had better taste in coffee than that.

R IGHT AFTER BREAKFAST the next morning, Tay went down to the lobby and checked out the desk clerks behind the long reception counter. They were all attractive young women who appeared to be in their twenties, but that was not why Tay was checking them out. He was looking for somebody who appeared deferential, somebody not likely to ask him too many questions.

When he had made his choice, he walked directly up to where the woman was working, her head down studying something on a computer screen.

"I'm Inspector Tay of the Singapore Police."

The woman's head snapped up and Tay saw her body tense. He held up his warrant card.

"Who is the hotel's security director?"

The woman's eye darted back and forth as if she was looking for help. Tay didn't want to give her time to find any.

"What is his name, please, madam?"

"Uh…" Her eyes darted back and forth again, but seemed to find nothing. "Khun Robert," she stammered. "Khun Robert is Director of Security."

Khun is a polite form of address Thais place in front of almost everyone's name, particularly people whom they think might be of superior status. Thais are good at keeping social and professional rankings of status straight. They have to be to live in Thailand.

But *Khun Robert?* Now it was Tay's turn to look startled.

"Your Director of Security isn't Thai?" Tay asked.

"Oh yes." The young woman nodded her head vigorously. "He Thai."

Odd. A Thai named Robert?

"Would you get him for me, please?"

The young woman hesitated. Her eyes did the flipping around thing again.

"Right now," Tay snapped in his best policeman's voice. He hoped it would intimidate the young woman without scaring the crap out of her.

It worked fine. She jerked up a telephone receiver without any further hesitation and said something in Thai that Tay thought included the name Khun Robert. She waited a few moments, glancing back at Tay and offering an uncertain smile, and then began to speak again in a tone that was decidedly deferential. Tay had little doubt that she had reached the Director of Security.

When she hung up, she said to Tay, "He coming."

Tay thanked her and walked across the lobby away from the reception desk where he stood looking out of the floor-to-ceiling windows at Pattaya Bay. He did that for three reasons. The first was that he didn't want to have this conversation in front of a desk clerk who would almost certainly be tempted to gossip about it later. The second was that he needed some time to size up the Director of Security before he had to make his pitch to him. And the third reason was that he wanted to check the lobby for cameras.

He found several and was just wondering whether there were others he couldn't find when he glanced back toward the reception desk and saw a middle-aged man in a dark blue suit talking to the young desk clerk. Any doubt as to who it was evaporated when the woman pointed toward Tay and the man turned to look. Tay beat back the impulse to wave.

Tay made him for mid-fifties. He looked to be around six feet tall and heavily built, and his shaved head glimmered in the morning sun streaming into the lobby. He made Tay think of an athlete who had grown older and heavier and had shaved his head when he started going bald. The man's face looked generically Asian with something else thrown in, but his skin was brown and his face was deeply lined. Tay would never have picked him as a Thai. Maybe he wasn't and the woman on the reception desk only assumed he must be.

"Inspector?" he asked when he had crossed the lobby to where Tay was waiting. "I'm Robert Jackson, the Director of Security. I'm sorry, but the receptionist didn't remember your name."

Which suited Tay just fine.

"Inspector Samuel Tay. I'm with Singapore CID." Tay extended his hand.

After they had shaken, Jackson extracted a business card from the breast pocket of his jacket. He offered it to Tay with both hands in the Asian manner. Tay accepted it the same way and pretended to study it for a moment in the expected gesture of respect. After he pocketed the business card, he took out his warrant card and held it up. Jackson bent forward slightly and inspected it, but he followed the accepted protocol and didn't attempt to take it.

"Forgive me, but I'm a little surprised that the Director of Security isn't a Thai."

"Oh, I'm Thai all right," Jackson chuckled. "That's how I got this job."

"It probably helped that your English is very good."

"It should be. I was born in L.A. and I was an L.A. cop for twenty years." He placed his forefinger against his cheek. "That's where all these lines came from."

Now it was Tay's turn to chuckle as he knew he was expected to. "So, now I suppose you must be—"

"Happily retired. When I had my twenty in, I pulled the pin as quickly as I could and went looking for a better way to live. I found it here."

"Too many assumptions. Now I'm a little embarrassed."

"Don't be, Inspector. It's not exactly painted on my forehead."

Jackson smiled and Tay was a little surprised at the warmth in it. He figured there might be some mileage in the old cop-to-cop pitch. Jackson probably didn't see many foreign cops here.

"How may I help you, Inspector?"

"We're trying to locate a woman who we think may have stayed here a little less than a week ago."

"What makes you think she was here?"

"We have sightings in Pattaya that appear to suggest she moved between this area and other parts of town."

"Is there an outstanding warrant on her?"

"No, nothing like that. She's more of a witness. At least she might be."

Close enough for government work.

"We just need to talk to her," Tay hurried on, "and I'm trying to establish her movements so we can locate her. That's why I'm here… informally."

Tay knew that word *informally* would signal to a retired L.A. cop that they were keeping this investigation away from the Thai police. He also knew that a retired L.A. cop who was the security director of the Hilton in Pattaya would understand exactly why they were doing that. The Thai cops had considerably less than an impeccable reputation for discretion, a poor reputation for diligence, and no reputation at all for integrity.

"Then she's not here now?"

"Not as far as I know."

Jackson fished a notebook and pen out of the inside pocket of his jacket. "May I know her name?"

"I wish I could tell you, but all I have is a description. I was hoping you would let me review your CCTV data and see if I can pick her up."

Jackson hesitated and Tay held his breath. If Jackson asked for formal authorization from CID in Singapore, then this little adventure was over before it even started.

But he didn't.

"Sure," Jackson said after a moment. "I guess that wouldn't be a problem. Let's just call it a cop-to-cop favor."

A cop-to-cop favor. Right. Let's call it that.

"Why don't you come back to my office?"

TWENTY-SIX

I T TOOK ALMOST three hours and a full pot of coffee, but Tay eventually found her. At least he was pretty sure it was her.

How many slim, expensive-looking foreign women wearing jeans and snow-white shirts buttoned at the cuffs and carrying green leather messenger bags could there have been in Pattaya at exactly the time August met the messenger at Secrets? Tay was reasonably certain what the right answer to that question was.

Jackson had hung around for a while when Tay started going through the hotel's video archives for the right period. He said he wanted to help Tay understand how to operate the software and retrieve the video, but Tay thought it more likely that Jackson just wanted to make sure Tay was doing what he said he was doing. Tay could tell that Jackson knew perfectly well he wasn't being told the truth concerning what this was really all about, at least not the whole truth, but it didn't appear to bother him. He seemed to Tay to be more curious than concerned.

After a while Jackson got bored and went out and came back with a pot of coffee and two mugs, but after drinking less than half of his coffee Jackson got bored again, made some kind of lame excuse, and left for a second time. Tay certainly didn't blame him.

The coffee was extremely good, a lot better than the coffee Tay had gotten from room service, and he wondered briefly if the hotel staff put aside the good stuff for themselves while the guests got the standard commercial bilge. Maybe that was being overly suspicious, Tay decided after he thought about it briefly. He knew he was probably inclined to look at far too many things from a standpoint of suspicion and mistrust. Probably this pot of coffee was just fresher. He decided to stop thinking about it.

Tay had set the search parameters to a period an hour either side of the time that August and the messenger had met at Secrets. It was no more than a fifteen-minute walk between the Hilton and Secrets, even if you were walking slowly because of the heat and humidity, so he was pretty sure that was a big enough window to catch the woman either coming or going from the hotel. Or maybe both. That is, it would be if she was actually staying at the Hilton at all. If she wasn't, a week's worth of video wasn't going to do him any good.

It was slow, tedious work. The Hilton had a lot of cameras, and even at double and triple speed, Tay had to review forty to sixty minutes of video for each camera he accessed to cover the whole timeframe.

It was a stroke of good luck that he found the woman in the archives of the fourth camera he looked at. He tried three outdoor cameras first, ones that covered the side of the hotel near the motorcycle taxi stand where the two drivers claimed to have seen her, but he found nothing. He was anything but surprised. There were so many ways into and out of the hotel that she could have passed in full view of the motorcycle taxi drivers taking a dozen different routes.

But then Tay switched to the lobby camera that covered the elevators coming down from the guest room floors and he found the woman almost immediately. He nearly missed her. Trying to identify someone on video while watching people move by at double-speed required unwavering concentration, and Tay's was flagging badly after nearly three hours of watching outside cameras with wide-angle lenses that showed hundreds and hundreds of people moving through their fields of vision.

The camera focused on the elevators, however, was at the end of an interior lobby just big enough for three elevators to open into it. People stepped out of the elevators into the small space, turned and walked directly toward the camera, and then turned again to go either into the lobby or in the opposite direction toward another bank of elevators that took them down into the shopping mall beneath the hotel.

The woman wore a blue baseball cap with the New York Yankees logo on it and she had it pulled down to just above her eyes with her head tilted toward the floor. Tay could tell the woman knew the camera was there and wasn't going to let it get a clear picture of her face. If a classy-looking foreign woman hadn't been as conspicuous in Pattaya as a camel in the Kentucky Derby, Tay probably would have missed her entirely.

Tay froze the video at the moment the camera provided the best view of the woman. He was disappointed that it wasn't a very good image. Certainly not good enough for anyone to make an identification from it. With her head tilted down and the bill of the Yankees cap covering her face, the woman had given them nothing anyone could use to identify her, which had obviously been her intention. Still, that didn't make the image entirely useless.

Now Tay had two things he had not had before.

First, he knew the woman was almost certainly a guest at the Hilton. There might have been other reasons for her to be coming down in the elevators from the guest room floors, of course, but the most obvious reason was still the most likely one. She was staying there.

And second, he knew an exact time when the woman had walked through a precise location in the lobby. With a time and a location, now he could track the woman's movements on the other hotel cameras without spending God only knew how many tedious hours searching locations and times more or less at random.

TAY FIDDLED WITH the camera menu trying to remember the instructions Jackson had given him for printing a frame.

Across the room, a printer clicked to life and whirred for a moment. Tay walked over, lifted the sheet of paper from the tray, and examined it. It was a clear, sharp reproduction of the image from the screen.

The Hilton's video surveillance system was pretty slick and the software that managed it offered more ways of viewing and organizing the archived video than Tay could ever hope to understand. Fortunately, he had at least worked out how to search the video archives by time so he put in a time one minute following the woman leaving the elevator and almost immediately struck gold.

The woman appeared on the video recorded by a wide-angle camera that was focused on the reception desk in the lobby. She stood quietly waiting until a desk clerk was free, then went up to the clerk and initiated a brief conversation.

Toward the end of the conversation, she handed the clerk something. The clerk bent down as if she was reaching under the desk, then handed something back. The angle made it impossible to see what was changing hands, but Tay's guess was that nothing sinister was going on. Probably it was the same sort of interaction that at least a hundred guests a day had with the desk at the Hilton. They asked for directions or perhaps changed some money into local currency.

Tay sorted through all the other cameras focused on the area around the reception desk looking for a better angle, but he couldn't find one. The woman was obviously very conscious of cameras and very careful about keeping them from picking up her face. Tay could see her on three of the other video feeds, but none of those feeds had captured an image adequate for identification either.

Two of the feeds did, however, have something else of interest to Tay: a clear image of the desk clerk with whom the woman had talked. She was young, probably no more than twenty-five. She was slim and attractive with her shiny black hair cut short and brushed tight to her head and she wore dark red eyeglasses with big round lenses.

Tay printed off stills of the young woman from both feeds and had just gotten up to retrieve them from the printer when Jackson walked back in.

"Did you find her?" Jackson asked when he saw Tay at the printer.

Tay took the sheets out of the printer tray and handed them to Jackson.

"Who's that?"

Jackson looked back and forth from one picture to the other and shook his head.

"How should I know? You can't see her face anyway."

"Not the woman. The desk clerk."

"Why are you interested in the desk clerk?"

"Because she's talking to the woman I'm looking for and maybe she'll remember something that will help me find her."

Jackson studied Tay for a moment before he answered, searching for some sign of hidden meaning in his comment. Finally, he shrugged.

"I don't know her real name. Everybody calls her Apple."

"Apple? Seriously?"

"Thais have weird nicknames. What can I tell you?"

"If you can find her for me, I want to ask her—"

"She's working today. You want me to talk to her?"

Tay considered that for a moment. His first thought had been to get Jackson to find the clerk so he could ask her if she remembered anything about the woman. But maybe letting Jackson talk to her would be better.

He knew Thais weren't all that comfortable talking to foreigners. Since Jackson was a recognizable face, she would probably feel more relaxed talking to him. If he got anything at all, Tay could always go back then and push the clerk for more.

"Good idea," Tay said. "Show her those pictures and see if she remembers the woman. Maybe she can think of something that might help me."

"Yes, boss."

Jackson tossed Tay a salute and headed out the door.

TAY USED THE software's search function to bring up all the camera archives from one minute after the woman left the reception desk. He methodically worked his way through each of the feeds, shuttling them back and forth for a minute or two around the targeted time, but he could find no further trace of the woman.

Had she been so careful about locating the cameras and so concerned about keeping her face away from all of them that she had been able to leave the hotel without appearing on any other feed? If she had, it gave Tay pause. Who was that capable, that professional, that good? Somebody with a lot of training, of course. Maybe law enforcement, or some government agency.

He was still thinking about that when Jackson returned and handed Tay the printouts without a word.

"That's disappointing," Tay said. "She didn't remember anything, huh?"

Jackson just looked at him and pointed to the printouts.

That was when Tay realized he was holding a thicker stack of paper than he had given to Jackson. He flipped past the two pictures he had captured from the video feed and found himself looking at a copy of a Canadian passport. The next page was a copy of an American Express card and a registration card, and the third page was a copy of the woman's hotel bill.

"This is her?"

"In the flesh, so to speak. Apple checked her in so she remembered her."

The passport bore a picture of a pleasant-looking woman who had apparently gone to some pains to play down her natural attractiveness. It said her name was Susan Brandstetter. It said she was a Canadian citizen born January 19, 1972. Tay doubted any of that was true, of course.

He glanced at the hotel bill. One night's lodging, a room service breakfast, and nothing else. No phone calls, no faxes, no movie charges. Phone calls would have made it too easy, wouldn't it? How much luck could he expect to have?

The American Express card, however, was much more promising. It was naturally also in the name of Susan Brandstetter, but the hotel would have confirmed that the account was valid when the woman checked in just as it would with any guest. Then, when she checked out, it would have sent her charges to the same account for payment, and American Express must have accepted those charges.

That meant the account was real. It belonged to *somebody*, somebody who paid the bills using a check or a direct bank debit that would be traceable. It wasn't much maybe, but it was a thread tied to things that were both concrete and tangible. Pull on that thread and it might just unravel the whole question of who August's mystery messenger really was.

"I owe you one, Robert."

"You sure do, man. If I ever get busted for anything in Singapore, I'm going to start screaming your name as soon as they cuff me."

Tay didn't have the heart to tell Jackson he didn't think that was a particularly good idea. Most likely it would get him sent away for life.

TWENTY-SEVEN

I N ORDER TO trace the American Express account and who was paying it, you needed resources to which Tay no longer had access.

John August, Tay was certain, did have access to resources like that. In fact, he probably had access to resources Tay couldn't even imagine. That meant all he had to do was get copies of the pictures, passport, American Express card, and registration form to August and he was done. He would be out of it. He could go home.

Upstairs in his hotel room, Tay retrieved the telephone August had given him from his bag. He opened the contacts directory and, sure enough, there was only one number in it just as August had said there was.

The number was labeled *September.*

Cute. Really cute.

"John? It's Sam."

"You've found her already?"

"I think so, yes."

"So, what have you got?"

"I've got her on video at the Hilton several times, but she was very cagey. She never shows her face clearly so there's nothing you can run through any kind of a facial recognition database."

"That's disappointing."

"Don't get ahead of me here. One of the front desk clerks remembered her and the hotel's security director made copies of the woman's check-in records for me."

"You identified yourself to the hotel's security director and told him who you were looking for?"

"John, I'm not completely stupid. He thinks I'm a Singapore cop trying to find someone without involving the Thai police. Now do you want to hear what I've got, or don't you?"

August said nothing, and after a moment Tay continued.

"I have a copy of the passport she presented to the hotel. It says she's a Canadian in her mid-forties whose name is Susan Brandstetter."

"That's almost certainly a fake."

"Of course, but it's a very, very good fake. She didn't buy it in Cambodia. What does that tell you?"

August didn't respond.

"I've also got her registration card, her bill, and, best of all, a copy of the American Express card the hotel used for billing when she checked out. That means it's got to be a real account and connect to somebody, but I don't have access to the resources I need to run it any longer. I assume you do."

"Yes, I can do that."

Tay waited for August to fill in the details, but he didn't.

"Okay, John," Tay eventually said with a shrug in his voice, "what do you want me to do now?"

"Do you have copies of the hotel's video feeds?"

"I printed stills from the parts where you can see her most clearly, but I didn't ask for copies of the full feeds. They're really not of any value."

"Okay, then. Put the stills you have together with the passport copy and the other stuff into an envelope. I'll send someone to pick it up."

"That sounds to me like a lot of trouble for nothing. I could just photograph the pages with the camera in this phone and—"

"Forget it. I don't want anything digital. We're doing this old school. Pieces of paper never duplicate themselves and fly halfway around the world without you knowing it."

"Fine with me if you really think that's necessary. My room number is—"

"Forget that, too. I'll have somebody there in fifteen minutes. Go downstairs to the mall. On the third floor, on the end facing the ocean, you'll find a Carl's Jr. I want you to—"

"I'll find a *what?*"

"A Carl's Jr. You mean you don't know what that is?"

"I have absolutely no idea."

"It's a fast food place, Sam. They sell burgers, milkshakes, fries, that sort of thing. You eat burgers and fries, don't you?"

"Not really."

August sighed. "I should have fucking guessed."

"Don't worry, John, I do know what burgers and fries look like. I'm sure I can find the place, but why can't you just send your messenger to my room? Don't you think you might be getting a little carried away with all this spy shit?"

"No, Sam, I don't think I'm getting carried away with all this spy shit. Now get an envelope, put all that stuff inside, and take it downstairs to Carl's Jr. Maybe order yourself a chocolate milkshake. Hell, man, live a little! I'll have somebody there in fifteen minutes."

"And then that's it? After that I can go home?"

"Probably, but wait until tomorrow, huh? Just in case. Hell, all the single men on the planet and half the married ones would love nothing better than a night in Pattaya on their own and here you are trying to get back to boring old Singapore as quickly as you can. Go out tonight, Sam. Have a good time for once in your life, man!"

"If it's all the same to you—"

"Let me look at the stuff you found, make some calls, and then we'll talk about what to do next."

"Listen to me, John. I've found the woman for you. I think it would be better if you took it from here. This is out of my league."

"Just think of it like any other criminal investigation."

"It's *not* like any other criminal investigation."

"What is it then?"

"It's out of my league."

August chuckled.

"Keep this phone with you. We'll talk soon about where we go from here."

Then August hung up.

CARL'S JR. WAS exactly where August had said it was, of course, on the third floor of the mall facing the Gulf of Thailand.

It occupied a little glassed-in finger that poked out from the front of the mall toward the beach and even had an open-air terrace that wrapped all the way around the restaurant and provided a spectacular one hundred eighty degree view of Pattaya Beach and the ocean beyond.

Tay went to the counter and ordered a Coke, but while he was waiting for it he realized he hadn't eaten since breakfast and he had to admit the fries smelled pretty enticing. He changed his order to something called a Big Carl and an order of fries, and then he added a chocolate milkshake, too. He was a little bit embarrassed by how American all that was, but who was going to see him?"

When his order was ready, he took the tray outside and selected a table looking down on the beach. It was a beautiful day with just enough puffy white clouds scattered over the sky to keep the heat under control, and the burger and milkshake were unexpectedly good. Tay even found himself thinking that maybe this was what retirement was actually supposed to be all about. Relaxing in the sunshine at a beach somewhere with a milkshake in his hand. After decades as a cop in the big city, could he really do something like that?

It only took him a few seconds to decide.

No, he couldn't.

"*Khun* Tay?"

Lost in his reverie about idle days at some beach, he hadn't noticed the man approach his table.

He was short, dressed in a black Polo shirt and jeans, and he had a brown canvas messenger bag strapped across his chest. He looked young, but then Thais always looked young to Tay. He was smiling shyly in the self-effacing way that Thais usually did when forced to communicate with foreigners.

"Yes, I'm Tay."

"I from *Khun* John."

Tay gave the young man the envelope and he took it and tucked it into the messenger bag. He *waied* Tay, bringing his palms together in front of his face in the traditional Thai gesture of courtesy, bobbed his head quickly, and was gone.

And that, Tay devoutly hoped, would be that.

But in his heart he knew it wasn't going to be nearly that simple.

He finished his milkshake, wiped his hands on a napkin, and went back upstairs to his room.

TAY HAD BEEN surprised and not particularly happy when he checked into the Hilton to discover that it only offered nonsmoking rooms. The busybodies and nannies were winning everywhere, weren't they? There was even talk in Singapore now of banning smoking entirely, even in your own home. How did that make any sense?

Not so long ago most people had been reasonably content to live their lives and leave everyone else alone, and we all got along pretty well. These days a great many people insist that others behave exactly as they are told regardless of what they really want to do, and we all hate each other for it. Tay thought the lesson was obvious, but most people appeared to ignore it.

It was far too early to settle in for the evening. He had nothing with him that he particularly wanted to read and watching Thai television was a fate too horrible to contemplate. Maybe a walk along the beach? At least that was a place where he could smoke without anyone bothering him. Tay took his cigarettes and matches, stuffed August's telephone in his pocket just in case he called, and headed back downstairs.

The sun had already slipped behind a bank of clouds in the west and a gentle twilight had descended on Pattaya. Tay lit a Marlboro, cupping his hand around the match to protect the flame from a warm breeze coming off the Gulf of Thailand, and he drew in the smoke and felt the first welcome tingling of the nicotine hitting his bloodstream. He really was going to have to look into quitting one of these days. He understood that, so maybe he would. Or maybe he wouldn't.

Tay crossed over Beach Road and turned north on the broad walkway that ran along the ocean. In contrast to what he had seen on his walk to Secrets in the other direction, there were far fewer women working the beach walk this way.

Instead of lines of prostitutes being pursued by roving packs of Indians, he found himself sharing the walkway with a remarkably normal looking group of people: tourists out for an early evening stroll, elderly people enjoying their daily constitutional, bicyclists out for a ride, and even a few joggers sweating heavily from their exertion in the heat and humidity. All nationalities, ages, sizes, and shapes were represented. It was a symphony of ordinariness, and the longer Tay spent in it, the better he felt.

He strolled along at a moderate pace while he smoked, and almost before he knew it he had arrived at the end of the beach where the road and the walkway curved away from the ocean toward far less interesting and scenic places. Tay sat for a while on a concrete bench and watched a chubby middle-aged Thai woman fold and stack the brightly colored canvas beach chairs which she had spent her day renting out to tourists.

When she finished, she spread a black plastic tarp over the pile and carefully weighted down its edges with large rocks. She looked up, satisfied with her work, and noticed Tay watching her. Flashing a wide smile, she gave him a big thumbs up. Tay smiled back and waved.

It was a small moment of human contact between perfect strangers from different cultures and it meant nothing at all. Or maybe it meant everything. That such small, empathetic encounters still occurred in a world roiled by anger and torn by turmoil made Sam Tay feel better about the planet he inhabited. And that was enough meaning for him.

Tay lit another Marlboro and walked slowly back to the Hilton.

TWENTY-EIGHT

TAY SURFACED SLOWLY out of a dream he would never be able to remember. For a moment he wasn't sure where he was.

He raised his head off the pillow and shifted his eyes around the room. The light seeping between the drapes was pale and watery and rendered his room in a dim palette of grays. He rolled his head toward the source of the cold, dim glow beside his bed and he saw the time displayed in a cloud of green luminescence.

2:57am.

Then he remembered.

He was in Pattaya. In a room at the Hilton. He was waiting for John August to review what he had unearthed about the woman who had set August up to be killed and to tell him he could go back home to Singapore.

But what was it that had waked him from a sound sleep?

Knock, knock, knock.

The rapping on the door was firm, not at all tentative. It was a sound meant to wake him.

Tay gathered there had probably been another knock a few moments before and that was what had tugged him out of his dream. Automatically, he glanced back at the bedside clock again.

Now 2:58am.

Could that be August at the door? Surely not. If August had something to tell Tay, he would have just telephoned, wouldn't he? There was no reason to drive all the way from wherever he was to Pattaya and pound on Tay's hotel room door in the middle of the night.

Knock, knock, knock, knock!

The rapping had taken on an aggressive edge. It was clearly a demand that he come to the door, a demand that was not negotiable.

"Just a minute!" Tay shouted.

Tay pushed himself out of bed, hung his foot on the duvet, and stumbled. He caught himself on the side of the bed before he fell and shouted again.

"I'm coming, I'm coming!"

He looked around for the bathrobe he had discarded the night before, found it on a chair, and slipped it on. As he walked toward the door, he tied the belt around his waist.

"Who is it?" he called.

No one replied so he put his eye to the viewer in the door. The lens was smudged and smeared, and it offered such a distorted view that all he could tell for sure was that several human forms lurked in the hallway outside his door. At least he assumed they were human forms. When he combined the crummy image through the viewer with his own state of limited wakefulness, he would not be prepared to take an oath on that.

"You have the wrong room. Go away!"

After a slight pause, a male voice spoke from the other side of the door.

"You are Inspector Tay, yes?"

The voice was strong and assertive, a voice accustomed to being obeyed. The accent was Thai.

Could it be the police? It sounded like the police, but why

would the Thai police want to talk to him in the middle of the night?

"Yes, I'm Tay, but it's three o'clock in the morning, for God's sake. Come back tomorrow."

"Open door! Open door now!"

Tay tried the viewer again, but he still couldn't see shit.

He sighed heavily and opened the door half certain now that it was the cops, but he still had no idea at all what the Thai police could possibly want with him.

It wasn't the cops.

It was worse than the cops.

Four armed soldiers stood in the hallway.

TAY KNEW, OF COURSE, that the military had taken over Thailand in a coup d'état a few years back, dismissed the elected government, and cancelled all future elections, and he understood that the military was running the country now.

He just wasn't entirely certain that he knew what that meant in real life, and he had never cared enough to find out. He had heard stories somewhere about students being arrested for criticizing the military on Facebook and political dissidents disappearing into re-education camps, but he had never thought much about that either.

At least he hadn't until now.

The four men outside his door wore crisp khaki uniforms adorned with enough gold braid to outfit the entire University of Texas marching band. The two at the back sported white combat helmets with wide red stripes circling them, but Tay's eyes went immediately to the black Heckler & Koch MP5 submachine guns each of them held at the ready across his chest.

"You are Inspector Tay?"

Tay's eyes shifted to the man who had spoken. He was one of the two soldiers standing closest to the door. From the uniforms and hats those two wore it was clear enough that they were the officers in charge of this raiding party, or whatever it was. Tay decided the one who had spoken had to be the senior officer. He wore so many medals that he could probably have been defeated by a good-sized magnet.

Unfortunately, Tay didn't have a magnet, but he did have… his eyes flicked toward the room safe where he had stashed the revolver Max had given him.

But that was crazy. He certainly wasn't going to grab the gun and start shooting at four armed soldiers, even if that were possible, which it wasn't.

Then something hugely troubling occurred to him. He might have a problem, a really big problem, if they searched his room and found the gun. At the very least he would have some explaining to do and he knew his Singapore Police warrant card wouldn't hold up any longer than it took Field Marshall Major Mucky Muck here to make a telephone call, and that was something he would almost certainly do immediately.

Shit.

Tay thought quickly, but nothing even remotely helpful came to him.

So, he cleared his throat and tried to look unconcerned, or at least as unconcerned as anyone could look after being rousted out of his bed in the middle of the night by four heavily armed soldiers.

"Yes, I'm Tay. What can I do for you?"

"You come with us. Now."

"Come with you where?"

"Now. You come."

The officer covered in medals stepped back slightly and gestured Tay into the hallway.

"I'm not going anywhere until you tell me what this is all about."

The army officer was expressionless.

"You must come! Must come now!"

"I'm wearing a fucking bathrobe, you idiot!" Tay shouted and jerked the lapels toward the man in case he didn't understand. "You want me to go somewhere in the middle of the night wearing a fucking bathrobe!?"

"Okay, you put on clothes. And you pack, too. Bring everything with you."

"I'd rather leave my things here until I get back."

"No," the army officer shook his head. "You not coming back."

Uh-oh.

B OTH OFFICERS SEEMED to have every intention of coming into the room to watch Tay get dressed, but he adamantly refused to let them in and they didn't insist. They didn't seem happy about it, but they let Tay close the door without any further protest.

Tay dressed quickly, and it took him only a few minutes to collect his things in the one small bag he had brought with him. He took his passport out of the safe and shoved it in his back pocket, then stood looking at the revolver and ammunition wrapped in the white plastic bags. What the hell was he going to do with them? He could hardly flush them down the toilet, could he?

If he just left them in the room safe a maid would surely discover them when the hotel serviced his room and he would be pretty well screwed. On the other hand, if he took them with him and the army searched his bag for any reason, he would be pretty well screwed that way, too. He remembered those happy-talk policing seminars he had been forced to sit through in Singapore and the way the lecturers preached about creating win-win scenarios. He just didn't recall anyone ever saying what to do when he found himself in a lose-lose scenario.

Well, shit, Tay sighed. He stopped thinking about it, grabbed the plastic bag out of the room safe, and stuffed it down in the bottom of his case underneath his dirty laundry before he changed his mind. Then he opened the door again.

"Am I under arrest?" Tay asked the officer who appeared to be in charge.

"You come now," the man said, which Tay couldn't help but notice wasn't much of an answer to his question.

The officer pointed to Tay's bag and one of the subma-chine-gun-wielding flunkies stepped forward, slipped the sling of his rifle across his chest, and took the bag out of Tay's hand. Tay figured that was an encouraging sign. Even in a military dictatorship, he doubted that people placed under arrest were provided luggage service.

When they got downstairs, he found another encouraging sign. Instead of the prison van that had begun to take shape in his imagination, a large black Mercedes with dark windows was waiting for them.

One of the flunkies opened each of the rear passenger doors. The soldier with the largest oversupply of medals pointed Tay toward one door, then got into the car through the other door himself. The two soldiers with the submachine guns took Tay's bag and got into some kind of a dark SUV parked right behind them. The other officer sat in the front passenger seat of the Mercedes, said something to the driver which of course Tay didn't understand, and the little caravan moved out onto Beach Road.

"ARE YOU GOING to tell me now where you're taking me?"

Tay put the question to the officer riding in the back seat with him, the one who was clearly in charge, but the man didn't reply. He didn't even glance over at Tay. He just stared straight ahead, as did both the soldiers in the front.

What in the world was happening here?

Tay had no idea at all.

Had the Hilton security guy gotten cold feet and blown the whistle on him? That didn't make any sense. Even if he had represented himself as a Singapore cop in order to check some security cameras at the Hilton, that wouldn't have turned out a whole squad of armed soldiers.

Maybe either Max's inquiries trying to trace the mystery woman's movements in Pattaya or his digging through the Hilton's security tapes hit some kind of hidden trip wire that triggered the army to respond, but what could that have been? What did the Thai army have to do with all this? It wasn't possible that it was really the Thai army that was behind the attempt to kill August with a bomb in Hong Kong, was it? That made no sense at all.

The Mercedes rolled quickly through the dark early-morning streets of Pattaya. Tay assumed they must be going to Bangkok even if the army officers wouldn't admit they were. Everything that was important in Thailand happened in Bangkok. And these four very serious guys and this motorcade certainly suggested that whatever this was all about, it was something that was very important to someone.

But they weren't going to Bangkok. Instead of turning north, the car continued to the south and Tay watched the beach and the dark waters of the Gulf of Thailand off to the right. The light was just beginning to rise, gray and reluctant, when they turned east on a narrow two-lane road.

They passed a Thai temple, its fanciful orange and green peaked-roofs looming out of the dim half-light like a whimsical mirage. Saffron-robed monks carrying their alms bowls were silently filing out of the wat's front gate in a long line to begin their daily rounds during which good Buddhists sought credit in this life by making offerings of food to the monks.

It all seemed so peaceful, so serene, that Tay had to remind himself that he wasn't having a religious experience. Instead, he was in a speeding Mercedes surrounded by armed Thai soldiers being taken God only knew where.

After another ten or fifteen minutes they came to a bigger highway and turned south again. By now it was full dawn, although the light seemed strained and watery as if it wasn't sure it should be there at all. Tay knew exactly how it felt.

Abruptly, the car slowed and turned into a wide driveway leading to a big hospital building. Had something happened to August? Was he in the hospital and had somehow gotten the Thai military to bring Tay there to see him? Apparently not, because the car passed right by the hospital's entrance and drove around the building to the back.

That was when Tay heard a sound that was familiar, but one he couldn't immediately identify. It was vaguely industrial, like a large piece of machinery running.

Whoomp whoomp.

As the Mercedes rounded the hospital, the sound became louder, and Tay saw its source.

A helicopter.

It had military markings and was sitting on the hospital's helicopter pad, rotor blades turning slowly.

Whoomp whoomp whoomp.

The Mercedes stopped about fifty feet from the helicopter and almost immediately the pilot began to power up the rotors. As the sound level rose, one of the armed guards from the SUV that had been trailing them opened Tay's door and pointed toward the helicopter. He held Tay's bag in his free hand.

Tay got out, but didn't move fast enough for the soldier's liking and the man took his elbow and began tugging him toward the helicopter. A hand reached out of the sliding door in the helicopter's side and helped Tay up while the soldier lifted his bag and pushed it inside. The hand turned out to belong to a soldier who was dressed casually in an open-neck khaki shirt and khaki pants. No medals, no brass, no insignia. He even looked reasonably friendly. He smiled, dipped his head, and gave Tay a respectful *wai*.

The man gestured toward a comfortable-looking padded

seat and Tay settled himself there while the man slammed and locked the helicopter's door. The man buckled the seat's harness around Tay, lifted a pair of heavily padded earphones off a hook at the back, and placed them over Tay's ears. He snapped off a salute, vanished into the cockpit, and almost at once the pitch of the engine rose sharply.

Tay glanced around. The interior of the helicopter was plush and comfortable. There were four big seats upholstered in soft, brown leather, although he was the only passenger. It certainly didn't look like the sort of conveyance the military would use to haul prisoners.

The helicopter shuddered slightly and, with a high-pitched burst of noise so loud that Tay felt more than heard it, the helicopter lifted slowly off the pad. It hung there for a moment, a foot or two in the air, and Tay looked toward where the Mercedes was parked. The four soldiers who had rousted him out of his room were still there as well. They were right in front of it, standing at attention in a straight line, all of them holding crisp salutes.

Then all at once the helicopter shot straight up like an express elevator. The pilot pushed the nose over to gain speed and they rumbled away into the gray half light of the new day.

TWENTY-NINE

TAY COULDN'T IMAGINE where they were going and he had no doubt that asking the pilots would be useless even if he could figure out how the headset worked and communicate with them over the engine noise.

And who was flying the helicopter anyway? The men who showed up at his hotel were all dressed in Thai army uniforms which made who they were plain enough, but the pilot who strapped him into the helicopter had been wearing plain khaki without any insignia at all. He had made Tay think of someone from the military who was on a covert mission, but the moment that thought crossed Tay's mind he had quickly pushed it away again.

Tay looked out the windows on his side of the helicopter, craned his neck, and tried to locate the sun to figure out the direction they were flying. He couldn't find it, but what difference did it really make? Other than being aware that Bangkok was somewhere north of Pattaya, his knowledge of Thai geography was pretty close to nonexistent. Even if he knew the direction they were traveling, he still wouldn't have any idea where they were going.

Surely, Tay thought, there was something he could do rather

than just sit there passively, but the more he thought about it the less of an idea he had as to what it might be. Admitting he was essentially helpless felt like an abject surrender, but what choice did he have? Just sitting there and waiting to find out what was to become of him felt like a lousy choice, but life was full of lousy choices, wasn't it?

So far Tay had managed to rise above them. He wanted to believe he could continue to do that, but he wasn't so sure anymore.

A FTER A LITTLE more than half an hour, Tay heard the pitch of the engine change and he felt the helicopter begin to descend.

Outside the windows on his side he could see a few scattered buildings off in the distance, but none that looked even remotely familiar. He bent down and looked across the cabin through the windows on the other side and saw an even greater number of very tall buildings. He didn't recognize any of those buildings either, but that had to mean they were somewhere near Bangkok. There certainly wasn't anywhere else that looked anything like this that they could reach in a half hour of flying from the area around Pattaya.

The helicopter leveled off at what seemed to be about a thousand feet, swung around, and began a slow, elevator-like descent to the ground. Tay could see far off to the right an airport terminal building with several Thai Airways airplanes parked around it, and on the expanse of concrete toward which they were descending six sleek and lethal-looking military jet fighters were parked in a straight line. Most surreal of all, the space between what must have been a civilian airport and what looked like a military airport was occupied by a golf course.

The only airport he knew around Bangkok was Suvarnab-humi, the city's major international airport, but this certainly wasn't it. Did Bangkok have another airport he had never heard of? One with a military facility and a golf course? Apparently, it did.

The helicopter bumped against the concrete, swung slightly to one side, and then settled. The pilots cut the engine and the rotor blades whirred to a stop. The same young man who had buckled Tay in reappeared, removed the headset he wore, and helped him out of the shoulder harness.

"Where are we?" Tay asked.

The young man didn't respond. He just smiled and opened the door. Tay stood up and the young man took his elbow to help him out. Tay shook him off. He wasn't *that* old, at least not yet.

Tay jumped to the ground. It wasn't that hard. It was no more than eighteen inches away. The young man collected Tay's bag and jumped down right behind him.

They were parked in front of a building that appeared to be a private terminal facility of some kind. It didn't look particularly busy, and through the windows Tay could see several men wearing what appeared to be military uniforms. Regardless of the pilot's lack of insignia, it seemed that he was still firmly in the hands of the Thai military.

With a sigh, Tay started walking toward the building.

"Sir? Sir?"

Tay looked back at the pilot who was pointing away from the building and out onto the aircraft parking apron. Tay's eyes went to where the kid was pointing and he saw a sleek private jet waiting. His mouth dropped open.

The kid walked toward the jet carrying Tay's bag and gesturing with his free hand for Tay to follow.

It was a big plane, white with a red stripe that ran all the way down the fuselage and up the tail. There was a number and some letters painted on the tail under the stripe, but Tay could see no other identification or markings on it. The plane wasn't as big as a commercial airliner, of course, but it was certainly bigger than most of the private planes Tay had seen parked at the airport in Singapore. Of course, he knew next to nothing about such things, but this looked like a serious airplane to him, one big enough to fly a dozen or more people almost anywhere in the world they wanted to go.

The forward door of the airplane was standing open and its boarding stairs were extended down to the parking apron. It looked almost as if it was just sitting there waiting for him, and he was beginning to understand that was exactly what it *was* doing.

At the foot of the plane's steps, the kid handed Tay his bag. Then he drew himself to attention, slapped his heels together with a crack as sharp as a gunshot, and snapped off a salute.

Having no better idea what to do, Tay returned the salute. Then he dragged his bag up the boarding steps and into the airplane.

"HEY, MAN."
John August was sprawled on a leather sofa on the left side of the cabin chewing on a small cigar.

"You certainly took your own fucking time getting here," he said.

It was one of the very few occasions in his entire life on which Sam Tay found himself absolutely speechless.

He stood in the doorway of the airplane and gaped at August, not able to summon up even a single coherent sentence. August looked back at him with something that was almost but not quite a smile playing at the corners of his mouth, and quietly chewed on his cigar.

"You'd probably be more comfortable sitting down," August said after a moment and pointed to a big chair opposite the couch where he was reclining.

Then he took the cigar out of his mouth, turned his head toward the half-open cockpit door, and shouted, "Let's move it, Fritz! Get this thing in the air!"

Tay walked a few steps and sank slowly into the chair without taking his eyes off of August.

The cockpit door opened and a stocky man wearing black pants and a white shirt with epaulets emerged. He opened a panel next to the main boarding door and held down a big black button until the stairs retracted and the door closed. Without speaking or even glancing at anyone in the passenger cabin, the man shut the panel, returned to the cockpit, and closed the door.

Tay felt himself regaining the power of speech. "I don't know what to say, John. You never mentioned anything about owning an airplane."

"I don't. This one belongs to a Manila charter company we use a lot. They think they're flying for the CIA, and we don't tell them any different."

August chuckled.

"I guess that makes us the first organization in the history of the world to use the CIA as a cover."

Tay heard the sound of the plane's engines starting. August raised his voice above the noise and pointed toward the back of the cabin.

"Say hello to the rest of the crew."

Tay turned his head where August was pointing and realized for the first time that they weren't alone on the plane. Near the back of the cabin, a man and a woman sat on opposite sides of the center aisle in seats similar to the one Tay was occupying. The woman raised her hand and gave Tay a wave with her fingers. The man sat perfectly still and just looked at him.

"I think you know Claire," August continued. "The friendly-looking guy with the beard is Woods, but he's not nearly as friendly as he appears."

Tay recognized Claire, of course. She was one of August's people who had been tracking a terrorist bent on staging an attack in Singapore a little while back, the same terrorist Tay had been tracking. She and Tay had become accidental partners in running the man to ground. Working together they got the job done and stopped an attack that might have killed hundreds or even thousands. The price for doing that had been high, and Tay wasn't at all sure it had been a price worth paying.

Naturally Claire wasn't her real name, at least Tay didn't think it was, but it was the one she had used in Singapore and he had gotten used to it. The truth was he thought it was a rather nice name, and working with a woman as attractive as Claire had been... well, that part had been nice, too.

She was tall, lean and fit looking, and she had long blond hair which she kept pulled back into a ponytail. When they worked together in Singapore she had generally dressed in a slightly masculine way, usually jeans and boots with a khaki shirt and aviator sunglasses. Tay thought the look was rather sexy, at least Claire made it look sexy. Did all American women dress to look a little masculine? Maybe they did. Thankfully, his experience with American women was limited, really limited since he'd had none at all, so he couldn't say for sure, but he really wouldn't be surprised.

He and Claire had gotten on well, and he had to admit the easy familiarity they had struck up had meant something to him. Still, it had never occurred to Tay that he would ever see Claire again after that, her being one of August's crew of ghosts and all, so he had filed her away as just another entry in his long and disappointing catalog of missed opportunities.

Tay had no idea who Woods was. The man was big and obviously fit, but he looked gentle and friendly enough, like the fellow in the neighborhood who always took time to play with the kids. Still, if the guy was nearly as formidable as Claire, and Tay had no doubt that he was or he wouldn't be here on this airplane with August, he was someone to be reckoned with.

The sound of the engines abruptly rose to a high-pitched whine and the airplane began to move. Tay glanced out the window and saw that they were rolling slowly toward the runways.

"I could have taken a commercial flight back to Singapore, John. You didn't have to go to all this trouble."

August chuckled. He propped his cigar up in an ashtray attached to the armrest of the couch, then he sat up and buckled a seatbelt around his waist.

"We're not going to Singapore, Sam."

Tay wasn't exactly thrilled to hear that, but he wasn't entirely astonished either. It had already begun to dawn on him that he wasn't going to be on his way home anytime soon. He waited for August to tell him the rest. It came quickly.

"We're going to Washington."

"Washington D.C.?"

August nodded.

"In the United States?"

August nodded again. "The land of the free and the home of the brave."

"I don't want to go to the United States."

"Why not?"

"I don't like Americans. You know that."

"I'm an American. You like me."

"Who told you that?"

"And Claire's an American. You like her, don't you?"

Tay knew he was just being baited so he ignored August's question and asked one of his own.

"Why would I want to go to America?"

"Because you're the kind of man who finishes what he starts. And that's where you have to go to finish this."

"You've identified the woman I found on the Hilton surveillance video."

"We have. Naturally her name isn't Susan Brandstetter, and she's not Canadian. But I'm sure you've already assumed that."

Tay had indeed assumed that. He also assumed August was about to tell him who the woman really was and so he waited for it.

"Her name is Rebecca Sternwood," August said. "She's an American."

The pitch of the engines rose another notch and the airplane shuddered slightly as if it were impatient to get into the air.

"And this woman is in Washington D.C.?" Tay asked.

"That's where she is," August nodded.

"Why?"

"Why is she in Washington D.C.?"

Tay nodded.

"Because she works for the Agency."

"What agency?" Tay asked, but almost immediately he realized how stupid that sounded.

"You mean *the* Agency?"

August nodded again.

"The CIA?"

This time August didn't even bother to nod.

"Are you telling me, John, that it's the fucking CIA that's trying to kill you?"

"Well… probably not the *whole* CIA."

August grinned and cut Tay an enormous wink.

"Fasten your seatbelt, Sam."

Tay wondered in what sense August was offering him that advice. Was he simply issuing the usual warning given before takeoff on all airplanes, or was August engaging in an unlikely eruption of metaphorical fancy?

Both, Tay decided almost immediately.

I'm pretty sure it's both.

THIRTY

T HE AIRPLANE TURNED onto the end of the
runway and accelerated into its takeoff roll without
stopping.

It climbed into the sky far more steeply than Tay ever
remembered experiencing before on an airplane. It was almost
as if their departure had been given priority by the airport over
all the other traffic, and after everything else that had happened
Tay wouldn't have been surprised if it had.

Tay had never flown in a private jet before. It was far more
comfortable than flying in a commercial aircraft, of course, and
getting to skip all the security nonsense that airports put people
through these days was a nice bonus, but he really wasn't all that
thrilled about being on a plane that was so small.

He wasn't particularly fond of flying in airplanes of any size,
but in this one all the sensations of flight that Tay would rather
not think about were exaggerated: the speed, the climb, the
distance above the ground. It was the difference between
speeding down the highway in a bus and then suddenly finally
yourself doing it on a motorcycle.

It seemed to Tay that the whole idea of human flight was a
fragile concept. When he was strapped into a seat in the middle

of a huge commercial aircraft, he might feel cramped and it might be unpleasant, but at least those discomforts pushed the thought that he was suspended in the air several miles above solid ground well out of his mind. In this smaller aircraft with its plush leather seats and big windows, the idea that he was strapped into a narrow aluminum tube whizzing at great speed far above the surface of the earth came front and center.

After ten minutes or so the plane's nose tilted down and Tay's sense of balance told him they were leveling off. August unsnapped his seat belt, stood up, and stretched.

"No flight attendants, I'm afraid, Sam. If you want anything, you'll have to get it yourself."

"How long is it going to take for us to get there?"

"You might as well get comfortable. It's going to be a while."

"A while?"

"We're routing first to Chitose Airbase. It's a Japanese Self-Defense Forces base on Hokkaido in the north of Japan that the Japanese government uses for its aircraft operations. That ought to take about seven hours. We'll top off the fuel there, which will take an hour or two depending on how busy they are, and after that it's another fourteen or fifteen hours to Washington. So that's something like twenty-four hours all in, give or take. There are three pilots in the cockpit so they'll take turns resting and we can go straight through."

Tay was flabbergasted. Twenty-four hours on an airplane? That sounded crazy. He realized they were flying halfway around the world, and he supposed if he thought about it he'd realize that was how long it took to fly halfway around the world, but he had tried hard not to think about things like that before. And he really didn't want to start now.

"I'm going to make some coffee," Tay heard a woman say.

He glanced up and saw Claire standing in the aisle right next to him.

"How do you take yours, Sam?"

"Black is fine," he said.

Claire smiled and disappeared behind a curtain at the front of the aircraft.

"You can smoke if you like," August said. "That's only one of many things that make this better than flying United."

Tay looked at August and saw him lighting the little cigar he had been chewing on before takeoff.

He opened his bag and took out what was left of a crumpled pack of Marlboros and a box of matches. That was just his luck, wasn't it? For the first time in more years than he could remember he could smoke on an airplane and he only had three cigarettes to last him for twenty-four hours. August must have seen him looking at the pack and guessed exactly what he was thinking.

"Don't worry, Sam. You can buy American cigarettes at Chitose. You won't have to ration those."

Tay said nothing. He wasn't about to admit to August that he had read his mind precisely.

A FEW MINUTES later Claire returned and set a white china cup and saucer on the table next to Tay's seat.

"The rest of the pot's on a warmer in the galley, Sam. Help yourself when you're ready for more."

Tay took that as a subtle declaration from Claire that she had no intention of playing stewardess for the next twenty-four hours just because she was the only woman on the plane. He wondered what it said about him that she had felt the need to make that clear to him.

"There are some sandwiches and fruit up there, too," August added. "It's not fine cuisine, but it will keep you from starving. They'll cater some Japanese food for us while we're refueling. It's usually pretty good stuff."

Tay tried the coffee. It was unexpectedly rich and tasty so he lit a Marlboro, leaned back in his seat, and thought about how it could possibly have come to be that he was enjoying his morning coffee and cigarette sitting on an unimaginably expensive private jet seven miles or so over the Pacific Ocean bound for Washington D.C. The more he thought about it, the more improbable it sounded, so he decided the best thing to do was simply to ask.

"Why am I here, John?"

"Don't you want to be?"

"No."

August chuckled. "You set all this in motion, Sam. You're responsible for finding the right string to pull on here, and my guess is you want to know what's on the other end of it just as much as I do."

"If that's your guess, then your guess is wrong."

"You mean like a minute ago when I guessed you were worried about running out of cigarettes?"

Tay said nothing.

"I really don't know what's going on here, Sam, and I want your help in putting the pieces together."

"The CIA wants to kill you. Somehow I don't find that all that hard to understand."

August shrugged and took a puff on his cigar.

"If you wanted my help, John, all you had to do was ask for it. You didn't have to get the Thai army to kidnap me in the middle of the night."

"I didn't want to waste time arguing with you. So, I asked a Thai general who owed me a favor to get you to the airport as quickly as he could. Maybe your escorts didn't explain that as clearly as they should have."

"They didn't explain anything at all. Why didn't you just call me? When you're in a country run by a military dictatorship and armed soldiers show up at your door at three o'clock in the morning, you normally don't assume there's an innocent explanation."

"Yeah, I get that. Sorry."

They each sat and smoked quietly after that. Tay finished his cigarette first and then his coffee, and then he stood up. He glanced toward the back of the cabin and saw Claire and Woods talking quietly over their own coffee cups.

"Anybody want more coffee?" he called out.

When they both shook their heads, Tay went up to the galley to refill his own cup. He didn't offer to get August any. He wasn't a stewardess either.

A UGUST WAS LOOKING at something on an iPad when Tay got back. Tay sipped his coffee and waited for August to finish what he was doing, but when he didn't show any signs of doing that Tay grew impatient.

"Why does the CIA want to kill you, John?"

August closed the iPad case and put it down on the sofa.

"I don't know. Maybe it's not the CIA that's really behind this at all."

"Didn't you just tell me that you've identified this woman as Rebecca Sternwood?"

August nodded.

"And that Rebecca Sternwood works for the CIA?"

"That doesn't mean the whole Agency wants to kill me. Maybe there's some other reason she's involved in this."

"Like what?"

"Figuring that out is why I need you, Sam."

"You think it could be personal?"

August shrugged.

"Have you ever tried to kill this woman?"

August gave Tay a dead-eyed look and said nothing.

"And you don't know of any other reason she would have a personal grudge against you?"

"No."

"I really can't see this being a personal thing, John. If someone did have a grudge against you, they wouldn't have to blow up a hotel in Hong Kong. There have to be an awful lot of easier ways to get to you."

August took another puff on his cigar and stubbed it out in the ashtray attached to the end of the couch.

"Look, Sam, I didn't get much sleep last night and I'm too whacked right now to think about this anymore so I'm going to sack out until we get to Japan. That seat you're in goes completely flat and there are some pillows and blankets in that closet up at the front so you can sack out, too. If you're not sleepy and you want to watch a movie, just push that button on the side of the table next to you and the top lifts up to become a touch screen video monitor. Or there's another iPad in the top drawer of the table and the Wi-Fi works pretty well so you can hit the net if you want. Whatever you do, we're going to have plenty of time to chew this over before we get to Washington. Right now, I need some sleep."

And with that August kicked off his shoes, stretched out on the couch, and rolled over with his back to Tay. It looked to Tay as if August was fast asleep in less than a minute.

THE REST OF the trip went faster than Tay expected. While the plane was being refueled in Japan, they went into the lounge and he bought three packs of Marlboros and a paperback copy of a Don Winslow novel called *The Force* that he had been meaning to read.

After the aircraft took off again, they all went into the galley and each of them helped themselves to the sushi, teriyaki chicken, miso soup, and Japanese beer that had been boarded during the fueling operation. It was as good as August had promised and somehow the subject of the CIA wanting to kill all of them didn't come up again while they were eating.

After the dishes had been returned to the galley, Tay turned on his reading light and was happy to find it was bright enough for him to read comfortably in spite of his rapidly deteriorating vision. After a while he closed the book and tried watching a movie, but with his reading light off and the cabin in near darkness he had trouble staying awake. Finally, he stopped fighting it. He went up to the closet and got himself a blanket and a couple of pillows, then he moved his seat into the flat position and was asleep in minutes.

When he woke, the navigation map displayed on the monitor on the front bulkhead said they were somewhere over Lake Huron a couple of hours out of Washington. Everyone else looked like they were still asleep, so Tay went up to the galley, found the coffee, and figured out how to work the coffeemaker. While it was running, he went to the toilet, then he poured himself a cup of the fresh coffee and returned to his seat.

"Stewardess! Oh, stewardess!" August called out from the couch without bothering to roll over. "I'll take a cup of coffee, too, please."

Tay put the cup he was carrying down next to the couch for August, then went back to the galley and got himself another one. When he came back, August was sitting up, rubbing his eyes, drinking the coffee.

"Damn, Sam, that's really good coffee. You're going to make somebody a fine wife one of these days."

Tay just grunted. It was far too early in the morning to get into a verbal joust with August. Or too late at night. Or too something.

"What happens when we get into Washington?" Tay asked instead.

August appeared to turn that over in his mind while he finished his coffee.

"We're landing at a small airport in Virginia just south of Washington. It's in a place called Manassas. You ever heard of Manassas?"

Tay shook his head.

"The first major battle of the American Civil War took

place there. The Union army thought all it had to do was stroll down to Richmond, kick some ass, and the rebellion would collapse in a week. The Confederates met them at Manassas and crushed the Union army, which then retreated to Washington in a disorganized route. Some people say the Confederates might have taken Washington if they had kept the pressure on the Union army right at that moment, but they didn't. They hesitated, and eventually they lost the war."

"Why do I get the feeling there was supposed to be a lesson somewhere in that story?"

"There was. Never hesitate. Push your advantage and you can take Washington."

"We have an advantage?"

"Sure, we have an advantage, and we're going to use it to take Washington.

"What's our advantage?"

"We're not here. We can't be. We're dead."

"Speak for yourself."

August grinned. "That's why we're coming in at night. I don't want anyone spotting us by accident. The longer we can keep them thinking they succeeded in Hong Kong, the better our chances of getting to them will be."

"Exactly who is this *they* and *them* you keep talking about?"

"Ah well, that's where you come in, Sam. You're going to figure that out for me."

Tay started to ask how he was supposed to do that. He knew nothing about Washington. He had never even been there before. And he knew nothing about how Washington worked. What he had read and heard from time to time about the functioning of the government of the United States made absolutely no sense to him. Maybe you had to be an American to understand a place like Washington.

But he didn't tell August any of that. He felt far too goofy from spending the last twenty-four hours on an airplane to conduct a serious conversation. That would have to wait for tomorrow.

"What happens after we land?" Tay asked instead.

"A couple of vehicles will be waiting at the plane to take us to a safe house the Band maintains near the offices."

A safe house? Seriously?

Was August pulling his leg? Tay felt like he had gone to sleep and woken up in the middle of a spy movie, the plot of which didn't make the slightest sense.

"Don't we have to go into the terminal and go through customs and immigration first?" Tay asked.

August just looked at him.

"Oh," Tay said, "I get it. You don't do customs and immigration. The usual rules don't apply to you."

August smiled. "And as long as you're with us, Sam, they don't apply to you either."

"What do we do after we get to this safe house?"

Tay almost snickered when he said *safe house*, but with the application of iron self-discipline he was able to avoid it.

"Get a shower, some food, a little sleep, and wake up tomorrow ready to kick ass and take names."

"I suppose you have a plan for how we're going to go about doing that."

"To tell you the truth, Sam, I've got no fucking clue. What we know for sure now, thanks to you, is that Rebecca Sternwood set us up to be killed by that bomb in Hong Kong. She works for the Agency and she's out there somewhere. I guess maybe we find her, look her up, and ask her why she did it."

Woods walked past them in the aisle on his way to the galley to get some coffee.

"Sounds like a plan to me," he muttered.

THIRTY-ONE

T HEY LANDED IN darkness somewhere that didn't really seem to Tay to be anywhere.

Two big, black SUVs of some American make he couldn't identify were waiting for them on the tarmac. Their plane taxied right up to the vehicles and while the whine of the engines was still dying away they were bundled into them, then driven by silent, formidable-looking men out of the airport, along mostly nondescript suburban streets, and down character-less freeways.

What Tay saw outside the windows looked utterly inter-changeable with probably thousands of other streets and free-ways in hundreds of other towns and cities. The only way he knew he was in Washington D.C. was because August had told him he was.

A little over half an hour after pulling away from the plane, the two vehicles entered a dignified neighborhood of traditional row houses lining cobblestoned streets and brick sidewalks. Many of the houses flew American flags from staffs mounted alongside front doors or between second-floor windows. The flags gave the area the air of a historical theme park, and for all Tay knew maybe it was.

The neighborhood reminded Tay a little of the area where he lived in Singapore, but it seemed older, more anchored in a time that Tay instinctively thought had to have been better than this one. Singapore didn't have much of a history, it hadn't been around long enough to have one, and Tay blamed that for the sense of being untethered from place and time that occasionally threatened to overwhelm him.

Both vehicles pulled to the curb in front of a three-story, red-brick row house. Two brass carriage lanterns with flickering gas flames flanked a black lacquered door with a huge gold knocker in the shape of a horse's head at its center. Flower boxes over-flowing with bright red geraniums hung under every window. Very agreeable, very gracious, very elegant.

If this is what safe houses are like, Tay thought, *it's a shame no one ever invited me to stay in one before.*

The door opened and a middle-aged woman wearing a white apron over a black dress stood smiling in the light dancing from the gas flames of the carriage lanterns.

"Sally will show you to your room, Sam." August put a hand on Tay's shoulder and handed him his bag. "If you want a sandwich or a drink, just ask her."

"What happens now?"

"We take a shower. We get some sleep. We all make ourselves human again. Then in the morning, we'll figure out where we go from here."

In spite of the graciousness of the surroundings, Tay was overwhelmed by a sense of disorientation. His head was full of cotton wool from the twenty-four-hour flight, and everything was made much worse by the twelve-hour time change. Nothing seemed quite real as he followed the woman up the staircase to the third floor.

There is a point at which the effects of fatigue are almost indistinguishable from the effects of alcohol. Judgment is impaired, reactions slow, and temper is hard to control. He was nearly there so he just plodded on up the stairs, putting one foot in front of the other, and tried to concentrate on not biting the head off the next person who spoke to him.

At the third-floor landing, the woman ushered Tay through a polished mahogany door and he found himself in a bedroom with a distinctly masculine feel to it. A dark-stained wooden floor covered with a worn red and blue oriental rug, two brown leather chairs flanking a table in front of a fireplace, a huge double-doored wardrobe cabinet, and a large bed covered by a dark green duvet.

"Can I get you something to eat, sir?" the woman asked.

Tay was slightly surprised to hear the woman speaking with a distinct English accent.

"You're British?" he asked. "Not American?"

The woman smiled slightly. "Perhaps a drink, sir?"

Well, Tay thought, he probably deserved to have his stupid question ignored, didn't he? America was the least homogenous nation on earth. Americans came from everywhere and spoke with every known accent. To assume someone wasn't an American just because they spoke with an English accent was silly.

Tay mentally slapped himself and said, "Nothing, thank you."

"Bathroom's through there," the woman said, indicating a door across the room. "You'll find a bathrobe and extra towels in the wardrobe. And if you need anything at all, there's a call button next to your bed."

Tay dropped his travel bag on an upholstered bench at the end of the bed.

"I'm sure I'll be fine. Thank you."

"I'll wish you a very good night then, sir."

When the woman closed the door behind her, Tay walked over and examined it. Somewhat to his surprise, he found there was a hotel-style locking bolt on the inside and when he closed it there was a solid *clunking* sound. He wasn't sure why he even bothered to close it. He had no idea what kind of security the house had, but he imagined it was formidable. After all, a safe house had to be safe, didn't it? That was the whole idea. Surely a bolt inside the door of a third-floor bedroom didn't make much practical difference one way or another.

Tay took off his shoes and stretched out on the bed. Was he tired? Utterly exhausted. Was he sleepy? Not a bit.

Tay looked at his watch and realized that he didn't even know what time it was. His watch said it was a little after six, but was that six in the morning or six at night? It was dark so surely it was six at night. Or was it? If his watch was still on Bangkok time, it was probably telling him that it was six in the morning in Bangkok, which was of no value to him at all.

He was reasonably sure his watch must still be on Bangkok time because he must have reset it to local time at some point when he was in Thailand. Or maybe he hadn't. Maybe he had never gotten around to resetting his watch at all and it was still showing Singapore time. The more he thought about it, the more confused he got.

He supposed he could have asked the woman what time it was, but he hadn't thought of it and, now that she was gone, he realized he really didn't care.

Tay got up and rummaged through his bag until he found one of the packs of cigarettes and the Don Winslow novel he had bought when they refueled in Japan. He had tried to start the book on the plane, but his concentration had failed and he honestly couldn't remember anything of what he had read so he decided to start it over from the beginning. He noticed there was an ashtray and a box of matches on the table next to the bed and he wondered if all the bedrooms had ashtrays or if that was just for him.

He had read forty pages and smoked two cigarettes when fatigue finally overcame him. He undressed, dumped his clothes on one of the chairs in front of the fireplace, and cut off the room lights, then he crawled back into bed and pulled the duvet up to his chin. He thought about reading a little more, but he quickly gave up the idea and turned off the bedside lamp.

Within minutes, he was fast asleep.

TAY EMERGED FROM sleep like a man crawling out of a cave. At first, he had no idea where he was, of course, and he lay without moving and prodded his memory to provide him with some explanation of his situation.

Slowly images began to bubble up from the depths of his recollection, slide around in his mind, and assemble themselves like an animated jigsaw puzzle. The soldiers appearing at his hotel room door in the middle of the night, the helicopter ride to some airport, the private jet flight with August and the others, and the black SUVs that brought them to this house which August had said was somewhere near Washington D.C.

Once Tay had satisfactorily established his relationship to his surroundings, he got up and showered and used the toothbrush and shaving gear he found in the bathroom. While he shaved, he inspected himself critically in the mirror as he often did.

His eyes were clear, probably the beneficiaries of a decent night's sleep, but he thought the wrinkles at the corners of his eyes had attained a new state of prominence. Was that because of the mad dash from Thailand through Japan and on to Washington, or was he just getting old? Of course, he was getting old, but he was beginning to think he was getting old at a faster rate these days. That was what gave him pause.

When he was done, he dressed in the only clean clothes he had left in his bag, opened the door, and stepped out into the hallway. Almost immediately he smelled the aroma of fresh coffee and heard the murmur of voices from somewhere downstairs. The voices were too faint for him to recognize any of them, but he really didn't care who it was. If it was somebody who had coffee, that's where he was going.

· · ·

W HEN TAY FOLLOWED the smell to the kitchen he found August, Claire, and Woods gathered around a big wooden table with a fourth man he didn't know.

The first thing he noticed was that Claire looked good, really good. She was wearing black jeans tucked into high black boots and a man's white dress shirt with the sleeves rolled up. Tay wasn't absolutely sure whether he was even allowed to notice a woman's appearance these days. Americans had been getting goofier and goofier about that sort of thing the last few years and he had the impression that just thinking a woman looked attractive now amounted to a felony in America.

So arrest me, Tay thought to himself, but he only nodded at Claire. Just to be on the safe side, he wasn't about to mention her appearance one way or another.

The woman who had shown him up to his room last night was clearing away plates and pouring more coffee.

"How do you take your coffee, sir?" she asked him.

"Black and soon."

"Sleep well, Sam?" August asked.

Tay nodded.

"I guess you did. I thought I was going to have to come upstairs and tickle your feet to get you up."

"You need to remember that I've got a gun."

Nobody laughed. Maybe they thought he was serious.

Then he remembered he *was* serious. The gun Mad Max had given him was still tucked into the bottom of his bag. Was having a gun in America legal? Tay's general impression was that it might even be mandatory.

"What time is it here?" Tay asked. "My watch is still on some other time zone."

"A little after nine."

Tay started to work out the time change between what his watch said and what August was telling him, but he quickly decided that wasn't going to happen before he'd had coffee so he just reset his watch and let it go. He was where he was and the time was what it was. There was nothing he could do about either.

The woman returned and placed a mug of black coffee in front of an empty place at the table. The aroma began to pump new life into him even before he had his first sip.

That's the ticket, Tay thought as he sat down and savored his first sips. *Take it slow and drink coffee.*

"Sam," August said, "I'd like you to meet the Conductor."

It was all Tay could do not to laugh out loud. This code name stuff was like a bunch of children playing in a treehouse. The man Tay didn't know half rose from his seat and offered his hand. Tay shook it.

"So, you're the famous Inspector Tay," the Conductor said.

"I'm retired. It's just plain Samuel Tay now."

Tay thought the Conductor was an unremarkable looking man and guessed he was somewhere around seventy. He looked like a small-town grocer or the man who ran the drug store. He could be anybody. Maybe that was the occupational qualification a spy needed in order to achieve his sort of longevity.

The woman who had served Tay his coffee stood next to his chair with her hands folded in front of her. "Would you like some breakfast, sir?"

All at once Tay realized how hungry he was.

"What do you have?"

"Fruit, muffins, Danish pastry, bagels, toast, cereal of all sorts, and of course I can prepare eggs and bacon for you."

"Ah…" Tay thought for a moment. "Fruit and maybe some scrambled eggs on toast?"

"Certainly, sir."

"More coffee?"

"Absolutely."

"Disgustingly healthy, Sam," August put in. "You're in America now. You ought to have a bowl of Fruit Loops in honor of the occasion."

Tay had no idea what Fruit Loops were so he said nothing.

The woman came back to refill Tay's coffee cup. When she left to prepare Tay's eggs and toast, the Conductor cleared his throat.

"Thank you for coming to help us, Sam."

"I don't really deserve any credit. I was more or less kidnapped."

"Nevertheless, you have already performed a great service for us. If you hadn't identified the messenger, we wouldn't have anything at all to work with."

"It wasn't very hard. John could have done it himself."

"Not and stay dead," August pointed out.

Tay didn't argue. He just drank some more coffee, then looked at the Conductor and said, "Can I ask you something?"

The Conductor nodded.

"Why am I here?"

"We need your help to find out who is trying to kill our people."

"You must have people more qualified to do that than I am. I know nothing about your business, and I don't want to."

"I understand that."

"I don't even know anything about Washington. I'm not the guy you need to ask to do this."

"Possibly not, but you're John's choice because he trusts you. And that counts for more than a working knowledge of the geography of Washington D.C."

Tay wasn't sure what to say to that so he did what he usually did when confronted by something that didn't make much sense to him. He said nothing, drank a little coffee, and waited for someone to tell him what was really going on here.

THIRTY-TWO

"REBECCA STERNWOOD IS part of something the Agency calls the East Asian Mission Center," August explained to Tay.

"Part of?"

"She's the DAD."

"Do you people consciously use acronyms as a torture technique, or is it that you just can't help yourselves?"

"She's the Deputy Assistant Director. Of the East Asian Mission Center."

"That sounds pretty high up."

"It's an upper middle position in the bureaucracy," the Conductor put in. "The Agency has a lot of divisions and mission centers and task forces, and most of them have a director and an assistant director and several deputy assistant directors."

"So, you're telling me she's not a senior official, but she's not exactly a foot soldier either."

"That's right," the Conductor said. "Think of her as a Master Sergeant. Just the level of person you'd get to run an operation that's important, but one that you want to be able to disown if it turns to crap."

"Then this really *was* a CIA operation. It was the CIA that planted that bomb in Hong Kong."

"No," the Conductor shook his head. "We're certain it wasn't an official op."

"I don't understand that. This woman obviously had help setting up the attack in Hong Kong. She didn't do it on her weekend off. She didn't build a bomb and plant it in that hotel all by herself. She's either part of an operation being run by the CIA, or she's running an operation for the CIA. Which is it?"

"We don't think it was either," August said.

"Get real, John. You can't be certain this wasn't an official operation of the CIA."

"It simply doesn't make any sense that—"

"No, you're right, we're not certain," the Conductor interrupted. "We don't think it was a sanctioned operation, but we can't be absolutely certain."

"How are you going to find out?"

The Conductor cleared his throat. "I thought you might do that for us, Sam."

The woman preparing their breakfast returned with Tay's scrambled eggs on toast just then. The timing couldn't have been better, at least from Tay's point of view. He picked up his knife and fork, attacked his eggs, and waited to see where this was all going.

"Look, Sam," August said. "This wasn't an attack on me. It was an attack on the Band. Somebody wants to put us out of business."

"I thought almost nobody knew the Band existed."

"They don't. But more people know I exist, and they can guess that I'm connected to some organization even if they don't know exactly what it is."

Tay chewed thoughtfully on his eggs and considered that.

"Tell me why somebody might come after the Band," he said after a moment.

"It's easy to imagine a lot of reasons."

"Such as?"

"Revenge against us for something we did. Bureaucratic jealousy. It could be anything. We don't know enough yet to guess at the real reason."

"You don't know very much, do you?"

"Maybe not, but there are really only three possibilities."

August held up three fingers as if Tay might not be familiar with the number.

"The first is that this really was an op officially run by the Agency to shut down the Band, in which case I don't even want to think about where that goes. The second is that this woman is acting essentially on her own for some reason and has gathered up a few other people she can rely on for help in targeting either me or the Band. And the third is that this woman was acting under instructions from someone higher up in the Agency in an op that was not officially sanctioned but which she probably thought was."

"And which of those three possibilities do you think is more likely?"

"The third one," the Conductor said. "She was following instructions from someone higher up."

"How much higher up?" Tay asked.

The Conductor just looked at him.

"That high up, huh?" Tay muttered, finishing the last bite of his eggs and pushing his plate aside.

"She's the only string we've got to pull on here, Sam. Whether she's the head of the snake or just a piece somewhere in the middle doesn't really matter. She's still the only way into this."

"So, what do you have in mind? Calling her up and asking her why she set John and the others up to be killed?"

"Not exactly. We're going to scare her."

"Scare her?"

"We're going to scare the unholy fuck out of her. If she's in this with somebody else, she'll run straight to them. If she's doing this on her own, she will come back against us. Either way, we'll find out what this is all about."

"I assume you've concocted some cockamamie plan for how you're going to go about doing that."

Neither the Conductor nor August said anything. The Conductor was expressionless, but August looked at Tay with a half-smile on his face.

"Why do I get the feeling I don't really want to hear this part?" Tay sighed.

THE CONDUCTOR SHUFFLED through some files that were stacked in front of him and came up with a flat manila envelope about the size of a hardback book. He pushed it across the table to Tay.

"For you," he said.

Tay opened the envelope and dumped out the contents. A black passport booklet with silver embossing, and a slim black leather folder that appeared scratched and scarred from use.

Tay picked up the passport and looked at the cover. At the top, in both English and Arabic script, it said **INTERPOL** with the Interpol logo right below, and following that was the word for passport in four languages: English, French, Spanish, and Arabic. Inside the front cover was a page that said International Criminal Police Organization in the same four languages, and below that was Tay's picture, his description, his place of birth, and his job title. Criminal Intelligence Officer.

Tay opened the leather folder, but he already knew what he would find. It was a badge case. On the right side of the folder was a gold badge that said **INTERPOL OFFICER** and on the left was an identification card with his picture that identified him as a Criminal Intelligence Officer. It looked a lot like Tay's Singapore warrant card.

"I won't even bother to ask where you got the photos," Tay said.

Nobody said anything, but then Tay really hadn't expected them to.

"Are these legitimate Interpol credentials?" he asked.

"We got them from a movie prop house in New York and stuck your photos in," August said.

"Seriously?"

"Of course not, Sam. They're real. We're not total idiots."

THE WOMAN WHO had been serving them breakfast had disappeared so Tay stood up, took his cup over to the coffee maker, and refilled it himself.

"Anybody else?" he asked before he returned the pot to the warming plate.

"I wouldn't mind some," Claire said.

Tay walked over with the glass carafe and refilled her cup. It was the first time Claire had spoken since Tay had come into the kitchen, and Woods had yet to say a single word. He assumed that reflected the pecking order. The Conductor was the boss, August was the underboss, and Woods and Claire were the soldiers. Tay wondered what that made him. He returned the carafe to the warming plate and sat back down with his fresh cup of coffee.

"This is your big plan? I tell this woman that Interpol is investigating her and she goes limp and tells me everything. Seriously?"

"I'm sure this woman has never dealt with anyone from Interpol in her whole life," August said. "When you suddenly show up and start asking questions about Hong Kong, it will be a total ambush. She'll freak out."

"For God's sake, John, she's a CIA officer. She's not going to go all gaga just because someone tells her he's from Interpol and starts asking her questions. She'll just smile at me and say she knows nothing about it."

"Look at it from her point of view. Whether she set the bomb herself or not—"

"Almost certainly she didn't," Tay interrupted.

"I doubt she did either, but she sent us there. She was still at least partly responsible for a bombing in Hong Kong that did extensive damage to the Cordis Hotel and killed three people."

"But the three of you aren't actually dead."

"Three bodies were found in the rubble," the Conductor said. "I have no idea who they were, but Rebecca and whoever she's connected with are naturally assuming they were John, Claire, and Woods. So, there *are* three people dead, even if it's the wrong three people."

"Depending on how you want to define who the wrong three people are," August added.

"Yes," the Conductor nodded. "Depending on that."

"When Interpol come sniffing around, Sam," August said, tapping his finger on the table, "and tells this woman they know she's responsible for three deaths, she's going to panic. China would love nothing more than to publicly out a CIA officer for murdering three people. She's not going to want to be the scapegoat here."

"What if she doesn't panic?"

"She will. She's a CIA bureaucrat, and I know bureaucrats. When something goes wrong, they spread the blame around as quickly as they can. You can make book on it."

"So, I just stroll into CIA headquarters, flash these fake Interpol credentials, and push my way into her office?"

"Don't be silly."

The Conductor dipped back into the files he had stacked in front of him and came up with two sheets of plain white paper. He pulled them out and slid them across the table to Tay.

"We've developed some background on Miss Sternwood and have a sense of what her daily routine is like. Using that information, we want you to watch her for a while and find a way to approach her when she is outside her office, someplace where she is alone and vulnerable."

"You mean at home?"

"Maybe, but maybe somewhere else. That's up to you. You find the place she would least expect to be approached, introduce yourself as an Interpol investigator, and tell her you've connected her to the Hong Kong bombing."

Tay looked down at the pieces of paper on the table in front of him. On the top sheet, he saw Rebecca Sternwood's office address. It was in someplace called Crystal City. Probably a Washington suburb. It was an enticing name for a suburb, but Tay suspected Crystal City sounded a lot more interesting than it would actually turn out to be.

Her home address was there, too, and a description of her living arrangements. Single, living alone, no cats or dogs. There was even a description of her car and its license number. But what really stopped him was the detailed log of her activities for the last three days.

"Where did you get all this?" Tay asked while he was still reading.

No one answered him and he glanced up at August.

"Does the Band have spies at the CIA, John?"

August said nothing.

The Conductor cleared his throat. "I'd prefer to call them friends."

"Whatever you call them, it looks to me like the same thing. The Band is spying on the CIA."

"I suppose you can look at it that way. If you want to."

"I thought you and the CIA were on the same side."

"So did I."

Tay shook his head. "Look, I'm just a simple policeman. These spy games you people play go right over my head."

"Somehow I doubt that," the Conductor said. "And they're not games. We simply live in a world that functions a little differently from the one in which most people live."

"*A wilderness of mirrors*," Tay quoted. "T.S. Eliot. But I'm sure you know that."

The Conductor smiled slightly, but said nothing.

"So, you want me to stalk this woman, ambush her, and frighten her enough to get her to tell me why she set your people up to be killed."

"We want you to confront her and identify yourself as an Interpol investigator looking into the Hong Kong bombing. That will put the cat among the proverbial pigeons. And, yes, maybe she will simply tell you why she did this."

"That makes me think of another line from the same Eliot poem."

"What's that?"

"*After such knowledge, what forgiveness?*"

Tay looked from the Conductor to August and back to the Conductor again, but neither of them seemed to have anything to say.

TAY CLEARED HIS throat to break the silence. "So, you want me to watch this woman as she moves around here in Washington?"

The Conductor nodded.

"I gather you don't expect me to do that on foot."

"Of course not. We have a car for you."

"Ah, well, a car." Tay seemed to think that over. "Then I guess that just leaves one problem."

The Conductor waited, his face assuming a polite expression of curiosity.

"I don't have a driver's license," Tay told him.

"Seriously? You really don't?"

"No. I grew up in Singapore."

"I don't understand. What's that got to do with it?"

"A lot of people in Singapore don't drive. Driving a car might be a life skill for Americans, and owning a car might be as common here as owning a pair of shoes, but it's not that way in Singapore."

"Are you telling me you don't know *how* to drive?"

"Of course, I know how. I'm just not a very good driver."

"Nobody in Washington is a good driver. You'll fit right in."

"You drive on the wrong side of the road here."

"The right side."

"Yes, the wrong side."

"This conversation is turning into an Abbott and Costello routine," the Conductor chuckled.

"Who're Abbott and Costello?" Claire asked.

Everyone looked at her.

"You're not serious," the Conductor said.

"I'm perfectly serious."

"You're also making me feel as old as dirt."

"Can we get back to the subject now?" Tay asked. "I'm sorry, but I just don't feel comfortable trying to drive here on the wrong side of the road."

"You mean the right side."

"Yes, the wrong side."

"For fuck's sake," August interrupted, "don't start that shit again!"

A silence fell. Tay wasn't about to break it since he was enjoying it too much. And neither August nor the Conductor knew *how* to break it since they couldn't figure out what to do.

Eventually, Claire spoke up.

"I'll drive Sam around Washington."

"You need to stay dead," August said.

"I'll wear dark glasses."

August just looked at her.

"No one in Washington knows me, John. There's no risk anyone who sees me is going to connect me to Hong Kong."

August thought about that for a moment. He looked at the Conductor.

"It could work," the Conductor said. "I don't have a better idea."

And so it was settled.

"ONE OTHER THING bothers me," Tay said.

"Only one thing?" August asked.

"How is Interpol supposed to have connected the Hong Kong explosion to Rebecca Sternwood?"

"Doesn't matter," August said. "You don't have to tell her even if she asks. You're an investigator following up leads just like you have a thousand times before. Since when do cops worry about telling the people you interview what information led you to them and where you got it?"

Tay had to admit August was right about that, but he said nothing.

"It's perfect, Sam. You're an investigator from Interpol following up leads on the Hong Kong bombing. Since you're Singaporean, this woman is going to jump to the conclusion that this investigation is being pushed by the Chinese government. She'll assume the Hong Kong cops found something that connects the bombing to her and that's what has brought you to her doorstep. Since you know she's CIA, she will immediately see what this is really all about. Using her to nail the Agency."

Tay said nothing.

"If Interpol and the Chinese have connected Miss Stern-wood to the bombing, Sam, this woman is looking at murder charges and the Agency is looking at major international embarrassment. She's going to panic and go straight to whoever set this whole operation in motion to tell him you're somehow onto them. When she does, we'll be watching."

"But what if she just walks down the hall to another office and talks to someone there? How will you ever know?"

"Whoever is really running this will be keeping it entirely off campus. They're not going to be sitting around Agency offices and talking about killing off American citizens who work for another organization. There'll be no phone contact, no email, nothing electronic at all. They'll be using the same technique we use to guarantee secrecy. All contact will be in person, and it will be in some off-campus location."

"And what if you're wrong? What if she really *is* doing this on her own? What if she's just got some grudge against you personally for reasons you've long forgotten?"

"She'll still panic. Her career, even her freedom will be at risk, and she'll push back."

"Push back? What does that mean?"

"Well…"

August tilted his head back and consulted the ceiling as if an explanation might be written there. After a moment he said, "She'll probably look for a way to put an end to your investigation."

"Like by putting an end to me."

August nodded.

"Then let's just put this plainly then, shall we, John? What you intend to do is dangle me in front of Rebecca Sternwood as live bait. You want to see if she bites me or if somebody else bites me. And assuming I don't get swallowed whole, you'll figure out what to do after that. Do I have that about right?"

"Gosh, Sam, when you put it that way you make it sound so wrong."

For a moment Tay found himself wondering if he could really trust August. He had never wondered that before, never had any reason to, but suddenly there the thought was, and try as he might he could not make it murmur an apology for the interruption and disappear.

Was August turning him into a goat tethered to a stake and waiting for the lion to turn up? And if he was the goat, who the hell was the lion? Was it the CIA, or was it something else entirely, something he couldn't even imagine existed? He had no idea.

The next move was apparently to be Tay's, so Tay lit a Marl-boro and thought about what August had just told him. It hadn't been the whole story. Of course it hadn't, but he had no idea what was missing. Still, he had to give August credit. He knew how to spin a tale that would reel him in.

All those years he had been a policeman, he had never tired of the mysteries that were brought to him, but he had tired of the solutions. In almost every case, those solutions turned out to be insipid, disappointing, and commonplace.

If he'd had a flaw as a detective, it was his tendency to imag-ine, or perhaps hope, that at the end of each trail he would find something compelling or at least interesting. There never really was. The human drama more often than not wound up as nothing more than unintended comedy. The motivations for human action were depressingly trivial.

Maybe it was time to take his skills and use them for some-thing that offered more promise, something that might actually turn out to matter. Maybe this was his chance to solve a mystery with real consequences. If not now, when?

Tay scooped up the fake Interpol passport and credentials, pushed them back into the manila envelope, and looked around the table.

"Well, shit," he shrugged. "I guess you've got me."

THIRTY-THREE

A FTER BREAKFAST, AUGUST and the Conductor adjourned to a room at the back of the house that had been kitted out as a secure meeting area.

The space had soundproofed walls, no windows, and a single door, also soundproofed. August had always suspected the space had originally been constructed as a servants' room, which felt entirely fitting every time the Conductor hauled him into it to work him over about the details of some operation.

August and the Conductor sat at a round wooden table in small and somewhat uncomfortable straight-backed metal chairs with hard plastic seats. There were four other identical chairs at the table, all empty.

"Do you really think your friend Tay can do this, John?"

"I don't know. Maybe."

"It's not too late to call it off, you know. We can find another way to deal with this."

"I don't have another way, sir. I can't just call up the Agency and ask who there would like to kill me. Half of Langley would put up a hand."

"And you're absolutely certain there's no chance this was simply personal?"

"That doesn't make any sense. I'm visible enough. If someone just wanted me, they could have sent someone into Secrets most any time and popped me. They didn't have to go through all this. No, whoever is behind this wants to kill the Band, not just me."

The Conductor nodded, but he didn't say anything.

"Besides," August continued, "the way the bomb's trigger mechanism was designed makes it clear that they wanted to be sure all three of us were inside before it detonated. They wanted to get the whole team."

"Perhaps they just wanted to make sure *you* were inside the room. After all, they had no idea the order in which the three of you would enter it."

"The whole plot was way too complicated just to take out one person. The bomb in Hong Kong was set up to take out an entire team in a very public way. Somebody thought it would expose the Band and cripple us, maybe even shut us down altogether."

August fidgeted for a moment, not certain he should ask the question that was in his mind, but then he just asked it.

"Is there something going on here in Washington that I should know, sir? Something that might explain why the Band is under attack?"

"This president doesn't much like the Agency. He doesn't trust them." The Conductor paused and thought for a moment. "This president does like the Band. He does trust us."

"But the Band can't replace the whole Central Intelligence Agency. Nobody in his right mind would think that was possible."

"Not many people know what we can do and what we cannot do. Over the years we've become something of a myth."

"A myth?"

"Nobody really knows who we are or how we operate. A few people know the president has some sort of means by which he can take action without going through the normal mechanisms of government, but they don't know what it is. And that scares the crap out of absolutely everybody."

"I can understand why the Agency might feel threatened by us, sir, but it's hard to believe they would try to protect themselves by killing Americans who are essentially in the same business they are."

"Who was it who said, *No matter how cynical you get in Washington, it's hard to keep up?*"

"I think that was you, sir."

The Conductor pursed his lips and tilted his head slightly as if struggling to bring something into focus in spite of having forgotten his glasses.

"It was, wasn't it?"

August smiled, but he didn't say anything.

"This town is defined by power, John. If you have it, you matter. If you don't have it, you don't matter. There are some people at the Agency who might do almost anything if they thought the Agency was going to lose power, and therefore *they* were going to lose power."

"Like Rebecca Sternwood?"

"She's just a bureaucrat. Somebody spun her a story. They might have told her, for example, that you and your people were former intelligence officers turned mercenaries who were trying to kidnap an American double agent being planted with the Chinese. Then they had her put together an operation to take you out and make it look like the Chinese had done it to eliminate the agent. You would have believed a story like that, wouldn't you, John?"

"I would have if it had come from you, sir."

"I think that's more or less what happened with Miss Sternwood as well. Her superiors laid out a convincing scenario as to why they wanted her to mount an operation to kill you. She probably felt all warm and fuzzy that they were willing to trust her with such an important job, and she went after you as hard as she could."

"Then you think she's just an innocent here?"

"I wouldn't put it that way. I just don't think she came up with this operation herself."

"Then who did?"

"No idea."

"Do you know who this woman's superiors are?"

"We know who the organization charts say they are, but that doesn't help very much. We have to get Rebecca Sternwood to tell us why she did this, and we have to get her to tell us who directed her to do it. Whether she knows that she's telling us doesn't matter, but we need to hear it directly from her."

"And when we find out for sure who was behind the Hong Kong bombing, what are we going to do, sir?"

"I guess that's the real question, isn't it, John? What do you think we should do?"

"I'm sure you already know the answer to that, sir."

"I feel pretty much the same way, but this may not be quite that simple."

"I think it's exactly that simple. Somebody tried to kill me and my team. When they find out they failed, they're not likely just to shrug it off and go out for a nice dinner. Unless we put them out of business, they'll come after us again. What's complicated about that?"

"You may be right. Let me think about it."

The Conductor pushed back his chair and stood up, signaling to August their meeting was over, but then he hesitated.

"I haven't questioned your decision to bring Tay into this, John, but I have to tell you I'm not entirely comfortable with it."

"He has skills I don't have, sir, skills I need right now, and I trust him absolutely."

"Maybe you do, but bringing in strangers isn't how we work around here."

"Sam isn't a stranger. Not to me."

"Maybe not, but he is to me, and the worst thing about this business is that you learn to doubt everything and everybody."

"Do you doubt me?"

"Of course not."

"Then trust me about bringing Tay in just like you trust me about everything else."

"For God's sake, John, there aren't two dozen people in the whole government of the United States who know for sure that we exist, let alone who we are and what we really do, and now Tay knows all about us. He's not even an American."

"Yes, he is. His father was an American."

"Tay has an American passport? He's an American citizen?"

August hesitated. "Not technically."

"Not technically? What does that mean? Either he is or he isn't."

"Sam doesn't have an American passport because he never formally claimed American citizenship."

"Why not?"

"I guess he doesn't really like Americans all that much, sir."

The Conductor sighed heavily and shook his head.

"He's your responsibility, John. If I have to hang him, I'm going to string you up right alongside him."

August figured the Conductor was just kidding.

Probably.

PART 4
CONCLUSIONE

THIRTY-FOUR

"T HIS IS A nice car," Tay said as Claire drove out of the alleyway behind the safe house and pulled into traffic. "Is it yours?"

She glanced at Tay out of the corner of her eye to see if he was joking. He didn't look like he was.

"The Band never has any trouble coming up with whatever we need," Claire said. "Cars, airplanes, weapons, you name it."

When he had been a cop in Singapore, Tay had had to jump up and down and flap his arms every time he needed a new ballpoint pen. Americans had it too easy. And what really annoyed him was how they seemed to feel entitled to have it easy.

"What kind of car is this?" he asked.

"It's a Mustang."

Tay had never heard of a Mustang. They didn't have them in Singapore and he didn't know anything about American cars. Not about any kind of cars from anywhere, to be entirely truthful, since he had never owned a car and had never wanted to. Singapore was an island with a decent mass transit system and a lot of taxis. Cars were more of a nuisance there than anything. Where was he going to drive to? Indonesia?

Tay had to admit the Mustang was sharp looking, shiny black on the outside and saddle-tan leather on the inside. He could certainly understand its appeal to some people. It even had an unexpected appeal to him.

"Maybe I'll get one," Tay said.

"You probably ought to think about getting a driver's license first."

"I can do that. Driving's not exactly rocket science. Say, do you suppose I can get a Mustang with the steering wheel on the other side where it's supposed to be?"

Claire gave him a look, but she said nothing.

Tay was just messing with Claire, of course. He had no intention of buying any kind of a car, and certainly not an American one. On the other hand, there *was* something about the Mustang. Maybe he ought to at least think about it a little before he blew off the idea completely.

THE MUSTANG WAS a bit on the small and intimate side, but there were a lot of worse things, Tay thought, than being trapped in a small and intimate car with Claire. As long as he didn't stumble into some unexpected way to make a fool out of himself, it was an arrangement that held real possibilities.

Tay had never been very good with women. Maybe it was mostly a matter of proximity and practice. He hadn't been around that many women in his life, at least not at close quarters such as the Mustang provided, so he hadn't had much experience in trying to figure out how not to come across as a complete meatball on those occasions when he did get up close with them. So here he was now, sitting less than an arm's length away from a genuinely attractive and interesting woman, and his customary feelings of apprehension were bubbling away energetically right beneath the surface.

In spite of his nervousness, however, things seemed to be

working out okay so far. Here he and Claire were, right next to each other, and they were carrying on a perfectly normal conversation and behaving like old and intimate friends. Well... intimate, he supposed, if you used the word in its very broadest sense, of course.

Maybe it was the car that was making all this feel so normal. Maybe if he had bought a Mustang twenty years ago, he would be a different man today.

Probably not.

Claire was much too young for him. He completely understood that. Still, for just a moment, Tay felt himself wishing he were a younger and better-looking man. For just a moment, he wanted to be everything other than what he was. The folly of age spared no one, he realized, not even him.

Oh Lord, Tay thought to himself, *don't let me turn into an old fool here.*

Then the feeling passed as quickly as it had appeared. Wanting something you couldn't have, and trying to be something you could never be, were a way of life for some people. Tay just wasn't one of them.

THEY DROVE SOUTH on the George Washington Parkway past Arlington Cemetery and turned off into a bland-looking neighborhood where the streets were lined with undistinguished medium-size apartment buildings, all of which looked more or less alike to Tay.

"Rebecca Sternwood's apartment building is up here on the left," Claire said.

She scooped her iPhone up off the Mustang's console, glanced at it out of the corner of her eye, and tapped an icon with her thumb.

"Her car is in the garage at her apartment building so she's still probably at home. We don't have any information to suggest that she rides with anyone else or uses public transportation."

"And your phone just told you all that?"

Claire handed the phone to Tay. He looked down at the screen and saw a map with a blinking green dot on it.

"Tracker. Woods put it on her car last night."

Where would Americans be without their toys?

That was what Tay thought, but he kept it to himself. He just nodded and put Rebecca's phone back down on the console.

"That's her building there," Claire said, pointing through the windshield.

The building she indicated was new-looking, five stories tall and constructed of red brick with large black-framed windows divided into small panes. The effect was to make it look vaguely like some industrial warehouse which had been reclaimed and turned into apartments for high-salaried young urban professionals.

The building's main entrance was at the exact center of its front, but it didn't look like a building where many of the residents came and went on foot. Like most Americans, Tay guessed, they drove themselves wherever they went in automobiles, frequently quite large ones. The real action would be the residents coming and going through the garage. He wondered where it was.

"The garage entrance is on the next cross street," Claire said just then, almost as if she were reading his mind. "Look off to the right."

Sure enough, Tay looked to the right and saw a white Mercedes sedan drive up a ramp from what was obviously an underground garage and turn away from them.

The neighborhood didn't look promising as a place to take the woman unaware. He wouldn't be surprised if she never set foot on the streets here at all. They were utilitarian passageways for automobiles, not centers of urban life like the streets in his neighborhood in Singapore. He doubted anyone spent any more time on them than they absolutely had to.

"Can we do a couple of loops through the neighborhood?" Tay asked, "just to get an idea of how she probably lives around here."

But Tay was just being thorough. He could see already.

Rebecca Sternwood *didn't* live around here. Nobody lived around here. It was one of those American neighborhoods in which upper middle-income workers were warehoused, but in which very little real, actual living was done.

They drove the streets around the building for ten minutes or so, but Tay saw nothing to cause him to change his mind.

Maybe he ought to just walk up to her apartment and ring the doorbell. After all, the simplest approach to a problem was usually the best. Complicated, well planned undertakings frequently ended up biting you in the ass. It was the simple plans that worked.

"Where's her office from here?" Tay asked.

"Everybody always thinks of Langley, Virginia, when they think of the CIA, but the Agency has expanded so much since 9/11 that now it's spread all over this area in dozens of different buildings. Rebecca Sternwood's office is in a building on Richmond Highway, close to Reagan Airport. The area's called Crystal City."

"Is that close to here?"

"Maybe fifteen minutes south."

"So, she just gets into her car in the garage of her apartment building every morning and drives fifteen minutes south to her office, then she drives fifteen minutes back home every evening. Does she ever go anywhere else?"

"According to the intelligence we have, she stops for breakfast a couple of mornings every week at an IHOP near here."

"What in the world is that?"

"You don't have IHOP's in Singapore?"

"*I hop?* What in God's name are you talking about?"

"Not I hop, IHOP. It's an acronym. International House of Pancakes. It's a sort of diner. But they don't call it International

House of Pancakes anymore. They just call it IHOP. I guess they thought that sounded better."

"How could anyone be dumb enough to think that?"

Tay knew that if he lived to be a hundred he would never understand Americans. *IHOP?* Good God.

"You want to check it out?" Claire asked.

"How could I possibly resist going to see a place named I hop?"

THE IHOP TURNED out to be a bland looking one-story structure set at the front of a Target Store parking lot.

The walls were whitewashed concrete, and blue canvas awnings shaded each of the large windows providing diners a view of very little other than cars scattered over a parking lot. The main entrance was capped by an out-of-proportion tower with a blue peaked roof that made the whole building look as if it had been drawn by a child.

"Let's drive all the way around it," Tay suggested. "Maybe there's another entrance on the other side."

There wasn't. There was a dumpster with a metal door next to it that appeared to provide access to the kitchen, but there was no other entrance.

They drove back to the front, parked, and looked around.

"Is the parking lot always this empty?" Tay asked Claire.

"I don't know. Probably more or less. It's a pretty big lot."

"Then we could approach her when she parks her car without anyone else around," Tay said. "I like it."

"Inside might work better."

Tay peered doubtfully at the building, but he couldn't see into it very well from where they were.

"If she thinks other people are listening to us," he said, "that will affect what she says. Out here in the parking lot she'll know that we're not being overheard."

"But she might feel conspicuous standing here talking to you and that won't help either."

Tay still looked doubtful.

"Maybe the place won't be crowded when she gets here," Claire said. "Let's go in and look around."

INSIDE, THE IHOP was a lot bigger than it looked. Two double lines of booths upholstered in brown plastic were laid out in an L-shape around a kitchen and service area. There must have been sixty or more of them in all and only a dozen were occupied.

"Let's sit down," Claire said. "I'm hungry."

"I don't like pancakes."

"They have all sorts of stuff, not just pancakes. Come on."

Claire walked a short distance down the row of booths closest to the windows and slid into one well away from any of the other customers. Tay sat opposite her and picked up one of the plastic-coated menus lying on the table. It was illustrated with impossibly colorful pictures of all sorts of very American-looking food and was so lengthy that Tay was still turning the pages when a young black woman wearing a blue apron came over to their booth.

"Welcome to IHOP," she announced, and her warm and apparently genuine smile made the phrase come across as less automatic than it probably was. "Can I get you something to drink?"

"Coffee for me," Claire said.

The waitress looked at Tay.

"I'll have a coffee, too," he said.

That caused her to smile some more.

"I love your accent, honey. Where you from?"

"I'm from Singapore."

The woman's face took on a look of puzzlement. "Where?"

"Singapore. It's near…"

JAKE NEEDHAM

Tay looked at Claire for help.

"It's near China," Claire finished.

"It is?" Tay asked.

Now the waitress looked thoroughly baffled.

"Well, wherever it is, you sure got a cute accent, honey. You all ready to order?"

Tay's mouth opened in astonishment as Claire ordered something she called a Rooty Tooty Fresh and Fruity.

"You just made that up," he said to her.

"No, really. It's on the menu. Pancakes with fruit."

"I don't believe you."

"It's real good, honey," the waitress put in. "Really. You ought to try it."

Claire was grinning so hugely that Tay thought her face might be in danger of cracking.

"I'll just have plain pancakes," Tay said. "With bacon, please."

"I thought you didn't like pancakes," Claire said.

Tay just grunted. He knew he had said that, but the truth was he didn't actually remember ever eating any pancakes before, although of course he knew what they were.

"Okay," the waitress said. "Then that's one stack of pancakes with bacon, and one Rooty Tooty Fresh and Fruity. Coffee coming up right away."

"Near China?" Tay asked when the waitress had gone.

"That's the easiest way to explain it. Most Americans think Asia is China and nowhere else in Asia amounts to anything."

"They're pretty much right about that," Tay grumbled.

THE FOOD CAME so quickly Tay couldn't believe it. He might not be too fond of most things American, but he had to give Americans their due. Most everything worked better in America than anywhere else in the world.

Tay and Claire chatted inconsequentially while they ate. It

260

had been a while since Tay had eaten a meal alone with a beautiful woman and he had to admit he was rather enjoying it. He had forgotten how much pleasure a warm, melodious voice and a gentle, companionable smile added to even the simplest of meals. The pancakes tasted better than he expected, too.

At the same time Tay was eating and taking pleasure in Claire's company, however, he was doing his job, too. He was watching and taking careful note of the pattern of activity in the dining room.

"This could work if it's no more crowded than this," he said when they had refilled their coffee cups from the carafe the waitress had left them. "She comes here all the time so she'll be comfortable and off guard. If there's no one sitting in the booths on either side of us or directly across the aisle, we're not going to be overheard."

"If it's too crowded, we always have the parking lot as a backup."

"How often does she eat here?" Tay asked.

"The intelligence profile says she has breakfast here once or twice a week."

Tay peered at the empty plate smeared with syrup on which his stack of pancakes had been served.

"If it was any more often than that, she'd probably be the size of a small house," he sighed. "Do we know the last time she was here?"

"That's not in the profile. I can ask."

"Don't bother. Whenever it was, either we're going to get lucky or we're not. Let's give it a couple of days. If she hasn't turned up by then, we'll just walk right up to the door of her apartment and knock on it."

"Works for me."

. . .

B UT THEY DIDN'T have to go to her apartment and knock on the door.

Because they *were* lucky.

The very next morning, Rebecca Sternwood left her apartment just before eight o'clock. Tay and Claire watched her car roll out of the underground garage and followed her as she drove straight to the IHOP, parked out front, and went inside for breakfast.

She didn't have the slightest inkling that the life she had so carefully built for herself was all but over.

THIRTY-FIVE

"**M**ISS STERNWOOD?"

When Rebecca Sternwood glanced up, Tay's first thought was how interesting looking she was. He had caught glimpses of her in the Pattaya surveillance videos, of course, and he had surmised she was an attractive woman, but he wasn't entirely prepared for how arresting her appearance actually was now that she was right in front of him.

She had a high forehead with sculptured brows, and her shiny black hair was pulled back tightly against her head and wrapped into a tight bun at the back. Her complexion was so pale that her oval face, accented by high, wide cheekbones and ending in an oddly square, mannish-looking chin, appeared nearly translucent.

But it was her eyes that drew most of Tay's attention. Big, almond-shaped eyes that were more green than brown and were scattered with golden flecks. They were a cat's eyes, and they utterly riveted him.

She wore a dark blue blazer cut wide on her shoulders and under it a white turtleneck that appeared to be cashmere. It was an expensive look, one well suited to a woman who looked just as expensive.

Attractive women in Tay's experience knew they were attractive and were accustomed to using their attractiveness to manipulate the people they dealt with, the men in particular, of course. He was supposed to put *her* off balance, not the other way around, so it wouldn't do for Rebecca Sternwood to dismiss him as a typical male seeking her attention and approval before he had even spoken a word to her.

What Tay wanted was to plant in her a tiny seed of unease as to what this was all about, so as he stood there beside the booth looking down at her he worked to keep his face completely still and his eyes utterly empty. He wondered if he succeeded.

Rebecca Sternwood looked back at him, her face as empty as he hoped his was, and pursed her lips slightly, either trying to remember who he was or striking a pose that was supposed to demonstrate that she was doing her best to remember. After a moment, she leaned forward against the table on her forearms and nudged her coffee cup slightly to one side. When she finally spoke, it was in a voice that was low pitched and throaty. Tay wondered if she was a smoker.

"I'm sorry," she said. "I'm terrible with faces. You'll have to remind me who you are."

Tay doubted she was terrible with faces. He really did.

He sat down in the booth directly opposite her and mirrored her posture of leaning forward on the table with folded arms.

"We've never met," he said.

"Whoever you are then, you're very rude. I didn't invite you to sit here."

Tay liked her voice, particularly its slightly husky tone. The sound of it made him think of Lauren Bacall in some old black and white film he had seen once on late night television, although he couldn't come up with the name of the film right off the top of his head.

"I thought you would prefer to have this conversation away from your office," Tay said, "but I'm happy to go there if you prefer. You're in Crystal City, aren't you? Or, here's an idea, maybe you could reserve a conference room at Langley and we could have our conversation there. That would save you a trip to explain everything to your superiors when we're done talking."

She was good. Tay had to give her that. She never even blinked at his demonstration that he not only knew who she was but he also knew that she worked for the CIA and even where her office was. She just looked back at him and smiled and frowned at the same time.

"Who are you?"

"I'm Inspector Samuel Tay."

"Inspector? You're some kind of policeman?"

"I'm an investigator for Interpol."

She nodded slightly and seemed to think about that.

"Do you have identification?" she asked.

Tay removed the leather badge case that the Conductor had given him from his inside jacket pocket, opened it, and placed it on the table in front of her. Her eyes went first to the gold badge that said INTERPOL and then to the identification card with his picture that identified him as a Criminal Intelligence Officer.

Without unfolding her arms, she pulled the badge case toward her with one finger. She appeared to study the identification card with some care, but she did not pick it up. After a few moments, Tay reached over, closed the badge case, and put it back in his pocket.

Had she bought the Interpol scam? He supposed he would find out soon enough now.

For a long while, Rebecca Sternwood said nothing at all. She simply sat, arms still folded on the table in front of her, and looked at Tay with that half smile, half frown on her face like she was trying to decide how much potential he might have. She made up her mind far more quickly than he would really have liked. She appeared to conclude that he had little or none.

"What do you want?" she asked in that smoky voice Tay had already decided he quite liked.

"You are aware of the explosion that occurred about two weeks ago at the Cordis Hotel in Hong Kong, are you not?"

And just like that Rebecca Sternwood blinked. Her facial expression never changed, but Tay saw it for just a moment in her eyes. She blinked.

"I may have heard or seen something about it," she said, looking away. "I really don't remember."

"Does your job include any responsibility for the Agency's activities in Hong Kong?"

She tilted back her head and laughed, apparently quite genuinely. "Come now, Inspector. Surely you know I'm not going to answer that."

"The explosion was caused by a bomb."

"Was it? I don't recall hearing that before, I really don't, but if you say so."

"The bomb was placed in room 1121."

Rebecca Sternwood's face remained still, but Tay saw the blink again in her eyes.

"Was that bomb a CIA operation?" he asked her.

"Oh my, Inspector, why would you even *think* of asking me something like that?"

"Because I figured you should have a chance to get out in front of this. Three people are dead. We want to know who is responsible for that and we're starting with you."

Just at that moment the waitress appeared with her breakfast order. A plate of sliced fruit and a buttered English muffin.

"More coffee, honey?" the waitress asked. When Rebecca nodded, she refilled her cup from an aluminum carafe and then put the carafe on the table.

"Would you like something, sir?" the waitress asked Tay.

"No, nothing."

"Just some coffee maybe?"

"No."

"Bring him a cup," Rebecca Sternwood cut in.

They sat in silence until the waitress had returned with the cup for Tay, filled it from the aluminum carafe, and left them again.

The coffee smelled good. Tay had only had one cup that morning and frankly he needed more. Tay took a sip, then another.

"I have to tell you I'm very impressed, Inspector. I still have no idea how you found me here. If I did work for the Agency, I'm sure I would be equally curious how you found that out, too. Nevertheless, I'm sure you must already realize I'm not going to answer any of the questions you're asking me, so may I ask you one instead?"

Tay nodded slightly, but said nothing.

"What is it you really want?"

"I've already told you. I want to give you a chance to get in front of this before it pulls you down."

"But why would you possibly think that I would know anything at all about this explosion in Hong Kong, regardless of who you think I am and who I might or might not work for?"

"Because we have you on surveillance video."

Rebecca Sternwood laughed again. Then she ate a slice of plum, drank some coffee, and took a bite out of the English muffin.

"This is all becoming clear now, Inspector. You have obviously mistaken me for somebody else. Didn't you say this explosion occurred in Hong Kong a few weeks ago?"

Tay nodded.

"I haven't been in Hong Kong for at least a year, probably longer. It couldn't possibly be me on your video."

Her face reflected nothing, but Tay could see the relief in her eyes as she ate some more of the muffin and followed it with a slice of orange.

That was when he leaned back, folded his hands in his lap, and delivered the kill shot.

"The surveillance video we have is from the Pattaya Hilton. It was taken when you were in Thailand setting up the victims."

This time even Rebecca Sternwood couldn't cover her reaction. She looked as if she had been poleaxed. Her mouth opened slightly and her eyes flicked from side to side like she was contemplating fleeing.

"We have most of it now," Tay said, "and I'll get the rest. Then it will be too late for you to help yourself."

She lifted her coffee cup and Tay watched her hand to see if it was shaking. It wasn't. The coolness of her natural demeanor had reestablished itself with remarkable speed. Tay found himself admiring that a little.

"You have no legal jurisdiction here, Inspector."

"That's true. Just think of me as like Batman. I drop in, grab you, and hold you for the local cops. In this case, the FBI."

"Batman, huh?" Rebecca Sternwood chuckled in a throaty way that Tay couldn't help noticing was extremely sexy. "I'd always pictured Batman as taller. And younger."

That last part hurt. Boy, did it hurt, but he tried hard not to show it.

Tay reached into his shirt pocket, took out a white card about the size of a business card, and placed it on the table. She glanced down and saw that it was blank except for a single telephone number written on it in black ink.

"That's the number of the phone I'm using here in the US. Call me if you change your mind and decide you want to talk to me."

"Maybe I could just turn on the Bat Signal."

Tay didn't even smile.

"I won't change my mind, you know."

Tay shrugged and stood up.

"It's your funeral, Miss Sternwood. We're going to hang some people for this. I'm sorry you have to be one of them. Thanks for the coffee."

Then he walked away from the booth and out of the dining room and was gone.

. . .

TAY CROSSED THE parking lot and slid into the passenger seat of the Mustang.

"Well, what do you think?" Claire asked.

"I don't know. She was surprised, of course, but..." Tay trailed off. "I'm not sure I sold it," he finished quickly.

"You mean she didn't believe the whole Interpol thing?"

"Oh, she believed that all right, but she didn't panic when I told her I was investigating the Hong Kong bombing. She's a cool one."

"She wasn't shocked?"

"She only flinched a couple of times and it was hardly noticeable. Mostly she just sat there with a little half smile on her face and looked at me. You know, I never realized from the surveillance video what an arresting-looking woman she is."

Tay glanced over at Claire and then did a double take. She was staring at him like he had suddenly grown an extra pair of ears.

"What?" he asked.

"I've never heard you say before that you thought a woman was attractive."

"You don't think she is?"

"It's not that. I thought you were gay."

For a moment, Tay wasn't sure he had heard Claire correctly.

"I mean," she continued, "you've never married and you never seem to take any interest in women, so I just assumed—"

"That I'm *gay*?" Tay sputtered. "You can't be serious."

Claire pulled a face and looked away.

"Now I've put my foot in it," she said. "I really didn't mean to insult you."

"You didn't insult me. I mean, I'm not gay, but it's not an insult for you to think I might be. There's nothing wrong with being gay. Absolutely nothing. I know a lot of... actually, no, I don't know a lot of people who are gay, at least I don't think I

269

do, but if I did know a lot of people who were gay then I'm sure I would think that every one of them was an absolutely fine—"

Claire giggled. "You're babbling, Sam."

Tay abruptly stopped talking and looked at his hands.

"Yes, I guess I am, but you bowled me over there and I'm still reeling a little from that. No one has ever said they thought I was gay before."

"Maybe they didn't say it to your face, but a fiftyish guy who's never been married? A lot of people always think he's gay whether they say so or not."

Tay's mouth slowly began to open. Could that really be true? Was it possible that behind his back people had been speculating for years, decades even, over whether he might be gay and no one had ever said anything to him about it? Surely that couldn't be, could it?

"You're not gay then? Not even a little bit?"

Tay was baffled as to how to respond to that.

A little bit gay? What in the world did that mean? How could anyone be *a little bit gay?*

He decided this conversation was complicated enough already, so he wasn't about to ask. He just went with the simplest possible answer.

"No, I'm not gay. Not even a little bit."

"Okay, then I was wrong. I apologize."

"No need to apologize. I told you that, if I were gay, I—"

"Let's not go through all that again. I'll take your word that you're not prejudiced against gay men, okay? Just tell me what this really attractive woman said when you told her you were investigating the Hong Kong bombing for Interpol and that the investigation had led you to her."

"She didn't say much. She just smiled."

"Which I'm sure you loved."

"What's that supposed to mean?"

Claire made a little snorting noise.

"Jesus, you men are such goddamned simpletons! Put you in

front of a good-looking woman and you all become little boys again, squirming around and hoping for her approval. Maybe we would have gotten a better result if you *were* gay."

"I suppose I ought to resent that."

"Resent it or not. I don't really care. You were supposed to beat her up, Sam. Slap her around. Scare the crap out of her."

"What I told her will either scare her or it won't," Tay shrugged. "The tone of voice I used or whether I smiled has nothing to do with it. She thinks now that Interpol has somehow connected her to the bombing. Me screaming and frowning wouldn't add anything to it."

Claire made that snorting sound again, but she said nothing else.

"August has her phones covered, a tracker on her car, and a team of watchers ready to go." Tay shrugged again. "Now she does what she does."

"You seem awfully fatalistic about this. What if it doesn't work?"

"It doesn't matter whether I think it will work. It's still what we've got."

Claire sat looking out the window across the parking lot.

"Look, Claire, you and I come at the world from entirely different places. You're an operator. You try to shape the world, to make it behave the way you want it to. I'm an investigator. I just observe the world. I watch and collect and put information together. An investigation goes where it goes and I follow."

"And what if this one goes nowhere?"

"Then I'll have a smoke and think up another way to do whatever I'm trying to do."

Tay fished in his jacket pocket until he found his Marlboros and a box of matches.

"Relax, Claire. Stop trying to pound the world into submission. You'll never do it."

THIRTY-SIX

REBECCA KNEW SHE had to do something to kill this investigation before it went anywhere, but she wasn't quite sure what that should be. She sat still and thought about it while she drank some more coffee she didn't really want.

How had Interpol connected the Agency and, perhaps more pressing right at the moment, how had it connected her personally to the Hong Kong bombing? She hadn't set foot in Hong Kong at any time when the operation was being carried out. Other than meeting John August in Pattaya to give him the phony assignment that sent him to Hong Kong, she had never gone anywhere near the operation.

Now, barely two weeks after the bombing, this Interpol investigator suddenly shows up when she's having breakfast near her apartment in Washington D.C. *At the IHOP for God's sake.* Not only had he somehow connected her to the bombing, he knew she worked for the Agency, he knew where she lived, and he knew where she had breakfast.

What was his name? Tan? No, that wasn't right. Tay. That was it: Tay.

Tay was a Singaporean name, wasn't it? Did it have any

significance that Interpol had assigned a Singaporean to the case? Was it a message that the Chinese government was determined to nail the Agency for this? Tay didn't really look that Chinese, not really, but Singapore was almost a Chinese city, wasn't it? Or pretty much the next thing to it.

She wasn't sure what to make of Tay. He was such a bland and nondescript human being that he could disappear in a telephone booth, or he could if telephone booths still existed. That made him an easy man to dismiss as insignificant, but her instincts were screaming at her not to do that. There was something about him that reminded her of... well, what?

Then she realized what it was.

That old television show from twenty or thirty years ago that she used to see on late night television when she was in school and trying to avoid studying. *Columbo*, it was called. Who was that actor, the guy with the glass eye... Peter Falk. Yeah, that was it. Peter Falk played a rumpled, bumbling detective most people thought was an insignificant jerk, but he wasn't really bumbling at all and he always ended up bringing people down because they didn't take him seriously.

Tay reminded her of the Peter Falk character in that show. He even looked a little like Peter Falk, now that she thought about it. All he needed was the wrinkled trench coat.

Tay said he had surveillance video of her at the Pattaya Hilton. That meant he had not only connected her to the bombing, but he knew exactly how and when and where she had set it up. Only three people knew she had gone to Pattaya to send John August and his team to Hong Kong. Only three people. And she was absolutely certain neither of the other two had told anyone since it would make them just as culpable in this thing as she was.

It was plainly impossible that Interpol could have found out she had been in Pattaya and connected her to the bombing.

But, just as plainly, somehow Tay had.

· · ·

S HE PUT A twenty on the table to cover the check. Way too much, but she really didn't feel like talking to a waitress right then, not even to ask for the check and pay it, so she left more than enough to cover whatever her breakfast had cost and wrote off the excess as a contribution to her general wellbeing.

As she walked across the parking lot to her car, her eyes swept the area, but she saw no sign of Tay. If he knew so much about her that he could walk in on her while she was having breakfast at the IHOP, then he probably didn't need to watch her. She shuddered slightly as she slid into the driver's seat of her car. She felt naked and exposed, which she knew was exactly how Tay wanted her to feel.

Looking out over the beautiful IHOP parking lot, she took several deep breaths, got a grip on herself, and started thinking again.

She had used Agency personnel in Hong Kong for the mechanics of the operation. Local operators had obtained and placed the bomb at the Cordis Hotel, but her contact had been limited to one man and he had directed everyone else. Frank Ward was the only person in Hong Kong who could connect her with the operation.

The story she gave to Frank was similar to the one she gave to August, that a defector was going to expose dozens of American agents and his defection had to be stopped before he disappeared into the vastness of China. Ward hadn't questioned the operation. She had known him long enough that he had simply assumed that, coming from her, it had to have been authorized at the highest level. Besides, there was nothing in the operation so unusual that it raised eyebrows.

The bomb was a little showy maybe, that part did stand out a bit, but there were a lot of explanations for the way she had chosen to deal with the problem. Maybe she was just trying to create a superficial level of deniability. An explosion at the hotel could be explained away as a gas leak if no one looked too closely, or perhaps it could even be blamed on the defector himself who could have been trying to cover his tracks and screwed it up. A bullet in the back of his head, however, would have been what it was. No possible ambiguity there, superficial or otherwise.

Could Frank Ward have dropped the dime on her with Interpol? That didn't even bear thinking about. Frank was an old pro. If anyone had started sniffing around Agency personnel and asking questions about the explosion, Frank would have faded right away. There wasn't a chance in hell he would have admitted knowing anything about it, much less offered up her name. Still, she was going to have to cover that base, at least find out what kind of inquiries Interpol had made of the Agency in Hong Kong.

She looked at her watch. It was only a little after eight. Was Hong Kong twelve or thirteen hours ahead of Washington at this time of year? Thirteen, she was pretty sure, which meant it would be after nine o'clock at night there.

She would have to wait twelve hours to reach Frank through the secure communications at the station and she didn't want to wait twelve hours. And maybe leaving a record of her talking to Hong Kong Station immediately after she had been rousted by Tay wasn't such a good idea anyway, but the only alternative was to call Frank at home tonight using a non-secure phone. She mulled that over for a moment and came to an easy conclusion.

Fuck security.

She wanted to know what Interpol knew about the station's involvement, and she wanted to know it right fucking now.

S HE MIGHT BE willing to run a small risk with security by talking to Frank on an open line, but she wasn't an idiot. There were still some basic precautions she could easily take.

The IHOP was located in the parking lot of a Target Store and five minutes later she was inside Target buying a cheap, prepaid mobile phone. She didn't even know flip phones were still being made, but there they were, half a dozen different brands of them.

She grabbed one at random, made certain it was a standard unlocked GSM phone, then picked up something T-Mobile called a Tourist SIM Kit. It contained a prepaid SIM card good for three weeks and loaded with more talk time than she had any use for. She paid cash for the phone and the SIM and as soon as she was back in her car she punched out the SIM and inserted it into the phone. Good to go.

She checked the number assigned to the SIM she had just bought, looked up Frank's number in the Agency phone she had with her, and sent a text.

Call 406-555-1278 immediately. Langley.

She didn't want to have her name in a text that could conceivably be retrieved someday, and she figured using Langley as a signature would be good enough to get Frank to take the text seriously and call the number. Hong Kong Station did so much flaky shit that her text probably wouldn't even move the needle on Frank's weirdness gauge.

Frank could be anywhere, she knew, but it was after nine at night and with just a little luck he would be in Hong Kong and at home. She had no doubt that Frank kept a few burners at home and surely he had at least one he'd never used before. With him on an unused prepaid and her on the one she had just bought, that was about as secure as they could hope to be without using Agency communication facilities, and she had no intention of doing that.

It was less than five minutes before the phone she had just bought rang. She hadn't bothered to set a ring tone for it, but now she wished she had. It went off with a noise that sounded like a World War Two air raid siren. Why in God's name did anyone think that was a good idea?

"Hello, Frank. I'm sure you recognize my voice, but please don't use my name."

There was a long pause, which made sense, and then after maybe ten seconds Frank Ward said, "Okay."

"And when we've finished this conversation, please destroy the phone you are using now. The number I'm on is for one-time use. Are we clear?"

"Crystal."

Rebecca described being ambushed in the IHOP by the man who identified himself as Inspector Tay of Interpol, and she described Tay's interest in the explosion at the Cordis Hotel.

"I have no idea why he would be asking me about that," she concluded carefully, "but since you're there in Hong Kong I thought I'd at least ask you what you've heard from Interpol."

"Not a thing," Ward said. "Are you sure this guy was kosher?"

"He certainly wasn't some guy off the street. He…"

She paused, looking for the right way to put it.

"…appeared to know a lot about my, ah, circumstances, and his ID looked good."

"Well, it would, wouldn't it?"

"What are you saying, Frank? If Tay wasn't really Interpol, who the hell was he?"

"No idea, but no one from Interpol has been asking any questions around here. I would know if they had been."

Rebecca didn't know what to make of that. If Tay was really Interpol, why would he have come straight to her without poking around Hong Kong at all? That didn't make any sense. But if he wasn't really Interpol, how did he know as much as he obviously knew?

"What's happened with the investigation there?"

"I haven't been asking my police sources any direct questions for obvious reasons so I'm just getting a bit of gossip. It sounds like they're not even sure of the cause yet. There's a view that it was an accident of some kind, but there's also another view that a bomb was placed in a guest room. About all they know for certain is that they have three bodies."

"Have they identified the bodies yet?"

"Nope. No guests in the part of the hotel that exploded are unaccounted for, although there are a few guests who were in undamaged sections of the hotel who disappeared after the explosion. The cops don't seem to be too bothered by that. I'm sure they think there're always a certain number of people in every hotel in Hong Kong who don't particularly want to be identified, and of course they'd be right about that."

"So, you're telling me that you haven't heard from Interpol and the local cops don't have shit yet."

"That's pretty much it. They can't find the cause of the explosion. They can't even decide if it was accidental or something else. All they've really got are the bodies of the three women they can't identify."

"Wait… what?"

"I already told you. They haven't identified any of the bodies."

"But… you said they were all women?"

"Yes," Frank Ward said. "Three women. All Chinese."

When Rebecca said nothing, Ward cleared his throat.

"Does that surprise you for some reason?" he asked carefully.

"I'm not sure," Rebecca said, and then fell silent.

That made no sense at all, of course, but Ward was smart enough not to ask any questions and Rebecca had no intention of telling him anything anyway, even if he did ask. Ward had managed to put in twenty years at the Agency by not asking questions he didn't need to ask, and he was hoping for maybe another ten. So, he said nothing.

"Look, Frank, if you catch any whiff of Interpol sniffing around, let me know right away, would you?"

"Sure, but…" He paused to think about how best to put it.

"Do you want me to let you know through official channels or—"

"Call me on my personal cell number. You have it, don't you?"

"Yes, I have it."

"Just leave a general message. Say something like *Your friends have been here,* and then I'll get back to you for the details."

"Got it."

That left nothing else to say and, not being one for small talk, Rebecca immediately cut the connection.

S HE SAT IN her car thinking over the conversation she'd just had with Frank Ward as she popped the SIM out of the burner phone and snapped it between her fingers.

Three unidentified bodies.

All Chinese.

All women.

That obviously meant August was alive, and he was out there somewhere.

It wouldn't surprise her one bit if he was already looking for her.

And judging from the sudden appearance of whoever this was claiming to be an investigator from Interpol, he might have just found her.

So, was this guy Tay who claimed to be an Interpol investigator really an Interpol investigator, or was he working with August?

If it was the former, her arrest by the FBI was certainly within the realm of possibility. If it was the latter, John August would just turn up one day and kill her.

Either way, she was well and truly screwed, wasn't she?

Fuck.

THIRTY-SEVEN

OR HER NEXT call, Rebecca didn't bother with security. She was way beyond that now. She pulled her own phone from her purse and dialed a number she had memorized, a number the man she was calling didn't know she had.

When he answered, she said, "We have a problem."

"What? Who is—"

"I said we have a problem. Right now, I have the problem, but I'm about to make it your problem, too. And then *we* will have a problem."

"Rebecca?"

She said nothing.

"Is that you, Rebecca?"

"Of course it's me."

"How did you get this number?"

"I think you ought to be a lot more worried about the problem we have. I sure would if I were you."

"We're not talking on secure phones here, Rebecca. I certainly don't want to discuss—"

"I really don't give a damn right now what you want to

discuss or don't want to discuss. I am not going to go down for this alone!"

"Calm down, Rebecca. Just calm down."

"Given what just happened to me, I think I am remarkably calm. Do you want to hear what just happened to me?"

"Naturally I do, Rebecca." The man spoke in the kind of voice he might use to try to talk someone down off the ledge of a very tall building, which was exactly where Rebecca Sternwood sounded like she was right then. "I just don't think this—"

"Meet me in the same place where we met last time. Exactly the same place. One hour from now."

"One hour? I can't leave here now, Rebecca. I really can't. There are all sorts of things going on. Let me call you tomorrow morning and—"

"One hour. If you're not there, don't bother calling me tomorrow. You can just read about everything in *The Washington Post*."

"Now look here, don't you threaten—"

She cut the connection and dumped the telephone back in her purse.

D URING THE AMERICAN Civil War, a good deal of effort went into protecting Washington D.C. from invasion by the Army of the Confederacy since it lay barely fifty miles north of the rebel capital in Richmond, Virginia.

A line of earthwork fortifications reinforced with batteries of cannon was built along the south bank of the Potomac River in 1861 and 1862 and one of those fortifications was located atop a promontory called Prospect Hill which overlooked Chain Bridge, a primary route of access to Washington from Northern Virginia. This particular fortification was named Fort Marcy in honor of Randolph Marcy, the chief of staff to the Union commander, General George McClellan.

The site of old Fort Marcy is now a park administered by the National Park Service. It is a peaceful place, heavily wooded with towering trees and a carpet of pine needles covering the ground.

It is mostly silent other than for the sound of the river rushing through the narrow gorge underneath Chain Bridge and the distant whoosh of traffic on the George Washington Memorial Parkway. A few picnic tables are scattered here and there, watched over by a couple of old cannons presumably dating back to the Civil War, but the brush is thick between the trees and it largely obstructs the sight lines between the tables. There could be a couple of dozen people in the park and they would never see each other except when they arrived and departed from the parking area.

That parking area has become a popular spot for workmen and other people who spend a lot of the day with their cars. People like that take breaks there, drink a soda, maybe sneak a cigarette or look at their phone for a while, but the park itself isn't used very much, particularly not in the middle of the day. There are seldom more than a handful of people in it, and often none at all. That's why it's such a good place for a quiet conversation.

It's a good place for another reason, too. Fort Marcy Park lies between the Potomac River and the George Washington Memorial Parkway not far from the center of the city and only about a fifteen-minute drive north of the White House. More important in these particular circumstances, it is less than a mile from CIA Headquarters in Langley, Virginia.

R EBECCA STERNWOOD SAT in her car in the parking area at Fort Marcy Park and waited, although not patiently.

It had been an hour and fifteen minutes since she had made her call and the man wasn't here. What would she do if he ignored her and didn't show up? She didn't really mean what she had said about going to *The Washington Post*, at least she didn't think she did, but she certainly couldn't go to anyone higher up in the Agency. Maybe she would have to pull a Snowden and make a run for it with all the classified data she could carry. No, of course she wasn't going to do that either, but what alternatives were there left for her to get the weight of this off her?

She had undertaken an operation to kill a rogue operative who was ex-Agency and was threatening to bring down the Agency's whole Chinese network. She knew what she was doing was illegal, but it had been for a patriotic purpose, and she had done it under instructions that came from the very top of the Agency's executive leadership, at least she thought they did.

What if they tried to cut her loose now and portray *her* as the rogue? What if they tried to protect themselves by claiming they had never given her any instructions to do anything? What proof did she have that she had been acting on instructions? The more she thought about it, the lonelier and more vulnerable she felt.

The parking area was nearly deserted. A dirty white van with a collection of ladders tied to a roof carrier was parked a hundred feet or so away from her. Behind the wheel she could see a man wearing what looked like a painter's cap and coveralls who was eating a sandwich and drinking from a thermos.

The only other car in the lot was a black Mustang parked forty or fifty feet past the workman's van. A couple in the front was engaged in what appeared at a distance to be an earnest conversation. The woman was behind the wheel and she seemed to be doing all the talking, although she held a cell phone in one hand and looked as if she might be talking both to someone on the phone and to the man in the passenger seat at the same time. Or maybe she was on the phone and he was simply waiting for her to finish. She couldn't see his face since he was half turned away from the passenger window, but he didn't appear to be saying much.

Rebecca wondered for a moment if they were having a break-up conversation. Was she breaking it off with him or was he breaking it off with her? The longer she watched, the more convinced she became that it had to be one or the other.

Rebecca looked at her watch. It had been nearly an hour and a half since she had called and he still wasn't there. Was it possible he would just blow her off and not show up? Surely not. His neck was on this block as much as hers was, probably more since the operation had originated with him. If he didn't fix this or at the very least try to keep her sweet while he figured out what to do, she was a huge risk to him. He wasn't going to blow her off and hope for the best. He would be here.

Still, how much longer was she going to give him before she drove away and… well, what? That was the problem, wasn't it? Since she had no idea what she would do if she let herself get so pissed off that she left, she ground her teeth and continued to wait.

"IS THAT WHITE van one of your people?" Tay asked Claire, "or is that just some innocent jerk who wants to be left alone to eat his lunch?"

"That's strictly need to know, Sam, and you don't need to know."

"Oh, for Christ's sake, cut out the spy crap, would you? It's getting downright irritating."

Claire cut Tay a huge wink and wiggled her eyebrows. "If you're a good boy, maybe I'll give you the password to our clubhouse."

Tay shook his head, looked away, and changed the subject.

"I'm still not sure this is a good idea for us to be here. If that woman recognizes me from this morning, she'll drive off and the whole plan is in the toilet."

"She's more than a hundred feet away and can't see anything but your shoulders and the back of your head through a tinted automobile window. How obsessed with you would she have to be to recognize you just from that?"

"That's not what—"

"Yeah, that's exactly what you meant, hot shot. You men are all alike. You think every woman you come in contact with starts seeing you in her dreams."

Tay wasn't sure what to say to that so he said nothing at all.

Suddenly Claire sat up a little straighter and moved her cell phone closer to her face.

"Here we go," she said. "This could be show time."

Tay risked a quick glance back over his shoulder. A car had pulled up next to Rebecca's and parked. It was a BMW sedan in an odd color, a sort of brown-green.

"What would you call that color?" Claire asked.

"I don't know. It's more or less the same color as—"

"A goose turd."

"That's disgusting."

"Yeah, it is, isn't it?" Claire wiggled her eyebrows again. "But I'll bet that's exactly what Beemer calls it: Goose Turd Green."

A man got out of the BMW and walked around to the driver's window of Rebecca's car. He was in every way unremarkable and looked exactly like every other man Tay had seen so far around Washington: middle-aged, ordinary, forgettable.

"He's too far away for you to get a clear picture."

"Don't be silly," Claire said. "We've got more cool gadgets than you cops have ever seen. The tech people who get this file will be able to count his nose hairs if they want to."

That was an image Tay could have lived a long time without.

"What's happening?" he asked when Claire kept her eyes on the screen of her phone and said nothing else. "I don't want to keep looking back at them."

"She's getting out of the car and they're walking into the

park." Claire panned her cell phone slightly to the left. "Now they're out of sight."

Tay watched as Claire lowered her telephone and worked the buttons on its face.

"Done," she said after a moment. "Now August can send this to our tech people and they'll find a way to identify the guy."

"Surely that won't be easy. It's going to take a while, isn't it?"

Before Claire could answer, her telephone rang, almost as if it were admonishing Tay for his lack of faith.

"That was fast, John," she said when she answered.

She listened for a moment.

"Holy shit, are you *serious*?"

She listened some more.

"Okay. I understand. No, he didn't pay attention to us and he doesn't have anyone with him. He's definitely alone. No doubt about it."

More listening.

"Got it. We'll leave right now and come straight back there. Can I tell Sam?"

Then after a couple of moments she cut the connection without saying anything else.

"Can you tell me what?" Tay asked.

"Who Rebecca is talking to in the park."

"How did August find out so quickly?"

"John is with the Conductor, and the Conductor recognized the man."

"Don't keep me in suspense. Are you going to be allowed to tell me who he is?"

"His name is Zac Reed."

"That doesn't give me much to go on. Who in the world is Zac Reed?"

"Zac Reed works for the Agency."

Tay thought about that, but he didn't have to think about it for very long.

"I gather then that eliminates the possibly that Rebecca was doing this on her own. So, you now think she did what she did at the direction of the Agency?"

"Uh-huh."

"And you think her instructions came from this Zac Reed fellow?"

"Not likely. He has no operational responsibility."

"You lost me. So how does that help us?"

"August and the Conductor think the orders probably came from the man Zac Reed works for. He's the executive assistant to someone much higher up who *would* be able to set an operation like this in motion."

"How high up?"

Rebecca lifted her forefinger and pointed to the sky. "Way, way high up, Sam."

Tay waited.

"Zac Reed is the Executive Assistant to the DCI," she said after a moment.

"I don't know what that means. Do you people ever speak in actual words instead of using acronyms for everything?"

"DCI stands for Director Central Intelligence."

"The Director?"

Claire nodded tightly.

"Of the whole damn Central Intelligence Agency?"

Claire nodded again.

"You're telling me August thinks the orders to kill all of you came from the fucking Director of the fucking Central Intelligence Agency."

"That's exactly what I'm telling you."

Tay exhaled slowly between his teeth.

"Oh shit," he muttered.

"Yes," Claire said. "Exactly."

THIRTY-EIGHT

R EBECCA THOUGHT IT was hard to imagine anyone more out of place walking through the woods of Fort Marcy Park than Zac Reed.

In his gray suit, white shirt, striped tie, and brown wingtips, he looked exactly like half the briefcase-carrying lawyers you encountered on K Street almost every day in Washington. But these woods were a long way from being K Street, and Reed was a long way from being just another workaday lawyer.

He wasn't a large man, nor was he particularly small. His very ordinariness was perhaps his most outstanding personal characteristic. The only really memorable thing about Zac Reed was his eyes. His eyes were bright blue, a cold metallic blue, and they moved in sharp, quick jerks like a bird's, darting from one thing to another, then coming back to you again. Those restless, unfeeling eyes gave him something of a menacing quality. They were a reminder to Rebecca to stay wary and not to be deceived by his otherwise bland appearance.

Reed led the way along a pine-needle covered path that wound deep inside the park and Rebecca followed a pace behind his right shoulder. It had rained in the night and the damp straw gave off a rich, organic odor that reminded

Rebecca of the mulch her father collected in a huge pile at the end of their garden back when she had been a child. It was a smell she had always thought took birth and decay together in equal parts and somehow combined it into a single aroma. It had always held a soothing quality for her.

The straw was also slick in spots. When the path tilted down a slight slope toward the river, one of Rebecca's feet slipped and instinctively she reached out and grabbed Reed's shoulder to catch her balance.

He stopped walking and turned his head toward her, and his eyes darted around on her face in such a way that she felt like she was being pecked at by a sparrow. His face twisted into something that was almost a smile, but his blue eyes glinted like ice.

Off somewhere in front of them the river made a throbbing sound as it surged through the gorge below on its way to the Atlantic. It sounded to Rebecca like it would wash away all her sins if only she could reach it in time, but she knew she couldn't.

"Sorry," she said. "I slipped."

Reed turned away without a word and continued walking.

"Okay, I'm here," he said without looking back. "What's this all about?"

"It's about life without parole in a Chinese prison."

"What is that supposed to mean?"

"Do they even have parole in China? Maybe they'll just shoot us."

"What in the world are you talking about, Rebecca?"

"Interpol has connected me to the bomb at the Cordis Hotel in Hong Kong."

Abruptly, Reed stopped walking and turned around.

"What the fuck do you mean by that?" he snapped. "That's not funny."

"No," she said, "it's not."

The sound of the river off in the distance was so peaceful that she didn't want to ruin it by telling Reed what had happened and she briefly considered not doing so, but she knew that was ridiculous. She took a deep breath.

"An investigator from Interpol contacted me this morning. He said they have connected me to the Hong Kong bombing. He wanted to know if it was an Agency operation."

"*What?* Some Interpol cop came to your *office?*"

"No, actually he walked up to my table when I was having breakfast at the IHOP in Arlington this morning and sat down. He introduced himself and then he asked me if the bombing was an Agency operation."

Rebecca leaned toward Reed and tapped her index finger on his chest.

"He knows where I have *breakfast*, Zac. If he knows that, can you imagine what else he must know?"

Reed looked so stricken Rebecca wondered for a moment if he was going to faint right there in Fort Marcy Park. She glanced around and saw a picnic table just off to the side of the path and about thirty feet away.

"Let's sit down," she said, taking him by the elbow and steering him toward the table.

The picnic table looked old and weathered enough to have been there when Fort Marcy was still fighting the Civil War. It had once been green, or something close to it, but only a few stubborn flakes of paint still clung tenaciously to the table top and the two wooden benches attached to it.

Not far from the table an iron cannon on two wooden wheels sat all by itself among piles of leaves and pine straw whipped up by the wind. Presumably it had once fought battles during the Civil War and its barrel had showered fire and fury on those at whom it had been pointed.

But that was a long time ago. Now it just looked forlorn and abandoned. Rebecca knew just how it felt.

"Tell me everything," Reed said when they were both seated at the picnic table.

. . .

"HE SAID HIS name was Tay. I think he was a Singaporean. He wasn't a very impressive man. Quiet, polite, even diffident. His credentials said he was an inspector in Interpol, whatever that means."

"And he knew you work for the Agency?"

Rebecca nodded.

"Did he say how he knew?"

"No, he didn't."

"That's a little frightening."

"Yes, it is, isn't it?"

"Okay, go on."

"He asked me if I had heard about the explosion at the Cordis Hotel in Hong Kong and I told him that I might have heard something about it. That was when he asked me if I had any responsibility for the Agency's activities in Hong Kong. I told him that I was certain he knew I wasn't going to answer that."

Reed watched her intently, but he didn't interrupt.

"Then this man said he knew the explosion had been caused by a bomb and that the bomb had been placed in room 1121 of the Cordis Hotel. He asked me if the bomb was an Agency operation."

"What room was the—"

"1121."

"Good Lord," Reed said, shaking his head.

They both sat quietly for a while after that. Reed just looked off into the forest and Rebecca knew he was working through the implications of what she had told him. Rebecca didn't bother working them through. She had already thought quite enough about what Tay's sudden appearance might mean to her, so she just sat and listened to the roar of the river.

All at once, Reed turned his head and those metallic blue eyes fixed her with a merciless stare. "Did you go to Hong Kong without telling me?"

"No. I haven't been in Hong Kong in more than a year."

"Then how did this man connect you with…" Reed hesitated, looking for the right word. "…the explosion," he finished quickly.

"You can call it a bombing, Zac. That's what it was. I think we're way past euphemism here."

"Stop worrying about what I'm calling it, Rebecca. Just tell me how he connected you to it."

Rebecca leaned back and folded her arms. She realized she was rather enjoying this in spite of everything. Maybe she just liked having Zac hanging on her every word.

"Well, that's really rather interesting. He said they had me on surveillance video."

"I don't understand. Didn't you just tell me you weren't *in* Hong Kong?"

"That's right. I wasn't. The surveillance video he says he has of me is from the Pattaya Hilton. That's where I stayed when I went to August's bar in Thailand pretending to be a messenger from the Band. That was when I sent him to Hong Kong."

Rebecca stifled a smile as she watched Reed's mouth slowly open.

"Good Lord," he said again. "How in God's name could he ever have been looking for you on surveillance video at a Hilton in Thailand?"

"I've been thinking about that and it seems to me obvious someone told him a woman met with August in Pattaya a couple of days before August and his people went to Hong Kong. Tay probably didn't have a name, just a description, and that's why he was looking through surveillance tapes. He was trying to find a woman who matched the description."

"But what good would that do him? Don't tell me you were registered under—"

"Zac, I'm not a fool. Of course, I wasn't registered under my own name."

"Then I still don't get it. Even if he was able to find you and find the name you were registered under, how did that lead them to you here in Washington?"

"Because he had my picture from the surveillance tape, Zac. And somebody recognized that picture and told him who I am."

"But who could have—"

"Think, for God's sakes, Zac. It must have been August who gave Tay my description. It couldn't have been anybody else. And then when Tay found me on the surveillance tape and August confirmed that it was me, August must have used his own resources to identify me. It couldn't have been that hard for him."

"But none of that could actually have happened. August is dead."

"Obviously, he isn't."

"Rebecca, that's ridiculous. Three bodies were recovered. August and the two members of his team he took with him."

"Did you confirm the identities of the bodies with Hong Kong Station?"

"No, of course I didn't. The last thing I wanted to do was leave a trail between Langley and what happened in Hong Kong."

"Why can't you just say it clearly, Zac? It's not something that *happened* in Hong Kong. It's the bomb that we set in Hong Kong. A bomb that we set for the purpose of killing people. Say it."

Reed looked away and said nothing.

"You can't, can you, Zac. People like you never can. You sit in your nice clean office and you move papers around with your nice clean hands and you talk on the phone while people like me do your dirty work for you."

Reed looked back at her and his blue eyes darted around her face, but he still said nothing.

"If you had thought hard about it, Zac, surely you could have found some pretext to use to inquire of the station. It would have been a useful thing for you to do because you would have found out something very interesting. Three bodies were recovered, that's true, but they weren't the bodies of August and his people. I did check with Hong Kong Station. The three bodies that were recovered were all Chinese women."

"Chinese women?" Reed repeated pointlessly.

"Yes, Chinese women. Not August and not any of his people. August is alive. That's how Interpol knew I was in Thailand and that's how they found out who I am."

ZAC REED PUSHED himself up from the bench of the picnic table.

He moved slowly, like an old man feeling the pain of his arthritis, and walked away down the path toward the river. Rebecca, not knowing what else to do, stood up and followed.

After a moment she caught up with him and, keeping her voice low in spite of no one being around, asked, "Why did you tell me to do this, Zac?"

Reed looked at her for a moment as if he had no idea what she was talking about, so she tried it another way.

"The story you gave me about August and his people going rogue was pure bullshit, wasn't it? Why did the Agency really want August and his people killed?"

"The Band had to be shut down, Rebecca."

"So, get somebody to shut it down. It's like any other part of the government, isn't it? Somebody has power over it. Somebody started it. Somebody could have stopped it. You didn't have to murder people to do that."

"It's an organization that's out of control. It's developed a life of its own and has to be pulled up by the roots. It's become a threat."

"A threat to what?"

"To national security, of course."

"A threat to national security or a threat to the Agency?"

Reed offered a tiny shrug. "Same thing. More or less."

"So, your solution was to start killing the people who worked for the Band."

"It wasn't *my* solution. It was…"

Reed abruptly stopped talking.

"Never mind, Rebecca. I'm not really prepared to discuss any of this with you. It's above your pay grade."

"But you were prepared to ask me to arrange to kill them. I guess my pay grade covers murder."

Reed shot her a sharp look, but he didn't say anything else. He just walked on and Rebecca walked with him.

A FTER A FEW minutes he stopped walking and looked back over his shoulder toward the parking lot, then ahead toward the river again. He appeared to Rebecca almost like he was searching for a particular location in the park, but she couldn't imagine what it could be.

They walked on, still not talking, and eventually Reed left the path and crossed over open ground to a slight rise covered in pine needles that was just in front of a line of three trees. There was a lovely view from there. Tree-covered slopes rolled down to a narrow granite gorge through which the Potomac River raced for two or three hundred yards spinning itself into plumes of foam and white water until the gorge opened up downriver as abruptly as it had begun and the river turned wide and lazy again.

"What are you going to do now?" Reed suddenly asked.

Rebecca noticed he wasn't looking at her.

"What am *I* going to do? I've already done my part here, Zac. What happens now is that you are going to fix this. Three innocent people are dead. They can charge us with murder if they want to. I am *not* going down alone for this."

"Don't threaten me, sweetie. You're not capable of backing it up."

"Call me *sweetie* one more time, you smarmy fuck, and you'll see what I'm capable of."

Reed slowly turned his head toward Rebecca and looked at her with empty eyes. She stared right back. After a moment he chuckled and raised both hands, palms out, in the age-old gesture of conciliation.

"Did you know that this is where they found Vince Foster?" Reed suddenly asked. "His body was right there."

He pointed to the pine-straw covered slope in front of the line of trees.

"What are you talking about? Who's Vince Foster?"

"You don't know who Vince Foster was, Rebecca? Really? I guess I forget how young you are."

She shook her head.

"He was a pal of the Clintons. He came here with them from Arkansas when Bill Clinton was elected president. He worked in the White House and built a reputation as a fixer for the Clintons. Some say he was responsible for killing off the Whitewater investigation and burying Travelgate, both scandals that threatened Hillary Clinton with felony charges. You know about that, don't you?"

Rebecca wasn't certain she did. It all sounded vaguely familiar, but she couldn't remember why. Bill Clinton was well before her time.

"Foster left his car about where we parked," Reed continued. "Then he walked in here, almost all the way to the river, and stretched out on the ground right over there."

Reed pointed again to the same spot.

"He shot himself once in the mouth with an old revolver that used to belong to his father. Or so they say."

Reed walked over to the slope and knelt down. He placed his palm gently against the pine straw as if he could feel the vibration of the past in it.

"Some people think Foster committed suicide because he knew too much about what Hillary Clinton had actually done and he was afraid he would be hounded by her enemies until he admitted what he knew. Other people think Foster didn't commit suicide at all. They think the Clintons had him murdered and the body was dumped here to make it look like a suicide."

Reed's eyes went to her face and Rebecca felt a chill go through her body.

"Either way, Vince Foster died for more or less the same reason. It wasn't about what he did. It was about what he knew."

In that moment they both went so still that Rebecca could swear she could feel the earth rotating beneath her feet.

"What do you think, Rebecca? Did Vince Foster kill himself or did the Clintons have him killed to be certain he would never talk?"

"How would I know?"

Rebecca had tried hard to keep her voice flat, but she could hear the squeak in it and she knew she had failed.

Reed smiled and looked away.

"I've got to go," he said. "Meetings. You know how it is."

"Why did you tell me that, Zac?"

"About the meetings?"

"About Vince Foster. Is there supposed to be some kind of a lesson for me in that story?"

"I just thought you would find it interesting, Rebecca. In Washington the past is always all around us. This is a city of ghosts. They're everywhere. Even lying on a pile of pine straw out here in the woods."

"Fuck you, Zac."

Zac Reed bobbed his head slightly.

"Yeah, fuck me."

Reed didn't say anything else. He just turned away and started back to the parking lot.

THIRTY-NINE

WHEN REBECCA RETURNED to her car, Zac and his green BMW were gone.

She got behind the wheel and started the engine, but then she shut it off again and just sat there staring at the woods. There had been a white van and a Mustang in the lot when she and Zac walked into the park, but now they were gone and the parking lot was completely empty. She was utterly alone, and she *felt* utterly alone.

What had Reed meant by that story about Vince Foster? Was it supposed to be a threat? Why else would he have told her? She didn't even know if the story was true, but it was hard to look at it as anything other than a threat aimed at her.

People in Washington who knew too much about other people in Washington sometimes ended up dead. That's what Reed was telling her.

She knew that Reed had directed her to set up August and his people from the Band to be killed, but now they were alive and somehow they had figured out she was the one who had put them in the room where the bomb went off. They knew about her and she knew about Zac Reed. It really *was* that simple, wasn't it?

When Reed came to her, he had told her these people had become a threat to national security and the Agency had been given the task of shutting them down by whatever means necessary. He told her that they were part of an organization called the Band, but he didn't tell her much else and at the time it hadn't seemed to matter.

Reed was the DCI's hit man. His job was to give the DCI separation from the really unpleasant tasks that ended up on his desk from time to time, and killing several Americans who might be a threat to national security certainly met the description of an unpleasant task. Worse, it was a task that could come back to bite somebody in the ass if it went wrong.

That was why Rebecca hadn't argued with Reed or questioned him when he came to her and laid out her instructions. On the contrary, she was proud to be trusted with such a sensitive undertaking. She had never doubted then, of course, that her instructions were really coming straight from the DCI. Reed was his closest aide. He spoke for the DCI. Everyone at the Agency knew that.

But now she found herself wondering if her instructions really *had* come from the DCI? They must have. Surely. Zac Reed wouldn't have launched an operation like that entirely on his own, would he? That simply didn't seem possible.

Rebecca had to admit she had no proof her instructions to see that August and his team were killed came from the DCI, but that was how it looked to her. And that was exactly the way it would look to anyone who found out that Reed had given her those instructions.

That was when a horrifying thought struck her. She had no proof Reed had given her those instructions either. There was nothing in writing. Of course, there wasn't. Nobody exactly sent out memos asking you to murder people, did they? What if Reed claimed he hadn't given her any instructions at all, that she had acted entirely on her own?

Just the thought of that made her shudder. If he did try to

deny it, she would only be able to protect herself by spilling everything she knew. And she knew a great deal.

Not only did she know enough to bring Zac Reed down, destroy his career, and possibly even put him in prison for murder, she probably knew enough to do the same thing to the Director of the Central Intelligence Agency, and he was a man with nearly unlimited power at his fingertips.

She knew Reed well enough to know he wouldn't sit around and hope for the best if he was threatened. She didn't know the DCI. She had never even met him. But you didn't get to be DCI by ignoring threats and hoping for the best either. You acted. You did something to neutralize a threat before it got to you.

And now she was that threat.

She didn't want to think about how vulnerable and alone she suddenly felt, but how could she not?

No matter how she looked at it, the bottom line here was stark.

She *was* alone. And she was pretty much fucked.

R EBECCA SEARCHED THROUGH her purse until she found the white card that Tay had given her back at the IHOP when this nightmare had begun for her.

Had that really only been a few hours ago? It hardly seemed possible.

When she located the card, she simply sat there in the car, holding it and not moving. She looked for a long time at the telephone number Tay had written on it.

That number was now her own personal Rubicon. She had never thought of comparing herself in any way to Caesar, but now they had at least this one thing in common. When Caesar crossed the Rubicon into Gaul, he was committed to war. After that, there was no going back for him. If she called that number and told Tay the truth, the whole truth, then there would be no going back for her either. She too would be committed to war.

And a war against people who would, and could, crush her without a second thought.

She had to admit Zac Reed's story about Vince Foster had shaken her just as she was certain Zac had intended for it to. Was he seriously suggesting to her that she commit suicide to protect the secret of where the operation to kill August had originated?

If he was, he didn't know her very well. She was about the worst candidate for suicide she knew. She was a fighter. Always had been, always would be. If Zac came after her, he would be in for the fight of his life. She had told him she wasn't going down alone, and she wasn't.

That still left the other part of the Vince Foster story, however. The part that had Foster being killed at the behest of the Clintons to protect them from Foster eventually breaking and telling what he knew about them and what they had done.

Did she seriously believe that the Clintons had arranged for Foster to be killed and his body dumped to look like a suicide? Rebecca knew what people in government were capable of, she knew how far they would go to preserve their power and protect their reputations, but a President of the United States was so powerful and had so many ways to bend people to his will that the crudeness of a fake suicide didn't ring true somehow.

Still, she supposed whether the Clintons actually had Foster killed or not had very little to do with her current predicament. What Zac was telling her was that people who became a threat could be eliminated by the people they threatened, and she knew that was true. You didn't have to be a conspiracy theorist wearing a tin foil hat to believe that such things happened in Washington every now and then.

She *knew* they did. After all, what had she been trying to do to August and his people, for Christ's sake? She was arranging the elimination of a threat by seeing that the people who posed the threat were killed.

So, was she in danger now?

Yes, she supposed she was. As far as she knew, she was the only link between the bombing in Hong Kong and the Agency. She was the only person who could point to Zac Reed as the source of her instructions, and everyone knew that Zac Reed was the Executive Assistant to the Director of the Central Intelligence Agency. Even if Zac tried to take responsibility all alone, no one would believe him. The DCI would go down, too.

The perfect solution for both Zac and the DCI here was obvious.

And that was for Rebecca to be dead.

As long as she was alive, they couldn't be certain of her. No matter how fervently she promised not to point a finger at either of them, she could always change her mind and, even if she didn't, what she might demand from them in return was always an open question.

No, the only foolproof solution was for her to be dead. Then they could push the whole thing onto her, call her a rogue employee with a personal agenda, and who was there to say anything different?

If she told Tay the truth, her career would be over and all kinds of hell would be unleashed, of course, but at least she would no longer be worth killing. Once her story was out there, she was protected. Killing her no longer achieved anything for the people she threatened and, worse, it made the spotlight that had been turned on them even brighter.

So, okay, telling Tay the truth would probably save her life, but would it leave her a life worth saving? Interpol couldn't arrest her or anyone else, of course, but they would report the results of their investigation to the FBI and that would unleash hell. She would spend the rest of her life testifying in Congressional hearings and then, eventually, in court, or at least it would feel like it was the rest of her life, but the more she thought about it the more she realized that was actually the good news.

The bad news was that she had committed a crime. No matter who had instructed her to do it, she had participated in and facilitated a conspiracy to murder three American citizens, a conspiracy that ended up killing three innocent strangers instead. She couldn't see that being brushed under the rug no matter who else she implicated in the conspiracy. In the end, she would go to prison. The little people always went to prison, didn't they? And the smaller they were, the longer they went to prison for.

The more she thought about it, the less she felt like she was left with any real choice in the matter.

She picked up her telephone, glanced again at the number on the card, and punched it in.

B UT SHE DIDN'T hit the *Talk* button. Instead, she put the phone down on the passenger seat.

Maybe there was another way.

She wasn't going to set herself up to be killed, but she wasn't going to prison either. There had to be another way.

So, what was she going to do instead? Run?

How far would she have to run to get away from the Director of the Central Intelligence Agency? Forget that. Nobody could run that far.

How about going to the press with her story? Wasn't that better than going to Interpol? Not really. The result would eventually be the same. Once the story was out there, she had admitted to a crime and they weren't going to give her a pass for it, not even if her admission had appeared first in *The Washington Post*. Maybe *especially* not if it appeared first in *The Washington Post*.

So what else?

She couldn't think of anything else, but she wasn't willing to give up. Not yet, at least.

The problem was that she didn't have much time. Zac was coming for her from one direction and Tay was coming from the other. Unless she intended simply to go limp and let the first

JAKE NEEDHAM

one to arrive have whatever was left of her, she had to make a choice. It might be a lousy choice to make, but it was still *her* choice. At least it would be if she made it soon.

She would give herself a little while longer to find a way out, but she would set a deadline for herself, one she couldn't weasel out of.

She picked the telephone up again, and this time she hit *Talk*.

"HELLO?"
"Inspector Tay?"
"Yes."
"This is—"
"I know who this is."
"Oh, okay, yes."

Rebecca paused and then firmly took the first step over the Rubicon.

"Look, Inspector, we need to meet. I want to talk to you."
"Fine. Where are you?"
"No, not now. Tomorrow. Tomorrow morning."
"Why tomorrow? Why not now?"
"Are you going to meet me tomorrow or not?"
"Yes, of course. I just thought—"
"I'll call this number around nine tomorrow and tell you where."
"I can come to your apartment if you like." Tay paused. "I know where it is."
"You don't need to remind me how much you know about me. I believe you."
"Then we'll meet at your apartment?"
"No. I won't be there tomorrow and, just in case you were wondering, I'm not there now either."
"You sound scared. *Are* you scared?"

304

Rebecca hesitated. She *was* scared, of course, but she still didn't much like the idea of sounding like she was.

All at once she didn't want to talk to Tay anymore. At least not right then. She had given herself until morning to find another way out of this, and she was going to use every damn minute she had. If she couldn't find another way, she would tell Tay everything. She might go to prison, but she wouldn't die. At least she didn't think she would.

"I'll call you tomorrow morning, Inspector. Be ready. I may not be near."

"What do you mean you may not—"

She hit the button to end the call. Then she turned her phone off, removed the battery, and dropped both the battery and the phone on the seat next to her.

FORTY

R EBECCA PULLED OUT of the parking lot heading north on the George Washington Memorial Parkway. She hadn't particularly intended to go north, but it was the only way you could turn when you came out of the Fort Marcy parking lot and, since she had no idea where she was going anyway, north was as good a direction as any.

She had always liked driving on the parkway. It traced the Potomac River from one side of the Washington Beltway to the other, and it was nothing like the rest of Washington. The parkway ran through a heavily wooded parkland for at least half its length and driving it you felt like you were wrapped in a peaceful cocoon far away from the mayhem and uproar of what people insisted on calling the most powerful city in the world.

She particularly loved using the parkway to drive into the District from the Agency's main campus in Langley. For the first couple of miles you were wrapped in a pine forest as dense and quiet as you would find anywhere in the wilds of Tennessee.

Then, all at once, you popped out on a bluff above the Potomac River and right there on the other side all of Washington was spread out before you. The granite cladding of the Washington Monument, the Lincoln Memorial, and the

Jefferson Memorial glinting impossibly white in the sunlight, and the White House and the Capitol Building radiating the strength and raw power always associated with them.

Each time Rebecca came upon Washington like that, it made her think of a child's model built on a tabletop. The city didn't look real. Its structures laid out in perfect geometrical patterns looked like toys carefully arranged by a kid with a serious obsessive-compulsive disorder. Looking at Washington that way, it seemed for a moment to be a pleasant and agreeable place to be, but that feeling never lasted for long.

The closer she drew, the more she sensed the malevolent lust for power that bubbled under the city like lava pooling under a volcano. This particular volcano had already erupted many times, and many times it had wiped out people, places, even whole civilizations. It would erupt again, and the people who lived on the volcano knew it. They understood the danger all too well, but they lived there anyway. The thing was, they thought the volcano's power would always destroy someone else. They never, none of them, thought the volcano would ever get them.

Rebecca could feel the first rumblings of an eruption beginning to roll the ground under her and reflexively she pushed harder at her car's accelerator. She had to get herself away before it exploded. She had to get away before the eruption got her.

The problem was that she had no idea if it was even possible to get away. So, she just kept driving, and she kept trying to think of someplace where she might be safe.

THE HAMPTON INN in Leesburg, Virginia, wasn't one of the places Rebecca would have put on any list of attractive sanctuaries she might have compiled at a more leisurely moment in her life.

In fact, she had never heard of it and didn't know it existed, but after driving west from Washington for more than an hour without any real destination in mind, it looked pretty good when she saw it. She parked, went in, and got a room.

The moment she closed the door behind her, a sense of peacefulness settled over her. She felt safe. No one in the entire world knew where she was.

They could find her if they looked hard enough, of course. She understood that. You couldn't check into a hotel anywhere in America without showing identification and a credit card, and both could be traced easily enough. But it wouldn't happen today. For today, she was in the wind.

Two double beds sat side by side, each covered with a fluffy white duvet and stacked with enough pillows to hold a decent slumber party. On the opposite wall was a long cabinet made of pine that was so light colored and polished to such a sheen that it looked almost yellow. Above the cabinet was a huge Samsung flat panel television set and at its far end was a small knee-hole desk with an office-style chair upholstered in orange fabric lined with a pattern of dark green squares.

It was an unexceptional although entirely pleasant room, but its very ordinariness made her feel better. She had been in hotel rooms just like it a hundred times and something about the sameness was reassuring. It was as close as she could get right now to being in a familiar place where she felt comfortable. The safety the room provided her was, of course, temporary. She knew that. But she welcomed the feeling, nevertheless, for however long it lasted.

Okay, what now?

She had driven away from Fort Marcy Park propelled by a desire to lose herself somewhere until she could decide what to do. She had had no destination in mind, had developed no plan of action. She just wanted to be... well, *away*. Now she *was* away, and something had to come after that.

She kicked off her shoes and pushed herself up into the

middle of the bed. Bunching up some of the pillows behind her, she leaned back against them and stretched her legs straight out.

Did she really believe she was in danger from the Agency? Maybe, but she doubted it. The Agency didn't kill its own people, at least not very often, but whether she might be in danger from Zac Reed was another matter altogether.

She was the only person who could link Reed to the operation that led to the bombing at the Cordis Hotel in Hong Kong, and linking Reed to the operation was as good as linking the DCI to the operation. Reed didn't have the weight to do something like that on his own. Nowhere close to it. It was inconceivable to her, as it would be to anyone else who heard the story, that the true originator of the operation could have been anyone other than the DCI himself.

If the bombing had succeeded, if August and his people had been killed like they should have been, probably no one would have cared. Three foreigners dead in Hong Kong in an explosion of unknown origins? The Hong Kong cops wouldn't have put much effort into that. But the real targets somehow escaped and three innocent local women were killed instead. That put the pressure on the cops to figure this thing out. And if Interpol had somehow linked the bombing to her and her to the Agency, the pressure would *really* be on the Hong Kong cops when they found that out.

The Central Fucking Intelligence Agency screwed up some cockamamie operation they were running and killed three Hong Kong grannies?

The cops would have to hang somebody up for that, and right now the only person they had to hang was Rebecca Sternwood.

She could change that, of course. She could give them Reed, and giving them Reed was the same thing as giving them the DCI, but that was both her salvation and her damnation.

Was Reed going to bet his career, even his freedom, that she was going to keep her mouth shut and take the fall all alone?

She couldn't see that. He would never believe she would do that for him, and in that he would be right. She sure as hell wouldn't.

And even if Reed were somehow willing to roll the dice that she might, it was the DCI who had the most to lose. He was the big fish here, and the moment the FBI had him in their sights everyone else would be forgotten. The DCI wasn't a man who would march to the gallows with his head held high. He would do everything he could to protect himself. And there was only one certain way to do that.

Get rid of Rebecca Sternwood.

Problem solved.

That didn't sound good, did it?

R EBECCA FIGURED SHE had a little time. Maybe not a lot, but a little.

She doubted there was a protocol in place for murdering an Agency employee who could send the DCI to prison. Not much time maybe, but surely a day or two. Reed would have to lay it all out for the DCI, they would have to make the decision to remove her as a threat, and then they would have to create a plan to do that. That would take a couple of days. But probably not any longer than that.

Still, she didn't need nearly that long. If she was going to tell her story to Inspector Tay, she could do that tomorrow, and as her price for telling him she could demand she be protected. Interpol could hardly refuse. After all, she was the only way they had to tie the bombing to higher ups at the Agency. They would want to keep her safe and sound.

Rebecca didn't like the idea of dropping a dime on Reed and the DCI, but what choice did she have? If she didn't, she would take the fall for this all alone, and why should she do that? She was just following Reed's instructions, doing her job as a dutiful employee of the Agency.

That thought gave her pause. It was starting to sound like the Nuremberg defense, wasn't it?

But, mein herr, I wass only following orders.

Still, it was true. She was following instructions from superiors at the Agency. It was what Agency employees did. The senior people there didn't, and shouldn't, have to convince every employee that they were doing the right thing every time they gave instructions. That's not how organizations functioned. The top people told the middle people what to do, and the middle people organized the bottom people to do it. How else could it possibly work?

She didn't really know for sure that this organization August and the others were supposed to be working for, this super-secret group that Reed claimed was such a threat to national security, even actually existed. Maybe there was something else going on entirely. Maybe Reed had just made up that story to keep from having to tell her the real truth. What the hell was she supposed to do? Investigate Reed's story before she did what he told her to do? No one could really expect her to do that, could they?

R EBECCA SIGHED HEAVILY, pushed the pillows away, and stretched out on the bed. She really only had one alternative, didn't she? She had to tell Tay the truth and get him to protect her until the truth became publicly known. Once that happened, she would no longer be at risk.

Would she be going to prison for what she had done anyway? After all, she hadn't actually killed anybody herself, had she?

The thought gave her no comfort. It was the thinnest of all possible excuses and she knew it. She had to accept there was a risk that the FBI would come down on her, but she thought the odds were in her favor. After all, they would need her to prosecute Reed and the DCI. There was no other way to link them to the operation, and they were both so much bigger fish than she was it made no sense that they would bury her along with them, did it? They *needed* her, right?

Rebecca looked around the room. She liked it here. She thought she could stay here forever.

But of course she couldn't.

She had told Tay she would call him tomorrow morning and give him a place to meet her, if she decided to meet him at all.

She knew now that she would.

At least she could give herself one more night of peace before everything hit the fan, and this room was as good a place as any to do it. Better really than most.

Maybe she should go back to her apartment and pack some fresh clothes and toiletries first. After all, she had no idea what would happen when she told Tay the truth. He wouldn't arrest her, of course. Interpol had no jurisdiction to arrest people on American soil. But he would immediately see the risk to her and therefore to his case so it seemed likely that at the very least he would want to stash her away somewhere. And if he didn't, she would insist on it herself. She needed to be prepared for that.

Was there any danger in going back to her apartment? What was she expecting? To find it surrounded by an Agency SWAT team?

Reed and the DCI were both bureaucrats. They had fancy titles, but that's still what they were. It had only been a few hours since she had seen Reed at Fort Marcy Park and told him that Interpol had tied her to the bomb in Hong Kong. In the history of the world, no bureaucrat had ever decided *anything* in a few hours. Reed may not even have talked to the DCI yet. Maybe the DCI was out of town, even out of the country. And there was no way Reed would do anything, certainly not move on an employee of the Agency, without first getting the DCI's support and authority.

So, it was settled, Rebecca told herself. She would go home, pack some things, and come back to the Hampton Inn to enjoy one more night of utter peace in a place where no one could find her. Then tomorrow morning, she would call Tay, arrange to meet him, and tell him everything.

After that, the world in which she had lived all of her thirty-seven years would burn to the ground.

It didn't seem fair, it didn't seem right, but that was simply the way it was.

FORTY-ONE

TAY WAS NOT an early riser by habit and that was why the effects of jet lag from the trip to Washington had been particularly hard on him.

He had been coming awake in the darkness every morning and finding himself unable to go back to sleep. Getting up at four or five in the morning was inconceivable to him so he had read some, but mostly he had just tossed and turned and felt miserable and frustrated.

This morning the jet lag seemed at last to have worn off. He had regained his ability to sleep to an hour he considered reasonably civilized so he was the last downstairs to breakfast. When he walked into the kitchen it looked to him like the others had already finished eating, but they were still gathered around the table drinking coffee. He poured himself a cup and took the empty chair, and everyone mumbled the usual morning greetings and then fell silent again.

The woman who looked after the safe house paused in clearing away the dirty plates.

"What would you like for breakfast, sir?" she asked Tay.

"Just coffee's fine."

"Everyone else had eggs and bacon," she prodded.

Tay shook his head and fished in his pockets. He came out with a crumpled pack of Marlboros and a box of matches. As he shook out a cigarette, he glanced up and saw that everyone was staring at him.

"Don't," he said, "just don't. A round of healthy-American anti-smoking bullshit before I've had at least three cups of coffee will lead to homicide. At least one. Probably more."

He lit his cigarette and looked around for some place to dump the match. He settled on August's egg-stained breakfast plate.

"When did she say she would call?" August asked.

Tay had no doubt that August remembered perfectly well, but he answered anyway.

"Around nine."

August cleared his throat and studied the tabletop. Tay realized something was coming.

"What?" Tay asked.

"I talked to our tech people to see if they could pin down the call Rebecca Sternwood made to you yesterday," August said.

Tay waited.

"They found out that her phone was pinging a cell tower on Dolly Madison Boulevard when she called."

"That's nice," Tay said. He drank some more coffee and took a long pull on his Marlboro.

"Actually," August went on, "it's not. Dolly Madison Boulevard is in McLean, Virginia, a little over eight miles from here. There's where the main entrance to the Central Intelligence Agency is."

"Rebecca Sternwood called me from the Central Intelligence Agency?"

"Personal phones aren't permitted in most of the buildings and under the circumstances I doubt she would have wanted to call you from inside anyway. My guess is she probably called you from her car when it was somewhere inside the Agency complex."

Tay thought about that for a moment, but wasn't sure what he was supposed to make of it.

"What are you telling me, John?"

"I'm telling you I think they took the bait. They need to stop this investigation and so they need to shut you down before it goes any further. I think the meeting she's going to ask you to come to will be a set-up."

"A set-up to do what?"

August just looked at Tay.

"Oh, come on, John. Do you honestly believe the CIA would kill an Interpol investigator right here in Washington just to try and stop an investigation?"

"Someone over there got Rebecca Sternwood to set us up to be killed because they wanted to shut down the Band, didn't they? Why should they get squeamish about using the same tactic to shut you down?"

"I don't believe it. It would draw far too much attention to them."

"It's easy to kill people and make it look like natural causes or an accident. I ought to know. I've done it often enough."

Tay stubbed out his Marlboro in the ashtray that the woman who ran the house had discreetly deposited at his elbow.

"I think you're wrong, John. This woman isn't a killer. I'm sure she isn't."

"Somebody over there is."

"Not her. She was scared when she called me. I think she's right on the edge of coming clean and giving us everything."

"You're being naïve."

"This is a silly conversation. Let's just wait for her to call and see what she says. Why speculate on what it's going to be? Let's hear it and then we can decide what it means."

By ten o'clock, Tay had finished his fourth cup of coffee and his third cigarette, but Rebecca Sternwood still hadn't called.

. . .

"**M**AYBE SHE CHANGED her mind," Claire said.
"Or maybe somebody changed it for her," August suggested.

Woods, as usual, said nothing.

Tay shook out another cigarette, but then he put it back without lighting it.

"I don't like this," he said. "Something's wrong. Do you have any way of locating her, John? Can you track her phone?"

"It's been turned off since yesterday afternoon. They said they'd call me if it logged on anywhere, but…" August shrugged.

"Don't you have a tracker on her car?"

"It went dead yesterday," August said. "That's the last time I'm using that cheap Korean shit. From now on, I'm buying American."

"My guess is she went back to her apartment," Claire put in. "Someplace she'd feel safe."

Tay thought about it. "Not likely. If she wants safe, she checks into a hotel under a false identity. She's only going back to her apartment if she has some important reason to be there."

"Which she would if the plan is to ambush you there," August said.

"That doesn't add up. I told her yesterday I'd meet her at her apartment, but she said she wasn't there. She told me to be ready this morning because she might not be near."

"Not near where?"

"Her apartment, I assumed. I didn't ask."

"I think we should check the apartment anyway," Claire said. "What have we got to lose?"

"Why not?" Tay picked up his cigarettes and stood. "It's not like I have something else to do."

"I don't want just the two of you there by yourselves if everything goes to shit."

"What are you talking about, John? Claire and I drive over there, I go up and knock on the door, and either she answers or she doesn't. What is there to go to shit?"

"Always the optimist, aren't you, Sam?"

"That's the first time anyone ever called me that."

"All four of us will go," August said and looked at Woods. "Get some gear together."

"We going heavy or going light?"

"I'd call it medium. Breaching equipment and silenced handguns. Nothing heavy-duty."

"Whoa, whoa," Tay said, waving his hands in front of him. "Silenced handguns? What in God's name are you talking about? We're just going to knock on the door, not start a war."

"When you knock on a door, you don't get to choose what's on the other side."

"Nothing is going to be on the other side. She won't be there. She's scared. She's in the wind."

"And you'd bet your life on that?"

Tay sighed, but he said nothing.

"I didn't think so."

August shifted his eyes back to Woods.

"We're out of here in five."

CLAIRE DROVE PAST Rebecca's apartment building at a normal rate of speed to avoid attracting any attention.

The five-story red-brick building with the big black-framed windows looked exactly like it had when they had been there before. Quiet and unremarkable. The sleepy residential neighborhood was probably at its sleepiest in midmorning, and they saw no one on the sidewalks in either direction.

"Go around to the garage entrance," Tay told Claire. "Tell John to park here in the front and wait for us."

Claire lifted a small encrypted radio transceiver off the Mustang's console and told August what they were doing. When

Tay looked over his shoulder, he saw the black Chevy Suburban with Woods at the wheel and August in the passenger seat pull to the curb and stop.

They were approaching the garage on the side street when Tay realized the gate was lifting and a dark blue Honda was nosing up the driveway from the underground garage.

Tay jerked forward as far as his seatbelt would let him and pointed to the driveway. "Get in there before the gate closes! Quick!"

Claire swung the Mustang in right behind the Honda as it turned out of the driveway. She got the nose of the Mustang under the gate just as it started to close, but the gate's sensors detected the car, immediately reversed the gate, and it opened again. Claire rolled into the garage.

"Tell August where we are and ask him to come in here and park," Tay said.

"How's he going to get in?"

"Gates like this always open automatically when cars approach from inside. When you see August turn into the driveway, just move up enough to open the gate for him, then roll back down the ramp."

Claire looked at Tay and smiled. "You're not just a pretty face, are you, Sam?"

"I'm a detective," he said. "I detected."

W HEN THE MUSTANG and the Suburban were both inside the garage and parked together as far away from the entrance to the lobby as they could get, the four of them got out.

Woods retrieved a brown leather valise from the back of the Suburban and, squatting down, he unzipped it and passed out pistols in black nylon paddle holsters. When he got to Tay, Tay held up both hands, palms out, and shook his head.

"A retired Singaporean cop getting into a gun battle with CIA employees in Washington D.C.? Forget it."

"It's not Washington D.C.," August said as he clipped the holster to his belt. "It's Arlington, Virginia."

Tay just looked at him.

August shrugged.

When the handguns were all safety tucked away, Woods picked up the valise and carried it to the lobby door. He tried the knob, but of course the door was locked.

Pulling a small black leather case out of the valise and unzipping it, Woods produced a stainless-steel lock-picking gun. He inserted the snout of the device into the keyhole in the door handle and pressed the button. A dull *whirring* noise sounded for a few seconds and then stopped. Woods withdrew the tool, turned the knob again, and this time the door opened.

"That's pretty cool," Tay chuckled. "Where can I get one of those?"

"Amazon."

"Seriously?" Tay asked, but no one answered him.

THE LOBBY WAS small and floored in red Mexican tile. A pair of clear glass doors on the front wall opened out to the street.

There were brass-colored mail boxes on one side and a long wooden table on the other. It looked vaguely Spanish in design and seemed to serve no purpose other than to collect the junk mail residents pulled out of their boxes and discarded. The gray metal door from the garage was in the lobby's back wall, as were the building's single elevator and another gray metal door with a small white sign on it that said STAIRS.

"Apartment number?" Woods asked when they were all inside.

"31B," August told him. "Third floor rear. Let's take the stairs."

They all trooped up the stairs keeping their body language casual in case they encountered anyone, but they didn't.

The third-floor hallway was painted a cream color and carpeted in dark green. Woods found the door to 31B while August and Claire made a quick check of the other half dozen or so apartment doors along the corridor, stopping for a few seconds in front of each and listening for any sound that might suggest they were occupied.

"Anything?" August whispered when they all reassembled in front of 31B with Woods.

Claire shook her head.

"Me neither," he said.

"Are you done with all the spy bullshit now?" Tay asked and reached out with his forefinger to press the doorbell.

August grabbed Tay's hand before it reached the button and shook his head.

"Go ahead," he whispered to Woods.

Woods removed a coiled black cable from the leather valise, took his iPhone out of his pocket, and plugged the cable into the phone. Then he went down on one knee and threaded a few inches of the other end of the cable underneath Rebecca's front door.

On the screen of Woods' iPhone, Tay saw a worm's eye view of the apartment. It was surprisingly bright and clear and, as Woods rotated the cable and moved it from side to side, Tay was able to see clearly that the room was empty.

"Wow, that's something," Tay said in a low voice. "You Americans really do have all the best toys. If I wanted to get something like that, where—"

"Amazon," Claire and Woods said almost simultaneously.

Tay didn't know whether they were pulling his leg or not, so he said nothing.

Woods looked back over his shoulder at August. "If it's an ambush, they're not waiting in the front room."

"Okay, Sam, then go ahead."

"Go ahead and do what?"

"Ring the doorbell like you were about to."

"You're not going to grab my hand again?"

"Ring the fucking doorbell."

As Tay put his finger on the bell and pushed, August and Claire flattened themselves on either side of the door with their right hands on the butts of their handguns.

After a few seconds, Woods said, "Nothing."

Tay glanced down at the screen of Woods' iPhone. The front room of the apartment showed no activity.

"Ring again," August said, and Tay did.

Woods watched for a moment, then said, "Still no movement."

"Okay," August told him. "Open it."

Woods pulled the black cable out from under the door, unplugged it from his phone, and stood up. He put his phone in his pocket, pushed the roll of cable back into the leather valise, and removed the lock-picking gun.

Rebecca's front door had a normal knob and keyhole lock as well as a separate deadbolt lock just above it. The keyhole lock took Woods two or three seconds to open. The deadbolt took longer. Maybe five or six seconds.

Woods turned the knob and pushed the door open.

And that was when everything went to hell.

FORTY-TWO

TAY KNEW IMMEDIATELY what they had found.

Death has a distinctive odor that is both instantly recognizable and impossible to forget. And God only knew how often he had smelled it in his lifetime. It is a sickly-sweet funk that seeps into everything, a combination of rotten eggs, spoiled garlic, boiling cabbage, vomit, and shit.

As Woods closed the door quietly behind them, August and Claire drew their handguns and cleared the apartment with a thoroughness and efficiency that came from long experience.

"Back here," Claire called quietly from down a hallway that ran off to the right just beyond the small kitchen.

When Tay got there, Claire was on one knee, her fingers feeling for a pulse. She looked back over her shoulder at Tay and shook her head. It really wasn't necessary. Tay had no doubt at all that Rebecca Sternwood was dead.

She was on her back just past a bathroom. Her feet and most of her body were in the hallway, but her head was just inside the doorway to what appeared to be the master bedroom. There were dark smears in several places on the gray carpet, bloodstains, but the smears were not large and there was no pooling of blood.

The right side of her face and her neck were mottled with gray-green bruises and her neck was covered with short, red scratches.

She did not look peaceful.

Claire stood up and stepped back, and Tay moved forward. He did not want to move forward, but after decades as a homicide investigator it was an automatic thing for him to crouch down and examine a body.

"How long?" August asked from somewhere behind him.

Tay lifted Rebecca's left arm slightly and examined the underside of it.

"Rigor is probably at maximum and lividity is fixed. I'd guess twelve to eighteen hours."

"So yesterday afternoon or last night?"

"Yes. Something like that."

All at once it occurred to Tay that Rebecca Sternwood was wearing the same clothes she had been wearing when he had ambushed her at breakfast yesterday.

At least he thought she was. Tay wasn't good about remembering women's clothes. As observant as he was about almost everything else, he normally drew a blank when it came to remembering what some woman had been wearing the last time he had seen her. He wasn't sure if he had a blind spot for clothes or if he had a blind spot for women, but he thought he could guess.

"Can you work out how it happened?" August asked.

Tay rose to his feet and stepped back. He let his eyes work the area while August and the others remained silent and waited to hear what he had to say.

He took two steps toward the open bathroom door and leaned inside without touching anything. His eyes immediately went to a pair of tall candlesticks on a shelf above the bathtub. They looked to be brass, and Tay didn't have to go any closer to see the patches of dried blood and skin scrapings smeared over the base of the one on the right.

"Someone was hiding in here when she came into the apartment," Tay said, pointing into the bathroom. "She walked down this hallway, probably going into the bedroom, and he stepped out and hit her in the side of the head with a metal candlestick. He hit her twice. When she went down after the second blow, he turned her over and straddled her. He pinned her arms to the floor with his knees and then strangled her with his hands. Then he put the candlestick back and left."

"Was he right-handed or left-handed?" Claire asked.

"Right-handed."

"I was just kidding."

"Kidding? What were you kidding about?"

"About how you can see all that. You're just standing here."

"It's what I said before," Tay shrugged, "I'm a detective. I detect."

"But what do you detect? All I see is a dead body lying on the floor."

"Look at the bruising to the right side of the face and head. The blows came from behind. Her attacker was almost certainly right-handed because no one would try to knock someone out with a candlestick by swinging it backhanded."

Tay stepped back and mimed first a right-handed swing, then a left-handed backhand.

"And as for the rest," he continued, "it's pretty obvious. There are bruises on the inner side of her arms from where he pinned her down with his knees, and you can see his finger marks on her neck."

"That's a shitty way to die."

"Every way to die is shitty."

August stepped past Tay and began moving silently around the body taking pictures with his telephone. Tay wondered why August was doing that, but something stopped him from asking. It shouldn't make any difference to him one way or another, but he still wondered about it.

Tay didn't want any pictures, but still he couldn't take his eyes off her body lying there on the gray carpet of her apartment. He wanted to look away. He really did. He just couldn't.

He had no doubt that Rebecca Sternwood had been killed because of him.

He told her Interpol had linked her to the bombing, and she must have told someone else that Interpol knew she was involved. And that someone else was almost certainly whoever it was at the CIA who had given her the instructions to do it.

Then they had killed her. With her dead, the connection to them was cut. Permanently.

Tay couldn't look away because he knew he was responsible for Rebecca Sternwood's murder. And bearing witness to what he had done was all he could do now.

"THE CALL TO the police probably ought to come from you, John. It would get messy if a former homicide investigator from Singapore is the one to tell the local cops they've got a body here."

August looked at Tay like he had begun speaking in tongues.

"Call the police? Are you out of your fucking mind, man?"

"I don't understand. What else can we do?"

"You and Claire are going to get the hell out of here right now, then Woods and I are going to wipe down anything we might have touched and we'll be right behind you."

"But, John, you can't just leave her—"

"Like hell I can't, Sam. You think I'm going to let the Band get sucked up in a local homicide investigation? Forget it."

"That's not right, John."

"Maybe it isn't, but that's the way it's going to be. You were never here. None of us were ever here."

"I can't go along with that."

"Look, I get it. You solve crimes, you bring justice for the dead and all that good shit. But that's small potatoes. This is a whole different league, pal."

"John, there is an innocent woman lying—"

"Not so innocent. She set the three of us up to be killed."

Tay took a deep breath and looked away. "That doesn't mean she deserved to be beaten and strangled."

"No, it doesn't, but that's what happened. That doesn't make us responsible for solving—"

"There's nothing to solve," Tay interrupted. "You know who did this."

"Of course I do, and that's exactly why we're not calling the police. What do you expect me to tell them?"

"Just tell them the truth."

"The truth? The *truth*? Good God, Sam, don't be so naïve!"

"I don't see anything naïve about that."

"You want me to tell the local homicide cops that the Director of the Central Intelligence Agency almost certainly had his executive assistant instruct Rebecca Sternwood to arrange for the killing of the three of us because he thought the President of the United States was starting to rely on the Band instead of the CIA and he wanted to put a stop to that by crippling the Band? And when we tried to flush them all out by claiming that Interpol had connected Rebecca Sternwood to the bombing in Hong Kong that was supposed to kill us, that then they killed her to keep Interpol from tying it back to them if she talked? Really? You expect me to tell that story to some local homicide cop?"

"I don't see what choice you've got."

"Get your head out of your ass, Sam. Do you really expect me to tell the cops that I'm a member of a super-secret organization that reports directly to the President of the United States, that the Director of the Central Intelligence Agency tried to use this woman to murder me, and that then he killed her to keep her from telling the truth to a fake Interpol cop? If I told them that story, they'd lock *me* up."

"Then what are you going to do?"

August took a deep breath and let it out in what was unmistakably a sigh of exasperation.

"Not a fucking thing," he said. "I'm not going to burn the Band over this."

"You're just going to walk out and leave this woman's body lying here on the floor?"

"Yep. Exactly. Just like she was willing to walk away and leave our bodies lying in the rubble of the Cordis Hotel in Hong Kong."

Tay understood how August felt about that, he even understood August's reluctance to tell the local cops about the Band, but still…

August walked over and draped an arm across Tay's shoulder.

"I know this doesn't sit well with you, Sam, but it's the only way. We can't go to the cops about this and tell them only part of the story. We can't be a little bit pregnant."

"Is this the part where you tell me there are bigger things at stake than a local murder?"

"I know you don't want to hear it, but there are. This is the big time, Sam, the top of the mountain. You can't even see one local murder from here."

"I can. I can see it plainly."

"I understand," August nodded, "I really do. But things are still the way they are. We're not here to solve local murders."

"So, they'll just get away with what they've done? This guy Reed and his boss and whoever else was involved in murdering Rebecca Sternwood can just go back to their lives and nobody will ever know what they've done?"

August dropped his hand from Tay's shoulder and walked over to the window.

The back of Rebecca Sternwood's apartment looked out toward the glass office towers of Rosslyn, Virginia, just across the Potomac River from Washington. August stood looking at the Capitol dome, impossibly white, peeking out from between two of the towers.

"I know it's not going to make you feel a lot better to hear this," he said without turning around, "but in my experience these things have a way of sorting themselves out. We know what these people have done. We know that they tried to murder us and killed three innocent people instead, and we know that they murdered Rebecca Sternwood to protect themselves. We know and we're not going to forget."

"But you're not going to do anything about it."

August turned and looked at Tay for a long moment in silence.

"Bigger things at stake, Sam," he said in a low voice. "Bigger fish to fry. Just remember what I said. These things have a way of working themselves out."

"I don't even know what that means."

"Neither do I," August admitted. "Not really."

The silence that fell after that was uncomfortable, but no one broke it.

Not until August eventually cleared his throat and pointed at Woods.

"Find a dishtowel or something and wipe down all the surfaces that any of us might have touched, then bring the towel with you and we'll get rid of it."

Woods nodded.

"Okay," August finished. "Now let's get the fuck out of here."

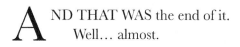 ND THAT WAS the end of it.
Well… almost.

PART 5
TOCCATA

FORTY-THREE

UGUST TOLD TAY he had a couple of things to do before they flew back so the plane wouldn't be leaving for a day or two. That meant that Tay could either go back on a commercial flight or hang around Washington until he was done and fly back with them.

Tay had more or less decided to take a commercial flight back to Singapore when Claire spoke up and offered to show him around Washington while they were waiting for August. All at once the hanging around thing sounded rather more appealing than it had before.

After all, he was in Washington D.C., a city filled with museums and monuments that he had seen in photographs all his life. Tay had never really been a traveler so he hadn't really been to all that many places. It wasn't that he lacked curiosity, certainly not, but he had always thought curiosity should be focused on a productive end of some sort, not squandered on slogging here and there in the world peering at landmarks for no reason at all other than that they were famous.

On the other hand, what else do I really have to do? Tay asked himself.

Isn't that what retired old farts are supposed to do? Travel pointlessly to places they don't have any reason to be and say they're seeing the world when they're really just killing time until they die?

It was such a depressing thought that Tay immediately put it out of his mind.

"A couple of days?" he asked August.

August nodded.

Tay looked at Claire.

"We'd visit the museums and some of the monuments while we're waiting for John to finish whatever he has to do?"

Claire nodded.

"Okay," Tay said. "Why not?"

Tay smoked a cigarette that night before he went to sleep and used his phone to trawl through some websites and think about the places in Washington where he might like to go.

The Smithsonian, of course, and the Library of Congress to see the Gutenberg Bible. The Mellon Gallery appeared to be worth a look, too, and he certainly would like to see the Lincoln and the Jefferson Memorials. He might even visit the Supreme Court building just to feel the sense of history there, but the Capitol and the White House he would just as soon skip.

He was sick of hearing about American politics and he certainly didn't want to go to places that were about nothing else. He sometimes wondered if Americans weren't just as sick of hearing about American politics as he was and, if they weren't, *why* they weren't.

Tay made a list of the places he wanted to go and it immediately made him feel better. Not the places. The list. He liked lists. Lists were islands of tidiness in an untidy world.

THE NEXT MORNING, Tay and Claire started out right after breakfast.

Claire had come up with a white SUV from somewhere and they drove north along the Potomac River directly toward the Washington Monument. Perhaps it was because he had seen so many photographs of the place before, but there was something about Washington that didn't feel real to Tay.

Now that he saw the sun gleaming on the white marble of its monuments and buildings just across the river, everything appeared smaller than he thought it ought to be. It was all too clean, too white, too perfect. It looked artificial. Like a theme park for people who wanted to visit Washington without having to cope with the bleak authenticity of the real thing.

They had a fine time wandering through the Smithsonian Air and Space Museum and the Natural History Museum, then they walked up the Mall and across the Capitol grounds to the Library of Congress. Tay stood mesmerized under the great dome of the main reading room in this greatest of all the temples to the printed word and wondered what would become of places like this now that most words were more often electronic than printed.

He looked at the Gutenberg Bible in its sealed glass case, the atmosphere a carefully controlled mix of oxygen and hydrogen to improve its preservation, and wondered if that was what all printed books would be in another century or so. Not words woven into magical canvases of ideas and emotions, but nothing more than curious artifacts left over from a long-forgotten age. Maybe it was good he wouldn't be around to see that.

On the second day they drove around past the monuments and, when they were lucky enough to stumble onto an empty parking place in East Potomac Park, they got out and walked up the steps of the Lincoln Memorial and stood for a while in front of the famous marble sculpture of Abraham Lincoln seated in a huge chair and peering resolutely up the Mall, past the Washington Monument, and all the way to the dome of the Capitol.

To Tay's surprise, he found it unexpectedly moving for some reason he couldn't quite put his finger on. Perhaps it was simply the majesty of it all, or maybe it was something else. Maybe it was its testimony to the conviction that belief in the ideal of your country was enough to transcend time. Maybe it really was. He wished at least a little that he could feel that way himself.

He and Claire were sitting on the steps of the Lincoln Memorial in the sunshine enjoying the view over the city when her phone buzzed. She pulled it out and looked at the screen.

"John wants us to meet him for lunch," she said.

"I can't imagine why. He knows I'm not happy about how all this ended."

"He wants to ask you something."

"Couldn't he just ask me on the phone?"

Claire shrugged, but she didn't offer an opinion.

"I don't guess we have anything that important to do anyway. Where does he want us to meet him?"

"At Bob and Edith's."

"Who in the world are Bob and Edith?"

"Not a who, a what. Bob and Edith's is a diner. It's over in Arlington not far from the Pentagon. John loves it, but I've always thought it was kind of crummy." Claire thought about it for a moment. "But I guess it's crummy in a homey way."

Tay wondered what crummy in a homey way was supposed to mean, but he didn't ask.

"John drags us there at least once every time we're in Washington. Always eats the same thing. Soft-boiled eggs and corned beef hash."

And that was how, at just after one o'clock on an otherwise ordinary Thursday afternoon, Samuel Tay found himself sitting next to Claire at Bob and Edith's looking across the table at John August and Woods sitting on the other side.

FORTY-FOUR

B OB AND EDITH'S was about the most American place Tay had ever been.

It had a yellow linoleum floor, four ranks of blue-painted booths with white Formica-covered tables and benches, and a line of blue and yellow plastic covered stools in front of a white tiled counter. On every table there were squeeze bottles of catsup and pancake syrup, salt and pepper shakers, and a rack of those little packets of jam and jelly that you can never get open without splashing some on yourself.

If Washington was a theme park for America, then Bob and Edith's was the theme park's featured restaurant.

The lunch rush had apparently come and gone and only a few people were left scattered around the room. The four of them had a booth off to themselves near the back.

The waitress was a skinny middle-aged woman with multi-colored tattoos peeking out of both sleeves of her uniform. Tay figured she had enough facial piercing to set off the security alarms at an airport before she even walked inside. Maybe she never flew anywhere.

Claire ordered first, then August, then Woods.

"And what you want, honey?" the woman asked Tay.

When Tay ordered a club sandwich and coffee, she stopped writing on her pad and stared at him.

"Why, don't you have the cutest accent, baby? Where you from?"

"Singapore," Tay said.

"Where?"

"Singapore," Tay repeated. "It's—"

"Oh, I know where Singapore is," the woman said. "It's one of them islands around Florida, ain't it?"

"Yes," Tay said. "Yes, it is."

"Well, sir, I gotta say you talk real nice even if you do come from Florida."

THE FOOD APPEARED promptly and Tay once again tipped his hat to the ferocious efficiency of Americans.

Nobody said much of anything while the food was served or even while they ate. August didn't seem inclined to make conversation and neither did Tay. Claire was equally quiet and, as for Woods, Tay had gotten used to his highly effective imitation of a wooden Indian.

The difference in feelings between August and Tay about what had happened here over the last few days ran deep. Tay was a policeman, and a policeman viewed the world in reasonably straightforward terms. You do the crime, you do the time. It had been Tay's job for twenty-seven years, his calling really, to do everything he could to make certain that always happened.

Maybe that was justice, and maybe that was only revenge, but either way it carried with it a sort of moral balance, a recognition that life might be unfair, but it was his duty to make it as fair as he could. That was the house in which Tay had lived for all of his life, and he was far too old to think about moving now.

Tay had no idea how someone like August saw the world, but he knew it wasn't nearly that straightforward. He imagined that August's world had so many shades of gray that it looked like a fantasy of some alien civilization. Which, now that Tay thought about it, was exactly the way he thought of the world in which August lived.

A policeman had no business getting involved with people in the spy business, Tay told himself for at least the hundredth time. Justice had nothing to do with foreign policy or intelligence gathering or, God forbid, politics. Justice was... well, justice. Everyone knew what it was even if they couldn't give you a definition of it, and everyone knew when it had been delivered. And when it hadn't.

In this case, it hadn't.

Two men had killed people to protect their own positions in the Washington power structure and they had been allowed to walk away. August had let them get away with what they had done. Even if that was good policy for somebody, it wasn't justice. And Tay didn't know how to get past that.

August polished off his eggs and corned beef hash, pushed his plate away, and drank some coffee. Then he cleared his throat.

"We're taking the plane back tonight, Sam. Are you still going with us?"

"Is that what you brought me here to ask?"

"Not really."

"Then whatever it is that you want to talk about, let's get to it."

August nodded slowly.

"Did you read *The Washington Post* this morning?" he asked after a moment.

"I don't read newspapers."

"Not ever?"

"No. Not ever. And I'm a happier man for it."

"I can understand that, but you probably ought to read this one today."

"Why? What happened? Has Singapore been wiped out?"

Woods picked a copy of the *Post* up off the seat next to him, carefully folded it over to a story on the front page, and laid it on the table. Tay pushed his plate away and pulled the paper toward him.

It was hard to miss the big headline over the three-column story right beneath the fold.

CIA DIRECTOR AND AIDE KILLED
IN ACCIDENT ON ACCESS ROAD
TO DULLES AIRPORT

Tay glanced up at August, then shifted his eyes to Woods. They were both expressionless.

He turned to Claire. "Did you know about this?"

Claire said nothing, and she wouldn't meet his eyes.

Tay glanced back down at the newspaper and began to read.

The Director of the Central Intelligence Agency, Adrian Small, and his executive assistant, Zac Reed, were both killed late last night when a car apparently driven by Mr. Reed was sideswiped by a truck on the Dulles Access Road, causing it to run head-on at high speed into a concrete retaining wall.

The truck was later found abandoned at Dulles Airport and sources say it had been stolen from a freight terminal in Richmond, although the theft had not yet been reported. It is not known why Mr. Small was being driven to Dulles Airport by an aide without his security detail.

The Central Intelligence Agency has acknowledged the Post's story and has confirmed the deaths of the Director and his executive assistant in a brief statement, but it has provided no other details. The White House released a statement saying...

Tay stopped reading. He picked up the paper, folded it over, and handed it back to August.

"Your handiwork?" Tay asked.

August tilted his head slightly toward Woods, but when Tay glanced at Woods his eyes were fixed somewhere just over Claire's head.

"You and I sometimes have different ideas of justice, Sam, but it seems to me we generally get to pretty much the same place in our own separate ways. Eventually."

The waitress returned just then carrying a stainless-steel coffee pot. While she refilled their cups one by one, they all waited in silence. After she was done, Tay smiled and thanked her.

"Sure thing, honey. You think one of these days maybe I could come visit you in Singapore?"

Tay didn't know what to say to that and his eyes darted frantically from August to Woods to Claire looking for help. He got none.

"I could listen to your accent forever, baby," she added and cut Tay a huge wink. Then, to Tay's immense relief, she walked away without saying anything else.

Claire was making little choking noises next to Tay, and he wouldn't look at her. If he did, he knew he would laugh right out loud, and he really didn't want to do that.

"SO, HOW ABOUT it, Sam?" August asked again. "You coming back with us?"

Tay drank some coffee and thought about his alternatives. They weren't particularly exciting.

"Might as well," he finally said. "You going to drop me off in Singapore or do I have to fly back there from Bangkok?"

"Well…"

August hesitated and made a show of thinking about that, but Tay knew it was all bullshit. August already knew exactly what he was going to say. Whatever it was, he had been leading up to it the whole time they had been sitting together in this booth at this diner.

"I've been thinking about changing the way we operate a little, Sam, and I've got a couple of things going that you could probably help us with. That is, if you want to."

What the fuck? Tay thought.

But that wasn't what he said. What he said was, "I thought this was just going to be a temporary job."

"It was, more or less. But I think we work together pretty well. Besides, you've got nothing else to do right now, have you?"

"I'm flattered, John, really I am, but that's ridiculous. I'm a cop, not a spy."

"You're not a cop anymore, my friend, and I'm not a spy either."

"No? Then just tell me in one simple sentence. What is it that your little group really does?"

August hesitated. He picked up his coffee mug and sipped absently from it while he considered the question. The expression on August's face almost made Tay laugh.

"You don't like philosophical questions, do you, John?"

"I guess I'm just not a very philosophical guy."

"Then forget the philosophy. Just give me the truth in one simple sentence."

"Okay, then I'll say this. We do things that need to be done."

"You kill people," Tay said.

"Sometimes that's what needs to be done."

"You know I can't do stuff like that, John. Maybe I'm not a cop anymore, but I still feel like one. It may sound corny to you, but I believe in law. I believe in justice. All that stuff."

"And I believe in what's right."

"A lot of people claim to believe in what's right. Then they do whatever they want to and say it was okay because they're the good guys."

"Yeah, Sam, but we really *are* the good guys."

Tay sighed and looked at his hands. But then he said something that not only surprised August a little, it surprised him as well.

"Tell me more about this job you're offering me."

Out of the corner of his eye Tay saw Claire shoot August a look, but he wasn't sure what it meant.

"I just want to have someone with your skills around occasionally."

"To do what?"

"Investigate things."

"So, you're talking about an investigation job?"

"Uh-huh."

"Not a killing people job."

"Uh-uh."

When Tay didn't immediately say anything else, August went on.

"Look, it's like this. The Conductor is willing to give us some latitude to expand the scope of our operations a bit and I've been thinking that we might freelance some here and there, take on a few things that somebody ought to be doing."

"What kind of things?"

August pursed his lips and seemed to think. Tay wondered if he was thinking about what the right answer to that question was or merely deciding what answer he ought to give.

"Okay, sort of like this. Last year two British kids in their early twenties were backpacking around Thailand. The girl was brutally raped and then both she and her boyfriend were beaten to death with hoes. It was an awful crime. Utterly savage. The local cops immediately picked up two young Burmese boys who were working illegally in Thailand. They got a quick trial and were sentenced to death. It was a travesty."

"You don't think they did it?"

"Nobody does, but they're going to be executed anyway. When tourists are attacked in Thailand, somebody's got to pay, and it's not going to be a Thai if the locals can help it."

"What's any of this got to do with you?"

"Nothing really. But it bothers me that the real rapists and murderers are still out there somewhere. They got away with it. I don't like people who get away with it."

"Do you have any idea who was really responsible?"

"Most people think it was somebody too important for the cops to mess with, or maybe a member of some well-connected family and now the cops are protecting him. I think that's possible. In Thailand it's more than just possible, but I don't like it at all."

"You mean the way you didn't like important people in Washington getting away with killing Rebecca Sternwood to keep her quiet and protect themselves?"

"Yeah," August said, "exactly like that."

Tay looked at August and after a moment August shrugged slightly and looked away. Tay could have sworn he even appeared a little embarrassed.

"We've got time between assignments," August continued. "We've got considerable resources, and we've got good contacts. Best of all, we've got a lot of experience in putting things right when there are no other alternatives."

Tay knew perfectly well what August meant by that, but he decided to let it go and offered no comment.

"The problem is, Sam, I haven't the faintest idea how to go about finding the people who really did the things they should go down for, like the people who killed these kids. You could do that. If we work together, I think we could add a little justice to the world."

When Tay remained silent, August tilted his head first toward Woods and then toward Claire. "These two figure it's a worthy cause," he said. "They're in."

Tay shifted his eyes to Claire and raised his eyebrows in a silent question.

She answered with a single tiny nod, one so small that Tay wasn't absolutely certain whether he had seen it or not.

Incredible, Tay thought. He felt as if he had walked into a tornado and been deposited in the Land of Oz.

Maybe if he went back to the safe house and slept, he would discover none of this had ever happened.

Maybe when he woke up he would be back in Singapore, lying in his own bed in his house on Emerald Hill Road, and he would still be a senior detective with the Singapore Police.

No, probably not.

Tay turned his head and looked out at the street through the big windows at the front of Bob and Edith's.

He watched the cars passing in both directions, people going somewhere with something to do they thought was important. People who had a purpose that they thought mattered.

Once he'd had a purpose he thought mattered, a purpose that *did* matter, but that was all gone now. He was no longer a policeman and it was unlikely he ever would be again.

And that left him… well, exactly where *did* that leave him?

It was true he had never really had anything in his life but his work. August had told him once that being a homicide detective hadn't only been his job, it had been who he was. If that were true, then who was he now?

Now that he didn't have his job anymore, did that mean he wasn't anybody?

Tay cleared his throat.

"What does this job pay?"

"Nothing. Not a cent."

"Can I smoke while I do it?"

"Sure. Foreigners can do pretty much anything they like in Thailand."

"Would I have to live in Pattaya?"

"God, no. Nobody lives in Pattaya unless they're on the lam from something. Move to fucking Malibu for all I care. I just need you to be available when and where I need you. I'm going to turn Secrets over to Woods anyway, and Claire and I will operate mostly out of Bangkok. Sometimes I miss life in a real city."

Although we usually don't notice them until long after they have passed, there are moments in life when everything hangs in the balance. There are moments when we really *can* change the future. When those moments come, either you lift your arms and fly, or you don't. There's nothing in between.

Some people fly anytime they get the chance simply because they can. They just do it, even if they don't know why the hell they're doing it. Perhaps *especially* if they don't know why the hell they're doing it.

Sam Tay was not one of those people.

Just breathe, he told himself. *In and out. Slow and steady. That's the ticket.*

That's how life happens. That's how you become whatever it is you become. Just breathing in and out, choosing whether or not to fly. Then just like that Tay chose. He chose to fly.

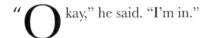"**O**kay," he said. "I'm in."

A PREVIEW

AN INSPECTOR TAY NOVEL - BOOK 6

A city that's falling apart, a man who's falling apart, and a girl with a secret past who has disappeared without a trace.

Here's a preview of the first chapter.

CHAPTER ONE

HONG KONG IS a city of splendor and sorrow. It is smooth, sophisticated, and sly, but it is also ruthless, scheming, and cruel. And it's as doomed as Jack Kennedy riding through Dallas in the back of an open car.

Most Americans know next to nothing about Hong Kong. Not many could find the place on a map if you threatened to kill their dog. A few people might remember hearing that the British fled Hong Kong in 1997 and turned over to the People's Republic of China what for a hundred and fifty years had been a colony of Great Britain. But ask them anything else about Hong Kong and all you're likely to get is a blank stare.

If you believe in omens, the ceremony in which Great Britain surrendered Hong Kong to China was a dilly. An unrelenting monsoon hammered the city and the ceremony was moved from the shoreline of the famous harbor to a slightly shabby auditorium inside the Hong Kong Convention Centre. Prince Charles and Tony Blair stood on the stage, emissaries from a threadbare colonial past, and watched stone-faced as China buried the British Empire forever.

When the flag of the once mighty Commonwealth was lowered for the last time, Hong Kong became the Hong Kong Special Administrative Region of the People's Republic of China. A fractured mishmash of words to describe a fractured mishmash of a city.

The British withdrawal from Hong Kong turned it into the Berlin of the twenty-first century, or maybe the Beirut. It became a patch over two worlds so disparate, so fundamentally at war with each other, that the strains underneath its surface were uncontrollable.

That was why no one was surprised when the riots started.

Just like Berlin and Beirut, Hong Kong always seemed on the verge of coming undone.

This time, maybe it really was.

SAMUEL TAY HAD only been in Hong Kong for ten minutes and he was already thinking about going home.

It certainly wasn't his first trip there. During all those years he had spent as a homicide detective with Singapore CID, more than a few cases had produced leads that took him to Hong Kong. He remembered a flying visit not long ago to interview a woman who had been a witness in a murder case, but he had been in and out then in one day and he didn't even have to stay overnight. For Tay, that was the next best thing to not going to Hong Kong at all.

Tay had never been much of a traveler. He had never found any place he liked more than his colonial-era row house in a quiet and dignified Singapore neighborhood called Emerald Hill. That was why mostly he just stayed home.

When Claire called and asked him to come to Hong Kong, his knee-jerk aversion to going anywhere at all kicked in almost at once, but his lack of enthusiasm went well beyond just his general reluctance to travel. He really didn't like Hong Kong very much.

The city wasn't as attractive as Singapore, and its overweening sense of self-importance drove him crazy. Hong Kong had a lot of soaring, glitzy buildings, of course, but now every city in Asia had soaring, glitzy buildings, and no matter how many garish buildings Hong Kong constructed, the city still felt trivial to him.

Underneath its façade of snazziness and glamour, there was

something insubstantial about Hong Kong. It was all flash and noise, and very little else. Tay hadn't been to Los Angeles and had never seen Hollywood, but he had heard people call Hollywood *Tinseltown*, and that was exactly the expression which came to mind every time he thought about Hong Kong.

If it had just been the summons to Hong Kong, Tay would have refused without a second thought. But there was another consideration.

Spending a few days helping Claire with whatever she was doing seemed quite appealing, even if he had to do it in Hong Kong. Tay didn't mix with very many women like Claire these days. If he were being honest about it, he supposed he never had. He and Claire seemed to get along well. It was a start, maybe, although a start on *what* Tay didn't quite know.

Claire wasn't even her real name. Tay knew that, but he had no idea what her real name actually was and he didn't know her last name either or even if she had one. Well, of course she had a last name. Everyone had a last name, didn't they?

John August had introduced him to Claire since she was one of the people who worked with him. August had simply called her Claire when he did. No other name was mentioned. Tay had gotten used to that. What difference did it make what name was on her birth certificate, anyway?

Claire was interesting, intelligent, and obviously good at her job. Tay understood her job included killing people occasionally, but no job was without at least a few aspects with which you could find fault, was it? Besides, he gathered she only killed people who needed killing so maybe it wasn't such a big deal.

Claire was also very attractive. There was that, too. He would have liked to tell himself it wasn't a consideration, but it was.

She was tall, lean, and fit with the most glorious dark eyes Tay had ever looked into, and she kept her long, dirty blonde hair pulled back into a no-nonsense ponytail. Tay thought

Claire looked like a girl not many years out of school who had played on the college volleyball team. He didn't know where Claire had gone to college, or even if she had gone to college at all, but he doubted she had played on a volleyball team if she had.

He thought she might have spent time in the military, but he wasn't certain about that. Still, she had her special skills and she had to have learned them somewhere. It certainly hadn't been at Miss Porter's School for Young Ladies.

When Claire called him, she hadn't been specific about why she wanted him to meet her in Hong Kong. She only told him it was important and asked him to get there as quickly as possible. A plane was waiting for him at Signature Flight Support, she said, which was at the private terminal across Changi Airport from the commercial terminals.

If Claire had said she wanted his help looking into a murder, he would have been a lot more enthusiastic about making the trip to Hong Kong. He would have gone to Timbuktu for a decent murder case. Well, maybe not Timbuktu, but one hell of a long way.

Still, he doubted Claire needed help investigating a murder case. She worked for John August. She and August didn't investigate murders. They committed them.

WHEN TAY GOT Claire's call that Monday morning, it had been a nice surprise. The part about her wanting him to come to Hong Kong hadn't been so great, but he thought he could get past it. Spending a few days with Claire almost anywhere would be a welcome relief from the boredom that had taken control of his life.

The retirement thing was a pile of warm shit. If it had been entirely his own idea, maybe he would have felt differently, but it hadn't been. He had always known the enemies his independent streak had accumulated for him among the senior ranks of the

Singapore Police would get him one day. It had just never occurred to him they would get him quite so soon.

When he had been forced out of CID and into reluctant retirement, it was John August who had hauled him from the scrapheap and put him back in the game. Tay had known August ever since the American ambassador's wife had turned up dead under rather embarrassing circumstances in a suite at the Singapore Marriott.

After that little imbroglio had been quietly resolved through their off-the-books collaboration, Tay had asked for August's help several other times when he was involved in difficult and sensitive investigations. August had asked no questions about any of the favors Tay sought nor had he asked for anything in return.

Not until somebody tried to kill him.

That was when August did ask for Tay's help. He wanted very much to find out who it was who was trying to make him dead, preferably before they succeeded, and he was smart enough to know he needed an investigator of Tay's talent to do it.

Until then, Tay hadn't known for certain who John August really was or who he worked for. He was a man who seemed able to get almost anything done, and he was obviously involved with the highest levels of the American military and intelligence communities, so the natural assumption to make was that August was CIA. But that had never felt right to Tay. He always figured August for being involved in something worse than the CIA.

When he eventually found out who August actually did work for, he realized he had been right all along. August was part of an organization few people even knew existed. Those who did know it existed inevitably referred to it simply as the Band. And the Band was a *lot* worse than the CIA.

Tay was flattered when August asked him to help the Band

out with a few things, but he couldn't see any real future in that. He was a homicide cop. Well, he *used* to be a homicide cop. Whatever it was he had turned into now, it wasn't a spy or an international man of mystery.

August and the Band dealt in the rise and fall of nations. Tay dealt in human tragedies, one human being at a time. What was a sophisticated team of international intelligence operators going to do that could possibly require the help of someone like Samuel Tay?

THE FLIGHT FROM Singapore to Hong Kong took a little less than four hours. Since Tay was the only passenger on a luxurious private jet, those four hours passed quite pleasantly.

There was no flight attendant, so one of the two pilots showed him how to find whatever refreshments he might want and where the toilet was. After takeoff, he got a bottle of water from the refrigerator in the galley, tilted his big leather seat all the way back, and looked out the window at the world slipping by below.

Tay didn't know what kind of plane he was flying on. He had thought about asking the pilot when he was pointing out the galley and the toilet, but he decided it would just mark him for the rube he was. Most people who flew on private jets already knew what they were flying on, didn't they? Why expose himself to the pilot as some putz who didn't rate a private plane often enough to know anything about them?

When they landed in Hong Kong, Tay found himself at another private terminal very much like the one they had departed from in Singapore. It was hushed and discreet, and the immigration and customs checks took place so unobtrusively Tay hardly realized they were taking place at all. He felt like he had stepped from the airplane directly into a plush private club which, when he thought about it, he supposed was exactly what he had done.

A chubby, cherub-faced driver was waiting for Tay just outside the terminal. The man was a Chinese of indeterminate age, and he was wearing a black suit and white shirt and holding up a sign that said Samuel Tey.

"It's Tay with an A," Tay said when he walked over. "Not Tey with an E."

The driver was a little puzzled by that, but he didn't see the point in investing any effort in trying to figure out what Tay was talking about. He had long ago realized trying to figure out what foreigners were talking about was almost always a waste of time. He just took the envelope he had been told to give his passenger and thrust it out without a word.

Tay tore open the flap and unfolded the single piece of white paper he found inside. There were two lines written on it in blue ink. There wasn't any signature, but there didn't need to be.

The driver will take you to the Cordis Hotel where you're staying. Meet me in the Garage Bar at six o'clock.

Tay contemplated the message for a moment.

The Cordis Hotel where you're staying.

The name of the hotel sounded familiar, although he couldn't think where he might have heard of it. That wasn't what bothered him.

It was the *where you're staying* part of the message on which he had his attention focused.

That had to mean Claire was staying someplace else. Not in the same hotel where he was staying, but someplace else. That was a rather inauspicious beginning to his trip, wasn't it?

He had been in Hong Kong for all of ten minutes and things were already going to shit.

Available at all Amazon stores worldwide
in both e-book and trade paperback editions

THE INSPECTOR SAMUEL TAY NOVELS

They steer a tight ship in squeaky-clean Singapore. No dissent, no opposition, no criticism. Disneyland with the death penalty, somebody once called it.

Samuel Tay is a little overweight, a little lonely, a little cranky, and he smokes way too much. He's worked almost his entire life as a senior homicide detective in Singapore CID, and he's the best investigator anyone there has ever seen.

Problem is, the senior officers of CID don't much like Tay. His father was an American and there's something about him that's just a little too American for most Singaporeans. Tay knows they'll get him someday, and eventually they do.

And that's when a whole new world of possibilities opens up for Samuel Tay.

THE AMBASSADOR'S WIFE - Book 1

THE UMBRELLA MAN - Book 2

THE DEAD AMERICAN - Book 3

THE GIRL IN THE WINDOW - Book 4

AND BROTHER IT'S STARTING TO RAIN - Book 5

MONGKOK STATION - Book 6

THE JACK SHEPHERD NOVELS

Jack Shepherd was a well-connected lawyer in Washington DC until he tossed it all in for the quiet life of a business school professor at Chulalongkorn University in Bangkok.

It was a pretty good gig until the university discovered the kind of notorious people Shepherd had gotten involved with in his law practice. That was when they suggested he'd probably be happier somewhere else.

These days, Shepherd lives and works in Hong Kong where he's the kind of lawyer people call a troubleshooter. At least that's what they call him when they're being polite.

Shepherd is the guy people go to when they have a problem too ugly to tell anyone else about. He locates the trouble, and then he shoots it.

Neat, huh? If his life were only that simple.

LAUNDRY MAN - Book 1

KILLING PLATO - Book 2

A WORLD OF TROUBLE - Book 3

THE KING OF MACAU - Book 4

DON'T GET CAUGHT - Book 5

THE NINETEEN - Book 6

"THE BIG MANGO is a classic!"
-- Crime Reads

$400 million is in the wind, ten tons of cash, the result of a bungled CIA operation to grab the foreign currency from the Bank of Vietnam when the Americans fled Saigon in 1975.

A few decades later, the word on the street is that all that money somehow ended up in Bangkok and a downwardly mobile lawyer from California named Eddie Dare is the only guy left alive who might still have a shot at finding it.

Eddie knows nothing about the missing money. At least, he doesn't think he does. But so many people claim he's got an inside track that he and an old marine buddy named Winnebago Jones decide to head for Bangkok anyway and do a little treasure hunting. What do they have to lose, huh? Their lives, as it turns out.

From the Big Apple, to the Big Orange, to the Big Mango. You have to admit it has a kind of nutty logic to it. Bangkok is about as far from California as Eddie can go without sailing completely over the edge of the world.

Although, at times, he wonders if that isn't exactly what he *has* done.

THE BIG MANGO

**available in paperback at Amazon
and as an ebook at all good online booksellers**

MEET JAKE NEEDHAM

Jake Needham is an American lawyer who became a screen and television writer through a series of coincidences too ridiculous for anyone to believe. When he realized how little he actually liked movies and television, he started writing crime novels.

Jake has lived in Asia for nearly thirty years and has published thirteen novels that have collectively sold nearly a million copies. He has twice been a finalist for the Barry Award for the Paperback Mystery of the Year and once a finalist for the International Thriller Writers' Award for Ebook Thriller of the Year. He and his wife, an Oxford graduate and prematurely retired concert pianist, now live in Bangkok.

Every month or two, Jake sends out one of his famous *Letters from Asia* to those readers who have asked to receive them. He often talks about the real people, places, and things that appear in his novels in fictional form and sometimes lets his readers know about new books he has coming soon or suggests books by other writers that he thinks they might like. If you'd like to be one of the readers who receives Jake's letters, you can go to this address and ask him to send them to you:

www.JakeNeedhamNovels.com/letter-to-readers

Excerpt from MONGKOK STATION, © 2020 by Jake Raymond Needham

Cover © 2019 by Jake Raymond Needham

Ebook edition ISBN 978-616-7611-38-9

Trade paper edition ISBN 978-616-7611-39-6

Printed in Great Britain
by Amazon